On Hawks & Harpies

From the Shelves
of the Noktern

Sean W. Bagan

On Hawks & Harpies
From the Shelves of the Noktern

<u>Other titles by Sean W. Bagan:</u>
On Ravens & Riddles

ISBN: 979-8-9929084-3-5

First edition, October 2025

Cover art done by Alexandre P.
Manufactured in the United States of America

You'll look differently at yourself and the challenge you endured when you give your pain a purpose.

For my Willow who has crossed the rainbow bridge. You will be forever missed, baby.

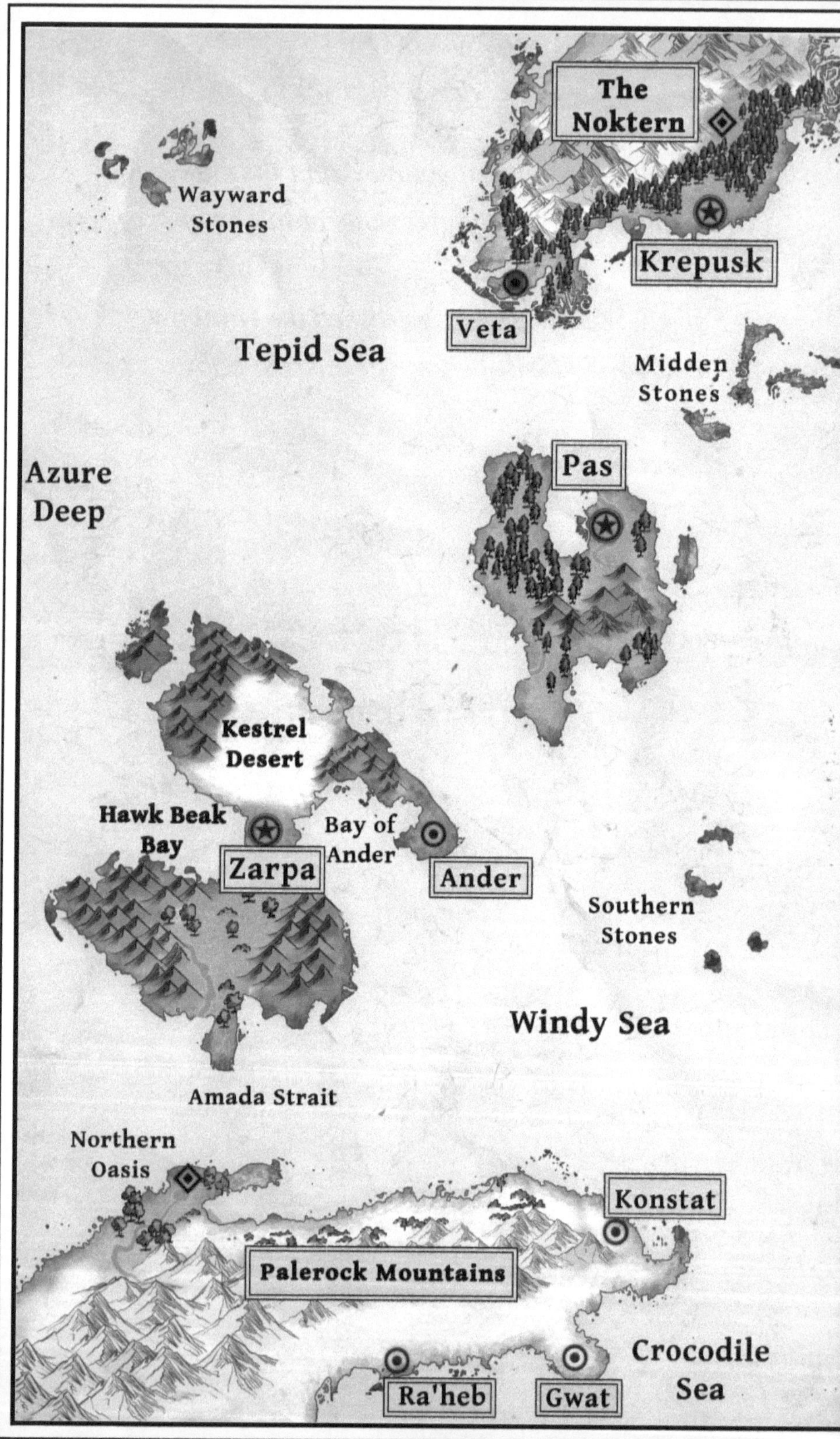

The Noktern
Wayward Stones
Krepusk
Veta
Midden Stones
Tepid Sea
Pas
Azure Deep
Kestrel Desert
Hawk Beak Bay
Bay of Ander
Zarpa
Ander
Southern Stones
Windy Sea
Amada Strait
Northern Oasis
Konstat
Palerock Mountains
Ra'heb
Gwat
Crocodile Sea

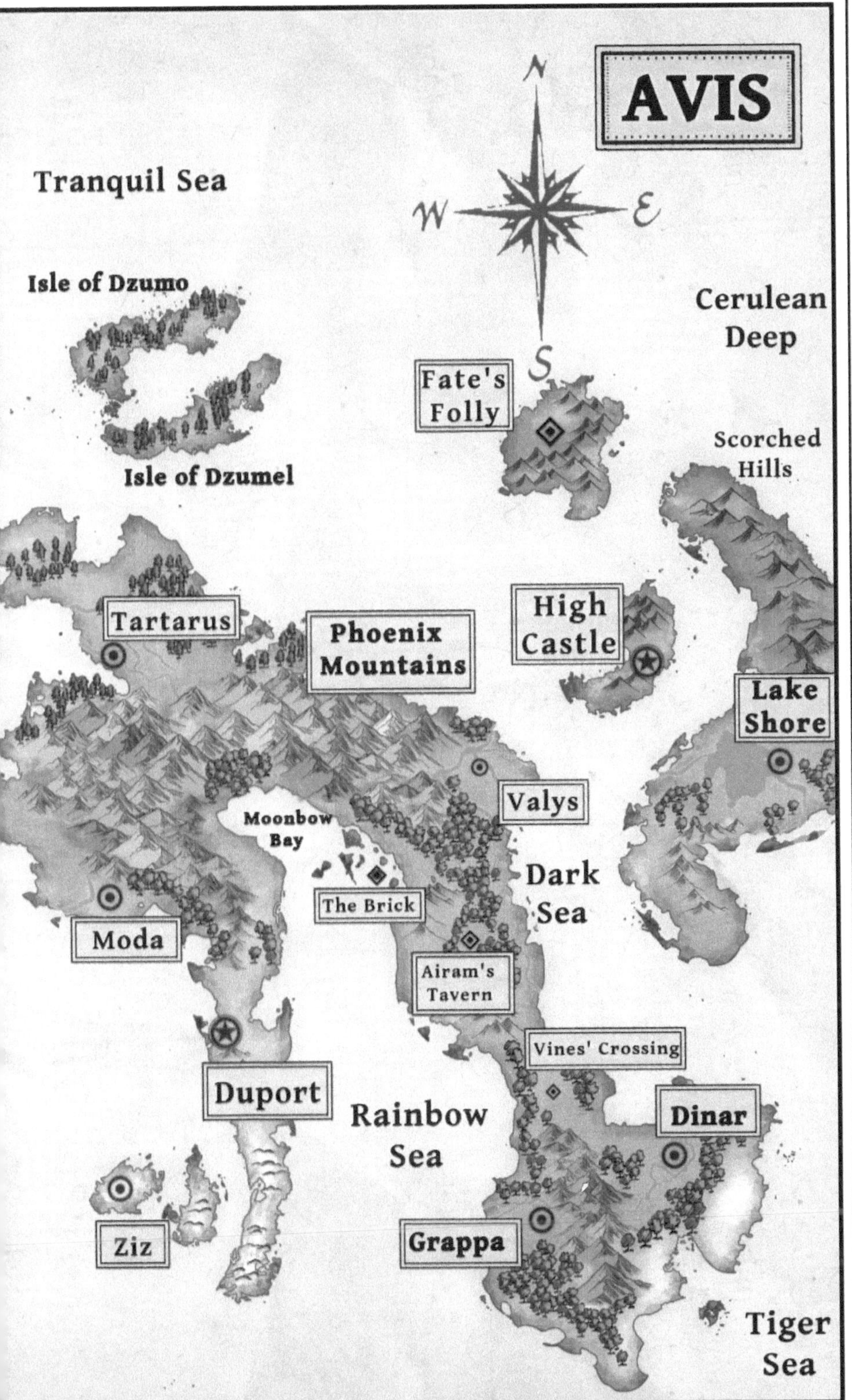

AVIS
Tranquil Sea
Isle of Dzumo
Isle of Dzumel
Cerulean Deep
Fate's Folly
Scorched Hills
Tartarus
Phoenix Mountains
High Castle
Lake Shore
Valys
Moonbow Bay
Dark Sea
The Brick
Moda
Airam's Tavern
Vines' Crossing
Dinar
Duport
Rainbow Sea
Grappa
Ziz
Tiger Sea
N
W
E
S

<u>Prologue</u>

From: Tvanor@Noktern.no.org
Sent: 01 June 15:43
To: Minkjænor@Noktern.no.org
Subject: Last Words

My Dearest Minka,

I don't have much time left and there's much to say, so I'm writing whatever comes to mind. Please bear with me.

He's gone. Primanor is dead.
Under any other circumstance, I'd be devastated. He was the closest thing to a father I ever had. Somehow, though, there's comfort in knowing I'll join him soon. In a way, he was fortunate. He got to go peacefully, while I...well...let's not dwell on it, shall we…

Do you know why a raven is like a writing desk? It may seem like a strange question, but it's important. Primanor asked me this the day we met. I was so taken aback at the time, but after a moment, I ventured: "Poe wrote on both."

He looked pleased enough, even though the answer was wrong. A few weeks later, he appointed me second in command, so I must've made him happy.

The real answer, by the way, is that they can both produce a few notes, though they are very flat; and it is nevar [sic] put with the wrong end in front. (I bet you scrunched your nose and tilted your head. I'm going to miss that cute, confused smile of yours).

Twenty years later, he's finally explained what the riddle means. It's literally nonsense. (How unsatisfying)

He must've sensed my skepticism because he told me: "Not everything in life needs to make sense. There was no sense behind this war that has destroyed our world." I couldn't argue with him there.

But by the end, his lucidity slipped away. He drifted back into visions of a boy who would save us all. His visions used to be crisp, now they're just tangled and obscure. My heart ached to listen, so I stopped.

On Hawks & Harpies

Then, in a sudden moment of strength and clarity, he gripped my hands with ice-cold fingers, sat upright in his bed, and fixed me with a fierce look I'd never seen before. He growled in my ear that I cannot be deceived by appearances and that there is more to someone than meets the eye. I think he wanted to go on, but the air caught in his throat as he crashed back onto the infirmary bed and closed his eyes for the last time.

I have so much more that I want to say, but the sirens have just sounded. I'm afraid I am out of time. There's one last thing I need you to know, so there's no room for mystery.

I love you, Minka.

Not just as a friend, but with everything I am. Your dark curls that catch the sun, your laugh like tinkling bells. I've been too afraid to tell you, worried about what others might think, afraid you might not feel the same. I suppressed these feelings for ten long years, but I never stopped loving you. My greatest regret is never knowing if you loved me back.

I guess it doesn't matter anymore. But at least now you know.

With courage and honor,
Tvanor.

—PS—

I need one final favor. I don't have time to email the Noktern admin. Share the answer to the riddle with them. I didn't write it down before, but now I know how important it is to Primanor's final vision.

Thank you, my love.

Goodbye.

Chapter One
Agnes

"You shouldn't let her bully us like this, Agnes," Marta chided. "You're her chaperone for goodness' sake, not some servant to be ordered about."

"Sister Marta," Agnes snapped, stomping her foot into the damp peat of the tundra. "If ye wish to tell Socorra and Fatima they can't come out to train because of a little mud and fog, then be my guest."

"A little mud and fog?" Marta bellowed, her wings flaring in agitation. "I can barely see the wrinkles on your face and I'm standing right in front of you! Why I–"

Agnes cut her off before she could protest further. "Until ye summon the courage to tell them yerself, kindly leave me the bloody 'ell alone."

"Agnes!" The petite Dove gasped, clutching the nape of her wimple. "You know such language is forbidden by the Order."

"Well, damn," Agnes muttered under her breath, snorting as she tried to contain her laughter.

Marta shot her a wicked glance, grinding her teeth as she waited for Agnes to yield. But the older Dove held her ground, meeting her glare with calm defiance.

"Anyway," Marta finally said, her cheeks flushing red. "Can you even believe the two of them?" Her judgment hung thick in the air.

"Ye'll 'ave to be more specific." Agnes turned away, her lips curling slyly as she traipsed through the muck, savoring her small victory.

"Come now," Marta sneered, fluttering forward to keep pace. "All of this nonsensical training: darting around the plains each day, throwing spears at one another, hand-to-hand combat. Do these sound like pursuits befitting young ladies?"

"Ye know what Mother Amelie says." Agnes wagged a finger, her other hand planted firmly on her hip. "Judge not and ye shall nae be judged."

"Do not condemn and you shall not be condemned," Marta spat in return with an exasperated air. "Yes, yes, I couldn't agree more. But surely you see how barbaric it is?"

Agnes slumped her shoulders and adjusted the folds of her starched robe. "I s'pose that really isn't up to us, now, is it? We're 'ere as the Owls' guests and Forranor 'as decided that the two of them should go about their training. And be easy on Socorra," she added somberly, her voice softening. "Today'll be 'ard on 'er."

Marta caught her by the arm, eyes wide with feigned concern. "Is that today? Poor, poor dear," she cooed, shaking her head.

"It's for the best," Agnes grunted, unable to hide her contempt for Marta's disingenuous display. "Socorra'll be leaving soon for Raven Rock, and Kyte'll be useless to 'er there. 'E might as well go 'ome and return to some semblance of normalcy."

"I couldn't imagine losing one of my wings," Marta murmured, stroking the tips of her cream-colored feathers. "But then, God works in mysterious ways."

"Amen," Agnes uttered automatically, more a reflex than a prayer.

"I just can't help but feel–" Marta started, but Agnes cut her off.

"Don't ye say it," she squawked. "That man did nae wrong, and 'e certainly wasn't punished. Ye saw the surveillance video. Kyte was trying to save that poor Finch boy when the lightning struck 'im. It was bad timing, not some beam of divine intervention."

"Oh, come Agnes. The other sisters and I have all been talking, and–"

"That's all ye ever do," Agnes boomed, jabbing an accusatory finger at Marta's chest. "For nearly a decade, I've 'ad to put up with listening to ye and the other sisters gossiping about anything and everything. We're meant to be 'ere to study so when we return to the Dovelands..."

Marta let out a high, sarcastic squeal. "Are you truly so naive to think we'll be returning to the Dovelands, Agnes? That's a laugh," she scoffed. "No dear. Mother Amelie has made it clear to me and the other sisters that Hierophant Gabriel has no intention of bringing us back to Pas."

Agnes's stomach knotted, but she squared her shoulders. "When did she tell ye that?"

"Last week," Marta answered flatly. "She sent a correspondence with all of the knowledge that we've acquired."

"So, the letter was blank?" Agnes rolled her eyes. "We've been limited to the most basic of functions 'ere. It's not like we're permitted to read any of their scholarly materials."

Marta exasperated. "And I couldn't bear to read about that girl in Wonderville, or whatever it's called, again if I had to."

Her lips spread to respond, Agnes froze as distant flapping rattled the mist. She squinted into the grey swirl, but the haze made it impossible to see past a few feet. Marta started to speak, but Agnes lifted a plump hand, urging her to keep silent.

The wings beat closer, whipping the fog into billowing eddies until Socorra burst through the gloom, the frenzied gust tugging at their wimples. Agnes grabbed her headdress, but Marta's flew free, revealing tufts of her fading orange hair.

"Socorra!" Marta roared, lunging for the drifting cloth, but it danced just out of reach of her manicured fingers. "What is wrong with that girl!?" she fumed. "I swear, I have half a mind to–" Before she could finish, a spear thudded into the peat, pinning Marta's habit. "Agnes!" she shrieked, spinning onto her back as mud splashed everywhere. "They tried to kill me! Do something!"

Her laughter bubbling, Agnes doubled over.

Scrambling upright, Marta wiped filthy streaks from her face. "It's not funny!" she wailed, pounding the soggy earth with her fists, sending another wave of fresh mud into the air. "These horrible girls! Fatima! Socorra!" She screamed at the top of her lungs.

On Hawks & Harpies

"Oh, calm yerself, ye wretched goat!" Agnes chuckled between breaths, shaking the last tears of mirth from her eyes. Finding firmer ground, she planted her feet and wrapped both hands around the spear's shaft. With a grunt and a few stubborn tugs, she freed it from the muddy earth.

Flustered, Marta scrambled to her feet and screamed into the fog again. "Enough of this foolishness!" She spun in place, making sure her voice carried across the field. "Get down here. Both of you!"

Agnes pursed her lips, suppressing a grin as Fatima's merry cackling rang out from somewhere unseen.

"These hooligans," Marta huffed, tapping her foot. "They've gone too far this time."

"Marta," Agnes exasperated. "It was an accident. There's nae a reason to be so irate."

"No reason?" Marta scoffed. "That little monster almost skewered me and you think I've no reason to be upset?"

Agnes opened her mouth to reply, but a distant, crackling voice cut through the fog.

"The caravan will be departing in fifteen minutes," Hermanor blared over the speaker. "I repeat: fifteen minutes until departure for Krepusk. Get your bums in gear and head to the main gate, ladies."

Agnes looked up just as Fatima's voice echoed through the mist: "Race you!"

"That's cheating!" Socorra called after her, and Agnes laughed. It warmed her to hear the Hawk in such good spirits, especially knowing what awaited them at the harbor in Krepusk.

"He can't be serious," Marta groaned, eyeing her wings in dismay. "We'll never make it back to the Noktern in time. I can't fly like this! I'm caked in mud!"

"Guess ye'll just 'ave to miss out," Agnes smirked, then took flight, leaving Marta red-faced and fuming in the clearing.

Chapter Two
GIDEON

"Mother."

Gideon bolted upright, the word a whimper on his lips, a jolt of pain exploding through his arm. He gasped, clutching his elbow as his vision swam. The sudden motion left him dizzy, breath shallow, limbs trembling. Disoriented, he blinked against the shadows pressing in around him. The room was cloaked in darkness. Thick curtains smothered the windows, allowing only the thinnest slivers of gray light to bleed through their seams.

"Ugh," he groaned, pushing himself up from the bed. Staggering to the window, every movement sent fresh jolts through his arm.

Why does it hurt? And my head...

He hadn't felt this foggy since the night Cas brought over that bottle of elderberry wine stolen from his mother's cellar. It had tasted divine, but the morning after was brutal. Gideon had sworn off drinking ever since.

"I don't think it was alcohol," he muttered, wincing. "But I don't remember..."

Thoughts scattering, his voice faded away. His memory felt slippery, dreamlike. He reached for the curtain, the metal rings screeching against the rod, each note slicing through his skull. Light flooded the room and a fresh stab of pain lanced behind his eyes. He winced, clamped his eyes shut, then cracked them open slowly. The glare dulled, and the world outside came into focus.

"What the...?" Gideon whispered, rubbing his eyes.

Through the window, towering concrete high-rises loomed, factory stacks vomiting smoke into the air. Finches darted through the smog-choked sky, weaving between buildings, all set against the jagged rise of the Phoenix Mountains.

I'm back in Moda.

"That's not possible," he breathed, the industrial rumble of the city washing over him like static.

Turning away from the window, he scanned the room. *His* room. Lifeless beige walls bore his sketches and scribbled quotes from his mother's old stories. At the foot of the wrought-iron bed stood a familiar desk. He crossed to it, eyeing the candelabra perched atop. The wax had melted into rivers, clinging to the brass sconces.

"How long has that been burning?" He snuffed the flame with a quick jet of breath. His gaze dropped to the desk's clutter and he picked up a worn, leather-bound book.

Alice's Adventure in Wonderland.

"This shouldn't be here," he stammered. "My mother's book...I left it..." He strained to recall, but the memory slipped from his grasp like water through his fingers.

"Gideon," came a voice from below, muffled through the door. "Breakfast!"

He flinched.

"She can't be here," he whispered, barely louder than the thudding in his chest. Bile rose in his throat as a flood of memories surged forward. He tried to move, but his body locked in place.

"Gideon!" his mother called again, sharper this time. Her voice carried a strange weight, pulling at something deep inside him. Against his will, his limbs obeyed. It had been five years since she'd left on an expedition to search for ancient Sapien tomes written before the Great End, and never returned.

"Didn't she?" he murmured, suddenly uncertain.

With a shaky breath, he gripped the door handle and stepped into the hallway. The air caught in his throat. Ferns and ivy spilled from planters lining the corridor, vibrant and lush. Between each set of greenery, ornate metal frames hung on the walls.

"What are these doing here?" He reached out, his fingers brushing the edge of a gilded frame. Inside was a photo of him and his mother when he was maybe ten years old, the two of them sitting on the floor as she read to him.

"I haven't seen this in years…" he lamented.

The plants had always withered when she left on her expeditions. His father never bothered to water them, and after she disappeared, he'd simply thrown them away. The photos were also packed away in boxes Gideon thought were long since forgotten.

"Gideon!" his mother called again, harsher still as she grew more impatient.

Snapping out of his daze, he hurried down the hall, then descended from the open balcony into the foyer, his wings hovering him to a halt.

"There you are!" She flashed him a grin that didn't quite reach her eyes, her lips twisted with false warmth. "I was starting to get worried."

Gideon froze, breath hitching. His eyes widened as he took her in, looking exactly the same as he remembered. Her blonde hair fell in soft waves across her bare shoulders, and the opal gown she wore shimmered like water in sunlight. Her feathers were sleek and pristine, groomed as meticulously as ever.

"You're back," Gideon beamed, his lip trembling.

Without a word, she took his hands and pulled him into a tight embrace. He clung to her, overwhelmed by her warmth and familiarity. For a moment, he let himself feel safe.

But his bliss was cut short, burned away by something acrid. A pungent, chemical stench stung his nostrils, turning his stomach. He reeled back, gagging, wiping his mouth on his sleeve.

"What is that?" he choked. He looked up and the scream ripped from him before he could stop it. Staggering back into the wall, he nearly slipped. Her face was still his mother's, but her eyes pulsed with an unnatural violet glow. Her once-lovely wings dissolved into jagged, obsidian shards. One hand contorted, the fingers elongated into a blackened talon.

No!

Squeezing his eyes shut, memories surged through his mind.

Crisp rain. Mud. The tundra plains. The sky cracked open, his mother descending like a wraith. His best friend lying on the ground, charred and lifeless.

"Cas," he whispered, voice thick with guilt. His arm throbbed as the memory of their battle flickered into place.

He opened his eyes and the vision was gone. His mother stood before him once more, immaculate and smiling, her eyes soft, wings pristine.

"What's wrong, my love?" She reached out to him.

He flinched, recoiling. "Nothing," he lied. "I just…" He sniffed the air. The chemical rot was gone, replaced by the comforting aroma of citrus and pastry. "Orange tarts?"

"Your favorite," she smiled sweetly. "I made a batch for you this morning. Wait here and I'll bring you a slice." She turned and vanished into the kitchen.

"A tart for breakfast?" he stuttered. But she was already gone, having disappeared through the kitchen's swinging doors.

Somethings wrong.

He could sense it, a thrumming beneath his skin. Horrific images—flickers of memory flashed behind his eyes: Owls, Hawks, Sapiens. "Have I ever even seen a Sapien before?" he asked himself aloud. The thoughts felt real, but distant, like a story someone else had told him.

Knock knock knock.

The heavy pounding at the front door made his heart leap.

"Can you get that?" his mother called from the kitchen. "I have another tart in the oven. I'd hate for it to burn."

Gideon hovered near the door, unease crawling up his spine. "This isn't right," he whispered, eyes fixed on the frame. Shuffling back a step, the hairs on his neck rose, feathers bristling as if the air itself had changed.

Knock knock knock.

The pulsing was urgent—louder this time, more desperate.

The Finch flipped open the small crest-shaped latch and peered through the narrow grate.

Nothing but fog.

"Who's there?" he called, voice unsteady.

Silence.

"Strange." Scrunching his nose, Gideon stepped back and peered through the sidelights. Peering out at different angles, he could see the high rises of the city laid out before him, smokestacks churning in the distance. But the stoop was completely empty.

KNOCK KNOCK KNOCK.

The sound boomed through the house as if it came from inside the walls.

"Aren't you going to get that?" His mother's voice chimed sweetly, but was laced with impatience. Flitting through the archway, she carried a plate with a slice of tart in one hand, a cake knife in the other.

"But there's no one there," Gideon stammered.

Knock knock knock.

"Of course there is," she replied flatly. "Don't leave them waiting. Open the door."

Each rap rattled the foyer, echoing off the tile.

"I don't think I—" he began, backing away.

"I said…open…the…door." Each word was as sharp as a dagger, every exclamation stoked with animus.

Gideon's heart thundered. Shuffling forward, his hand trembled as he brought it to the brass knob.

Everything in him screamed.

Don't do it!!

Then, an idea nipped at him.

Why can't she open the door herself?

He hesitated, his grip on the knob slipping. "Because she can't," he whispered.

"What's that?" Cecilia's head snapped up. Her perfect facade cracked; shoulders tensing, her wings flexed with warning.

"I won't." With a step back, Gideon let go of the knob. He met her gaze, steadying his legs so they wouldn't give out beneath him.

She might look like your mother, but she's still the Master.

He swallowed, voice surprisingly steady. "If you want the door open so badly, mother, then do it yourself." Even as a fledgling, he'd never dared defy her. Still, despite knowing what she'd done—abducting innocent Avians, torturing Cas—it felt treasonous, almost a betrayal to stand against her.

Don't let her get to you. Hold strong.

Cecilia's lips pressed into a thin line, the familiar purple spark crackling in her eyes. Whipping the plate violently over her head, she threw it, porcelain shattering in every direction. Silence fell, broken only by Gideon's ragged inhale and the soft hiss of Cecilia's wrath building in the stillness. Then she stepped forward, gripping the knife tightly at her side.

Gideon shook like a leaf.

Do I run? Fight?

His eyes darted around searching for any kind of weapon. But before he could move, she was in front of him, eye to eye. He could feel her breath, hot and damp against his skin. The bitter odor returned, curling through his nostrils. She raised the knife high over her head. Gideon gasped, throwing up his arms to shield himself, but the blow never came. Instead, a loud *crack* rang out. He opened one eye to find the knife was buried in the center of the door, mahogany split clean down the grain. Cecilia's face contorted in frustration as she yanked it free. But even as Gideon stared at the gash, the wood began to smooth over like ripples in water. Within seconds, the door was whole again.

"Why are you like this?" she growled, her hand trembling.

Gideon could only stare blankly.

"I don't understand why you have to be so difficult." Her voice echoed with fury. "When most people want to hide something, they put it behind a vault or a brick wall. Those are easy enough to break through. But this," she gestured to the door with her talons, "this is just ridiculous. A plain old door…not even locked, but for some reason I can't open it."

Gideon trembled, his throat dry. "And what am I meant to be hiding?"

"Memories," she seethed.

"Memories?" he repeated, trying to understand. "We're in my mind, aren't we?" The words tumbled out, breathless.

Of course.

The hallways, the plants, the photos. They weren't real. She couldn't know what the house looked like after she'd left.

"This is your problem, Gideon." Cecilia gave a dry, humorless chuckle. "You're too clever." Her lips curled into a grin, cold and calculating. "And I have no one to blame but myself. Your father was useless in that department. But me? I filled your head with all those stories. Built you an imagination so wild, it's turned your mind into a fortress I can't crack."

With a snap of her fingers, the house began to dissolve around them. The floor flaked away, walls fading to dust. Everything vanished until only the door remained, looming between them in the void.

Cecilia changed too; in a blink, her disguise melted. What stood before him was no longer his mother, but a nightmare. Her wings shimmered like translucent glass, nearly invisible in the blackness. Electric blue veins spiderwebbed through the plumage, pulsing with unnatural light. Her eyes burned, monstrous and unavian.

"Now," she said, her voice soft and eerily calm. "I'm growing quite tired of your defiance, Gideon. I've asked kindly more times than I can count."

"What're you talking about?" he shot back. "You've only asked me to open the door a few times."

Her lips thinned. "This isn't the first time we've played this game." She lifted a talon and gently traced it down his cheek, sharp and revolting; Gideon flinched at her touch. "We've done this at least a half-dozen times. You come down here. I ask kindly that you open the door, and you refuse. Every time, you find a new way to disobey me."

Gideon blinked, trying to process what she was saying. "Then why not just *make* me open it? Like you forced me to follow you from the Noktern?"

"If I could, I would," she growled. "But I can't hypnotize you here. Only in the waking world. And since your memories are all in *here*..." She spread her hands with theatrical helplessness. "That wouldn't do me any good."

Helpful to know.

"But that doesn't mean I won't get what I want."

In a flash, Cas appeared before them, emerging from the void like a ghost. His eyes flicked around, confused. As soon as his gaze locked onto Gideon, the confusion vanished, his brow furrowing into a raw fury.

"Cas!" Gideon gasped, reaching out for his friend.

With a snarl, Cas lunged, but Cecilia caught him mid-leap, wrapping her arms around his chest.

"Ah, ah," she warned, pressing the knife to his throat.

"No!" Gideon surged forward, wings outstretched.

"Don't come any closer," Cecilia squawked, dragging the knife higher.

Gideon froze, his body trembling with helplessness.

"Let go of me, you witch!" Cas spat, writhing in her grasp.

"Is that any way to speak to your Master?" she purred. "Now behave, or I'll slit your pretty throat. Right here. Right now."

On Hawks & Harpies

"This isn't real," Gideon whispered. He threw his hands to his temples, hoping to wake himself up. "It's all in my head. She can't hurt him. Not really."

"That's a lovely thought," she cooed. "But are you willing to bet *his* life on it?" She leaned in closer to Cas, eyes glittering. "Because even if I can't kill him here, I *can* kill him in the waking world." She laughed menacingly. "So, what'll it be, my dear?" Her tone turned mocking. "Are you going to be a good boy and open the door?"

Gideon tried to think, to come up with a plan, but his mind felt dim, his thoughts drowned in fog. Even the searing anxiety that had gripped him minutes ago had dulled, replaced by something worse—resignation.

He would do anything to protect Cas.

"Fine," he shot quietly, the word catching in his throat. "Just…tell me why."

"Why what, Gideon?" Her claws tightened around Cas.

He lifted his eyes, a deep pain scribbled on his face. "Why *all* of it?" His voice cracked. "You abandoned me. Then you came back, and now *all this*." He gestured vaguely, flailing his arms into the ether. "Holding my best friend hostage, digging through my head to get to my memories. I just want to know *why*."

For a heartbeat, her expression flickered; her pale lips parted, her eyes softening.

Was that guilt?

But it passed as quickly as it came, her mouth twisting back into a sneer.

"You're in no position to demand answers, my love." Her voice stiffened, coldness creeping back into her demeanor. "Do as I've asked and maybe, *just maybe*, I'll tell you. After I get what I want."

Gideon exhaled slowly and turned to Cas. He searched his friend's face, hoping for some miracle. Maybe Cas would break free, maybe time would stretch out and give Gideon a chance. But there was none to be had. He was trapped.

Stepping toward the door, he stretched out his hand and gripped the knob, the metal impossibly icy on his skin.

"Don't do it, Gid!" Cas cried out, thrashing in her grasp.

"Do it, or he dies," the Master shrieked.

Gideon twisted the knob and the door burst open, a deluge of memories exploding from within. Wind howled like a beast unleashed, ripping through the void with hurricane force. Debris of images, voices, flashes of feeling all spiraled out of the doorway.

"It's done!" The Master cackled. "I can finally see what those damned Owls are hiding!"

Pulling with all his might, Gideon tried to close the door, to silence the rising cacophony, but the flood pressed him back. A violet mist, thick and endless, surged into the void like a tide. It poured over the storm of memories, consuming everything in its path.

"No, no, no," Gideon whispered, a renewed sense of panic washing over him. He tried to back away, but the mist curled around his feet, tethering him in place. The muscles in his back twitched, but wouldn't respond as he attempted to lift his wings.

Trapped, a voice cut through the darkness, soft and distant, like a lullaby.

"Time to wake up, my dear."

Chapter Three

Pelanor

"Where the hell is Théo?" Pelanor's wings twitched with unease. He hovered twenty feet above the ground, rapping on the front door until his knuckles throbbed. Ten minutes passed. No answer.

Circling the house, he pressed to the windows, searching for movement. Still nothing. The place felt abandoned.

When he reached the bedroom window, his wings faltered, throwing him off balance.

"What…happened here?" The words slipped out before he could stop them.

The bed was flipped on its side, straw spilling in messy tufts. Shards of glass glittered faintly in the morning light. Stains darkened the floorboards in uneven streaks.

Pelanor's chest tightened, his heart thudding unevenly. He jerked away from the window and dropped to the ground, landing with a heavy thud beside one of the stilts that held the house aloft. He gripped it for balance, breath shallow, mind racing.

What I wouldn't give for a vision right now.

He squeezed his eyes shut, desperate for the familiar blur that signaled foresight. But, as always, his gift refused to come when he needed it. It never worked on command.

A slam rang out from somewhere nearby.

Pelanor snapped upright, wings half-spread, eyes darting for the source. A few houses down, a Dove woman launched herself from her porch, heading toward the city center.

"Hey!" Pelanor shouted, his voice cracking from panic.

Faltering mid-flight, the Dove's wings fluttered awkwardly before she steadied herself in the air.

Pelanor cleared his throat, forcing his tone into a calm. "Sorry to bother you," he called, more composed. "But have you happened to see Théo recently?"

"Théo?" she echoed, concern tightening her features even from afar. "You might want to check the tavern," she continued after a pause, an awkward note in her voice. "My guess is you'll find him there."

"The tavern?" Pelanor repeated, but she was already gone, fading into the mist above the rooftops. He remained beneath the house, the damp grass beginning to seep through his shoes, his thoughts churning.

The sun is barely up, what in the name of Mim would he be doing at the tavern? Théo's an early riser, sure, but not a drinker. Not unless there was something to celebrate. And what could possibly explain the wreckage in his bedroom?

A cool breeze bit into his dew-stained robe. With a final glance at the house, the Owl lifted into the air and took off toward the village center.

Flying over Tartarus, he couldn't help but marvel at the sprawl of new construction. Several buildings gleamed with unvarnished timber, their frames still raw and unfinished. It was a far cry from his first visit, when the village had been little more than a scatter of lean-tos, hastily assembled by a breakaway group of Doves.

He had come then with Valanor, the late leader of the Noktern scholars. The High Priests of Pas and Valys—the largest Dove cities—had feared the formation of a permanent settlement and tasked the scholars with negotiating a peace deal that precluded construction. But Tartarus's fledgling council wouldn't entertain the idea, citing years of relentless persecution: beatings, public denouncements, exile for loving the wrong people or rejecting the suffocating dogma of Dove religion. Since then, there's only been tentative peace between the two factions because the Noktern deemed Tartarus legitimate.

Reaching the city center, Pelanor touched down lightly on a narrow suspension bridge, its ropes creaking underfoot. The bridges, strung like braids between the oldest buildings, were a necessity here. Tartarus sat in a floodplain, and storms often rendered the ground im-passable. During periods of heavy rain, the bridges allowed the village to stay connected and permitted travel when the conditions were unideal for flight.

The tavern stood crookedly at the far end, its thatched roof lopsided and its faded sign clinging to the post above the door. Pelanor paused on the threshold, trying once more to will a vision to the surface. But there was nothing—no blur of color, no whispers of what was to come.

I hate going in blind.

It had been years since Pelanor last saw Théo—since their falling out. He had no idea how Théo might take the news he carried. Would he flare up in anger? Shut down in silence?

The longer Pelanor lingered, the more he felt eyes on him. Doves passed along the gangways, their glances quick but weighted, curiosity and caution mingling. None came close, yet their stares pressed in all the same.

He drew a steadying breath and pushed open the door. The smell struck him at once: sweat and stale ale, heavy and cloying. He'd been here before, long ago, but the memory hadn't preserved the way the scent seeped into everything. With no windows and no air to escape, it simply hung there, thick as fog.

He squinted into the dim interior and stepped inside.

"Well, well," a voice boomed from the shadows. "If it isn't Pelanor, the great scholar."

The Owl blinked against the weak candlelight, then caught the familiar rumble. "Théo," he ventured, forcing a smile as the Dove rose unsteadily from his stool. The tavern door shut behind Pelanor with a hard click, and the echo rattled across the slatted floor, making him flinch. "It's been a long time," the Owl managed, working to steady his nerves.

"Three long years, my friend," Théo replied, a broad, drunken grin spreading across his face.

Friend.

The word should have landed soft, a kindness after so long. Instead, it struck like a blow, lodging in Pelanor's chest. For a flicker of a moment, the floor seemed to tilt under him. He smoothed the reaction away as quickly as it came, forcing a weak smile. He had no claim to Théo anymore, no right to feel the sting. Yet it lingered, sharp and unwelcome, beneath his ribs.

"Ohhh, get over here!" Théo bellowed, throwing his massive arms around Pelanor and hauling him clean off the ground.

The Owl wheezed, pinned in the bear hug before he could react. "Yes, yes. Good to see you, too. Now kindly *put me down!*"

"Still as prudish as ever, I see." Théo set him down roughly and they both teetered before crashing to the floor in a tangle of feathers.

"For Mim's sake, Théo," Pelanor sniped scathingly. Wriggling free from beneath the Dove, he used a chair to haul himself up, brushing sawdust from his wings and patting dust off his robes. "The sun's barely up and you're three sheets to the wind. What's gotten into you?"

Théo straightened with unsettling speed. His warm humor evaporated, replaced by a rapid, raw fury. "I'll tell you what's gotten into me!" His voice cracked, tears springing to his eyes. "My mate's missing. We've searched everywhere. He's just...gone!"

Pelanor's heart clenched. He stepped forward and awkwardly enfolded Théo in a cautious hug. Collapsing against him, the Dove trembled as he sobbed; his rough spun tunic felt damp. Pelanor prayed it was sweat and not something worse.

"There, there," the Owl soothed, awkwardly patting Théo's back. He glanced around the near-deserted tavern.

The bartender was busy nursing her own drink and a Dove slumped unconscious in the corner.

Pelanor rolled his eyes.

No help in sight.

"For the love of Avis!" Pelanor squawked, shoving Théo back. He planted his hands on his hips, feathers bristling. "Just look at you. A husk. A hollow shell. You look like you haven't slept in days. Your feathers are matted with Mim only knows what and you reek like a dead animal."

From years of diplomacy work, he knew that he should stop there and wait for a reply. But the sight of Théo in such a state burned in his stomach, and the words came tumbling out without thinking better. "I know you loved him. But by the heavens, pull yourself together, man."

Théo's wailing suddenly ceased, his face twisting in a sneer that made Pelanor's blood run cold. The Dove planted himself between Pelanor and the door, the tavern's lone exit. With that towering frame and wingspan, there was no easy escape, especially if Théo decided to attack in retribution.

"What else should I have expected from you?" The Dove gnashed his teeth, the heat draining from his face, leaving only bitter disdain. "You don't know how to love. The only thing you've ever truly cared about is the Noktern. You proved that the day you left me."

The words struck hard, the air punched out of Pelanor's lungs, his chest caving under the weight of that truth. He would've preferred if Théo had chosen physical violence.

"Well?" Théo pressed, eyes blazing, nostrils flared. "Nothing to say?"

Pelanor forced a breath, rolling his shoulders back to steel himself. "You're too drunk for this conversation," he orated, voice steady, wings flaring slightly to project strength. "I didn't come here to relitigate the past. I came because I need your help." His voice softened, but only a touch. "I'm sorry about Rocque. I truly am. I know this must be—"

"What do you know?" Théo cut in, his voice suddenly hushed, almost reverent. "I know you, Pelanor. I *know* you. You're hiding something." His posture shifted. Some of the alcohol-fueled rage gave way to something sharper. A desperate clarity. "What do you know about Rocque?"

Pelanor opened his mouth, but the words jammed in his throat. He hadn't meant to say it. Not like this. But they spilled out before he could stop them. "He's dead."

Théo reeled. "That's not true," he gasped, backing away as if the revelation itself were something toxic. "It's not true," he repeated, stumbling into a frantic loop. "It's not true, it's not true—" He paced violently before the bar, striking his temples with the heels of his hands. The bartender glanced up, then looked away, weary; she'd clearly seen this too many times.

"You're lying!" Théo erupted, his voice breaking. Tears cut down his soot-streaked face, his fists trembling at his sides.

Pelanor didn't move, the bitter taste of failure curling on his tongue.

Stay calm.

He chided himself. He needed Théo's help. And now he'd shattered the Dove's last thread of hope. If he wanted to salvage anything, he'd have to control himself. Diplomacy, not emotion. Strategy, not guilt.

Easier said than done.

"I'm not lying." Pelanor averred softly. He rolled his shoulders back and stretched out his neck. "Théo, I need to tell you everything. Please, sit."

He reached for Théo's wrist, the Dove's skin hot to the touch. Gently, Pelanor steered him to a quiet corner of the tavern; he expected some kind of struggle, but Théo didn't resist. He slid into the chair with a heavy thud, gaze unfocused, and Pelanor's heart clenched at how lost he looked.

Settling opposite him, Pelanor took a steadying breath. He chose his words carefully, knowing Théo's mind was frayed. Over the next quarter-hour, he laid out the conspiracy of the Ravens, the Noktern's plan to turn Avis into a battlefield, and his own mission to find the Owls' champion, Gideon. Théo listened, eyes glazed, only once looking up when Pelanor described Rocque's fate. But even that was no more than a passing glance.

At last, Pelanor told how he'd escaped the Noktern. Three days ago, his world had shattered. He'd collapsed among the Midden Stones, too exhausted to fly farther; by the next dusk he'd forced himself onward, needing another day just to recover. And all the while, Forranor—now Head Owl after Valanor's death—was doubtlessly spinning lies to the tribal councils, branding Pelanor a traitor, implicating him in the disappearances.

He paused, letting the weight of everything settle between them.

"So you see," Pelanor started, angling his head to meet Théo's gaze, "you're the only Avian I can trust." He waited for any response, but Théo didn't answer. He sat motionless, expression unreadable. The silence stretched, heavy and uncomfortable. Pelanor wavered for a beat, but then pressed on. "I know this must be difficult to process, especially after what you've lost, but–"

"Don't." Théo's voice was barbed.

Pelanor reeled his head to see the Dove's face had twisted into a scowl; his lips thinned, eyes narrowed and nostrils flared.

"Don't even pretend to care about Rocque," Théo spat.

"You misunderstand, I–"

"You think I don't know you?" Théo snapped, pushing up from the chair with a screech of wood against wood. He swayed slightly but stood tall, his voice suddenly crisp with clarity. "I gather that this is a very serious situation, and I feel for the people in Avis who have suffered at the hands of these Ravens. But I won't help you, Pelanor. You only ever show up when it's *convenient*, when *you* need something. And you *always* hide it behind talk of the 'greater good.' You don't give a damn about what I've lost. You never have."

"Théo, please," Pelanor begged, rising. "I'm not here to reopen old wounds. What happened to Rocque, what the Master did…it's *monstrous.* But if you let this personal grudge blind you to what's coming, more people will suffer."

"Oh, spare me your righteousness." Turning toward the bar, Théo scoffed. A wild, toothy grin stretched from ear to ear. "This isn't about some noble cause."

Pelanor noticed a shift in the room. The bartender had stopped pretending she wasn't listening; the Dove who'd been passed out in the corner had finally stirred, his glossy eyes transfixed on them.

Théo turned and grabbed a bottle off the shelf, returning with slow, deliberate steps. He stopped just short of Pelanor, so close the Owl could smell the sour tang of alcohol and grief on his breath.

"You always did what was best for *you,*" Théo growled. "You chose the Noktern over me…you didn't even think about it! And now you want to drag me into another one of your crusades?" He leaned in. "You don't care about anyone, Pelanor. You never have. And you never will."

Pelanor didn't flinch, but inside, something buckled.

Bringing the bottle to his lips, Théo bit down on the cork before yanking it free with a pop that rang through the otherwise silent tavern. Tilting his head back, he drained three gulps of the amber liquor.

"You're running quite a tab, Théo," the bartender sneered. "Any plans to pay up one of these days?"

"Keep it open, Brigitte," he slurred, swaying on his heavy boots. "You know I'm good for it." He gave a conspiratorial wink. "After all, I *am* the mayor."

Turning back to Pelanor, Théo jabbed a finger into the Owl's chest. With a pause, he bit his lip and stared at the ceiling as if searching for strength. Finally, he exhaled, voice low and bitter: "I hope you find the help you're looking for," he exhaled with a bitter smile, "but you won't get it from me."

Without another word, he swaggered toward the door, tripping over the threshold as he left. The slam of wood echoed in the sudden stillness.

"Do you think this is what Rocque would've wanted for you?" Pelanor called out, voice cracking. "Being piss-drunk and broken over his memory? Or would he have wanted you to be the leader he knew you to be?"

Théo stopped with his hand on the door, but refused to turn around. Pushing forward, sunlight spilled into the tavern and Pelanor shielded his eyes. "Goodbye, Pelanor," Théo uttered in a flat tone. Then, he stepped back out and the door swung shut, plunging the tavern into darkness again.

"Fuck," Pelanor spat, fists slamming against the table. He had one chance to try and turn things around and he blew it. His chest tightened, hopelessness pooling in his gut.

"Pelanor, was it?" Brigitte approached, polishing a mug as she did. To Pelanor's dismay, she spat into it before wiping it clean. "Don't waste your pity on him," she continued. "He's been here almost every night for three months. He's not well." She shook her head, sorrow softening her voice. "I wouldn't take anything he says to heart."

Pelanor wanted to find solace in her words, but he couldn't. Théo had been right. He hadn't come to Tartarus to mourn Rocque, or even to protect the people here. He had come because his standing in the Noktern was compromised. Because he was afraid. And in his fear, he had dragged Gideon into the Master's talons, knowing full well the Finch boy was in over his head.

Was it really duty that brought him here? Or was it guilt? Maybe it was just his desperate urge to salvage his own reputation.

I don't even know anymore.

"Can I get you something to drink?" Brigitte offered gently.

With a sigh, Pelanor climbed onto a barstool, his wings drooping behind him to the floor like heavy drapery. "What do you recommend?"

Brigitte didn't answer; instead, she grabbed two glasses, reached for a bottle on the top shelf and poured a generous measure into each. Sliding one in front of him, she lifted her own.

"Santé," she cheered.

"Tchin-Tchin," he echoed before downing his drink.

The liquor burned like fire down his throat. He gagged, coughing into his sleeve as a strange warmth crawled behind his eyes, familiar fuzziness tugging at the corner of his vision.

"What's your name, boy?" a man's voice demanded authoritatively.

Pelanor staggered backward in the vision, breath hitching.

"Go suck a pig's teat," a fledgling spat, a young Dove, dirty and defiant.

A crack echoed as a guard's hand whipped across the boy's face. Pelanor recoiled with the force of the strike, staggering again in the real world, though his body remained seated. His hands clutched the bar, his knuckles white.

The boy crumpled, one hand pressed to his cheek. Two guards pinned his arms, while a third set the sword's tip against the tender place where his wings met his back. Their faces were warped; Pelanor couldn't make them out. But the emblem on their uniforms was clear. A flaming sword encircled in gold lettering.

Judica Causam Nostrorum.

Defend our cause.

The crest of the Inquisitors, a fanatical sect of Valysian Doves. They hunted down and punished anyone they considered to be heretics, *purifying* them.

But the Inquisitors were abolished over a century ago.

Or so Pelanor thought. At least, that's what he'd been taught by the historians at the Noktern.

"I won't ask again, boy," the man growled. The voice didn't echo in the air, it echoed in *Pelanor*. It vibrated in his chest like it came from his own lungs. He wasn't just watching anymore. He was *inside* this man, tethered to his senses.

"Yuri," the boy sniffled, blood dribbling from his split lip. He couldn't have been more than twelve. Small, skinny, far too young to be in chains.

What could the guards possibly want with him?

Pelanor searched the edges of the vision for clues. All he could see were trees, thick with towering trunks and hanging moss. Somewhere in the forests outside Valys, but where exactly, he couldn't say.

"Was that so hard, Yuri?" the man sneered. Spurs clanked with every slow and measured step. The vision turned with him as he walked, the world shifting from the boy to a battered wagon nearby. The voice continued, mocking and smooth. "Now, you're going to tell me where these supplies came from, and we can all go about our merry way. Can you do that?"

Pelanor's gaze dropped as the man looked over the wagon's cargo. A thick, gloved hand sifted through burlap sacks revealing wineskins, jars of honey, dried meats, a bundle of lavender, amid other sundries and provisions.

"I already told you," Yuri whimpered. "They're from Grappa. I'm delivering the cart to a private merchant in Moda."

The man shook his head. "See, Yuri, that's where you've lost me," he replied, voice dripping with cruelty. "Grappan vintners send their wares through the Finchlands by sea. Always have. Because they *know* we don't tolerate alcohol in the Dovelands."

Yuri opened his mouth to protest, but the man cut him off.

"Franz. Alexandre."

Two guards snapped to attention. "Aye, Sarge?"

"Take the boy away. Throw him in the Brick for questioning."

The Brick?

The word echoed like a thunderclap inside Pelanor's skull.

It can't be.

The Brick was a prison so vile, the terracotta walls cooked its inmates alive during daylight. Even the High Priests and Hierophants of the Dovelands had agreed it was an abomination. The Inquisitors were supposed to be gone, the Brick torn down.

But here they are.

"Once he cracks," the man—Sarge—continued coolly, "I'll finally have Airam's head on a spike. That witch is as good as mine." He turned back to the wagon. "Someone bring me a torch. This shipment isn't making it to Tartarus."

Orange light bloomed in the periphery of the vision as a fire erupted, spreading fast. Flames curled up the sides of the wagon, catching the burlap until they licked the sky. Heat roared through the vision, blistering and searing, pressing against Pelanor's temples like burning irons. Pelanor gasped as flames devoured everything.

"Sir!"

Heart pounding, Pelanor blinked back into the waking world. The fire vanished, heat evaporated, replaced by the damp air of the tavern.

"I've been screaming at you for five minutes," Brigitte scowled, shaking his shoulders. "Are you alright?"

"Never better," he muttered, brushing her hands off his robes as the haze in his eyes cleared.

She stared at him like he'd grown a second head. "What the hell happened to you?"

"I don't know what you mean." He forced a shrug. "But tell me something," he added, sidestepping her concern. "Do you know someone named Airam?"

Brigitte froze, blinking at him as if he'd asked something untoward. Her hand slipped from the mug she was holding, nearly dropping it before she caught herself. "Airam?" she echoed, her voice sharper than before. "Well... yes. She's where we get the goods we can't make ourselves in Tartarus. But how do *you*—"

"I'm an Owl." He flicked a wrist in dismissal, an exaggerated nonchalance in his reply, and to his relief, she seemed to accept that.

Brigitte frowned, still unsettled, but she gave a reluctant nod. "Right."

"Has she been reliable?"

"I...suppose."

Maybe it was the liquor, or maybe it was the lingering urgency of the vision, but something in Pelanor snapped into place. "Would you say she's the sort who can track down anything, no matter how obscure?"

Brigitte narrowed her eyes. "I guess? But what does–"

"I need you to tell me where I can find her." Pelanor didn't let her finish.

She hesitated, her eyes narrowing. Clearly, Airam's location wasn't something people just handed out.

Pelanor exhaled sharply.

Fine. No more diplomacy.

He tugged a coin purse from his sleeve and let it fall onto the bar. The soft thud and metallic clink carried more promise than words. "If you tell me where Airam is, I'll use this gold to clear Théo's debt. Deal?"

Brigitte arched a brow, skeptical. She lifted the pouch, testing its weight with a practiced hand. "That's not even close to what Théo owes me."

Pelanor's jaw tightened, but before he could answer, she added, "...But it's a start." With a deft flick, she emptied the coins into her apron pocket.

Chapter Four

GIDEON

Gideon fought against the wind, wings flailing as he tumbled through the storm of darkness and debris. A violent gust tore through his feathers pulling him down into the abyss. He gasped, but the air refused to stay in his lungs. The harder he struggled, the faster he fell.

"It's okay," his mother's voice cooed, soft yet piercing, reaching him through the gale like a thread of silk. "Just give in. Everything will be alright."

He faltered, his wings giving out beneath the tempest. As he succumbed, the wind died down and the mist dissolved; the world went still. He was alone, suspended in an infinite sea of black. No ground, no sky, neither up nor down. Gideon wanted to scream, to thrash and fight for control, but his body refused to move. His voice had no sound.

"Come out of it, my dear."

His eyes blinked open to a flicker of orange, a wisp from a flameless lantern, glowing softly in the dark. The air returned to his lungs, slow and shallow, as the room took shape: stone walls streaked with age, a slatted wooden ceiling above, the whitewash on the walls gray with neglect.

"There you are!" Cecilia greeted him warmly, her voice snapping into focus as her form appeared beside the bed.

Gideon jerked back, wings flaring against the wall behind him.

"I was afraid you wouldn't come out of it." Her lips curled gently. "But you look right as rain now."

"Don't touch me," he rasped, recoiling as she reached for his face.

Her joy faltered, annoyance flickering in her eyes, but she withdrew, the wooden chair creaking beneath her as she leaned away. "I'm sorry about the accommodations." Her tone was brittle and overly formal. "I didn't imagine I'd ever have the pleasure of hosting you. But I hope the room is to your liking."

Gideon's eyes flitted around the room, taking in the faded paintings and worn knickknacks that cluttered the dressers. Along the far wall, bookshelves groaned beneath the weight of ancient tomes, their cracked spines and dust-laced pages hinting at centuries of secrets. Under better circumstances, Gideon would have been eager to explore them.

But something else gnawed at his senses.

As his gaze lilted around the chamber, an eerie ticking buffeted Gideon's ears. Twisting his neck, he found an ancient clock mounted above the bed. Its wooden trim was blackened with rot, the once-delicate carvings now little more than ghosts of patterns long erased by time. The metal hands jittered out of sync, bent and twitching, gouging jagged trails into the face of the timepiece. The longer he stared, the louder the ticking became, hammering against his skull like the clocktower in Moda used to.

"You can look at me, you know." Cecilia broke into the memory, her voice soft and tinged with amusement.

"I'm not going to trance you. I've no reason to. You'll find that here at Fate's Folly, there's nowhere to run."

Fate's Folly?

The name rang through Gideon like a bell. He had only ever heard it in whispers—rumors traded in the academy courtyard, spooky tales meant to frighten fledglings. It was an ancient castle, built by the Sapiens before the Great End, isolated on Raven's Rock, a northern island buried deep in the Crowlands. Haunted. Cursed. Long forgotten.

A knot of anxiety tightened in his stomach, but he forced himself to remain composed. He wouldn't show weakness, not to her.

"So I'm a prisoner," he stated flatly.

"No, no, no, my love." She leaned forward, her onyx wings brushing the table behind her with a dry *thump*. "You're my boy. I'd never make you a prisoner."

"Then what would you call me, *mother*?"

She winced. "Must you call me that? 'Mother' sounds so...clinical, so sinister. "

"Then it's fitting."

"Oh, Gideon." Her smile wavered, partly in affection, the other pain. "Of course you still see me as the villain. And why wouldn't you? After everything that's happened. After I left you. After my...experiments."

"You *kidnapped* people!" Gideon spat. "You *tortured* them! You turned Cas into a *monster*!"

"Yes." The word was soft, sliding off her tongue. "I suppose I did." Leaning back in her chair, Cecilia twisted around and picked something off the table behind her. In one swift motion, she stood and tossed a worn book through the air. It landed at the foot of the cot with a *thud*, stirring the dust.

"What's this?" Gideon reached for the tome, the cover creaking as he opened it revealing a delicate script etched in one of the ancient Sapien languages.

Tvanor's Journal.

The title read in an elegant, deliberate script. He didn't recognize the name, but the aura of the text was unmistakable. It was an Owl's work. One from *before* the Great End.

"Where did you get this?"

"I found it during one of my excursions." She paused at the door. "It was tucked away in a building —looked like an old military base or something akin. Why don't you read page one-forty-five. It might help you understand. Maybe even see me as something more than the bad guy here."

Without another word, she turned on her heel and pulled the door shut, the ancient hinges screaming.

"Wait!" Gideon shouted. He lunged from the cot, cold stone biting at his bare feet. "Don't leave me in here!" he cried, but the door slammed shut, and the echoing *click* of a bolt sliding home cut through him like a blade. He tore at the handle and pounded against the wood, but the slab wouldn't budge.

"Damn it," he hissed.

Skin prickling with frustration, he let his forehead rest against the stone, too hard. "Ow," he grumbled, blinking back the sting. Fingers raked through his sandy hair as he tried to collect himself and form a plan.

"I have to get out of here," he whispered.

His eyes darted around the room. A single window. With three strides, he crossed to it and wrapped his fingers around the rusting bars. He pulled, straining, but they wouldn't budge, the iron sunk deep into the stone like the bones of the keep itself.

Angling his sight through the bars, he looked out on the desolate scene. Fate's Folly was built into the side of a jagged hill-peak, its foundation carved into the very spine of the land. Beyond the window, a barren moor unfolded like a wound. Craggy and gray, it was speckled with patches of hardy moss that clung to collapsed trunks of ancient trees. The world below looked long-forgotten, stretched thin beneath a sky choked with clouds. At the edge of the horizon, waves crashed against black cliffs, their rhythm a slow and sorrowful melody.

"Think, Gideon," he whispered, pacing the room. "Even if I got out of here, then what?"

His fingers trailed along the rugged stone as he circled the table, eyes scanning for solutions that wouldn't come. He'd head back to the Noktern, of course, but what about Cas?

"Where could he be?" he muttered, stopping mid-step.

The memory came in broken flashes: Cas crumpled on the ground, his skin scorched, the acrid stench of burnt feathers hanging in the air. Then the trance, his mother's voice wrapping around Gideon like a net, then the vision of

Cas rising, staggering, following them skyward. After that...nothing.

He has to be somewhere in the castle.

And if that was true, Gideon couldn't leave him.

Not again.

"That's not fair to yourself," he mumbled. He hadn't had a choice when the Ravens took Cas. He'd barely escaped Goldfinch's estate with his life. Still, Cas's anger haunted him. The way he'd looked at Gideon at the Noktern... "It doesn't matter." Gideon shook his head and pushed the guilt aside. "I'm not leaving here without him. So I might as well make myself at home."

He wandered to the bookshelves, brushing dust from the ancient spines. The leather bindings crackled beneath his touch.

"These must be ancient...even by Sapien standards." Most of the titles were in languages he couldn't read, their scripts curved, yet jagged, completely alien to him. Then, nestled between two crumbling tomes, he spotted one in familiar text.

The Prince.

Sliding the thin book free, he blew gently across the cover, revealing the faded title more clearly. Flipping to a random page, he read aloud:

> *"Upon this a question arises: whether it be better to be loved than feared or feared than loved?"*

"Ugh," Gideon groaned, snapping the book shut. "I can't handle Sapien politics right now."

He tossed it back irreverently on the shelf and returned to the cot, collapsing into the scratchy wool blanket. As he rolled onto his side, a soft *thud* jolted him upright.

The journal.

It had slipped from the bed and landed on the floor, the red leather stark against the gray stone. He leaned down and picked it up, brushing the dust from the cover with more care than he'd given *The Prince*.

"I almost forgot," he murmured. Settling in, he propped his back against the wall; wrapped in his wings, he studied the book. There was something intoxicating about it, as if it pulsed faintly in his hands, drawing him in. He couldn't tell if it was the journal itself, or what its contents might reveal.

"Let's see what all this is about, then."

Gideon flipped through the pages, reading arbitrary passages in the hope that something might jump out at him. He didn't expect much; he couldn't imagine anything that would spark his mother's pursuit of villainy, but a small part of him held onto the possibility that these brittle pages could offer some explanation.

Line after line, Gideon poured through the neat scrollwork, digesting all he could about the world before the Great End.

"They traveled to other planets?" he gawked, each revelation of the ancient Sapiens' accomplishments prompting a new outburst. There were so many things he couldn't fully understand: robots, airplanes, microwaves.

Things he had never seen or heard of anywhere outside of stories.

From what he could gather, Tvanor was second-in-command of the Avians, serving as the First Owl's right-hand. The First Owl, Primanor, was a powerful seer, a gift the ancient Sapiens had genetically engineered in him.

"Whatever that means," Gideon groaned, running his fingers over the faded ink.

Primanor had a vision of the Great End and decided that the Owls would create a sanctuary—the Noktern—that would refurnish the world after its destruction. Gideon had known that much, but the way Tvanor described it, the Owls were meant to be far more involved in restructuring the world. Gideon had always known the Owls to be reclusive, intervening only on the rarest occasions.

"Like when people started going missing," he whispered.

Having his fill of random passages, Gideon flicked to page one-forty-five as his mother had suggested, immediately noting the shift in tone. When the project began, he could sense her excitement as she laid out her ideals and the benefits the Noktern would bring to the new world. But as months turned into years; frustration bled onto the pages.

08 March

HOW DARE THEY DO THIS? Marcanor is nothing more than a misogynistic, pigheaded, stubborn oaf. I don't even understand why he was made a scholar. The Noktern is my project, and these men think they can just sweep in and take it over like they own it? I don't know why I should be surprised. They've been doing it for millennia, so why stop now at the end of the world? Well, Marcanor and his band of pretentious disciples (fuck them all) have decided that they will be writing out a new set of bylaws for how the Noktern will run once Operation AVIS is underway.

Gideon had seen several references to Operation AVIS: Allocation of Vital Infrastructure and Support.

They want to butcher the program! Scrap AVIS and call their new project Operation Innocence.

"Innocence," Gideon uttered, the word igniting a memory. "The Owl's prophecy…something about finding the champion before innocence is undone."

As if "Innocence" even begins to describe what they want. If anything, they're culpable of creating a world that will be crueler than it needs to be. They insist that by being open and transparent, we're ensuring that future generations will take advantage of the benefits we provide. Mind you, these benefits they're talking about are basic materials such as medicine. We've literally stockpiled at least three centuries worth of viable treatments for the most rudimentary of illnesses. Not to mention the materials and recipes needed to craft more. And they don't think that future inhabitants should have access to this. They believe that after rebuilding the environment, any survivors should fend for themselves.

"That's…cruel," Gideon murmured, recalling the marvels he'd seen in the fortress beneath the mountain: automated medical supplies, fireless lanterns, self-sustaining subterranean gardens. This technology *could* elevate the livelihoods of all tribes.

"But they've hidden it away. They kept it from us."

Why would the Owls think this was the best plan? How many people suffered because of it?

He kept reading, hoping the journal would provide more answers.

When I brought it up with Primanor, he told me that he understands my frustration, but that I would just have to get over it. Like I was a child, he tried to explain to me that collaboration requires sacrifice. That working with others demands that I give up my morality if it's the will of the majority. I was FLABBERGASTED! It's like he wants to treat the well-being of an entire race of people like some botched school project! Meanwhile, my entire proposal for Operation AVIS was built on his vision for the future!

Then these people come along and think they'll change everything. Well, it's absolute bullshit. Fortunately, Minka and I have secured a back-up plan to make sure that the new world flourishes with all of the advantages we hoped to afford them.

Before he could read any further, the lock clicked. With a *thud*, the door burst open as wood slammed against stone. His mother stood in the archway, her eyes glistening with that familiar violet light. There was a flash, harsh and blinding, and pain cracked through his skull like lightning. But just as quickly, it was gone.

A wicked smirk etched on her lips. "Ah, so you've read it."

"Stay out of my head!" he snapped, rubbing the back of his skull where a dull throb still lingered.

"And even after all that," she scoffed, ignoring his demand, "you still cling to your sympathies for the Noktern scholars."

Gideon's gaze drifted away, uncertain how to respond. He hadn't had enough time to process what he'd read. Tvanor's journal had shaken something in him, making him question the trust he'd placed in the scholars. He thought of Pelanor—how evasive the Owl had always been, how carefully he doled out information. Was that about protecting Innocence, or was it just Pelanor being Pelanor?

But no matter what the journal contained, Gideon couldn't understand how his mother used it to justify everything she'd done.

"Come," she bade, extending her untaloned hand. "I know this is a lot to take in. Let me explain."

Gideon hesitated, eyeing her with deep suspicion. He couldn't forget the atrocities she'd committed. Still, if Tvanor's words were true, maybe there was more to her plan than he understood.

Do I owe her a chance?

"But Cas," he whispered, anchoring himself.

No.

She'd mutilated his best friend, twisted him into a raging monster. Nothing could justify that. Gideon could never forgive her for what she did to him.

Even so, he wasn't in a position to argue. With a look, she could bend his will. For now, compliance was survival. He laid the journal down and stood, crossing the room slowly. When he reached her, she reached for his shoulder, but he recoiled from her touch.

"Where are we going?" His voice was flat, asserting his reluctance.

She withdrew her hand, her lips pursed in an indignant pout. "I want to show you something."

Chapter Five

Socorra

"Would ye whimperin' lot quit complainin' about yer blistered feet!" Agnes bellowed, bracing herself on the cab door as the carriage bounced along the uneven floor of the pine forest. "Ye've done nothin' but cry since we left the bloody Noktern! Give it a rest, would ye?" The carriage door crashed shut with a reverberating *thud*, echoing through the still forest. The horses startled, whinnying sharp protests before pressing onward, hooves crunching over roots as they forced their way through the tangled thicket.

"I want to be Agnes when I grow up," Fatima beamed with satisfaction.

Using her spear to press through the damp ever-green boughs, Socorra gave a half-hearted chuckle. "Me too."

Behind them, the Owl guards grumbled as they slogged through the muddy forest, still bitter over the half-day trek.

"I still don't get why we couldn't just fly," one muttered, keeping his voice low.

"I know," another nodded. "It's not like we're the ones who need the carriage. We could all have flown to Krepusk in less than two hours while that fat oaf and the–"

"Go ahead." Socorra's voice was gravely, crackling in her throat. She stopped short, spear clutched tight, and beat her wings violently. The gust slammed into the two guards, forcing them back a step. Her gaze pinned them in place, cold and unyielding. "Finish that sentence."

"He didn't mean it!" The guard's eyes widened as she stammered. Taking a few paces back, she lowered her shoulders and cowered in the crook of her wings, her feathers bristling.

Socorra's gaze locked on the remaining guard. He gaped at her, scrawny shoulders hunched tight against his neck as she closed in. Around them, the other Owls had fallen silent, their trek forgotten as they watched the commotion unfold. She didn't care. For weeks she had borne their sidelong glances, their hushed murmurs of pity.

What a shame Kyte lost his wing, they said, pretending to care. But Socorra had seen the pity behind their eyes, had heard it in their voices, thin and false, dripping from their tongues like rot.

She wasn't a fool. She knew what they really thought of Kyte—what they whispered behind her back as she sat by his bedside in the med wing after the battle at the Noktern.

Broken. Cripple. What good is an Avian who can't fly?

She wasn't going to let it slide again. Especially not from some sniveling boy bold enough to say it so brazenly.

"Now, what were you going to say?" The question seethed through clenched teeth. Her eyes locked on the guard; she watched his breath quicken, his gaze flitting side to side in search of escape. He started backing away, but Socorra pressed forward, preventing his retreat.

"You heard her!" Fatima's voice rang out behind them, cutting through the rustling boughs. "Answer the question!"

Startled, the Owl staggered back and hit the ground with a grunt. His wings flailed, scattering dead needles as he clawed for balance. A flicker of guilt coiled in Socorra's gut. She rolled her eyes, exhaling hard, then bit the inside of her cheek before thrusting out a hand.

The Owl froze, eyeing her warily.

Tired of waiting, Socorra bent down and grabbed him by the collar, yanking him up from the forest floor. Once on his feet, he blinked at her, dazed and unsure.

"I'm sorry," he stammered, brushing damp needles from his sleeves. "I didn't mean–"

"I'm sure," Socorra growled. She jabbed a finger into his chest. "Don't let it happen again." Her voice dropped, razor-sharp. "Next time I'll put you under the ground."

"Alright, alright," came a voice from behind them. Aldanor, the captain of the Owl guard. Her armor clanked as she stepped forward. "Let's break it up." She narrowed her eyes at Socorra. "And Socorra–" she added bitterly, brushing short hair from her face, "I trust I don't need to remind you that I expect to return with the same number of Owls I left with."

"Yes, ma'am," Socorra spat, finally tearing her glare away from the guard. She turned and stalked back to Fatima's side, simmering with rage as they pressed deeper into the seemingly endless forest.

"She didn't specify they needed to be alive," Fatima mumbled behind her.

But Socorra didn't respond. Keeping her head down, the Hawk strode through the trees at a brisk pace, trying to shake off the bitter encounter. But nothing worked. Even Fatima's idle chatter only drew the occasional grunt or a half-hearted *okay*. Nausea churned in her stomach, rising toward her throat. Every step dragged like an eternity, her thoughts pounding in her skull. The fire in her knuckles flared, forcing her to loosen her grip on the spear. As they pressed on, her pace slowed until, at last, the company reached the edge of the woods.

"That's Krepusk?" Fatima groaned, snapping Socorra out of her haze. "And I thought Konstat had problems."

Before Socorra could reply, Captain Aldanor's voice rang out from behind. "Cut down some of these branches, will you? The horses can't get through with the carriage."

Exhausted after their grueling trek south, the Owls muttered curses as they began hacking a path with their swords.

Pushing past them, Socorra brushed aside the last branches and stepped into the clearing beyond. She stopped short; this wasn't what she'd expected. After a few weeks in the Noktern, she'd grown used to its small luxuries, hot showers especially, the way steaming water worked the knots from her shoulders. But Krepusk was nothing like the stronghold. Smoke curled against the orange sky, rising from broken stone chimneys. The towering monoliths looked ready to collapse, their pinewood foundations rotting beneath a patchwork of warped rooftops and splintered beams.

Fatima stepped out of the forest and drew up beside Socorra. The Hawk had been so lost in thought she didn't notice the fledgling trembling until she spoke. "Do you think Omar and Nadia will recognize me?"

Socorra rolled her shoulders, easing the tightness at the base of her wings. "Why wouldn't they recognize you?" She turned to the Sapien and caught the glassy sheen in her eyes. Fatima stared out toward the horizon, unmoving. Curious, Socorra followed her gaze.

There, on the gray water of the Tranquil Sea, sat a lone Finch ironclad, cutting through the mist.

Socorra's stomach twisted.

The ship moved steadily toward the capital, steam hissing from its stacks. Kyte had arranged for it to bring Fatima's siblings to the Noktern after she'd been captured. Now, it would carry Kyte back to Zarpa. She knew it was for the best, but she had only just gotten him back. It felt like she was losing him all over again.

At least this time I know he's alive.

Looking back at Fatima, Socorra caught the glint of familiar sass on the Sapien's face.

"Oh, I don't know," Fatima mused, returning to their conversation. Grabbing the coverts of her wings and splaying her feathers in a grand display. "Maybe these have something to do with it?"

Despite the grief simmering in her chest, a hardy laugh burst from Socorra's throat. "Of course they'll recognize you!" She smiled wide, grateful for the stretch in her cheeks. "I bet they've missed you so much, they won't even notice."

"Pft," Fatima scoffed, though her tone was light. "I doubt it. They'll probably yank on them just to see if they're real. You don't know those two like I do."

Behind them, the low groan of wheels sloshing through muck signaled the carriage's arrival as it broke through the tree line. The horses' hooves slapped the wet ground with mounting irritation.

"All right!" Aldanor squawked, her voice sharp over the clatter. "Let's move out!"

At her order, the horses surged forward, dragging the carriage behind them, the wheels sloshing through the murky terrain. As it passed, Socorra caught a glimpse of Kyte through the small window, his face pale, drawn and distant. She lifted a hand in an attempt to wave, but he never looked up. A quiet exhale escaped her lips as she lowered her hand, falling back into step behind the Owl guards. Her heart felt heavy.

As they entered Krepusk, the stench of salted fish and charred coals struck her like a wave. Socorra wrinkled her nose; the reek clung to her, thick in the air and stubborn in her nostrils no matter how she tried to breathe through her mouth. She scanned the crumbling streets in disbelief. The Owls here wore rough-spun hides, their furs uneven and poorly tanned, threadbare at the seams. It startled her. These were the same people hailed across Avis as revered historians, the guiding hands of civilization after the Great

End. Yet that grandeur, she realized, belonged only to the Owls of the Noktern.

The caravan trundled deeper into the city's slums. Socorra and Fatima lingered near the rear, hopping from stone to stone to avoid the mud churned up in the carriage's wake. The Sapien kept talking, spinning stories of her family, and Socorra let the words wash over her, easing the tight ache in her chest. The distraction was welcome. After all the drills and trials of the past week, she'd had little chance to truly know Fatima; what free time she had was spent in the med wing, tending to Kyte.

"I'll never forget this one time," Fatima began with a jovial flair, "I was six, so Omar couldn't have been more than three. My baba decided it was time for me to go out into the desert and learn how to forage and hunt."

"That's a bit young, don't you think?" Socorra's brow furrowed slightly. "I mean, Hawks start pretty young, but even my father didn't take me out on practice hunts until I was ten."

"Yeah, well," Fatima shrugged, "we don't really have that luxury in the Desertlands. At that age, my baba taught me how to find, cut, and clean aloe; trap a hare; and tan the hide of a scaly-foot lizard."

"Sounds impressive." Socorra flickered through her memories of her own early days of training.

"We do what we have to in Konstat," Fatima added with a tilt of her head. "From what you've told me, the Hawks live in a real community. People look out for each other, help each other."

"And Sapiens don't?" Socorra asked, surprised.

"No, we don't," Fatima answered, her tone tightening. "If you're not kin, you don't matter in Konstat."

"But you're not like that," Socorra rebutted, though carefully. "You've helped Gideon and me more than once."

"It just gets tiring, you know?" Fatima lamented, brushing off the compliment. "After we lost our parents, I did everything I could to provide for my brother and sister. But it's almost impossible when everyone in your city is looking to take something from you."

"Whoa!" the driver of the carriage called out suddenly, his voice cutting through the conversation. The horses whinnied and stomped, their agitation breaking through Socorra's stupor. She looked around, startled to realize how close they'd come to the sea.

The harbor, if it could be called that, stood before them, a crooked skeleton of driftwood lashed together into a dock barely fit for a rowboat, let alone a Finch ironclad. And yet, here they were. Socorra swallowed hard, the briny wind slicing through the air. She hated how unaware she'd become of her surroundings.

What's happening to me?

She had always been attentive—ever alert. She knew her terrain left, right, and center, and never forgot to check her back. But ever since the battle at the Noktern, something inside her had shifted. Her fight with Craven had left bruises she couldn't see, but it was Kyte's condition that gutted her.

The last few days had been especially hard. She felt nauseous every time she thought about his departure. For years, Kyte had been her constant, her calm. And she, his. But since losing his wing, he'd shut her out completely.

She couldn't blame him, but it didn't make it easier. The weight was crushing. Kyte's care, Fatima's weapons and flight training, the shifting web of Noktern politics that Pelanor had left her tangled in. It was too much. She felt like she was constantly juggling daggers, and any moment now, one would fall and cut her open.

"You okay?" Fatima's tone was soft with genuine concern.

"I'm fine," Socorra lied, mustering a pitiful smile.

Fatima folded her arms and shot her a knowing glance. "And I'm the queen of the Desertlands. C'mon, tell me what's going on."

Before Socorra could respond, the carriage door slammed open.

"Good Lord, I can't feel me arse," Agnes bellowed as she stumbled down the steps onto the muddy ground. "Wake up, Kyte. We're finally 'ere."

Kyte appeared in the doorway behind her, his expression grim. He wobbled slightly as he stepped forward, unsteady on his feet.

Socorra moved to meet him, leaning her spear against the carriage. "Here, let me help you."

He hesitated, grimacing at the thought of needing help, but finally accepted her outstretched hand. His descent was slow, each step cautious and uneven.

"I thought those pills were supposed to wear off by now," he muttered, leaning into her as they made their way toward the dock. The rest of the caravan followed at a distance.

"Are you in pain?" Socorra asked quietly, keeping her voice low so only he could hear.

"No." He tore his gaze away from her. "No pain. Just wounded pride."

Socorra let out a soft sigh. "You still have every reason to be proud." She let her hand glide gently across his back, fingers brushing the stitches through the thin travel robe.

"Don't," he flinched.

She drew her hand back quickly. "Sorry, I just–"

Her words trailed off as Captain Aldanor approached, her armor clanking. She looked at Kyte with disinterest. "The ship you've arranged has launched a small boat to collect you. I suggest you start saying your goodbyes." Without waiting for a response, the Owl turned and walked back toward the carriage.

Socorra looked out to sea. Sure enough, a small craft was skimming over the foggy waters, towed by three Finches in tight formation. The wind off the ocean bit at her cheeks.

"Are you sure you don't want me to come back to Zarpa with you?" She asked, already knowing his answer.

Kyte turned toward her and took her hand, then leaned in to rest his forehead against hers, their noses brushing. "You know you can't do that." His voice tightened with sorrow, his lips thin. "There's still too much to do here. We've only taken down two of the Ravens. And someone has to bring Gideon home."

"The scholars–"

"Are not to be trusted," Kyte murmured, glancing around to ensure they weren't overheard. "That's what Pelanor said. And we need to trust *him*."

He stepped back as others began to gather around. "Besides," he added with a faint smile, "someone has to keep an eye on this troublemaker." He patted Fatima's shoulder as she stepped beside them.

The Sapien gave a wink, shrugging him off playfully. "I can take care of myself."

"Of course," Kyte nodded. "I wouldn't expect anything less." He unwound himself from Socorra and bent to embrace Fatima. Even then, she had to rise onto her toes to loop her arms around his neck.

"I wanted to say thanks again." Fatima stepped back. "You didn't have to go back to save my brother and sister, but…I'm grateful you did."

"It was nothing," Kyte replied gently as Socorra helped him back upright. "And don't worry, I'll take good care of them. Now why don't you fly out to the ship? Toulouse will want to set sail as soon as I'm aboard. You should spend as much time with them as you can."

Fatima's eyes widened as if it hadn't occurred to her that she no longer needed to wait for the ferry. With a sudden burst of joy, she threw herself into the air, wings slicing upward as she spiraled high above before gliding toward the ship.

"You sure you're up for this? Caring for Omar and Nadia in your condition." Socorra asked once Fatima was out of earshot. "We could still write to your mother, ask her to come help out."

Kyte shook his head. "I doubt she'll be thrilled with me harboring two Sapien fledglings. She's never had much affection for Sapiens, and the last thing I need is her flitting around the house calling them 'humans.'" He shrugged. "Besides, I'm not worried about the kids."

"No?"

"No. Jamal, on the other hand…" A crooked smile played on his lips. "That dromedary gave me hell wandering back through the desert. But I think I can win him over. Eventually."

An awkward silence stretched between them. Socorra grasped for something—anything—to say, but every excuse she had rehearsed over the past three days rang hollow now. No words she could muster would change his mind.

"Oh, Aggie," Kyte effused theatrically as Agnes ambled up the dock behind Socorra, "I think I'll miss you most of all."

"Shut up, ye right git," Agnes chuckled, catching his hand in a firm shake.

"I'm just sad Sister Marta couldn't join us." Kyte scrunched his lips and nose mockingly.

Socorra recalled the memory vividly: the orange-haired Dove standing at the Noktern gate, glaring icily as the caravan rolled away, leaving her a muddy mess in its wake.

"Yer a right pain," Agnes sniped, shaking her head. "But I'll certainly miss yer sarcasm."

On Hawks & Harpies

As the sister wandered off, Socorra and Kyte were left alone on the dock. The rest of the caravan lingered around the carriage, chatting quietly. Farther out, the faint lapping of the boat carried across the water, the Finches nearly there.

Socorra had been dreading saying goodbye.

As if sensing her hesitation, Kyte stepped forward and pulled her into a firm embrace, wrapping his arms around her shoulders. His skin radiated warmth against the chill air sweeping in from the tundra. For a moment, neither of them spoke. They stood together on the creaking dock, letting their silence say everything.

"You owe me big time for coming all the way up here just to drag your sorry ass back to Zarpa!" A voice fumed out across the water, a burly Finch with pink wings hovering just beyond the dock. "That damn dromedary ate all the fresh fruit we picked up in Duport!"

Still holding Socorra, Kyte didn't turn around. "Yeah, yeah, Toulouse."

After a beat, he stepped back, and the air between them cooled instantly. Socorra kept her chin high, but something inside her sank quiet and heavy.

At Kyte's signal, two Owl guards turned back to the carriage and unlatched the storage compartment. They heaved out two hefty sacks that clinked with coins. The dock groaned beneath their weight as they trudged to the edge and dumped the bags into the waiting boat with dull, metallic thuds.

"Happy?" Kyte called, his tone clipped. He gave Socorra's hand one final squeeze, then let go.

"No," the Finch snapped, rifling through one of the sacks. "But get in before I change my mind."

In a daze, Socorra watched as Kyte descended from the dock. The dinghy drifted steadily away, carried across the misty sea. After weeks of thinking he was dead, the idea of being apart from him again clawed at her insides, but she bit her tongue.

There was nothing left to say.

"Y'alright, Socorra?" Agnes's voice cut through the silence behind her.

Startled from her daze, Socorra turned, but found herself facing a crowd of stares. The Owl guards glared back, some indifferent, others curious. The hollow ache in her chest vanished, replaced by a flush of heat rising to her cheeks. She quickly averted her gaze, locking eyes with Sister Agnes alone.

"I'm fine," she lied again, her voice catching as she wiped sweaty palms on her breeches. "Let's just head back. We need to finalize the plans with Forranor. Raven Rock isn't going to invade itself."

She crouched, wings unfurling as she prepared to take flight, only to feel Agnes's strong hand clamp gently on her shoulder

"We'll get there," the Dove said, her tone kind but steady. "No need to go flyin' off before we're ready. Fatima hasn't returned from the ship, and the guards need a wee rest before headin' back."

Socorra exhaled sharply, shoulders sinking, but the tension remained. She itched to be moving, to be *doing* something. Anything to stop thinking about Kyte's departure. And Gideon was still missing. Raven Rock was their only lead, yet Forranor and the Parliament moved like they had all the time in the world.

"Socorra!"

Fatima's voice tore across the water, frantic and laden with terror.

Snapping her head back to the sea, Socorra spotted the silhouette of Fatima's black wings against the blush of the sunset. But what trailed behind her made Socorra's stomach drop. A massive cloud of Avians surged over the ship, racing toward the docks at breakneck speed.

"Socorra!" Fatima screamed again, her voice nearly lost beneath the roar of wings and shrieks.

The Hawk spun, taking in the Owls as they stirred—wings snapping open, hands reaching for bows and blades. Tension crackled in the air like lightning.

Where's my spear?

Her gaze darted frantically until it caught on the weapon leaning against the carriage. Just beyond it stood Agnes, her already pale face bleached ghost-white.

"Agnes!" Socorra bellowed, breath tight. "Find cover. Now."

She sprinted for the carriage, snatching up the spear; the grooved metal steadied her, pulling her back to herself.

Then she turned toward the sea. Fatima's wide, terrified eyes locked with hers as she closed in on the dock. Behind the girl, chaos surged—a tempest of screeching, monstrous Avians with teeth, claws, and malformed wings descending like a plague. Socorra's pulse thundered in her ears. And yet, in the rush of it, something shifted. The adrenaline no longer tasted of panic, but of purpose.

Just beyond the horde, through the whirl of wings and storm-dark sky, she caught sight of the ship. It appeared untouched, and a flicker of relief swept through her. She tightened her grip on the spear.

Let them come.

From somewhere behind her, Socorra heard Captain Aldanor squawk an order. "Lancers, in formation! Archers, get to the dock and ready your arrows. I've got a bad feeling about this."

She glanced back to see the Owl guards scrambling into position, then jerked her gaze to the sea. Fatima was nearly at the shore now, wings pumping hard. And behind her came the monstrous, twisted Avians, gaining fast. Socorra could finally see them clearly. Misshapen limbs, warped wings, eyes burning with feral hunger.

"Archers!" Aldanor's voice roared again.

The creak of bowstrings filled the air.

A sudden, cold awareness struck Socorra like a blade across the chest. There were so few of them—only a handful of Owl guards, a dozen archers between them.

Just them against the horde.

"Loose!"

The sky shuddered with motion as arrows screamed over the water. Socorra launched herself into the air after them, spear drawn, her wings slicing the wind.

"Socorra!" Aldanor shouted. "Get back here!"

But the Hawk didn't hear her. Not really. Her focus had narrowed to a single point—Fatima, just yards away, flying hard, every beat of her wings laced with fear. Socorra surged toward her.

Their eyes met. Sensing her intent, the Sapien dove, narrowly dodging the first wave of arrows.

Then the sky erupted with shrieks, a chorus of squawks and howls echoing out as the volley struck. Dozens of Avians spiraled downward, limbs flailing, wings crumpling like broken sails.

Socorra let out a breath of relief, but it vanished as quickly as it had come. For every Avian that fell, two more surged forward. The sky churned with wings, a dark swarm bearing down like a storm.

"What are you doing!?" Fatima's voice rang out as they met midair, her tone a mix of fear and disbelief.

Socorra halted in place, wings flaring wide, her breath catching as the truth crashed down on her.

I shouldn't be here.

It had all been an instinct, a feeling that surged her forward. But now, with the screeching hive behind them and the dwindling defenders below, she understood just how foolish it was.

She didn't hear whatever Fatima said next. The world dulled into a blur, her heart hammering against her ribs. With a sharp pivot, Socorra turned, racing back toward Krepusk, wind tearing at her feathers.

As she neared the shore, her eyes caught movement below. More Owls were flooding into the narrow, grimy streets of the city, drawn by the growing commotion. Civilians craned their necks, peering out from alleyways and rooftops.

"Get back inside!" Socorra bellowed, diving toward the ground. She drew a sharp breath, ready to shout again, but searing pain tore through her shoulder. Her body snapped backward, a scream tearing from her throat as talons clamped down. Her spear spun from her grasp, vanishing below as the creature yanked her skyward.

Dread crawled through her as the ground receded beneath her. Blood streamed down her arm, hot and fast. She twisted midair, catching a glimpse of the monster hauling her upward, its claws buried deep, grinding into bone. Another wave of agony scorched through her like fire.

Her fingers scrambled toward the hunting knife in her boot, but the beast's erratic flight tossed her around like a rag doll. She couldn't get a grip. In a last-ditch effort, she drove her nails into its clawed foot, digging and tearing to rend herself free.

It didn't even flinch.

Then a wet *crack* split the air.

The beast shrieked as its foot burst apart, pierced from below in a wet spray that spattered Socorra's face and hair. Its talons tore free of her shoulder, ripping fresh pain from her throat as she cried out. Her wings were still pinned by momentum, and she fell, tumbling. Desperate, she reached out for something, *anything*, and her hands closed around curved wood.

"What the–?"

She blinked. It was her spear, the blade still embedded in the beast's mangled heel. Stunned, Socorra turned her head back toward Krepusk.

On Hawks & Harpies

Agnes.

The Dove soared into the fray, flanked by a wave of Owl guards. Spears arced from her arms like missiles, each throw swift and deadly.

A fire sparked in Socorra's chest. Gritting her teeth against the pain, she locked her legs around the shaft of the spear, using it for leverage, kicking hard at the creature's calf. With a final, ragged squawk, the beast lost its grip, and the spear tore free. Socorra dropped, spinning. Wind rushed past her ears. Then, with a snap of her wings, she caught the air and righted herself, hovering mid-sky.

Bloodied, breathless, but burning with fury, she turned her gaze to the chaos around her.

The Owls were already swarmed, each one fending off two or three of the feral beasts. Their double swords flashed through the air, silver arcs slicing through wings and sinew. Above them, Agnes reigned from a distance, her aim lethal. Spears hurled through the fray, skewering monsters mid-flight and sending them tumbling into the Tranquil Sea.

Back on shore, the archers held their line, loosing volley after volley to keep the enemy at bay. But within the narrow streets of Krepusk, terror reigned. A handful of the creatures had broken past the front and now dived on unsuspecting citizens. Some Owls were ripped from their doorframes as they tried to flee indoors while others were plucked from the sky.

"Socorra!" Fatima's voice rang out behind her.

The Hawk spun just in time to dodge a feral assailant, its gaping mouth snapping inches from her throat.

With a swift pivot, she brought the butt of her spear down hard between its shoulder blades. Bone crunched. The beast screeched as it dropped into the sea.

"Thanks," Socorra rasped, catching her breath as Fatima drifted closer.

"What *are* these things?" the Sapien panted, panic tugging at the edges of her voice.

"No idea." Socorra shook her head.

"But I'd bet anything that Master bitch has something to do with it."

"Language, Fatima!" A booming voice cracked from above. "And I didn't know we were 'avin' a meeting up 'ere while devil's spawn tear us to shreds."

"Agnes," Socorra gasped. Her eyes locked on the fresh gash running from the brim of the Dove's wimple to her chin. Blood beaded beneath the smear of grime. "You're hurt."

"No more'n *ye!*" Agnes gave a cheeky grin, giving Socorra's bleeding shoulder a shove.

"*Ow,*" Socorra chuckled, despite the blaze of pain. But her laughter faded quickly as she scanned the battlefield. Avians on both sides fell from the sky, tumbling into the sea like broken dolls. A few Owls were dragged screaming into the clouds, vanishing into the encroaching dusk.

Her eyes found the ship on the horizon—the ironclad that carried Kyte and Fatima's siblings. Still undisturbed, sailing on to home.

A thin breath of relief passed through her.

At least they're safe.

"So, fearless leader." Agnes spun her final spear between her fingers, a sharp grin cutting through the viscera on her face. "What do we do now?"

A shiver ran through Socorra's wings. Their eyes were on her, awaiting her guidance. Behind them, the sky blackened with flapping wings and shrieking beasts.

Retreat, or stand?

"We take out as many of them as we can."

Chapter Six

GIDEON

Brass chandelier, staircase with a broken banister, moth-eaten tapestry.

Gideon kept a silent inventory of landmarks as he and his mother moved through the crumbling halls of Fate's Folly. If he ever managed to escape, he'd need to know every twist and turn of this place.

"You seem distracted." Cecilia's tone was coated in concern, though Gideon could hear the irritation brimming beneath the words.

"I'm listening," he replied quickly—a half-truth. He'd heard enough to piece together her argument. "You were saying you left me in Moda with my father because you didn't want me involved in all of this."

She raised an eyebrow, but pressed on. "I wanted to create a better world for you. All over Avis, people die from infections, injuries, sicknesses the Noktern could cure. Our people have clawed their way to survival while the scholars live in comfort under that mountain, hoarding everything. So I've decided to change that."

"I understand that much," Gideon retorted as they descended a creaking flight of stairs. "But does that really justify all of the terrible things you've done?" The words burned in Gideon's throat as he thought about Cas.

At the bottom of the steps, Cecilia stopped. Her boots clicked sharply on the stone floor as she turned to face him. "What would you have me do, Gideon?" Her voice was somber. "Do you think I *enjoy* this? Ripping people from their homes, separating families?" She shook her head. "Do you think that gives me pleasure?"

"Then why?" he asked quietly.

"Because I needed help." Her eyes searched his face. "And I couldn't just knock on the Noktern's door and ask for it. If I thought that would work, I would have tried it years ago"

"Why not go to the Finch council?"

Cecilia scoffed. "Those ancient mules? They'd never risk conflict with the Owls. And if I *did* convince them, they'd twist it for profit. Ration out medicine to the highest bidder. Only the wealthy Avians would benefit, as always."

"Which isn't much better," Gideon muttered, ashamed to give even a sliver of credence to his mother's fanaticism.

"No, it isn't," Cecilia agreed, already turning down the corridor again.

Gideon wanted to press her, but too many questions fought for priority in his mind. So he followed her in silence until they reached the end of the hall.

She pushed open a heavy door. The hinges groaned, and Gideon winced at the sound, already dreading what lay beyond.

It was a torture chamber.

Chains dangled from the ceiling, rusted machinery crowding the walls. Hooks and clamps and tools he didn't have names for lined the far side of the room like some macabre exhibit.

"Since I couldn't get the Finch council behind me," Cecilia continued, stepping inside as though it were any other room, "I decided I'd take on the Noktern myself. I started tinkering with the recipes in the journal on the enhanced abilities the ancient Sapiens developed."

"Like hypnosis." Gideon's eyes darted to a metal frame that looked like a restraint rack. "And the talons."

"Among others," she confirmed, trailing a clawed finger along the edge of the frame. "I didn't have all the right components Tvanor listed, but I researched substitutes. I remember being so excited when I finished the first batch…" She raised her arm and stared at her talon. "I injected it into myself immediately."

"You tested it on yourself?" Gideon blinked, surprised.

"I did." There was a tinge of regret in her voice, but it didn't last. "I know you hate what I've done, but I never meant for it to go this far. The first version was a disaster. I was trying to replicate the Bengalan's claws, but the transformation only took on one hand. My wings darkened, my body broke into fever. I was hallucinating, convulsing. I thought I was going to die. And all the work I'd done, all the sacrifices, would've been for nothing."

"So your solution," Gideon began, eyes narrowing, "was to start kidnapping people?"

"Not at first," she snapped. Her tone cut through the air causing Gideon to flinch. "I looked for willing participants," she continued, trying to steady herself.

"Willing?" he echoed, disbelieving.

"Yes." Her response was biting and defensive. "There were some. The desperate, the sick. People who believed in what I was trying to do." She paused, jaw tight. "I was out for weeks after that first injection, but once the fever passed, I got back to work." Turning away, she crossed to a shadowy corner of the room and knelt, fingers digging through the folds of her gown. Gideon stayed put, uncertain what she was about to reveal. She fiddled with something on the ground. Metal scraped, chains clinked. Then came a soft click and the groan of hidden hinges. "I couldn't risk something like that happening again."

Brushing dirt from her dress, Cecilia rose, and Gideon saw the trapdoor nestled seamlessly into the stone floor, nearly invisible.

"So why the kidnappings?" he pressed, his voice hot with fury. A foolish, aching part of him still yearned for some explanation that could make sense of it all. Something that might allow him to forgive even a piece of her. But he didn't dare let himself hope.

"My love," she sighed in that condescending tone he'd grown all too familiar with. "Once I had a few Ravens at my disposal, I could finally focus on my research. I can't be blamed if it wasn't in their nature to *cordially* invite others into the fold as I had."

"You're delusional," Gideon accused.

Her face contorted into a cold, devastating sneer. He braced himself. For a slap, a command, a talon at his throat. But none came. Instead, she simply tilted her head toward the trapdoor.

Swallowing the knot in his throat, Gideon crouched and slunk onto the floor. With a final glance at her expressionless face, he swung his legs over the edge of the trapdoor and began to descend the rickety ladder.

The shaft was tight, damp, and black as pitch. Even tucking his wings close, Gideon felt them brush the walls. Hand over hand, he climbed down, trying not to think about what lay beneath. When he glanced up, he saw his mother already following, the hem of her gown fluttering down after him like a ghost.

"So," he called up, more to fill the silence than out of curiosity, "how did you get anyone to volunteer for the change?"

"It wasn't as hard as you'd think." Her voice echoed strangely in the narrow shaft. "You just have to find people desperate enough."

His jaw clenched.

"So Craven and Zokya…" He let the names dangle between them, his feet brushing the floor.

"Correct." Landing beside him, her boots rang crisply against the stone. A soft click sounded, and a row of flameless lanterns flared to life along the ceiling, their glow casting long shadows down the corridor ahead. "And a dozen others before them," she added, already starting down the corridor.

"A dozen?" Gideon's voice cracked with fury. "How did you convince that many Avians to put themselves through *that*?"

"This is a sad world, my dear," she replied breezily, as though commenting on the weather. "All it takes is the hint of hope, and people will crawl through salt and barbed wire." Her lips twisted into a cruel smirk, the words dripping off her tongue without any hint of shame or reflection. "Craven was a sniveling mess when I found him in Ander—a half-Crow, taunted by the other Hawks, barely surviving. And Zokya...she was already a broken little thing, really. Just a shell when I offered her the change."

"And they just...agreed?" Gideon's voice trembled, his hoarse whisper laden with disgust.

"They *thanked* me! The two basically threw themselves at the power that I offered them." She shrugged. "Much good it did them. Even with Craven's powers, your little Hawk friend and the Sapien girl still managed to kill him."

Relief surged through Gideon; a small smile etched on his face.

Socorra and Fatima are alive.

"And that little witch…" Cecilia snapped her talons in frustration. "The Void take her if I ever find Zokya again."

"What happened to her?" Gideon pressed, startled. He hadn't seen any sign of Zokya since their confrontation in the Kestrel Desert.

"She's vanished," the Master growled. "I told her to watch the Sapien girl and she couldn't even manage that."

"Well, that's…" Gideon paused, grasping for the right word, "...interesting." He wasn't sure how to feel. Some small, vindictive part of him was thrilled at hearing his mother's plans had unraveled. But Zokya's powers of hypnosis were dangerous. If she'd gone rogue, what havoc could she be unleashing across Avis?

His thoughts broke off at the sound of something sharp echoing ahead. It was faint, like metal dragging over stone. It wasn't until they got closer he realized they were screams.

"What is that?" His voice cracked with unease.

"It's what I wanted to show you." With a nod, she continued down the hall, the clack of her boots echoing against the stone.

Despite the growing tension in his shoulders, he followed.

"My Ravens are gone," she went on, almost casually. "All except Cas."

Heat bloomed in Gideon's ears at the sound of his name.

"Unfortunately, he's too volatile now. He proved that at the Noktern, when you two fought. He nearly killed you because I lost control of him."

"You mean Cas *wanted* to kill me?" Gideon blurted.

"Oh yes," she answered, with disturbing calm. "Though I suppose that's my fault. Purely speculation, of course, but I believe the dose of the change I gave him had too much tyrosine. That could have overstimulated his adrenal medulla resulting in an overproduction of epinephrine, which would trigger a persistent and acute stress response."

Gideon's eyes widened. Her words landed like a barrage of stones—hard, fast, and incomprehensible.

"What does any of that mean?"

She waved a dismissive hand. "In the simplest terms, he's always angry now."

"Can't you fix him?" Gideon's throat tightened, a flicker of hope in his voice. "If you know what's wrong, couldn't you undo it?"

Cecilia gave him a remorseful glance but kept an even stride. "No," she answered flatly.

Gideon's shoulders sagged, his wings drooping until the tips brushed the floor.

"I wouldn't know where to begin," she added. "There's nothing in the journal that references reversing the change. I don't know if the ancient Sapiens ever bothered to try."

He stared at the stone beneath his feet, jaw clenched tight. Tears threatened to stream down his face, but he refused to break, not in front of the Master. He pushed the grief aside, but the screeches ahead kept rising, jagged and unnatural, like claws scraping the inside of his skull.

"We're here," Cecilia called over the din,

Rounding the corner, they came upon a pair of immense wooden doors bound in iron. Gideon flinched, covering his ears as the wails reached a maddening pitch. Howls that didn't sound entirely Avian. With a swift motion, Cecilia threw the bolt. The doors groaned open, their hinges shrieking in harmony with the noise inside.

The light was dim, but Gideon saw enough to make his stomach turn. In the center of the vast chamber rose a domed iron cage, tall as a house and rusted deep into the stone floor. Inside, winged silhouettes writhed and slamm-ed against the bars, shrieking like souls in torment.

"Silence!" Cecilia's voice rang out, layered with power, and Gideon was sure that hypnosis played a role. The effect was immediate. The creatures recoiled, retreating to the far edge of the cage, cowering together in a tangled horde of limbs and wings.

There has to be fifty of them crammed in there.

His feet felt like lead as he crossed the threshold. He let his hands drop from his ears and stepped into the chamber, marveling at the ceiling arched impossibly high above. The light of the sky filtered down from a distant oculus in the tower's crown, illuminating the cage in a ghastly glow.

"What are they?" His voice came out hoarse.

He edged closer, squinting into the gloom. They were Avian—or had been once. Now each one bore its own terrible, twisted corruption. Wings sagged in tatters, feathers colorless as ash. Some crawled on all fours like beasts, while others lurched upright, jagged claws jutting where hands and feet should be. A few were skeletal, ribs pressing sharp against skin; others swelled with grotesque muscle, shoulders broad as gates. Just like Rocque, the brute who had hunted him through the alleys of Duport.

"I call them, *Harpies*." Her tone was clinical, though a cruel smile curled at her lips. "And this isn't even all of them; just one cage. I've had to build quite a few to house them all. The results of my failed experiments."

"They're *what*?" Gideon choked out, his voice echoing up the tower walls. The sound riled the creatures. Several lunged forward with snarls and hissing breaths.

On Hawks & Harpies

"There's no need to get excited," she chided, and Gideon wasn't sure if she was speaking to him or the Harpies. "This is what happens when the change doesn't take properly. It was disappointing the first dozen times. I thought I'd have to put them down or forget about them entirely; I certainly couldn't let them loose in Avis. But over time, I discovered they were still useful. I've been training them to respond to hypnosis, even on longer journeys."

A chill traced the length of Gideon's wings. The implications clawed at the edge of his mind, too many questions rising all at once. For a fleeting moment, he wanted to believe this made it better, that perhaps the Harpies weren't just discarded lives.

But the longer he sat with it, the worse it felt.

"What about the Sapiens?" His heart sank.

"What about them?"

He craned his neck, searching the tangle of bodies for any hint of someone familiar. "The Sapiens you experimented on. Are they in there too?" His throat tightened as he thought of Fatima's mother, wondering if she could be hidden somewhere in that twisted mass.

"No." Her voice was hollow, but her stare was biting. "All the Sapiens I put through pteroplasty died. All except that one little bitch who escaped and got Craven killed." She exhaled violently, as though inconvenienced. "But what are a few humans in the grand scheme of things, I suppose?"

"You're a monster." The words escaped before he could stop, a tear cutting down his cheek. His stomach rose, but he didn't look away. "When you gave me that journal," his voice shook with anger, "I thought maybe there was something left in you worth saving." He threw his arms toward the cage. "But *this*? This is disgusting."

Cecilia didn't flinch.

"This is *progress*, my dear…"

"This is an *abomination!*" Gideon roared, his fury echoed by the shrieks of the Harpies. "These are Avians, not experiments. I don't care how twisted the Noktern scholars might be, there is *nothing* in this world that can justify what you've done!"

His breath came in ragged pulls, his whole body shaking. He couldn't hold it in anymore. His mother—no, the *Master*—watched him with flared nostrils, her face taut with fury. But he didn't care. Not after everything. Not after this.

The Harpies. The Sapiens. The lies. The torment. He couldn't even bear to *think* the word *mother* anymore.

"I'm sorry you feel that way, Gideon."

Her voice was tight, cold. A flicker of violet caught in her eyes, and before he could move, the power gripped him. Panic exploded in his chest as his body seized. He tried to scream, but no sound came; he couldn't even part his lips.

"I had hoped you'd come around." There was a note of disappointment in her tone. "That you'd see things my way when the time came. But it's clear now that you never will."

She turned away without another glance, boots cracking like gunfire against the stone as she strode to the far wall. The Harpies stirred, their squawks rising like a fever behind her. She paused by the lever embedded in the stone, then turned, her eyes blazing violet fire.

"Listen, and listen well," she commanded, her voice cracking through the chamber like a whip. The Harpies froze, their gnarled forms curling tighter, bristling like coiled springs. "You are to leave Raven Rock and fly to the Hawklands this time. Bring me new subjects for the change."

NO!

Gideon screamed inwardly, every nerve alight as he strained to move, but his body refused to obey.

"The ruddy Owls you brought me last time were useless."

With a mechanical groan, the Master yanked down on the lever. Rusted gears screamed in protest, and the dome split open. Iron bars peeled back like ribs. The Harpies screeched and scrambled, fighting to squeeze through the breach. Claws scraped metal. Wings beat the air.

Gideon's head exploded with pain as he strained against the Master's hold. Every nerve screamed as he fought for control, digging deep within himself, trying to twitch a finger, flex a wing, *anything*. But the harder he resisted, the more her grip tightened. It was like being crushed from the inside out, the world slipping away until even sound felt distant.

He could only watch, frozen in his own body, as the Harpies burst from their cage like a swarm of locusts. One after another, they jettisoned into the air, shrieking as they spread their twisted wings and spiraled up the tower. Their whoops and caws echoed off the stone walls like a war cry.

Over the cacophony, Gideon heard something worse than the screams. The Master's laughter, unrestrained, triumphant, and absolutely *wicked*.

"*Fly, fly, fly!*" she squawked, throwing her arms wide.

Her voice echoed like a curse, ricocheting around the chamber as the last of the Harpies vanished into the light above, leaving only the sound of beating wings and the gnawing horror in Gideon's chest.

Chapter Seven

Pelanor

The crunch of dried leaves beneath his feet sent pain spiraling through Pelanor's head; each step felt like someone driving a warm butter knife into the base of his skull. The visions had been relentless, more frequent and intense than ever before. Even in the shade of the trees, the Valysian forest was sweltering. Hunger gnawed at his belly, thirst clawing at his throat.

Still, he pushed forward, brambles scratching at the Owl's arms as he forced his way through the brush. He clung to Brigitte's cryptic advice like a lifeline:

"If you wander through the center of the southern forest, eventually, the Subrum Tavern will find you. That's where you'll find Airam."

She'd refused to say more; whether because she didn't know or wouldn't say, Pelanor couldn't tell. He'd nearly taken back the gold he paid her out of spite. But with no other lead, he'd chosen to trudge into the woods.

Pungent and acrid, a sudden whiff of smoke hit his nostrils, replacing the earthy scent of dry mud and moss. The smell turned his stomach. He staggered behind a tree, dry-heaving as his gut twisted into knots.

That must be the Doves I saw in my vision.

It was a grim thought. The scene came back to him in brutal detail: young Yuri's terrified eyes as his wares went up in flames…the boy's scream as he was dragged off to the brick.

This time, Pelanor couldn't stop it; he retched bile onto the roots at his feet, barely missing the hem of his robes.

At least I'm getting close.

Steadying himself against the wide trunk of an oak, he blinked sweat from his eyes, then stopped in his tracks. A shadow passed overhead, blotting out the filtered sun for only a heartbeat. He looked up instinctively, but saw nothing. Only swaying branches and sky.

His breath caught in his chest.

Something's wrong.

The forest had gone silent. He'd grown used to the humming of cicadas and the occasional snap of branches as squirrels and other small animals scurried in the underbrush. But now, there was nothing.

I'm being followed.

Panic bit at his throat.

No...stalked.

But by what?

Pelanor scanned the treetops, eyes flitting from branch to branch. Nothing. No wings slicing through the canopy. No rustling above.

Could it be an Avian?

He doubted it. An Avian couldn't move that silently through the trees, not without exposing their wings.

So, what kind of predator could glide through the forest with such speed and stealth?

Now's not the time for speculation. Move.

He started forward, trying to maintain a steady pace, feigning ignorance of the presence behind him. Sweat clung to the back of his neck, soaking into his collar. His heart thundered, and the pressure building at his temples became almost unbearable, but still, he pressed on.

Each step was measured, every breath shallow. He strained his ears for any sound—twigs snapping, branches shifting—but the forest held unnervingly still. Then, as he risked a glance skyward, his foot caught on an exposed root.

He stumbled forward, instinctively throwing open his wings to catch himself. But in his panic, he flapped downward instead, thrusting himself into the ground in a shower of leaves and twigs.

The impact stole the wind from his lungs. The world spun. The forest floor blurred and pulsed with color. He groaned, trying to lift himself, but his limbs were leaden and the dizziness anchored him down.

Then he heard footsteps, soft but purposeful.

Pelanor tried to push himself up, but something pressed hard between his wings, shoving him back into the dirt. He gasped. The weight was heavy, deliberate.

Craning his neck, he saw gleaming yellow eyes, slit-pupiled and fixed on him. They glowed from a face wreathed in black fur, framed by twitching whiskers and a low, rumbling growl.

A paw rested between his wings, claws lightly digging through the fabric of his robe. He could feel the beast's breath, warm and steady, against his ear.

"A Bengalan?" Pelanor choked. "A cat in Avis?"

His eyes went wide, then fluttered half-closed with strain. "Who are you? What are you going to do with me?"

"*Diam saja*," the cat purred in their native tongue, their voice soft but assertive. "Silence. That's not for me to decide, *burung*."

"Then who–?"

A sharp cry escaped him as the paw struck the side of his head. Pain bloomed. His vision fractured.

"*Tidur sekarang.*" The voice was a velvet murmur as the cat withdrew their paw and rose onto two feet. They padded to where Pelanor's head lay, standing over him as the forest dimmed around the edges.

"Sleep now."

*　　　*　　　*

Cold water splashed across Pelanor's face and chest, soaking through his robes. The icy shock bit at his skin; pain throbbed at his temples, radiating down his neck to the base of his wings. He shook his head gently, trying to clear the haze, but his vision swam.

"Who are you?" a powerful voice demanded. The sound came from directly in front of him.

"My name is Pelanor," he replied, steadying his breath as the room spiraled into view. He was in some kind of cavern—a wide, natural hollow with a vaulted ceiling that stretched into darkness. The light from a few scattered torches and candles painted the stone walls in flickering amber. A figure stood silhouetted before him.

He squinted, trying to make out her features, but the backlighting threw her into shadow.

"Are you…" Inhaling slowly through his nose, he tried to maintain an even tone, calming his pulse. "Airam?"

"Depends who's asking."

"Well," Pelanor muttered, giving a fruitless tug at his restraints, "let's just say an Owl tied to a chair was asking. What would you say then?"

"A smart-ass, I see." She paused, then scoffed softly. "I like that."

She set down the bucket and stepped forward, hips swaying with a kind of feral elegance. As she closed the distance, she slammed her hands on the arms of his chair. Her biceps flexed beneath tight sleeves, and her angular face emerged from the shadows, her jawline sharp, ice-blue eyes gleaming.

"I am indeed Airam. Welcome to my tavern."

Candlelight flickered across her plumage. Pelanor's breath caught in his throat. Her left wing shimmered like pearl, smooth and luminous, the right a void of black feathers, darker than a moonless night.

"Like what you see?" She tilted her head, a playful menace in her smile, her tongue running slowly along her teeth.

"I've just never seen dichromatism before." Pelanor shifted in his chair, the ropes biting deeper into his wrists as he tried to inch away from Airam. "I've read it was possible, but to see it in person…"

"Yeah, yeah." Airam snorted. Pushing off the chair, she adjusted her corset and sauntered across the cavern toward a cabinet in the corner, the *clack* of her boots echoing on the stone. "I've heard it all before. The stares get old fast."

"I'm guessing Crow and Dove parents?" Pelanor fidgeted again with the restraints, still getting nowhere.

"Very astute," she replied without looking back. The opaque glass door creaked open as she reached in and retrieved a pair of glasses. "As if that wasn't obvious. But you, Owl, are in no position to be asking questions."

She clinked the glasses down on a low wooden table and turned again to the cabinet.

"Can I offer you a drink?" Her voice was suddenly sweeter. "I like to give my guests a proper send-off." She glanced over her shoulder and gave him a playful wink, though her lips thinned in a serious line.

"Do you often kill your guests?" Despite the chill in the cavern, sweat began to bead at Pelanor's hairline.

"Only the ones who come looking to ruin my operation." She pulled an ornate bottle of amber liquid from the top shelf. "Which, in my experience, is most of them."

"That's not why I'm here."

"So you haven't been scratching at your restraints to escape?" Uncorking the bottle with a satisfying pop, she held it to her nose and inhaled deeply. "Oh yeah, that's the one."

Heat flushed Pelanor's cheeks, his jaw clamping tightly in frustration. Stilling his hands, he let them hang slack behind him; he could feel fibers stuck beneath his fingernails.

"Don't stop on my account," she added sweetly, pouring two glasses of the amber spirit. After sealing the bottle, she set it aside and picked up the glasses. Returning to Pelanor, she placed one at his feet, then took a long, unapologetic swig from her own. She barely flinched as the liquor slid down her throat.

Dragging a chair from one of the nearby tables, its legs scraping loudly across the stone, she spun it around and sat, knees crossing smoothly, just close enough for them to brush against his.

"You're not even going to untie me for that drink?" Pelanor asked, feigning nonchalance.

"You seem to be doing just fine on your own."

"So this is a test? You're waiting to see if I can break out?"

"It's not a test." Her shrug was almost lazy. "Even if you manage it, you won't get far."

Then, without warning, she released the glass.

Pelanor flinched, bracing for the inevitable crash. But no shatter came. Instead, a single, crystalline chime rang through the air. Airam's wing flicked, and a dagger gleamed in her grip. The glass rested neatly on the flat of its blade, balanced as if she'd set it to rest on a counter.

"Impressive," he breathed.

"That's not the only one I keep on me," she smirked, sliding the glass back into her grip and resheathing the dagger without breaking eye contact. "And even if I couldn't handle myself…" She downed the last of her drink in one smooth motion. "You'd still have to contend with Satu."

"And Satu would be?"

"*Kita sudah bertemu.*" The voice rolled from the cave's mouth, low and smooth, like a purr.

Pelanor jolted, his bound body straining forward. A moment ago, the entrance had seemed empty, but now his eyes caught the figure leaning against a stone column. Relaxed in posture, yet coiled beneath a blanket of fur that gleamed faintly in the torchlight, the stranger radiated a quiet menace.

"We've already met," the cat repeated in accented Avian.

"You're the Bengalan who attacked me in the woods." Pelanor's voice cut sharp with accusation.

Satu didn't respond. Instead, they leaned forward and dropped to all fours, calves flexing beneath snug breeches. The cat glided silently across the stone floor, a silhouette prowling through the gloom. Bengalans could walk upright, but they rarely chose to; instinct still ruled their posture. Their great ancestors, the wild cats of Bengala, had vanished long before the Great End, and their descendants seemed content to shed the trappings of Sapiens altogether.

Reaching the chair, Satu rubbed their muscled shoulders against the underside of Airam's seat. A low, resonant thrum vibrated from their chest as they collapsed onto the floor, curling their front paws possessively around Airam's ankles.

Only now did Pelanor catch the delicate pattern in the Bengalan's fur: smoky rosettes barely distinguishable from the inky black, revealed only in the flicker of candle-light. The effect was mesmerizing.

"Satu is my right hand." Airam's tone softened with pride. "They protect me, and I them."

Pelanor was almost drowning in the odd splendor of the pair that sat before him. Though Pelanor had met Bengalans during diplomatic missions, he'd never encountered one with full melanism. And to see one paired with a dichromatic Avian? The odds felt astronomical.

"So, handsome," Airam cooed, setting her empty glass beside her chair, across from Satu. "I'm going to give you one chance. Convince me not to kill you."

All the while, Pelanor's fingers worked steadily. Scratch by scratch, he wore down the fraying rope. The fibers had weakened under the strain; a few more moments, a final, forceful jerk—then the rope snapped with a dull snap, and his hands were free.

A low, primal growl rumbled in Satu's throat. Hackles bristled as they dropped into a crouch, long claws flexing against the stone floor.

Airam reached down and stroked the back of their neck, a soothing gesture that made Pelanor's skin crawl. "Let's wait to see what he does." There was a flourish of amusement in her stare, her eyes gleaming with antici-pation.

Pelanor carefully weighed his options, keeping his gaze fixed on Airam. Her expression was still, composed. She cradled her chin in one hand, a slender finger tracing the corner of her lips. But her other hand drifted slowly, almost lazily, down the curve of her thigh. Beneath the hem of her dress, Pelanor glimpsed the glint of a sheathed weapon.

Cautiously, the Owl leaned forward. The soft scrape of his movement stirred a low, warning growl from Satu.

He froze, his fingers hovering just above the glass at his feet. Slowly, deliberately, he reached down, eyes flicking to the Bengalan. Satu watched him through narrowed, slitted pupils, their back still tensed to pounce, but did not move.

Pelanor grasped the glass and eased back into the chair, his wings held tight to his back. Swirling the dark liquid, he took a hesitant sniff and winced at the burning sting of alcohol.

"I assure you, it isn't poison."

He gave Airam a dry glance, then tipped the drink back. The burn scalded his throat, but he didn't stop until it was half gone. A welcome heat spread down his neck and into his cheeks. The pounding at his temples softened, though dizziness still lapped at the edges of his vision.

"Now," her tone sharpened, "are you going to tell me what you're doing here?"

Pelanor exhaled hard through his nose. "I need to procure a few items. And from what I've heard, you're the woman who can make that happen."

Airam arched a brow, intrigue flickering beneath her cool exterior. "And what exactly are you hoping to get a hold of?"

"Saltpeter, charcoal, sulfur. Maybe a few other things."

Satu's ears twitched, their pupils dilating. Airam's lips thinned, her expression darkening. "And what, exactly, are you planning to do with those?"

"I think you already know," Pelanor answered evenly with a flick of his hair.

"Gunpowder." Her eyes hardened, the lines of her face tightening. "I'm sure you can guess that I'm not keen on putting something so volatile into the Noktern's hands."

"Who said it was for the Noktern?"

"Do you take me for a fool?" she scoffed, her voice chilling. "You're wearing scholar robes, albeit filthy ones. And given that the Noktern has long tolerated the position of the Valysian Inquisition, I have no reason to help you." She leaned forward, wings unfurling behind her in a sudden, striking display. Drawing the blade from beneath her skirt, she leveled the point at his chest. "You have one last chance to convince me not to gut you right here."

Pelanor's heart thudded, loud in his ears. The blade gleamed in the firelight, a trembling silver fang. Satu's posture remained coiled, eyes locked on him with animal focus. Still, he did not falter.

"I've left the Noktern." His eyes never left Airam. "The scholars have lost their way. I intend to make it right."

She didn't speak. But the knife stilled.

"I'll tell you everything," Pelanor continued. "But I think I'll need another drink first."

He extended the glass slowly, deliberately. As he leaned forward, the blade pressed into his chest, pricking skin, but he didn't flinch.

Airam's eyes flicked to Satu. The Bengalan met her gaze, tail flicking once. "*Saya percaya padanya,*" they purred in their low, velvety rumble. "I trust him."

Pelanor looked at Airam, his face knit with confusion, but she offered no explanation. Without a word, she slid the knife back into its sheath, retrieved the glass from his outstretched hand, and walked away to refill it.

"*Kami baru tahu.*" Satu rose fluidly onto two feet. They stretched, claws slipping from their fingertips with a quiet click. "Bengalans have an innate sense of *keyakinan* …trust. I can't explain it. But I know you're genuine. Even if you pretend to be *pria tangguh.*"

"What does that mean?"

Satu's wiry tail flicked through the slit in their trousers as they turned. In a few strides, the cat leapt onto one of the tables lining the cavern wall, nimble as ever. They weaved between scattered plates and candles before curling into a tight coil, chin resting on their front paws. Their eyes stayed fixed on Pelanor, unblinking.

"It means 'tough guy,'" Airam translated, returning with a fresh glass, which Pelanor accepted gratefully. "So, drop the act and explain yourself."

Pelanor gave a small nod, cradling the drink. "Do you have anything to eat?" His voice was rough with fatigue.

Without comment, Airam moved through the room, her wings twitching as she rummaged through crates and burlap sacks. She returned with a modest plate of bread and cheese, which Pelanor accepted like a lifeline.

On Hawks & Harpies

Between rapid, ravenous bites, he told her what she needed to know, sparing certain details, but giving enough. He spoke of the Noktern's shadowy investment in the kidnappings across Avis and the whispers of an Owl prophecy. He recounted his journey to the Finchlands, his meeting with Gideon, and their trek across the Desertlands. He described the scholar's fall from grace, Gideon's fight with the Ravens. At least what little he knew of it, not having been there himself.

"So, now that I've left the Noktern, I need to get Gideon back," Pelanor finished, draining the last of his drink. Between the food and the liquor, he felt clearer, steadier. More like himself again.

"And you need these materials because…" Airam's voice was flat. She hadn't spoken once through his whole retelling, and her face remained unreadable.

"I have a plan to break him out of Fate's Folly."

"You're going to blow up the castle," Airam stated, not a question.

"That's a gross simplification," Pelanor replied. "But yes, parts of it at least."

Airam leaned back, drumming her fingers against the arm of her chair. "Getting those materials won't be easy. But it's not impossible." She paused, sharpening her gaze. "One more question before I decide whether or not to kill you." She flashed a sympathetic smile as if to apologize. "I've managed to stay hidden from the Noktern all these years. The Valysian Inquisitors know I'm out here, but they'd rather pretend they don't. Too embarrassed to admit I've eluded them. So how did *you* find me?"

A sudden wave of lightheadedness surged through Pelanor. He blinked hard, rubbing his temples as the edges of his vision began to blur.

Not now.

"Brigitte," he snapped, as if saying it aloud could anchor him. "I was in Tartarus. She told me you might be able to help."

"*Bukan itu saja,*" Satu murmured from their perch, lifting their head from their paws. "That's not the whole truth."

Whatever Airam said next, Pelanor didn't hear. Pain exploded behind his eyes, streaking down his spine like lightning. His breath hitched as images surged through his mind, too fast, too caustic to control.

Twisted beasts spun through a smoke-choked sky. The shriek of metal dragging across stone filled his ears, and somewhere in the cacophony, he heard the caws of something far older, far darker than anything born of Avis.

Below, the city of Zarpa rushed toward him, the domed roofs of Accipiter Manor rising from the sea of terracotta. Hawks scrambled in the streets, grabbing what weapons they could. The Hawk Guard tried to rally them, shouting orders over the chaos. But it was too late. The creatures were upon them.

Pelanor watched, helpless as the monsters dove into the city. They plucked Avians from market stalls, tore defenders from the sky. Blood splashed across sandstone. Screams echoed through the narrow alleys. The vision pressed closer, faster, more visceral, more real with every second.

On Hawks & Harpies

Amid the chaos, a familiar voice rang out. "Kyte?" Pelanor muttered aloud.

Focusing what little energy he could muster, he pulled at the vision, twisting its flow toward the source of the voice. Sure enough, the one-winged Hawk had thrown himself into the heart of the fray. Shouting commands, Kyte rallied the nearby Hawks with sharp, confident orders. He snatched a bow from a nearby weapon-rack and began loosing arrows in rapid succession, providing cover as others dashed into Hepha's tent to gather whatever armaments they could.

In no time, Kyte had formed a rough battalion of archers, spearmen, swordsmen cobbled together from whoever could still stand. Under his command, they mounted a frantic defense, fending off the shrieking tide of winged horrors.

The vision fractured like watching battle through a shattered lens. Gory flashes strobed through Pelanor's mind. Hawks and beasts tumbled through the sky in torn, tangled spirals. He couldn't tell how long it lasted. Minutes? Hours? Eventually, the Hawks pushed the monsters back. But not without a cost. At least a half-dozen were carried off, caught in the talons of the retreating creatures as they vanished eastward, silhouettes against the setting sun.

On the ground, the survivors embraced, bloodied and breathless, but alive. A decorated officer of the Hawk Guard approached Kyte who stood with his bow slack at his side, sweat matting his feathers. The guard's words were muffled, but Pelanor caught fragments.

Then–

"*Hey!*" Airam's voice cracked like a whip. A sudden pressure shoved Pelanor back into himself as she pressed her forehead against his, her piercing stare stripping the haze from his eyes. "What the hell is wrong with you?"

Pelanor stared blankly at the half-Dove, the vision still echoing in his skull.

"*Dia seorang pelihat,*" Satu offered calmly, sliding from their perch, golden eyes locked on Pelanor.

"I don't know that word." Airam's voice was tinged with unease. "*Pelihat?*"

"He sees the future." There was no inflection in the cat's voice—nothing to betray their opinion on the statement. "I believe you Avians would call him *seer*."

Airam tilted her head, lips parting slightly as she craned her neck back toward Pelanor, the scent of alcohol warm on her breath.

"Well," she murmured, "that's an interesting development."

Pelanor wanted to deny it—call it a dizzy spell or dismiss the vision outright, but the words wouldn't come. His breath still staggered from the force of what he'd seen.

Tired of waiting, Airam braced her hands on the arms of his chair and pushed herself upright, a wisp of her graying hair brushing his cheek. She turned to Satu and the two exchanged a flurry of words in Bengalan. Pelanor caught a phrase here or there, but not enough to make sense of it.

"Then it's decided," Airam uttered at last, gesturing toward the cavern's exit.

Pelanor straightened, the uncertainty sending a flurry through his chest.

Satu dipped their head in acknowledgment, then dropped to all fours and padded silently toward the exit. They slipped into the shadows like mist rolling off the sea.

Pelanor rose unsteadily to his feet, the stiffness in his legs making him stumble. "What exactly was decided?"

Airam sauntered closer. "Your fate."

"Ominous and disconcerting," Pelanor mused, seemingly nonchalant despite his concern. "But it didn't really answer my question."

"Satu went to fetch your items." A smile twitched at the corners of her lips. The clack of her boots stopped just short of him.

"So, you'll help me?"

"That's what I said, yes."

Relief washed over the Owl. He exhaled deeply, tension unspooling from his shoulders. "And the terms?"

Airam let out a breathy snort. "Straight to business. I like that." She picked up her glass. "Can I get you another drink?"

Pelanor shook his head. The first two were still pulling at his temples.

"Suit yourself." She pursed her lip, refilling her own glass. "In exchange for my services, all I want is your help."

"My help?" Pelanor couldn't hide the surprise from his voice.

Airam gave a casual shrug. "Seeing as I'm getting you the basics for a round of explosives, I figure you must know what to do with them."

"Go on," Pelanor pressed cautiously.

She let out a sigh, then took a slow sip from her drink. "Sarge and his band of Valysian Inquisitors have been getting bold. They've been pressing deeper into my forest. Small parties, Satu can handle. But lately…" She met his eyes. "They've been sending battalions."

Pelanor's mind snapped back to Tartarus and the towering Inquisitor grinning as he torched the cart of supplies.

I'll finally have Airam's head on a spike. That witch is as good as mine this time.

"I've heard they're using the war between the Hawks and Crows as an excuse to move their forces into the area," Airam continued.

Pelanor's jaw tightened. "The Doves have joined the Hawks then?"

"Not in so many words," she dipped her head. "The Doves have demonstrated their support, but won't interact directly. *But* the Inquisitors are using it as cover to try and cut Tartarus off completely."

"And what could you possibly want from me?"

A glint sparked in Airam's eyes. "I want you to rig the woods with explosives."

Pelanor blinked. "I'm sorry, you want me to–?"

"You heard me," she cut in. "I've got the means to get you gunpowder. In exchange, you use that clever head of yours to booby trap these forests before you run off to rescue your friend."

The idea turned slowly in Pelanor's mind. It would cost him a day, maybe two. But it was also the perfect chance to practice making explosives, something he only understood in theory. And if the Inquisitors were moving to isolate Tartarus, could he really walk away?

"Deal!" The word sliced through the air between them. "How long before Satu gets everything?"

"About a week. Give or take a day."

"Perfect," Pelanor replied, feeling an energy surge back into him. "In the meantime, I've got a few errands to run. Assuming I'm free to leave?"

Chapter Eight

GIDEON

Tap tap tap.

The stark patter against the glass jolted Gideon upright, the rusted frame of his bed creaking in protest. He froze, breath held, trying to pinpoint the direction of the sound.

Tap tap tap.

This time, he could tell it was coming from the window. He slid off the tattered mattress, the cold floor biting at his bare feet. In a crouch, Gideon crept along the edge of the room, keeping below the sill, wary of whatever was outside.

"I've been at Fate's Folly long enough to know there's nothing good out there," he whispered to himself. But a sudden surge of hope quickened his breath. "What if it's a rescue?" He straightened up too quickly, heart hammering in his chest.

Tap tap tap.

"Don't be stupid, Gideon," he chided, trying to ground himself again. "The Owls probably think you're dead. No one's coming. It's probably just one of the damn Harpies."

He pressed himself against the wall beneath the window, fingertips grazing the cold grooves of the iron bars embedded in the stucco. Slowly, Gideon pulled himself up and peered through the slats, out into the fading sky stretched over the rotting husk of Raven Rock.

No one there.

On Hawks & Harpies

"Guess they left," he shrugged.

Tap tap tap.

The sound sliced through the silence. His head jerked up, eyes scanning the window again, then he let his gaze drift down.

No. No, that can't be right.

A chill crawled down his spine as he stepped closer to the window. "That's not possible," he breathed.

There, perched on the outer sill was a creature cloaked in soot-dark feathers, its outline wavering against the wind. It tilted its head, the movement too sharp, too deliberate.

"Bir–" The word caught in his throat. "The Great End wiped out all of the bi-birds."

They stared at one another in silence. The bird's eyes were tiny abysses, deep, obsidian, unblinking. Then, with a sharp jerk, it drove its stone-like beak against the glass again.

Tap tap tap.

A restless, if not impatient rhythm.

Gideon snapped out of his awe. "The windows don't open. Trust me, I've tried. Even without the grates, they're bolted from the outside."

A flush of embarrassment crept up his neck.

"Have you completely lost your mind, Gideon? You're talking to a bird. It can't understand you…" But the way the bird tilted its head just so sent a flicker of doubt through him. "Can you?"

The bird ruffled its feathers, smacking its wings once against its sides with what looked suspiciously like irritation. Then, with a crisp flutter, it hopped higher on the window frame, digging its talons into the weathered wood between the panes.

Gideon watched, dumbfounded, as the creature worked its beak into the seam of the window. A metallic *clink* echoed in the cell as one of the locking pins rolled to the far side of the sill.

"How did you…" Gideon began, words catching on disbelief. But the bird ignored him, hopping to another bolt. Within a minute, two more pins dropped to the stone floor with quiet pings.

Then it resumed its perch and gave the glass one final, expectant *tap tap tap*.

Mouth agape, Gideon slid his arm through the square gap between the bars, forcing his hand forward until it brushed the pane. With a grunt and a shove, the hinges creaked, then gave way, groaning from long neglect.

A cool wind swept in, stirring the stale air of the chamber. The bird slipped through the crack with practiced ease, but the bars were too narrow to let it pass further. It paced along the sill, strutting back and forth like a sentry awaiting orders.

"This has to be a dream," Gideon murmured. He slid his arm back in and, hesitantly, held out his hand. Expecting a peck, he flinched, but instead of her beak, he felt the soft brush of feathers against his fingers.

The bird leaned into his palm, nuzzling gently, with a kind of solemn tenderness. A gesture of recognition, perhaps trust.

Gideon swallowed. "What're you doing here?"

The bird pulled its head from Gideon's hand and began pecking at something attached to its leg.

"You're a carrier bird," Gideon breathed, stunned. He'd read stories of ancient Sapiens training birds to carry messages across vast distances, but he'd always assumed they were legends. Yet here was living proof.

"Pigeons," he murmured, crouching to inspect the small tube strapped to the creature's leg, his fingers fumbling to remove the scroll nestled inside. "I think that's what they were called. But you certainly don't look like the pigeons in my books," he added, eyeing the sleek black feathers and sharp beak.

A flutter of anxiety rose in his chest as he unfurled the crisp, white scroll. The script was rushed, but legible. He read through it once. Then again. A third time, trying to take it all in.

Gideon,
Mim willing, Nox will find you with this message.

"Nox?" He looked at the bird who met his eyes and flared her wings with what could only be described as pride. "That must be you." He stroked her head and she preened herself at his touch.

With the reports of these new monsters, I imagine the circumstances surrounding Fate's Folly must be extraordinarily difficult at the moment.

"They must be talking about the Harpies," Gideon thought aloud. "My moth--" He stopped, the word catching in his throat like a curse. "The Master ordered them to attack the Owlands, so you must have been sent here by the Noktern," he added, a renewed vigor in his voice.

There is much I wish to say, but in the interest of security, I must keep some things hidden. What I can tell you is that our plans for a rescue have been thwarted.

"Lovely," the Finch grimaced, any traces of hope were dashed in an instant.

I don't mean to frighten you.

"Too late for that."

Know that there are some who still believe in the champion. I don't have much else to offer, I'm afraid. Be careful as I work to free you. In the mean-time, any details that you can provide of the Master's plans could prove invaluable. Just slip your note into the tube on Nox's leg, and she will take care of the rest.

~ A Friend

"A friend?" Gideon repeated, still absentmindedly running his fingers through Nox's sleek feathers. "Who sent you?" he asked, though it was more to himself than her. "No way Pelanor would sign off as a friend. If anything, he's probably grateful to be rid of me." Waiting for some kind of response from the bird, Gideon let out a sigh, realizing he wouldn't get one.

"Well, who else could it be? I only met a handful of Owls–" A terrible thought struck him, making his stomach twist. "Please don't tell me...Hermanor." He grimaced at the memory of the petite Owl who'd clung to him like a hatchling to its favorite toy. "I'd rather be trapped here forever." He shuddered, then looked back to the scroll.

PS. If Nox gives you any trouble, she's probably just hungry.

"Ouch!" He yelped as he felt an abrupt pinch on the back of his hand. Nox gave him a pointed peck, as though she knew the line was about her. "Alright, alright," he huffed, laughing despite himself. "Point taken."

Retracting his hand from the bars, he tossed the scroll onto the battered desk that faced the wall, then grabbed the cold plate of food from the floor. With a chunk of mutton in one hand and a random book in the other, he returned to the window where Nox was already hopping excitedly.

Setting down the meat, he watched as she tore into it greedily, strips vanishing down her gullet in seconds.

"Enjoy." A small smile tugging at the corner of his mouth. He wiped his hand on the back of his breeches and returned to the desk. The chair creaked beneath him as he eased down, placing the book carefully beside the note before turning back to the stark white parchment.

With a resigned breath, he opened the book and flipped to one of the blank front pages. The paper was yellowed and brittle in his hands.

"I can't believe I'm about to do this." He drew in a sharp breath, his shoulders tightening, and ripped the page from the binding. The tear echoed louder than expected, like it was being torn straight from his chest.

Still holding the page, he glanced back at Nox, who had paused in her eating to eye him with something that looked suspiciously like judgment.

"Don't look at me like that," he snapped. "What else could I do? I needed paper."

Nox cocked her head as if to say *sure you did*, then resumed picking at her half-finished meal.

"Whatever," Gideon grumbled, shoving the book aside and repositioning himself in the high-backed chair. "It's not like I could read that one anyway."

He laid the paper flat and rifled through the desk drawers, half-expecting to find a reed or bone pen. Instead, his hand closed around a strange instrument lying beside the inkwell. At first glance it resembled a reed, but the tip gleamed oddly, harder than bone. He turned it over in his fingers, running his thumb along the narrow slit in the nib. No hollow shaft for the ink to pool, no feather shaft to grip—just a weighty barrel and a metal point.

Scrunching his nose, Gideon gave the tip a tentative scrape against the inkwell's rim, but nothing marked the page when he pressed it to the paper. He tried again, this time dipping the point directly into the ink. A thin black bead gathered and, when he touched the nib down, a delicate line followed. A small spark of satisfaction flickered through him.

"Details…" he muttered, tapping his fingers against the supple wood of the desktop. With a few swift scratches of ink, Gideon jotted down everything he thought might be useful. It wasn't elegant, but it was honest. "I hope that helps," he shrugged.

The harsh clack of heels echoed against stone, the unmistakable rhythm of the Master's steps ringing down the hall like a death knell.

Gideon's heart lurched. He snatched the letter from the desk and blew across the wet ink, dark streams running like veins as each breath sent them skittering toward the paper's edges.

He stood too quickly; his wings caught on the back of the chair, sending it toppling over with a sharp crack.

"Shit," he hissed, barely daring to breathe. "She definitely heard that." Panic set in as he scrambled for an excuse.

The chair broke. I was pacing and I tripped.

A sudden *tap tap tap* behind him yanked his focus. Nox was at the window, pecking frantically at the stone, her beady eyes narrowed with urgency.

Gideon rushed over, folding the letter with shaky hands, barely caring about the creases. The footsteps were closer now, too close.

He shoved his arms through the bars and slipped the note into the tube on Nox's leg. As soon as he pulled away, the bird launched into the air, wings slicing through the gloom as she disappeared into the dusk.

Still trembling, Gideon turned back to the mess. He swept the scraps of meat from the sill and brushed them out the window with hurried strokes. Then, pressing his face against the bars, he stretched to reach the window frame, fingertips just grazing the wood. With a grunt, he managed to pull it shut.

He spun around just as the door unlocked with a *click*.

"And what kind of ruckus are you making in here?" The Master's voice was calm but biting as the door flung open and smacked against the wall.

"I, uh–" Gideon stammered, his wings twitching involuntarily. "I was just reading when one of those Harpies showed up at my window and startled me." He took slow, measured breaths as he lied, though his heart pounded so violently he felt faint. "I jumped, knocked over the chair, came to check–" he motioned weakly toward the sill.

The Master raised an eyebrow.

"Sorry about that," he added, trying his best to sound contrite, though it felt forced.

She let out a low, skeptical groan, her form stiff with suspicion as her heeled boots tapped against the cobbled floor.

"And what, pray tell, were you reading?"

The question sank into Gideon's spine like a hooked claw. "It's just over there," his voice thinned. He cleared his throat, trying to summon courage. "On the desk. I don't remember the title." He winced. That was a mistake. He should've checked.

A heavy silence followed. Her stare bored through him, the tension stretching taut like wire between them. Then came the deliberate *clack-clack* of her steps as she crossed the room. Her indigo dress fanned behind her, regal and dangerous.

She lifted the book with a lazy curl of her clawed hand. "*Az Ajtó*," she read aloud, her tone edged with disbelief. "Since when can you read ancient Magyar?" She offered a snide smile.

Gideon's mind exploded in curses, though he bit down on each one. He knew well enough that Magyar must refer to the ancient Sapien language the book was written in, but he'd never heard of the language, much less knew how to read it.

"I mean–" he stammered, "–the languages you taught me have so many similarities." That much was true. "They share a lot of roots and patterns. I just…pieced some of it together." His gift for languages had always come easily, but it was a feeble lifeline now. "Enough to get through the first few pages."

The Master stared at him, expression unreadable: one brow lifted, lips slightly parted, the book resting limp in her talons.

Sweat gathered at Gideon's temples. His calves trembled. Any moment now, he expected to see her eyes flash violet, feel the shroud of her mind grip his thoughts and pull the truth from him like thread from a spindle.

If she reads my mind, I'm done for.

"Well," she exasperated, offering no comfort, "do let me know what you think if you press on with it, my love. It's a fascinating story ending in betrayal." The word hung in the air like a dagger. "But we don't have time for that now. Come, my dear, we've got work to do."

✳   ✳   ✳

"Ugh, what is that?" Gideon gagged as the double doors groaned open. He yanked the collar of his tunic over his nose, but it did nothing. The stench clawed at his sinuses, burning his eyes and scouring his skin with invisible fire. "It's awful."

"Bleach." She dropped the word like it explained anything, brusque and with finality. "Now, be a good boy and go stand by the wall."

"I thought you wanted my–"

His voice faltered as the sight before him came into focus.

The chamber beyond was dim, lit only by a few recessed bulbs that burned like distant stars in the vaulted ceiling. Shadows pooled thick along the walls, warped by the hulking shapes of enormous machines—steel beasts crouched in silence, their lights gleaming like eyes as if they watched his every move. The air was heavy with the scent of oil and cold metal beneath the sterile bleach.

At the center of it all stood a raised stone slab. Upon it lay an Avian, limbs bound, feathers matted and disheveled. Gideon couldn't see their face, but the low, pained groan that echoed through the chamber left no doubt that they were alive.

"You thought I wanted your help?" The Master's voice slithered to his side. She laughed, low and humorless. "Not in so many words. But I thought you might benefit from seeing the change yourself. With your own eyes. Maybe then you'll begin to appreciate the work I've sacrificed everything for."

There was a *click*, then *bzzzzzzzzzzzzz*.

The air vibrated with a sudden, furious hum, like a thousand hornets roused from their nest. The sound grew until it filled the room, alive and thrumming in his bones. And then, without warning, the world exploded into blinding white.

Gideon recoiled, burying his face in his tunic. His eyes seared, breath hissing through his teeth as he waited for the burning to ebb. Slowly, he lifted his head. Shapes bled back into focus: the towering machines, the stone slab, and the Avian writhing beneath the glare.

"An Owl?" he whispered; the word strangled in his throat as horror took root in his gut.

"Naturally," Cecilia answered, the click of her heels ringing through the lab. She brushed past Gideon, stepping into the inner circle of machinery. At a small wheeled table, she paused and retrieved a pair of rubber gloves with deliberate grace. "I'd hoped the Harpies would bring me a scholar or two. How poetic would that be," she mused, "to put one of those pompous bastards through the change."

Gloves donned, the Master clattered over to one of the machines and began pressing buttons and flipping switches. With a grinding whir, the slab shifted, rising and tilting backward.

The Owl groaned, his ragged breaths rising in a desperate crescendo. "Where am I?" he squawked, cursing under his breath, thrashing against the leather straps as the slab leveled out.

Ignoring the struggle, Cecilia wheeled her cart closer, the rubber wheels screeching against the stone. She halted beside the Owl and raised a gloved finger to her lips.

"*Shhhhhh.*"

A sudden flash of purple flickered in her eyes. The Owl's resistance faltered; his wild eyes glazed over, the fight draining from him. With her victim quelled, the Master's attention turned back to the cart. Her talons carefully extracted a vial and a large syringe. Gideon's eyes locked onto the thick, black liquid as she drew it into the needle.

A burning surge of anger welled in Gideon's throat. He wanted to leap forward, knock the vial free, scream for her to stop. But he knew better. Any rash move would invite her into his mind, breaking his fragile control.

If she learns about Nox's message, all hope would be lost.

"She'll probably figure it out anyway, but I can't do anything stupid."

"What was that?" The Master's voice snapped, catching his muttering, though she never diverted her attention from the needle.

Shit.

"Nothing," he blurted.

On Hawks & Harpies

"Do tell, dear. I'm all ears."

"It was just a line from Tvanor's journal about the change." Gideon managed to eke out a voice that was steadier than he felt. He was startled by how easily the lie slipped out; it was the second time he'd deceived her without remorse. Before she'd disappeared, lying was unthinkable. Now it was survival.

The Master's lips curled into something like approval. "I'm glad to see you taking an interest in my work." Flicking excess liquid from the syringe's tip, she turned back to the Owl strapped to the slab.

Without a moment's pause, she plunged the needle into the Owl's arm and pressed the plunger.

Frozen with nerves, Gideon watched as the thick black liquid snaked through the Owl's veins, crawling along his arms and neck. Sweat broke out on the Owl's forehead; his face contorted in agonizing pain. His eyes remained glazed, still tethered to the Master's control, but that did nothing to dull the torment.

A blood-curdling howl shattered the lab's silence. Gideon's knees buckled, his arms trembling uncontrollably as the Owl writhed violently, the leather straps straining to their breaking point. The Avian's skin began to gray; his proud speckled feathers shriveled into coarse black stubs. At his fingertips, skin peeled away, revealing jagged barbs that tore through his fingernails which fell like shards onto the cold floor.

"Another damn Harpy," Cecilia sighed, dropping the vial and syringe onto the cart with a heavy *thunk*. "These Owls just aren't cutting it. Not hardy enough for the change. I'll have to see about getting some Hawks in here. They'll probably take it better. Oh, well."

She yanked off her gloves and stalked to a control panel, flipping a switch with her elbow. The harsh overhead light flickered off, plunging the lab into a grim gloom.

"Sleep."

The Avian's thrashing slowed, then stopped, his body going limp, though the pain remained etched deep on his face.

Gideon took a tentative step forward, rage and disgust flooding his veins. His feathers bristled; his fists clenched so tightly his knuckles whitened.

"This has to stop," he hissed, cheeks flushed. He glanced toward the Master, hoping she hadn't heard, but she was engrossed in charts and notes.

What should I do?

His eyes settled back on the cart. There was a host of tools: scalpels, scissors, the syringe, all sharp and pristine, each silently beckoning him.

"Can I–" his voice faltered as he edged toward the rolling table, eyes locked warily on the Master's back. Each step was careful, deliberate; he had to be silent. All it would take was to grab one of the instruments, catch the Master off guard while she was distracted...and it could all be over.

Would it be though?

Gideon's fingers trembled as they brushed the cool, etched handle of a scalpel. Even if he killed the woman who he once called mother, the tribes teetered on the brink of war. The legion of Harpies was still under her thrall.

What would happen if her spell broke? Would he be unleashing a storm on an already fractured Avis?

There was no time for doubts. This could be his only chance.

Suddenly, a scuffle echoed from down the hall. The piercing squawks of Harpies mingled with grunts of pain and frustration.

"Excellent timing," the Master's voice rang out, punctuated by a sharp clap of her hands. She set down her papers and strode to the door. With a flourish, she flung open the double doors just as a squadron of Harpies poured in, their cries piercing the lab's cold air.

In the chaos, Gideon snatched a scalpel, sliding it carefully into his breeches, wrapping the blade in the fabric of his shirt to muffle any hint of metal. Secured, he turned back to face the Harpies, and his heart dropped.

Some dragged behind them battered Sapiens—men who barely clung to life, faces swollen and bloodied, their bodies a patchwork of gashes and bruises. Others carried weapons: long rifles slung across their backs, compact pistols gleaming at their sides, an arsenal as fearsome as the taloned hands that bore them.

"There's no way–" Gideon breathed, the memory flooding back to the sunbaked Desertlands shore, when he and Rune—Kyte—were ambushed by armed Sapiens. A bullet had lodged in Kyte's shoulder, and only Gideon's quick thinking had saved them both. Could this be the same ruthless group? It seemed too uncanny not to be.

"Get your hands off me!"

From the hallway, a struggle erupted. The last Harpy barged in, dragging a defiant Avian behind her. The woman's wrists were bound tightly, a burlap sack tied over her head, but her black wings thrashed furiously, desperate to break free from the grasp of her captor.

"All my days! I'd recognize that voice anywhere," the Master effused, a wicked smile curling across her lips. Gliding forward, Cecilia loomed over the hooded Avian and, with a sudden tug, ripped the sack from her head using her talons. "Zokya, dear. So nice to see you again."

"Bite me," the Raven spat, venom lacing her words.

"Don't tempt me," Cecilia sneered, tracing the sharp edge of her claw lightly along Zokya's cheek. The touch drew a harsh flinch, a thin rivulet of blood gleaming against the Raven's brown skin.

Gideon watched, his heart pounding as he waited for the Master's next move, anticipating the cruel punishment the runaway Raven might face. He avoided meeting Zokya's gaze directly, wary of any attempt to seize control of his mind. She seemed wholly focused on the Master, unaware or unconcerned by his presence. Through quick, cautious glances, he noticed the swollen side of Zokya's face, a permanent mark left by their last brutal clash in the Kestrel Desert.

"I wouldn't believe it if I didn't see it with my own eyes," Cecilia clicked her tongue, addressing Zokya like a scolding matron. "But I see you've stooped to hiding out with these humans."

"Sapiens," Gideon corrected sharply, the word bursting from him with fierce conviction. His chest flared with sudden fury at the insult. The Master's eyes snapped to him, scathing and dangerous, but she said nothing more, letting the moment hang thick with unspoken threat.

"Anyway," Cecilia's gaze flitted back to the disheveled Raven. Her voice was a venomous hiss, each syllable a barb. "I'm so glad you've returned home to us." The words dripped with malice, and Gideon could almost feel the sting of the hidden promise behind them.

"And with weapons, I see." The Master glided over to one of the Harpies, extending a clawed hand to accept the rifle he carried. "What a beautiful piece," she murmured, lifting the stock to her shoulder as a small cloud of sand and dust settled in the folds of her dress. "A true wonder from the ancients, don't you think?"

She brought her eye to the scope, swiveling it deliberately until the barrel pointed straight at Zokya.

"Don't shoot!" Zokya's voice cracked with desperation, struggling against the Harpy holding her wrists. "I swear I didn't have anything to do with that human bitch escaping. That filthy rat must've slipped out before I even got down to the dungeon. It wasn't my fault!"

Gideon clenched his jaw, disgust flaring at how casually Zokya spat on Fatima's name. He bit his tongue, unwilling to provoke another confrontation.

"Zokya, darling," the Master purred, a sly grin tugging at her lips. She grunt-turned the rifle back to the Harpy and glided back to the Raven. "You misunderstand me. I was fraught with worry when you disappeared on me."

"You—" Zokya's voice faltered, disbelief softening her icy glare. "You were?"

"Of course, love."

"So, you're not going to punish me?"

Cecilia cocked her head and tsked. "I never said that." With a sharp snap of her fingers, the Master signaled a Harpy, who replaced the burlap sack over Zokya's head. A cascade of muffled curses spilled from the Raven's lips, but Cecilia ignored them. "Put a blindfold on her eyes and take her to the dungeon. I have plans for this one."

Chapter Nine
Socorra

"Check," Socorra announced triumphantly, setting her queen down on the chessboard.

"Yer gettin' better at this." Agnes slid her bishop into place with a snarky grin, cutting off the Hawk's advance.

"It's not like I'm allowed to do anything else," the Hawk huffed, leaning forward to study the board. Her elbows landed with a soft thud on the smooth oak table. "Forranor hasn't let us out to train in almost a week." She seized her queen again and moved it with a flourish, capturing the piece Agnes had just moved. "Check."

"Bad move, lass," Agnes tsked flatly. With one deft sweep, she knocked Socorra's queen aside using her knight.

The Hawk groaned, feeling defeated. "You're too good at this, Agnes."

"Keep in mind, I've been stuck down 'ere a lot longer than ye 'ave."

Socorra opened her mouth to reply, but the sudden shouts of Owl Guards echoed from the balcony above the library. Around them, at least a dozen scholars lifted their heads from their tomes, curiosity piqued by the disturbance. Peering through the outer ring of shelves, she spotted the commotion. Fatima, flanked by a unit of broad-shouldered Owl Guards, was being hurried across the chamber's upper tier. The fledgling's furious voice rang out, even above the ever-present roar of the waterfalls.

"Let go of me!" Fatima thrashed against the guards. "I can't take it down here anymore! All you people do is read and bathe! It's absolute torture!"

Agnes rolled her eyes. "What's that make, now?"

"Eight escape attempts," Socorra replied, barely reacting. She rubbed her temple and tried to refocus on the board, though a pang of guilt tugged at her as Fatima's shouting faded into one of the tunnels beyond the main chamber.

"Honestly," Sister Marta piped up from her table across the aisle, setting aside her needlepoint, "I don't know why they don't just lock the little brat in her room and throw away the key."

Socorra's wings went rigid.

"Because bein' locked up in 'ere is cruel enough, ya heartless wretch," Agnes snapped, not even looking up. "That girl needs fresh air, not to be cooped up in this prison."

Socorra exhaled slowly, letting her shoulders ease. She was grateful Agnes had stood up on Fatima's behalf.

"Oh really, Agnes." Marta rose to her feet, her chair screeching against the floor. "You know as well as I do, she's been nothing but trouble since she arrived."

"And ye've been nothin' but a pain in me arse since forever." Agnes nudged a pawn forward. "So when're they gonna lock *ye* up?"

Marta's jaw dropped in an insincere gasp. "You know, Agnes, I don't know why I bother talking to you."

"That makes two of us."

"Fine." Marta snatched her embroidery from the table, shoving the hoop under one arm. Socorra caught a fleeting wince as the sister jabbed herself with a needle. "I can tell when I'm not wanted."

"Can ye?" Agnes flashed Socorra a quick wink, never shifting her attention from the game.

Marta's face flushed cherry red. Socorra covered a laugh with a cough, doing her best not to smirk. The sister stormed off, the hem of her habit swishing furiously behind her.

Agnes raised her voice just as Marta passed out of earshot. "I thought she'd never leave!" Socorra saw the sister's shoulders scrunch high, but she didn't stop. "Yer move, Socorra."

The Hawk studied the board. An opening. She moved her knight with care, placing it within reach of the king. "Check."

Without missing a beat, Agnes snatched her queen from Socorra's side and slid it across the board.

"And that's checkmate," she effused airily, a hint of disappointment in her voice.

Socorra slumped in her chair with a groan. "I thought I had you that time."

"And ye might've." Agnes settled back into her chair with arms folded. "Ye know where ye went wrong?"

Socorra leaned in, resting her elbows on the polished table as she studied the board. After a moment of silence, she shook her head.

"Ye were too brash," the Dove chided gently. "So busy goin' after my pieces, ye forgot to watch yer own defenses."

Socorra furrowed her brow, her shoulders tightening. "I get the feeling you're not just talking about our game."

"I'm talkin' about whatever *ye* want to talk about, Socorra."

The Hawk watched Agnes closely, searching the Dove's wizened face for any sign of what she really meant. But the older woman's expression remained unreadable.

"I've just been distracted."

"Is that why ye've been tryna break down Forranor's door e'ry day?" Agnes kept an even temperament.

"That man owes us answers," Socorra retorted, a dull bite in her voice. "Gideon is still out there, and he doesn't–"

"Why is finding this Gideon boy so important to *ye*?"

Socorra jerked back in her chair. "He's the champion. It's his job to–"

"'E's the *Owl's* champion." Agnes didn't raise her voice, but there was a hard edge beneath her calmness. "And Forranor doesn't seem all too bothered about gettin' the boy back. So again, why do *ye*, really?"

"It's his job to stop the Master." Socorra's voice cut through the chamber like a thrown blade. She lowered it, but the sharpness remained. "That monster has caused enough pain. How many more people have to suffer? Look at what she did to Fatima! And those things that attacked us? They were probably Avians once."

"And what she and the Ravens did to Kyte has nothin' to do with you feelin' distracted, I'm sure."

Socorra felt a lump in her throat as if she had swallowed a stone.

"The silence is very loud in 'ere, don't ye think?" Agnes began resetting the chessboard, her voice gentle but pointed. "I'm not tryin' to speak for ye, Socorra. But I've seen the way ye stare off, like yer a thousand miles from 'ere. I watched ye throw yerself into that sea of monsters at Krepusk. That wasn't the same warrior I saw fightin' the Ravens on the surveillance tapes."

Socorra turned away, pulling her knees to her chest and wrapping her wings tightly around herself. "Like I said," she muttered, "I've just been–"

"Distracted. I know," Agnes finished for her. "I imagine it's 'ard to focus with yer 'usband laid up and so far away. Maybe it feels easier to throw yerself into a rescue mission…'elps take yer mind off things."

"That's not–" Socorra stopped.

Wasn't it?

Since her battle with Craven, the Hawk had spent nearly every moment watching over Kyte, caring for him like a devoted mate should. But that wasn't the whole picture. When she couldn't be by his side, she'd thrown herself into training with Fatima, arguing strategy with the Owl Parliament. After her lockdown and the restrictive rules that Forranor set in place, Socorra worked hard to keep herself occupied, pushing through her agenda of rescuing Gideon. She poured over maps and came up with plans of her own, every day knocking at the offices of Parliament members to pitch her plans, but they never accepted an audience with her. She'd even started working on Fatima's early escape attempts just to feel like she was doing something. She hadn't been able to sit still or relax. She needed to feel like she was moving forward, making progress.

Have I just been shooing away my worries?

"Can I tell you something?" Socorra asked softly. "Without judgment?"

Agnes laced her fingers over her lap, leaning forward. Her stare softened. "Of course, lass."

Socorra scratched at her cuticles, her fingers trembling as she struggled to find the words. "This is going to sound horrible," she began, a pit forming in her stomach. "But sometimes...it was easier when I thought Kyte was dead."

The Dove tilted her head, but the kindness in her eyes didn't waver.

"I was beside myself with grief," the Hawk continued. "The thought of losing him hurt so much, but this–" her voice cracked. "This is a different kind of pain. Watching someone you love be broken…"

Agnes reached across the table, gently taking her hand. "Socorra, just because Kyte lost a wing doesn't mean 'e's a broken man."

"No, that's not what I meant," Socorra blurted, a sharp sniffle cutting her words. "Kyte could lose both wings, a leg, an arm, an eye, I wouldn't care. I'd love him until the day the Void took me." She tightened her grip on Agnes's hand, her knuckles whitening. "But what the Master did to him, it shattered something inside. Kyte has always been a snarky pain in my ass, and that's what I *love* about him. He's always found a way to laugh, to lift others, no matter how dark things got." Her voice faltered. "He still *pretends* for others. But in the med wing…when the doctors told him what happened, I watched the light leave his eyes. And somehow, that hurts a thousand times more."

Agnes lifted her chin and straightened. "So, what is it yer after, Socorra? Revenge?"

"Of course I want revenge." The Hawk pulled her hand back, heat radiating from her clenched fist. "Kyte means everything to me. And it kills me to see him suffer." She took a steadying breath. "But it's not just about revenge. I'm fighting this hard because it matters. Because it's right." Her voice grew firmer, though her eyes shimmered. "Saving Gideon. Stopping the Ravens. It's about more than just what they did to Kyte. It's about what they took from Fatima. It's about honoring Tama, and the sacrifice she made to save me." She paused, chest heavy, wings curled inward. "I've been pushing so hard…because no one else should have to suffer the way we have. Never again."

The Hawk fell silent, waiting for Agnes to speak.

After a brief pause, the Dove gave a curt nod. "I'm glad to 'ear that." Her voice was low but certain, the corners of her mouth curling into a faint, toothy smile.

Socorra watched her closely, expecting more, but the Dove just bobbed her head a little, her gaze drifting back to the board. "One more game?"

"Aye," Agnes replied, already reaching for the pieces. "Then I think ye ought to check in on Fatima… make sure she's alright."

*   *   *

"You alright in there?" Socorra knocked again, the chill of the metal door biting her fingers. She pressed her ear to the steel and caught the sound of a scuffle, muffled swearing, then a sharp clang.

"I hate these damn wings!"

Fatima's scream rattled the door. Socorra pulled back, arms crossed against the cold that crept even through her parka. The underground corridors were never warm, but today they felt glacial.

"Why this time?"

"I can't get through the vent," Fatima growled. There was a *clang* from what Socorra assumed was Fatima kicking the grate against the wall.

"You've been locked in your room for three hours," Socorra chuckled, shaking her head. "You're already trying to escape again?"

"There's no way I'm letting these Owls get the best of me." Frustration laced her words, but there was a spark beneath it, something like pride. "I'll be out of this place in no time. Wait and see!"

"Just make sure you come back for me when you do."

"Are you kidding? You're first on my prison-break team."

"You going to be alright in there for three days?" Her tone softened.

"I'll be fine," Fatima huffed. "They forgot to search me, so I've got my hunting knife. I'll probably just whittle this desk down into toothpicks while I wait."

"Sounds like a good plan." Socorra shook her head, a light sigh of a snicker escaping through her nostrils. "I'll come check in on your progress tomorrow?"

"Looking forward to the visit!"

Turning around, the Hawk padded back to her room a few doors down. She collapsed onto the bed, staring at the stone ceiling above her. Her mind churned. Agnes's words echoed in her head, looping until her thoughts blurred until she finally managed to fall asleep.

Socorra woke to the abrupt *click* of her door unlocking from the outside. She stirred on the mattress, her hand groping in the dark until her fingers found the shaft of her spear beneath the bed. Gripping it tight, she sat up, blinking blearily as the door creaked open. Pale fluorescent light spilled into the small chamber, casting a long shadow across the floor.

"Agnes?" Socorra rubbed the sleep from her eyes.

"Shh." The Dove held a finger to her lips. "Come with me."

"What's going—"

"Keep quiet and follow me," Agnes shot in a whisper.

Socorra blinked the tiredness and confusion from her eyes. She had so many questions, but the mystery was too great to walk away from. Lifting herself off the bed, Socorra pushed past the Dove into the hallway, the frigid air biting at her exposed arms.

Agnes shut the door behind them and locked it with a silver key.

"Where did you get–"

A single, scathing look from Agnes silenced her. The Dove tucked her hands into the deep chest pocket of her habit and moved swiftly down the hall. Her footsteps, usually so heavy and sure, were eerily light.

Socorra hurried after her, rubbing the sleep from her eyes. As they turned a corner, she spotted Fatima leaning casually against her door, arms crossed.

The Hawk gave her an inquisitive look. Fatima only shrugged and fell in beside her.

"What's going on?" the fledgling whispered hoarsely.

Agnes spun around, and both girls froze mid-step.

"Do neither of ye understand what it means to be quiet?" she hissed, soft but sharp. "Don't answer that. Just stay silent until we get there."

Socorra wanted to ask where *there* was, but she knew better than to test the limits of the Dove's patience. She and Fatima followed wordlessly behind Agnes as they weaved through the fortress's labyrinthine corridors. The chilled air bit at Socorra's exposed arms, and she crossed them tightly over her chest. Beside her, Fatima tugged her abaya closer, visibly shivering.

They turned corner after corner, until they reached a dead end. The shallow offshoot looked utterly useless. There were no doors, no windows, just the same sterile teal tile that lined the rest of the passage.

Before either could speak, Agnes glanced both ways down the corridor, then stepped toward the blank wall. She pressed her hand flat against it, and a square segment of tile shifted under her touch, lifting to reveal a nest of wires and blinking panels.

From the folds of her habit, Agnes produced the silver key she'd used to lock Socorra's room and placed it against a narrow slot on the control panel. With a soft beep and a flash of green light, something clicked from deep within the wall. The Dove planted her shoulder against the stone. With a groan of hidden hinges, the wall swung open.

Out of the corner of her eye, Socorra caught Fatima's wide-eyed stare, her mouth agape in wonder.

Without a word, Agnes motioned them forward with brisk waves of her hand. Socorra stepped in first, followed closely by Fatima, and the two slipped into a narrow tunnel carved into the stone. Agnes entered last, easing the wall shut behind them. The door sealed with a faint *thunk,* plunging them into near darkness.

A trail of dim amber lights flickered to life along the tunnel's edges, glowing like clusters of torchbugs from the Zarpan plains and casting a soft golden shimmer across the walls. Socorra stiffened when a hand brushed her back, but it was only Agnes, urging her onward. Tightening her grip on her spear, Socorra pressed forward through the winding passage. The floor was uneven, the stone damp beneath her boots, but warm gusts of air whispered through the tunnel, easing the chill.

They didn't have to walk far before the tunnel opened into a vast grotto. Vaulted ceilings loomed above, supported by thick stone columns that rose straight from the mountain floor. Hanging bulbs hung in loose clusters overhead, casting gentle starlight across the chamber. The walls vibrated with a faint hum, and here and there, short bursts of steam hissed from pipes that jutted from the rock like ancient roots.

Despite the cavern's rough-hewn appearance, it somehow felt homey. Worn sofas and threadbare rugs softened the ground, mismatched pillows heaped across them in cozy disarray. And at the center of it all stood a lone, ancient Owl, hunched over a cane wound with delicate, living flowers.

"*Ordranor?*" Fatima gasped, her voice ricocheting through the chamber.

"Ah," the Owl beamed, his yellowing teeth flashing behind cracked lips. "So you *do* remember me, little one."

Socorra glanced between Fatima and the frail figure, her brow furrowed. "You know him?"

"He watched over me when I first got here." Fatima's voice dipped in reverence. "He read me stories."

"I wasn't sure if you'd remember." Ordranor shuffled forward, the *clack* of his cane echoing off the stone. "You were unconscious for most of it. I didn't know if anything I said would reach you."

"It did." Fatima nodded solemnly.

The Owl turned to Socorra with a twinkle in his eye. "We, however, have not been properly introduced." He extended a frail, trembling hand.

"Socorra." She reached to shake his hand, but was caught off guard when the Owl grasped her by the forearm instead. Instinctively, she tried to pull back, her other hand tightening around the shaft of her spear, but then she caught the warmth in Ordranor's eyes. The tension eased from her shoulders; she adjusted her grip, returning the gesture as the Owl pulled her gently into a traditional Hawk greeting, their foreheads pressed together. It was unexpected, but comforting and familiar, putting Socorra at ease.

"You'll have to forgive me for not meeting you sooner." Ordranor pulled back. "Unfortunately, I've been a bit...occupied."

"'E's been in 'iding," Agnes muttered, sidling up beside Socorra.

"Hiding is such a harsh word." The Owl's lips curled slyly. "Let's say I've been lying low. Waiting for the dust to settle."

"And what dust is that?" Socorra's curiosity piqued.

"Well," Ordranor chuckled. "I may have liberated a hostile fugitive from the Noktern."

"Badass!" Fatima blurted.

There was a beat of silence as all three turned to look at her.

"What?" Agnes and Socorra balked in unison.

"You know..." Fatima gave them a confused look. "Badass. Like...incredible! Cool, what a rebel..."

"You Sapiens certainly have colorful lingo," Ordranor chuckled. "I'll have to remember that. *Badass.* I like it."

"This was 'ardly *badass*," Agnes snorted, rolling her eyes. "All 'e did was help yer friend Pelanor escape after the battle with the Ravens."

"It's not as exciting when you tell it *that* way," Ordranor grumbled.

"It's still pretty badass to me." Socorra gave Ordranor a wink and a curt nod, causing the old Owl to blush.

But before he could reply, a shrill cry tore through the cavern, high-pitched and piercing, ricocheting off the chiseled stone. Socorra dropped into a crouch, spear at the ready. Fatima darted back a step, her hunting knife already drawn from her boot.

"Oh, you two don't need to worry." Ordranor waved a dismissive hand and turned back toward the center of the chamber. With a few clicks of his cane, he hobbled to what looked like a wooden perch. "It's only Nox."

As if on cue, a winged creature swooped in through a square porthole in the wall. Socorra lowered her spear, her breath catching in her throat as the animal soared overhead, circling the cavern once before gliding to a graceful landing on the perch.

"I can't believe it," she whispered, mouth agape. "It's a bird. A real bird."

"A raven, to be precise," Ordranor corrected, his eyes glistening with fondness.

"I'm sorry," Fatima said sharply. "Did you say *a Raven?*"

"I know what you're thinking," the Owl replied, soothing. "But Nox here is nothing like the Ravens you've faced. Those creatures are twisted and cursed, shadows of their former selves, products of our Sapien ancestors' tampering…no offense."

"None taken." Fatima sucked her teeth.

"This raven," Ordranor continued, "is descended from the wild birds that once ruled the skies before the Great End. My family has bred and cared for them across generations."

He grasped the top of his cane and twisted it, revealing a hidden compartment. With care, he dipped his fingers into the small opening and retrieved a handful of tiny seeds. Sealing the cane once more, he stroked Nox's sleek plumage and offered the seeds from his palm, murmuring gentle praise as she pecked delicately at the offering.

"Back when the world was ending and no one knew what would remain, the Noktern initiated a program to preserve the species. One of their early leaders pushed for it as a way to scout for survivors after the skies cleared, without endangering Avian search parties. The ravens were trained to carry messages."

He tugged gently at the thread tied around Nox's leg, inspecting it.

"Of course, the program's long since fallen out of fashion. Forgotten, really. Now I maintain it out of my own interest."

"If you're breeding them," Fatima's eyes scanned the chamber, "shouldn't there be more than one?"

Ordranor's lips thinned. His eyes dropped to the stone floor, shoulders sagging with a quiet ache.

"Nox had a mate," he answered softly. "Erebus. I sent him with a message just after the battle, but he never returned."

"So that means…" Socorra's voice trailed off, a wistful look in her eyes.

Ordranor offered a gentle smile. "Fortunately, Nox laid five beautiful eggs before Erebus disappeared. They're fertilized and healthy; I've been tending to them since. So yes, it's sad, but not extinction."

As he finally loosened the string around Nox's leg, the raven gave a brief flutter and flew up to a wooden ledge where a nest was nestled. A metal ladder leaned casually against the wall beneath it. Nox circled the nest once, twice, then settled in with a soft rustle of feathers.

"Let's see what news she's brought us, shall we?" Ordranor unfolded the tiny letter and scanned its contents, muttering as his eyes darted across the page. "Tvanor's journal? Hmm. Less than excellent. Harpies…of course. Just as I feared. The Master's experiments…Well, this does not bode well."

Ordranor looked up, carefully tucking the note into his robe. "The good news is Gideon is alive. And relatively well."

A wave of relief swept over Socorra. She hadn't realized she was holding her breath. "That's great news! Then why the panic?"

The Owl sighed. "Because it appears the Master… is Gideon's mother."

"What!?" The word punched from Socorra's chest. The hairs on her arms stood on end. A sick, burning weight twisted in her stomach. All the trouble and turmoil that poor boy had gone through only to learn that *she* had been behind it all?

Her heart ached for Gideon.

"She's been keeping him locked away in one of the towers of Fate's Folly," Ordranor continued, relaying what he could from the message, peppered with his own deductions. By the time he finished, the air in the cavern felt heavier.

"So you see," the Owl concluded, "it's imperative we get the two of you out of here. Gideon needs you."

"Wait." Socorra blinked. "You're helping us *escape*?"

"Pretty badass, right?" Ordranor lifted his furry eyebrows and waggled them, eyes darting between Socorra and Fatima like a fledgling waiting for approval.

"Very badass," Fatima grinned, her whole face lighting up. "So how're we doing this? Storm the front gate? Start a riot? I've tried pretty much everything short of digging a tunnel with my spoon."

"Yes, so I've heard." Ordranor exchanged a knowing glance with Agnes. "Nothing quite so dramatic as your past attempts, I'm afraid. But the Noktern *does* have a back door." He raised his cane and pointed to the stone vent where Nox had flown in. "That shaft leads straight to the surface, about halfway up the mountain. It's far beyond any of the Noktern's cameras."

Fatima scowled, crossing her arms over her chest. "Well, that's no fun."

"What's the plan once we're out?" Socorra brushed past Fatima's comment. "I don't mean to sound ungrateful, but our original mission involved the full support of the Noktern and the Owl Guard. I don't know how much the three of us–"

"Two, lass," Agnes cut in. "Just ye and Fatima are goin'."

Socorra blinked. "You're not coming with us?"

"Be reasonable." The Dove gently patted her stomach. "This thing's not squeezin' through that tunnel."

"Fair enough." Socorra rubbed the back of her neck. "But then what are *we* supposed to do against the Master and her entire legion of Harpies?"

Ordranor's expression turned solemn. "I wish I had a good answer. But if I were you, I'd find Pelanor. He left here with a plan to rescue Gideon. I'm sure he could use some help."

"Where do we find him?" Fatima asked.

"Your best bet would be Tartarus," Ordranor replied. "If he's anywhere, it'll be there." Shuffling over to a stone table at the far end of the cavern, he returned with two packed knapsacks. "Here. Take these and head out. Dawn's just a few hours off. You'll want to be clear of the ridge before first light."

Fatima snatched one of the bags and hurried toward the vent. "I can already taste the fresh air!"

In turn, Socorra took her pack, pausing to meet the kindness in the old Owl's eyes. "Why are you helping us?"

"I'd go rescue Gideon myself if I could," Ordranor shrugged. "But I'm too old. Wouldn't make it far. *You*, though…" He laid a frail hand on her shoulder. "You're strong. Kind. Resilient. From what I can tell, everyone who meets you walks away changed for the better."

Socorra tilted her head. "How's that?"

"Come now, Socorra. Surely you see it. Fatima idolizes you; she's learned to channel her fire because of you. Pelanor believed you'd do great things for Avis. And if you haven't noticed, Pelanor doesn't think *highly* of anyone."

The Hawk snorted, trying to shake away the warmth curling in her chest. She was still upset at Ordranor for keeping Kyte's survival a secret, but praise from Pelanor? That was hard to dismiss.

"Then there's Kyte."

The breath caught in Socorra's throat. "What about Kyte?"

"I've never met a man who cared about anything the way he cares about you." Ordranor's tone was gentle. "I didn't speak to him after the accident, but from what Agnes told me…I doubt he would've pulled through without you."

Socorra felt the sting of tears. She coughed, trying to cover as her breath hitched and a sob slipped through.

"As for why I'm helping you," Ordranor gripped her hand with surprising strength, "I've never met anyone more *badass*. You help people, Socorra. And right now, Gideon needs you."

She nodded, wiping her cheek with the back of her hand. "Thank you," she whispered.

On Hawks & Harpies

Shouldering her pack, Socorra turned to Agnes, offering her a final nod. The Dove gave a soft smile in return. Then the Hawk climbed into the vent. As her boots scraped against stone and darkness swallowed her, she heard a whisper drift after her like a prayer.

"May 'eaven be on your side, Socorra."

Chapter Ten
Agnes

"I almost forgot to return your key." Agnes set her tea on the side table beside the couch, fishing the skeleton key from the front of her habit.

"Keep it," Ordranor beamed from across the room. "I have a spare." He pressed a finger to the side of his cane. With a click, a hidden compartment flipped open, revealing a matching key nestled in the groove.

"That cane really is a marvel."

"It serves its purposes, I guess." Ordranor laid the cane across his lap, his fingers running along the etched vines in the stone. "Though it comes with its own curse."

Agnes waited, unblinking.

"Don't you want to know about the curse, Agnes?" Ordranor sheepishly tapped the tips of his wizened fingers together.

"Ye can read me mind," she snapped. "Ye know full well I want to know. Why do I 'ave to say it?"

"It's not as fun a story if you don't ask."

Agnes exhaled sharply with mock drama. "Oh me, oh my, a curse 'e doth say? Please, do tell!"

"You're a killjoy," the Owl huffed. "Remind me why I keep you around?"

"Because no one else in this God-forsaken place is willin' to risk their neck sneakin' ye pastries from the kitchens while you're in 'iding."

"Fair enough." Ordranor chuckled.

"So?" Agnes leaned forward. "Ye gonna tell me about this curse or nae?"

"In time." He leaned haphazardly across the couch to grab his tea, the cup clattering against the saucer in his shaky hands. "But that's not really what you're here to talk about, is it?"

"Nae, I guess not."

"You want to know what I saw in Socorra's mind. If what she told you in the library was true."

"If ye'd be so kind."

"You care for her, like the daughter you always wanted but weren't allowed to–"

"Oi, don' get all sappy on me," Agnes scoffed. "Just tell me what ye saw."

Ordranor took a long sip of his tea, slurping as he did.

"Oh c'mon," the Dove griped. "Ye know damn well I've been waitin' on yer assessment and now ye want to keep me in suspense?"

Still holding the saucer, Ordranor rested the cup in his lap, his wrists draped over the cane. "Socorra told you the truth."

Agnes exhaled and sank deeper into the couch, the worn plush wrapping around her like a hug.

"Her mind and heart are in the right place," Ordranor continued listlessly. "I have no reason to believe that she's invested for the wrong reasons. Socorra has a very clear sense of right and wrong, and she's going to do whatever it takes to get Gideon back."

"Do ya think they'll be able to find Pelanor?"

On Hawks & Harpies

"I should think so, so long as Pelanor wants to be found." Ordranor gave a light shrug. "I'm sure he'll eventually have a vision that they're coming…at least, I hope he will."

"Ye *'ope* 'e will?" Agnes choked on her tea, coughing violently until she could speak again. "So ye don't even know if this plan will work? We may've just sent them on some wild 'unt for Pelanor?"

"To be fair, being psychic isn't exactly a science." Ordranor lifted his hands in a gesture of helpless honesty. I've had years of practice and study, and my grandmother was able to mentor me in reading other people's minds because it's a gift we shared. But as far as I know, we haven't had a seer in the family…since…probably the First Owl himself."

"Wait–"

Ordranor perked up at Agnes's interjection, rolling his shoulders back until he sat completely erect.

"Pelanor is yer family?" Agnes shook her head.

"My grandson, actually."

"Why 'aven't ye told me this before?"

Ordranor cast his eyes to the floor. "Because I haven't even told him. He has no idea."

Agnes's jaw fell open.

"Yes, I know it's not ideal."

"If that isn't the bloody *understatement* of the century."

"It was just never the right time." Ordranor muttered, brushing the guilt from his expression. "Pelanor came to the Noktern much younger than I expected. Then his power started manifesting and I—I didn't know how to help him. The seer's gift is so rare, there was almost nothing in the research I poured through for years to find a way to help him. I had my nose buried in books for so long that time just slipped away from me."

"Ye didn't think to tell 'im before 'e ran away from the Noktern?" Agnes crossed her arms, leaning forward, elbows on her knees.

"There wouldn't have been much of a point. Pelanor's place is out there, fighting the good fight. Eventually, he'll inherit the family responsibility, but it doesn't need to be right now."

"Family responsibility?" Agnes raised an eyebrow. "You mean taking care of the birds?"

"That's only one of the responsibilities my family has been charged with."

Agnes stared intently at the Owl, waiting for more. "Ye're just gonna leave it at that?"

"I wouldn't even know where to begin." The Owl let out a sigh. "My family has been charged with guarding the kill code."

Agnes shifted in her seat waiting for the Owl to continue. "Ordranor, sometimes I wonder if ye really can read minds. Cause if'n ye could, ye'd know that I ain't got a bloody clue what a *kill code* is!"

"My apologies, Agnes. The kill code is a special program developed by my ancient relative, Minkjaenor. When activated from the Noktern's mainframe, it initiates a full system shutdown: life support, containment, commun-ications, everything."

"And that's bad," she uttered, somewhere between a question and a statement.

"That depends on your view of the Noktern and its work in Avis through the centuries." The Owl gave Agnes a peculiar glance, his tone measured. "But yes, it'd be bad; at least for us scholars. It would render this base completely uninhabitable. The systems that maintain our technology, our climate control, our food supplies…they'd all shut down. We'd have no choice but to learn to live as the other tribes do, without our comforts or safeguards, and that'd greatly diminish the sphere of influence the Parliament has held."

"Well, that's a pretty 'eavy responsibility."

"Indeed."

"I've 'eard you rail against this administration time and time again." Agnes gestured toward the cavern ceiling. "So why's this wretched building still standin'? If yer family was meant to shut it down, why haven't *ye* used the code?"

"Because it may not be that simple." Ordranor hesitated. "The code was written long ago, before the Noktern became the network it is today. I've never seen the program itself, and there's almost nothing written about it, just fragments of oral history passed down through the generations."

He ran a thumb across the carved petals on his cane.

"If the code is limited to the mainframe here, the damage would be immense, but containable. However…" His voice dropped slightly. "If it reaches the subsidiary systems—if it disables all of Project Innocence—then it won't just be the scholars who suffer. It could doom all of Avis."

Agnes's eyes widened. "Then why nae destroy it?"

Ordranor took a final sip of tea. Setting the saucer down, he exhaled slowly. "My duty was never to destroy it." He looked up at her, gaze steady. "Only to protect it, in case Avis were ever ready to be free of the Noktern's influence."

Agnes leaned forward, brows knit. "But how can ye keep it around if it's that dangerous?"

"Because one day soon, it'll be needed." Ordranor's smile vanished. "Pelanor has seen it be used."

Agnes's eyes widened. "Ye mean, 'e saw the Noktern fall? And you were there to see it in 'is vision?"

"Yes, though I doubt he remembers it. It was a long time ago, and he didn't yet understand what his power was."

"What'd 'e see?"

The Owl didn't answer at first. His gaze drifted to a distant spot in the cavern behind her, his thoughts somewhere far away. When he finally spoke, his voice was quiet, haunted.

"There was thunder and lightning…but inside the Noktern. Rain poured down through the halls, flooding the shelves and riverways. Then something emerged; a beast. Not one of these Harpy creatures…no, something far worse. Something feral and contorted, cloaked in violet mist. It came from the shadows and tore through scholar after scholar, its roar echoing off the stone. And then…everything went dark. The only sound was the tapping of computer keys. A light blinked on, and the kill code appeared on the screen, the program already running. Everything flashed red. Owls stormed from the Noktern, screaming."

"But if that's what ye saw, 'ow do you justify keepin' it 'ere?'"

Ordranor gave a heavy sigh, the air rattling in his chest. "Because I cannot change the future. Destiny comes in many forms, and the worst we can do is to alter it too much. If the code is to be used, the only thing I can do is to try and make sure it stays in the right hands, and out of the wrong ones."

Agnes wanted to press for more, but the distant sound of a horn rang low through the chamber.

"Shite," she cursed, pushing herself up from the couch with effort. "They've already sounded the bloody alarm. I was supposed to be back in my room before it went off, else they'll suspect I had a hand in their escape."

"Go," Ordranor urged, flicking his hand toward the exit. "There'll be time enough for stories later."

The Dove hobbled to the mouth of the tunnel, where the siren's wail grew sharper, closer. She paused, placing a hand on the wall. Faint tremors pulsed against her palm, stone vibrating like a distant heartbeat. She turned back, casting one last look at the Owl.

"Will ye be alright?" Her voice was softer, laced with concern. "The Parliament'll be watchin' after this. I don't know when I'll be able to visit ye again."

"Yes, yes, I'll manage." Ordranor waved her off, already turning his back.

He clicked his tongue softly and extended his arm. From the shadows of her nest, Nox stirred, her sleek head rising before she swept down in a silent arc. The raven landed lightly on the Owl's wrist, burying her beak into the folds of his sleeve.

"I should probably write to Gideon anyway," Ordranor murmured, stroking the bird's neck. "Let him know that help is already on the way."

Chapter Eleven
Kyte

Chop. Whittle. Sand. Repeat.

Kyte laid another wooden slat on top of the growing pile beneath the large holm oak at the edge of his property. The work was tedious and boring, but it gave him a break from the abyss that was his mind. The motions had become familiar, the crack of the wood silencing his thoughts long enough to find a sliver of peace.

"What can I do to help?" Nadia asked. Her voice was resolute, unwilling to be shooed away again. She rocked back and forth on the balls of her bare feet, her dress billowing slightly in the light breeze of the Zarpan afternoon.

"That depends," Kyte answered, wiping sweat from the nape of his neck. "Think you can handle making some rope?"

"I don't know how," she admitted, furrowing her brow.

Kyte gave her a weak smile. "Don't worry, I'll show you."

No matter how awful Kyte felt, he always tried to show the Sapien fledglings kindness. What happened to him wasn't their fault. They hadn't called down the lightning that seared away his wing. They hadn't made him an outcast.

On the other side of the tree sat a pile of hemp stacks he'd gathered over the last few days. He plopped down, resting his back against the trunk, the rough bark digging into the tender scar tissue where his wing had once been.

"Are you alright?" Nadia's eyes widened as the Hawk let out a few quiet grunts.

"Fine," Kyte huffed through gritted teeth.

He rolled his shoulders, trying to find a comfortable position, while Nadia sat cross-legged beside him. For the next few minutes, Kyte worked with her, teaching her how to tweeze out the plant fibers, roll them into thin cords, and braid them into makeshift twine.

"Why don't you get your brother to help with this?" Kyte scanned the area but didn't see Omar anywhere. A mild tug of panic pulled at him. He'd been so caught up in the work, he'd lost track of the boy. "Where is he?"

Still fiddling with a handful of hemp, Nadia silently pointed toward the anise fields, where Omar was busy picking flowers and weaving them into crowns.

"Thank the Void," Kyte effused, the air flooding out of his chest. "Go grab him, and the two of you can get to work." Returning to his woodpile, a familiar voice cut through the breeze as he bent to lift his hatchet from the ground.

"You're a natural with fledglings."

Kyte turned to find Pelanor approaching. Even in the oak's shade, the normally polished Owl looked worn, his travel robes frayed at the hem, his face drawn and gaunt.

"Any plans for you and Socorra to settle down and have your own?"

With a ferocious exhale, Kyte grabbed a log from the pile and began carving into it with the hatchet. "Whenever she's done saving Avis, I guess," he muttered, the disinterest plain in his tone. "But I'm guessing you didn't come all this way to ask about my future."

"On the contrary, that's exactly why I'm here." Despite his rugged state, Pelanor still wore the smug expression Kyte had come to know all too well. "But we've got a little time before that becomes a necessary conversation. What are you building?"

Raising an eyebrow, Kyte paused, letting the hatchet hang loosely at his side. "A ladder," he answered, voice clipped.

"Because...?"

"Because I'm tired of sleeping on a hay bale on the first floor," Kyte grumbled.

"Ah, that's right," the Owl mused aloud. "You Hawks build your homes without stairs. It's ergonomic, sure, but I imagine it's inconvenient, given your condition."

The coldness in the Owl's words bit deep.

"And what condition would that be?" Kyte's fingers tightened around the handle of the hatchet.

"Not being able to fly, of course." Pelanor picked up one of the finished wooden slats, examining it. "Not that it seems to inhibit you much."

"Doesn't inhibit me?" Kyte sneered. "I can't do shit! I can't hunt, I can't fight..." His breathing hitched. "I couldn't even protect–"

"Socorra?" Pelanor interjected gently. "You know better than anyone she doesn't need anyone protecting her."

Kyte looked away, eyes fixed on the dirt, a faint, reluctant smile tugging at the corners of his mouth.

"I saw how you handled yourself when those monsters attacked Zarpa," Pelanor persisted. "Harpies, I believe they're called."

"Right place, right time," Kyte shrugged, lifting a log and setting it upright.

"I also saw that the Hawk Guard offered you a leftenantship in the Crowlands."

"Of course you did." Raising the hatchet, the Hawk brought it down hard. The wood split with a crack, a splintered chunk flying past Pelanor's head.

"You don't seem happy about it," Pelanor noted, unfazed.

"Should I be?"

"Why wouldn't you be?" The Owl tossed the slat he'd been holding back onto the pile. "It's a distinct honor. I'd have thought it might make you feel better."

Kyte turned his head, shooting Pelanor a sideways glance. "Feel better about what, exactly?"

"Nothing in particular," Pelanor's voice softened. A stretch of silence lingered between them; the Owl shifted his weight, jutting his hip to the side. After a moment, he chewed his lip, eyes studying Kyte. "I'm just sensing… some negative emotions."

A pressure bloomed behind the Hawk's eyes, his grip tightening on the hatchet. "I'm not depressed."

"I didn't say you were." Pelanor's voice was soft, but the words seemed disingenuous, almost clinical. "I'm merely suggesting you're projecting some self-doubt, and I thought—"

"I'm not depressed," Kyte snapped more harshly.

"Then why didn't you take the offer?"

The Hawk didn't answer. He just kept chopping, wood splintering beneath each strike.

"I think it's because you feel stuck," Pelanor continued, calm and measured as ever. "Being back here without Socorra is hard, I imagine. And being flightless in the Hawklands…that can't be easy."

Kyte slammed the hatchet into the dirt, rising sharply. His posture was rigid, soldierly. "So what would you have me do, Pelanor? Go play broken-soldier in a war that you and I both know is meaningless?"

"First of all," Pelanor cut in, "you're not broken." Just because you can't fly doesn't mean you have nothing to offer."

Kyte opened his mouth to fire back, but the Owl raised his voice, pressing on. "Who's Condor?"

The Hawk stiffened. His shoulders drew back as the muscles in his remaining wing flexed involuntarily. "Why?"

"He was there with you that day." There was a softness in Pelanor's tone. "You fought the Harpies together, side-by-side."

Kyte narrowed his eyes, unsure where this was going. "We were friends as fledglings. Our fathers were both Ospreys, so we grew up fishing together…before I became a hunter."

"Does Condor have fledglings?"

"Twin girls," Kyte's voice softened despite himself. "They're almost ten now. Same age as Nadia over there." He flicked his head toward the Sapien child who sat together on the other side of the tree, the pair laughing at some unheard joke as they spiraled together the strands of hemp.

"And because of your actions, Condor got to go home to his daughters." Pelanor inhaled deeply, a soft smile tugging at the corner of his lips, replacing the arrogant smirk Kyte was used to. "How many other Avians were saved because of your actions that day? How many parents got to go home to their fledglings because of your leadership?"

The Owl's words gave Kyte pause. The Hawk never took his eyes off Pelanor, his face set in stern resolve; but inside, a numbness began to spread through his chest, cooling him from the inside out. A subtle tingling crept down his arms.

"I can't." Kyte's words came out firm, but they made him feel hollow. His stomach twisted, and a tremor rose in his calves as he stood his ground before the Owl.

Pelanor shook his head. "I was hoping to convince you based on your merit," he sighed, retiring the sentimentality from his tone. "But the truth is, the situation's more dire than I originally let on, and you don't really have another choice. You're going to have to leave Zarpa."

Kyte's jaw clenched. The muscles in his neck pulsed. "What did you do?"

On Hawks & Harpies

"Don't look at me like that," Pelanor huffed. "It's Socorra."

A bolt of fear shot through Kyte's chest, his eyes bulging. "What happened? Is she alright?"

"Are any of us really alright?" the Owl mused with a bitter twist.

"Just answer the damn question, Pelanor." Kyte exasperated.

"She's fine," the Owl relented. "She and Fatima just escaped from the Noktern."

"Escaped?" Kyte echoed, a new wave of tension drawing deep lines across his brow. "What do you mean, *escaped*?"

"It's pretty simple, Kyte." Pelanor gave the Hawk a scathing look. "They were told they couldn't leave, and they left…"

Kyte folded his arms. "And I have to leave Zarpa because…?"

"What do you think Forranor's going to do once he realizes Socorra and Fatima are gone?"

"Pelanor," Kyte growled. "I'm not in the mood for one of your guessing games. Just get to the point."

"His first move will be to declare them outlaws." Pelanor let that hang in the air a moment. "Word will spread to Zarpa and the other major cities soon enough. When it does, I'm willing to bet the Hawk Council won't hesitate to drag you in for questioning."

Kyte narrowed his eyes. "What makes you think they won't just come after me in Vines' Crossing then?"

"First, the Noktern has no reason to believe Socorra would head into the war zone, so they won't bother wasting resources alerting the Hawk generals. Second…" Pelanor eyed Kyte from head to toe. "Even if I'm wrong, and I'm not, the odds of you harboring a Noktern criminal in the middle of an active war zone are slim. And given your…"

Kyte shot him a hard look.

"…condition," Pelanor finished, unapologetically. "Let's just say there are members of the Council who don't expect you'd make it back alive."

"They think I'm going to die?"

Pelanor shrugged, his face stern.

"I hate to be this guy," Kyte bemoaned, "but you're aware this is the *second* time you've told me I was going to die. I think we both remember how that turned out."

"A miscalculation." Pelanor countered. "I saw the lightning hit you, and based on the prophecy…"

"'Though the shield be lost…'" Kyte recited, his tone sharp with sarcasm. "Yeah. We've covered that already."

"What do you want me to say, Kyte?" Pelanor's voice turned cold, distant. "Do you want an apology? I thought you were going to die, so I'm terribly sorry that you survived."

"It doesn't matter," Kyte muttered, running a hand through his thick chestnut hair. "Just tell me what you need me to do."

"Right now, I need someone in the Crowlands who can shift the direction of this war. If you can do that, then you'll be playing a role in not only stopping the Master, but you can also blunt the Noktern's power."

Kyte fell silent, chewing over the Owl's words. "So what, you want me to help slaughter a bunch of innocent Crows in a pointless war?"

"Quite the opposite," Pelanor countered. "The war may be a lie, but it's going to happen regardless. The Noktern made sure of that. But with you in command, you might be able to steer the Hawks toward a more tactical route. You're the best chance we've got to cut the bloodshed, and maybe…just maybe, save lives."

Casting his eyes to the ground, Kyte turned the idea over in his mind. "What about the fledglings?" He glanced toward Omar and Nadia. "I can't just abandon them. And someone has to keep an eye on Jamal."

"Already taken care of!" Pelanor declared, twirling his hands with exaggerated flair. "Estus has agreed to look after Omar and Nadia while you're away."

"Estus?" Kyte scoffed. "Hepha's new apprentice? He doesn't exactly strike me as the nurturing type."

"Trust me, I don't think he's thrilled either. But the alternative was telling Hepha 'no.'"

"You managed to rope *Hepha* into this?" Kyte groaned.

"Wasn't even that hard." Pelanor puffed out his chest with pride. "She was apparently pretty salty when she found out you turned down the leftenant position."

"That's putting it mildly."

"So when I told her I *might* be able to convince you to go, she graciously volunteered Estus's services."

"Sounds like Hepha."

"Speaking of the old-bird, I have something for you." The Owl reached into his sleeve and produced a small leather purse. With a casual toss, it landed in Kyte's outstretched palm, jingling softly. "For your ladder, I assume."

Kyte opened the drawstrings and peered inside to find at least a dozen roughly smithed nails.

"You'll want to get that finished by day's end," Pelanor motioned toward the pile of slats. "There's a ship leaving Ander in three days. Hepha's on it, transporting her armaments to Vines' Crossing. She's booked your passage."

"I haven't agreed to anything," Kyte retorted, but even he heard the falter in his voice.

Pelanor took a few steps back, spreading his speckled wings. Loose pebbles lifted into the air, striking Kyte's shins as the Owl launched himself upward.

"I trust you'll do the right thing."

"I *hate* it when you do this!" Kyte shouted over the rush of air from Pelanor's wings.

The Owl dipped into a hover a few yards above the ground, smirking. "Do what, exactly?"

"Show up out of the blue with everything already planned, all smug and confident like you *know* I'll go along with it. It's not good for your ego."

"You *love* it and you know it," Pelanor laughed dryly. "You're just mad I stole your bit. How many times did you pull the same stunt on Gideon?"

Kyte glowered as the Owl flew away.

Chapter Twelve

Fatima

A thin mist crept through the Tartarean countryside. Vapor clung to the raised platform like fingers slipping through the wooden slats. Tree branches sagged under the weight of moisture, heavy and glistening, while the dampness leached into the fibers of Fatima's clothes. Every time she licked her lips, the salt of her skin clashed with the sweet tang of pine that perfumed the clearing where the village lay.

Through the haze, she could just make out the first tendrils of sunrise. Pale yellow light danced along the mist, casting hauntingly beautiful shadows through the stilts beneath the buildings.

"What's the deal with Tartarus?" Fatima's voice broke the stillness of the sleeping village. The only other sound was the soft clomp of their boots on the wooden planks as they moved forward. "A lot of Sapiens back in Konstat used to talk about it, but they wouldn't really say much in front of kids. Always said we were too young to understand."

"That's ridiculous," Socorra scoffed. The butt of her spear knocked against the walkway. Her other hand gripped the rope railing of the rickety bridge that linked the main buildings of the Dove settlement. "There's nothing going on here that even a fledgling couldn't understand."

She rubbed at her eyes and gave her head a small shake, auburn hair swaying loose in the morning breeze. "A few years ago, before you were even born, a group of

Doves left the capital, Pas, to escape religious persecution from the High Priests."

"What'd they do?" Fatima tilted her head. "What could be so terrible that they had to flee into the wilds?"

"It's not really about what they did," Socorra sighed. "It's who they were. Who they *are*," she corrected.

The two rounded a corner in silence. Socorra seemed to gather her thoughts, her voice quieter when she continued.

"Today, Tartarus is home to Doves who don't want to live by the strict rules laid down by the High Priests. But it was first founded as a sanctuary. A place for Dove men and women who happen to love…well…other Dove men and women, respectively…" Her voice trailed off into the mist.

"So, they're gay refugees?" Fatima asked without reservation, then instantly regretted it. Socorra wasn't easily rattled. That was why the subtle arch of the Hawk's brow startled Fatima more than it should have.

"We don't use that term in Zarpa." the Hawk stated, her voice even. She took a breath. "The idea that we *have* to label someone like that assumes they're different or lesser. At least that's how the Hawk tribe has always viewed it."

"Good to know." Fatima's response was quiet, but respectful. She nodded, chewing on the words, mulling over Socorra's point. "Being…different…isn't exactly welcome in the Desertlands either." Her voice carried a bleakness, but she didn't elaborate.

"It's a shame." It was a simple utterance; the words seemed to close the thought like the hush of a wind through feathers.

They crossed another bridge, mist curling around their boots as a faint flicker of flame appeared ahead.

"I'd bet that's a tavern," Fatima squinted at the glow. "If Pelanor's here, that's probably the best place to start asking around."

Even if he's not, they probably have a few beds to rent," Socorra yawned, brushing away the beads of condensation on her face.

Fatima glanced over. There was a glassiness to Socorra's eyes, a faint sway in her step.

"Good point," Fatima murmured, stifling a yawn as the exhaustion from their overnight flight finally hit her.

They started toward the door, but just as Fatima reached for the handle, the sharp crash of breaking glass split the air, followed by muffled shouting from within.

"Well that's not good," she muttered, raising her eyebrows.

Exchanging a quick glance, the pair moved toward the entrance. Before Socorra could open the door, it burst outward, and a portly Dove man stumbled into the threshold, teetering on the edge.

"Timber!" he bellowed cheerfully, toppling forward, only to catch himself against Socorra's shoulders.

"Are you alright, sir?" Socorra instinctively steadied him with one arm while gripping the thick wool of his cloak in the other. Cradling her spear in the crook of her elbow, she pushed against the man's chest with her shoulder, the edge of her blade coming dangerously close to the weathered skin beneath his graying beard.

"A'course I am!" he hiccupped with a hearty guffaw, breath ripe with alcohol. "Was jus' tryin' t'get me some air when you two popped up outta nowhere!" He rocked backward, catching himself on the ruggedly carved doorway and steadying his balance with thick, calloused fingers. "But thanks fer catchin' me," he added, swaying slightly. "Yer a real swell lass. Name's Fergus. Wha' can I do ye fer?"

From somewhere behind him, the noise inside continued: the unmistakable sounds of a man and a woman screaming at each other.

"We heard…" Fatima started, trailing off. Rising on tiptoe, she tried to peer past Fergus's broad frame, but saw only the dim, smoke-hazed interior.

"Aye," Fergus cocked his head. "That'd be Théo and me wife, Brigitte. The two of 'em get t'brawlin' when they're this blootered."

"Blootered?" Fatima echoed, head cocked to the side.

"I know, I know, lassie. I *told* Brigitte we ought nae be drinkin' our own with supplies runnin' low, but we *must* be, to be toleratin' Théo while he's goin' through it."

Socorra opened her mouth to ask more, but Fatima cut in sharply.

"Back up a second. Did you say *your wife*?"

"Pshaw, aye," Fergus beamed, chest puffing. "Lovely creature, that one. All the beau'y o' the sunrise and the brawn of a mother bear. Warms me 'eart, she does."

"That's very sweet." Fatima forced a smile. "I just thought–" she paused, choosing her words with care. "Aren't Tartarean men supposed to… y'know…?" She gave Socorra a sidelong glance. Even in the dim light, she could see the Hawk's olive skin flush red.

"Ah, wha' a wee lil skunk ya are," Fergus cackled, wagging a thick finger at her. Socorra let out a small breath, her shoulders easing. "Ya see, I met good ol' Brigitte many moons ago. I was sellin' me turnips on the streets o' Pas. Hauled 'em all the way up from me wee cottage in me midder's wheelbarrow. Tha's when me eye caught sigh' of the most beau'iful Dove–" His tone darkened briefly, a scowl curling beneath his whiskers. "–buyin' taters from tha' huddy McAndrews lad…"

As Fergus rambled on, Fatima leaned to one side, trying to peek past him. But the Dove filled the entire frame of the doorway like a particularly tipsy barn door. Bending at the waist, she ducked slightly and spotted two Doves still shouting at each other in front of the bar. The air inside shimmered with heat and lamp-glow, and the floor was a battlefield of broken glasses, scattered crockery, and a few overturned stools.

"Y'alright, lassie?" Fergus uttered suddenly, catching her off guard. "Ye drop summin'?"

"No, sorry," Fatima responded quickly, straightening again. "Don't you think someone should do something about the two of them?"

"Pfft, *nae!*" Fergus dismissed the idea with both hands flapping. "This 'appens e'ry night. No need t'worry yerself. They'll sort it out soon enough. Now, where was

I?" He scratched through his scruffy, pepper-flecked hair, looking mildly lost.

"Yer wife." Fatima matched his tone with a cheeky grin, even mimicking his brogue just enough to draw a sharp laugh from Socorra, who quickly smothered it with a cough.

"A'course!" Fergus clapped his hands, a toothy grin spreading beneath his beard. "Well, I s'pose tha's really none o' *ma* business to be tellin' ye."

"What!?" Fatima groaned. "After all that, you won't even tell us? What a rip-off."

"Sorry, lassie." Fergus shrugged, the motion almost toppling him. "Ye'll have to ask Brigitte yerself."

With a dramatic sway, he leaned back and flung one burly arm toward the interior of the tavern. "Now why don' ye two come in? Take a seat at the bar and grab a drink. No alcohol for ye, lil' one," he added, jabbing a thick finger toward Fatima.

She scowled. "Rude."

"Then ye can get yerselves cleaned up an' maybe sleep off whatever storm brought ye here. Yer lookin' a bit rough 'round the edges."

With a tight jaw, Socorra stepped past him into the tavern, her boots thudding against the wooden floor. Fatima followed. The air was thick with the scent of lacquered pine and old liquor, the dull snap of the fireplace barely audible beneath the tension.

"What the hell, Ferg?" a voice boomed.

A broad-shouldered Dove at the bar turned toward them, eyes bloodshot and wild. "I told you, no more outsiders until we get our shit together!"

"We?" Brigitte squawked, her voice biting. She bent to scoop shards of glass into her tweed apron, movements practiced and tight. "I guess all *your* drinking and debts are Tartarus's problems now."

She dumped the glass into a tin bin behind the bar with a clatter that echoed through the quiet tavern.

"Know what?" Théo snarled, his speech slurring at the edges. "Yeah, it *is* Tartarus's problem. I'm drinking all the booze because I'm pissed! And I *deserve* to be, after what's happened." He slammed his arms onto the bar, veins bulging, rattling a pair of empty mugs.

Socorra started to move forward, but a firm hand clamped onto her shoulder.

"I woul' nae do tha', lassie," Fergus warned, his tone gone somber.

Across the room, Brigitte sucked her teeth and shook her head. "Théo," she sniped, calm but biting, "you've done this shite every night for the past month ever since Rocque disappeared."

Fatima felt something twist in her chest at the name. She glanced up at Socorra and caught the faint flicker in her expression, the flash of recognition. She recalled the Hawk's story of Tama, the Dove who had nursed Socorra back to health when she was Craven's prisoner. Rocque had been Tama's son, a marred boy who had been disfigured by the Ravens.

"I've been patient with you, but frankly, I've had enough," Brigitte pressed. "I know it's fresh, but at least you finally know what happened to him. You'll never admit it, but thanks to Pelanor, you have closure."

Socorra opened her mouth to speak, but Théo erupted before she could get a word out.

"I don't need closure!" he roared. "I need my husband! And now he's dead. And as for that damned Owl, it should've been *him*!" With shocking speed, he swept his arm across the bar, sending half a dozen glasses crashing against the far wall, shards exploding in all directions.

"That's it!" Brigitte's voice cracked like thunder. Her cheeks flushed a furious red as she grabbed a full bottle of brown liquor from the shelf and marched toward him. She shoved it into his chest with both hands. "Take this and *get out.* Drink yourself stupid if you want. Just *go!*" Sliding behind him, she seized a fistful of his feathers and yanked him from behind the bar.

"Aren't you going to do something?" Fatima shot Fergus a look of disbelief.

"Nae." He shook his head. "Truth be told, I dunno which of 'em scares me more when they get like this." A deep, rumbling laugh bubbled from his belly.

Despite standing a full head taller, Théo let Brigitte tug him toward the door like a stubborn mule. But before they made it halfway, he dug in his heels and pulled free.

"Whatever," he spat. Spinning around, he flared his wings to their full span, toppling chairs as he jabbed a finger toward her face. "But I'll have you know—"

With a grip like a trap, Brigitte caught him by the ear mid-sentence. "No," she snapped.

Théo's knees buckled, his wings drooping like sodden laundry.

"I'll have *you* know that if you ever stick that finger in my face again, I'll rip it off, shove it in a bottle, and serve it neat to every patron in Tartarus."

Fatima grinned. "Oh, I like her."

Fergus winked. "Ain't she jus' charmin' when she's actin' like a wee fire-breathin' dragon?"

Brigitte ground her teeth, flinging Théo's arm aside like a ragdoll. "Now get out!"

Spinning on her heel, she stormed back behind the bar. Yanking her apron over her head, she tossed it into an empty bucket. "Fergus!" she screeched, her tone sharp as broken glass. "I need a hot bath and then I'm going to bed. Grab a broom and clean up that mess, would you?"

Fatima watched as Théo staggered out of the tavern. At the threshold, he clenched the bottle's cork between his teeth and spat it into the fog beyond the plank balcony. The bottle sloshed in his grip, his silhouette swallowed by mist.

"Don' ge' me wrong, lassie," Fergus grumbled behind her, raising his voice, "Pelanor's a fine boy, sure, but we 'ad Théo two or t'ree days away from quittin' the drinkin' an' sobbin' e'ery night…"

Socorra, seated next to him at the bar, nodded absently. She glanced back and caught Fatima's eye, then rolled her own with clear irritation. Mouthing, *Go. I'll find out about Pelanor,* she turned back toward Fergus, one elbow braced on the counter.

On Hawks & Harpies

Taking the cue, Fatima stepped through the doorway and onto the balcony. The morning fog swallowed her whole. Moisture clung to her abaya, beading on her sleeves and seeping into the hair beneath her head dress. The mist curled around her like ghostly dancers, blurring the edges of her world.

In the distance, she heard the town begin to stir. Doors creaked open, the muted calls of "good morrow" echoing from unseen porches. But nothing sharp enough to pierce the fog completely.

A low groan drifted from the right. Fatima turned, squinting through the mist until she made out the faint outline of a figure slumped against the rope railing. She drew a breath, steeling herself. Every step across the creaking planks sounded too loud, giving her far too much time to consider what to say.

Hey, I know your husband's dead, but so are my parents. Think you can help us?

She winced. "Ugh. Why am I like this?" she muttered under her breath. Shaking her head, she kept walking.

The closer she got, the clearer Théo became, his tall frame bowed against the handrail, the bottle dangling loosely from his fingers. His dark skin stood out starkly against the milk-white haze, the mist curling around him like smoke.

"What do you want?" he moaned, voice low and broken. The sound vibrated through the fog, through the planks beneath her feet, like thunder trapped in wood.

Fatima stepped beside him. "I wanted to know who did your braids." She crossed her arms and leaned on the rope railing, wings folded tightly behind her. "They're gorgeous. I was thinking of getting them done myself."

Théo didn't so much as glance at her. He tipped the bottle back instead, taking a long pull.

"It's funny," she went on, "'cause my hair's covered by a–"

"I got it," he mumbled. "Hilarious."

"Oh, see, I wouldn't have known. Usually when I make a joke, people *laugh*."

He straightened a little, turning toward her with a tired kind of menace. "What do you want, girl?" His arms tensed, chest puffed, like he thought she might be scared of him.

"Just out for a walk." She tossed her shoulders. "Trying to shake off the weight of the world."

"You're just a fledgling." He sneered. "What do *you* know about the world?"

She gave his arm a shove, playful but firm; not that he moved an inch. "Everyone's got demons, Théo."

"Yeah, okay," he scoffed. "What could *you* possibly be dealing with?"

"Oh, I dunno." She exhaled sharply. Folding her arms, she came to rest on the rope guardrail. "You try being twelve, losing both of your parents, getting kidnapped, and having someone else's wings sliced off and sewn into your back. Then after all that, get yourself involved in a massive battle that'll decide the fate of Avis. Meanwhile, the one person who's supposed to do anything about this disaster disappears and is probably being held captive by an evil witch and her insane minions with magic powers. On top of all that, you become a political prisoner of the Noktern until you shimmy your way out through an air shaft that probably hasn't been cleaned out since the Great End." She turned her head, lips tight, eyes unwavering as she glared at him. "But sure, my problems aren't that bad."

"Damn!" Théo's eyes went wide, matching the gape of his mouth. "You're taking the piss."

"You're right," Fatima shrugged. "I'm actually forty-seven. Just short for my age."

"Shit." Théo took another swig, then held out the bottle.

"No thank you." She looked away, eyes drifting toward the floorboards.

"Why not?" A smirk tugged at the corners of his mouth.

She shot him a serious look, her eyes brimming with incredulity. "I'm literally a child."

There was a moment of confusion etched on Théo's face, but it quickly disappeared with an irreverent shrug. "Always figured Crows were born with a wine glass in their hand. Didn't think it'd matter that you're a fledgling."

"That'd make sense if I were a–" She caught the squint in his eye as he glanced at her wings. "Never mind," she exasperated. "I just know my parents would kill me if I tried to drown my pain like this."

"Well," Théo sighed, "consider yourself lucky. At least your parents cared about you." He leaned into the railing, bottle dangling from his hand. "That's why I built Tartarus. So someone *could* give a damn."

"I do consider myself lucky," Fatima said gently. "And you should too. You've got people here who care about you. I mean, if you weren't important to them, I think Brigitte would've killed you a long time ago."

That drew a crooked grin from him. "Yeah. Probably true."

"You're not the only one who the Ravens have hurt, you know. They're the ones who killed my parents." Fatima could feel a pit growing in her chest, a swirling eddy of fear and anger that had been lingering since her battle with the Harpies at Krepusk. "They killed my father at least. I don't know about my mother. For all I know they could've turned her just like your mate. Maybe she's out there right now, scooping up some poor soul and tearing them away from someone they love."

Théo didn't speak, but the tension in his shoulders eased. His face slackened, no longer hardened with grief but cast in quiet reflection.

"That fear and hate will never go away." She felt the riptide in her heart, a crashing sense of anger breaking the air in her lungs. "But we can't let it control us." She took a deep breath. "Not when there are people counting on us to be strong. People who need us."

The glade stretched out in silence before them. Mist curled around the treetops, slowly dissolving as the sun pushed through. A breeze stirred the sweat-soaked linen on Théo's back, ruffling his wings as he drew a long, steady breath.

Then, without a word, he extended the bottle.

"What?" she stammered. She started to refuse again, but the suddenness of it threw her. She took the bottle with an awkward grip, uncertain what else to do. "I just told you I didn't want this."

"I know." He flashed a manic grin. "So take it back to Brigitte for all I care. I need to get some sleep. And you do too. You look awful."

Before she could reply, Théo thrust his wings and lifted into the air. Like a fish out of water, he floundered awkwardly until he reached a large stilted house perched on a hill at the edge of the fen.

"Good talk." Fatima ran her tongue over her teeth, shook her head, and stamped back toward the tavern door, her face still flushed. "It's not like I just poured my heart out or anything. The least you could do is acknowledge that."

Despite herself, the heat in her cheeks eased as she placed her hand on the door handle. Replaying their exchange in her mind, she caught the calm in his tone, the quiet gratitude in his eyes.

"He's gonna be okay," she smiled softly. "Ugh, I'm having feelings," she groaned. With a stretch, she let out a long, satisfying yawn.

"I should sleep." She gripped the handle with both hands, then paused, chuckling to herself. "I really need to stop talking to myself. I'm letting Gideon get to me."

Chapter Thirteen

Socorra

"Remind me why we can't just fly?" Fatima groaned, curling into herself and gripping her sides with white knuckles.

"Because the Phoenix Mountains are too high for you," Socorra answered between heavy breaths. "The air gets thinner, and the temperature drops the higher we climb. You've only been flying a few weeks; you don't know how to handle this yet."

"We have mountains in the Desertlands, you know."

"Yes, I know." Socorra wiped sweat from her arms as goosebumps rose on her skin. "But these are higher. When's the last time you flew through the Palerocks?"

"Why don't you just tell me what to do?" Fatima whinged like a fledgling testing her wings. "You could at least let me try."

"I could," Socorra responded tersely. "But I'd prefer your lungs don't explode."

"Wait, seriously? That can happen?" Fatima's eyes went wide. "Brutal."

"Very." Socorra chuckled, though a biting stab of pain cut through her abdomen. "Once we reach the apex of the pass, we should be able to glide down over the forest." She tried to sound reassuring. "From there, we just need to keep our eyes peeled for the tavern."

"What do you think Brigitte meant, by the way?" Curiosity brightened Fatima's voice. "'You don't find Airam's tavern, it finds you.' What does that even mean?"

"I'm not sure," Socorra admitted. "If Airam's the supplier for Tartarus, it makes sense she'd keep herself hidden. But how a tavern could 'find' someone? I don't know." She shrugged. "I guess we'll find out when we get there."

The route was long and unforgiving. Jagged peaks rose like the teeth of a Croc, their summits stabbing at the sky. They were too steep to fly through easily, and impassable on foot. Even the flatter passes were treacherous, with loose shale and slick moss-covered stones.

The sun had long since slipped behind the mountains, leaving the northern face swallowed by shadows. Socorra and Fatima pushed on through the rough terrain, pausing only to catch their breath. When the last gleam of light faded and stars began to sprinkle the darkening sky, they reached a flat outcropping dotted with scant grass and wildflowers, a rare oasis amid the harsh rock.

"Let's camp here for the night." Socorra dropped her rucksack with a sigh. She pulled out her waterskin and took a long draught.

"Finally!" Fatima exclaimed, breaking into a trot as she dropped her rough pack on the loose dirt. "I've needed to pop-a-squat for the last two hours!"

Socorra rolled her eyes, but chuckled to herself as Fatima dashed toward the nearest thicket. "I'll be right over here!" she called after her. "And watch out for stinging nettle!"

"Got it!"

Gathering a few dry scraps of timber, Socorra arranged them into a small pile. Fingers rifling through her knapsack found the chiseled flint block just as an abrupt screech shattered the stillness across the plateau.

"I warned you about those nettles!" Socorra snickered, waiting for a response. "You okay?" she called out. Silence. "Fatima?" She called again, but all she heard was the crackle of branches underfoot.

A cold weight settled in Socorra's stomach. Instinctively, her hand reached for the spear lying on the ground behind her. She grabbed it with both hands, rising to her feet. Wings spread wide, rigid at her sides.

"Who's out there?" Her voice wavered, the chill creeping into her lungs. The rustling stopped. Planting her feet firmly, she forced herself to speak again, voice steadier. "Show yourself, coward!"

Silence.

The pale starlight barely illuminated the glade. Socorra strained her eyes, barely making out the pile of sticks she'd arranged moments ago. Every muscle tensed as she stepped cautiously forward, shadows billowing like hungry smoke across the plateau, threatening to swallow her whole.

Suddenly, behind her, soft footsteps scraped against the earth. She whipped around, swinging her spear in a wide arc, but caught nothing but air.

Heart pounding, she scanned the darkness. A fleeting shadow darted along the plateau's edge.

"Stop!" she screamed, lunging forward in pursuit. The figure slipped into a thicket of trees. She skidded to a halt, searching frantically for any sign of it, cheeks burning despite the cold night.

Footsteps came again, closer this time. She whirled, eyes blazing with fierce determination, spotting the shadow once more. Her chase quickened, adrenaline surging, but like smoke, it vanished, leaving her grasping at emptiness.

The cycle repeated: the sharp scrape of footsteps, a flicker of shadow, the frustrating miss as the phantom slipped just beyond her spear's reach, each time edging closer. Desperation fueled Socorra's speed and agility, her muscles coiling tighter, but the elusive figure danced always just out of reach.

Amid the scuffle, Socorra caught the distinct sound of wings beating against the air. She turned to find the silhouette of an Avian plastered against the speckled sky.

"Finally," she whispered.

She planted her feet firmly, coiling her fingers around the spear's shaft like a javelin. Her muscles tensed, pulsing with raw energy, the wooden shaft humming faintly with anticipation. The shadow advanced, wings beating in rhythm, precise and pointed.

Her gaze tracked the creature as it began to dissolve into the mountain's looming darkness. With every ounce of strength, Socorra lunged forward and threw.

The spear sliced past her face, but before she could follow through, a sudden, searing blow exploded at the back of her skull. The world flipped.

Pain exploded down her spine and into her legs. One hand flew instinctively to the strike as she crumpled to the cold earth. Her limbs betrayed her. Numb, useless, she flailed helplessly. Nausea washed over her in dizzying waves as the world spun into a blur of color.

Her eyelids fluttered open to the cold, dim world. Over the ringing in her ears came the unmistakable crunch of footsteps, dozens of them, closing in.

Through the haze of fading consciousness, she caught the clipped Valysian voices. "Get back and tell Sarge we've got two of 'em."

∗   ∗   ∗

"Let me out of here!"

The shout slammed into Socorra, dragging her back to consciousness like a lash. The iron clang that followed reverberated through her skull. She bolted upright, but the pain was instant. Agony cascaded down her spine, a fiery throb blooming at the base of her neck. Her wings flared instinctively, kicking up a cloud of dust that clung to the dry air and caught in her throat.

Coughing violently, she struggled to breathe. The arid atmosphere was suffocating, each gasp scraping her lungs like sandpaper. Her limbs screamed. Her thoughts blurred. Darkness licked at the edges of her vision again, threatening to drag her under.

"Songbird's awake," came a voice, raspy and cold, mocking. Behind her, laughter slithered through the space like a snake through weeds.

Socorra gritted her teeth and forced herself upright. Her body howled in protest, her throat raw. She blinked hard, trying to steady her vision, but the iron bars of her cell wobbled in a drunken spin.

Staggering forward, she collapsed against the nearest wall. Its surface was black clay, baking-hot, and as her palms met it, pain flared up her arms like fire.

"Son of a–" she hissed, jerking back and crumpling to her knees. She looked down, her hands seared red, angry welts forming fast.

"Stupid girl!" someone jeered through the bars, their voice shrill with cruel delight.

"I love it when they cook!" another cackled, echoed by a chorus of snickers from the dark beyond.

Seeking relief, Socorra blew a shaky stream of cool air across her blistered palms, then lifted her eyes to take in her surroundings.

Beyond the bars of her cell stood three Doves clad in leather armor draped over loose togas. Sunlight spilled through the stained-glass windows lining the chamber walls, blazing reds and yellows casting wild flickers across the stone, as if the prison itself were on fire.

"Get outta there!" Fatima squawked from the adjacent cell. She tried to wedge herself between the iron rungs, but they were too tight, even for her slight frame.

Her command went ignored. The guards rummaged through their belongings like vultures, one of them slipping Socorra's canvas coin purse into his tunic. The rest of her gear was deemed worthless, flung aside with casual disdain.

Socorra instinctively reached for her spear, but her hand grasped only air. A sharp pang clenched her chest. Her eyes darted in panic, ignoring the flare of pain in her neck until she spotted it: the glint of her blade propped against a counter near the guards.

"When I get out of here," Fatima growled, "I'm gonna rip your feathers out and stuff my pillow with them!"

"Shut your mouth, you filthy girl!" one of the guards snarled. Drawing his sword, he sauntered toward her cell, sneering beneath his leather helm. "You're giving me a headache." He slammed the flat of the blade against the bars, catching Fatima's fingers in the strike.

She yelped in pain while the guards howled and hooted.

"Enough!" Socorra blustered. But she quickly caught herself, swallowing her fury. Drawing in a slow breath through her nose, she softened her voice. "There's been a mistake. Let us explain, and we'll be out of your way."

More laughter from the guards sifting through their supplies; but the third, the quiet one, turned to her. His smug expression shifted from a scowl to a faint, pompous grin.

"The prisoner speaks with such conviction." His voice was calm and cold. "You'll get your chance to explain. Sarge'll make sure of that. But don't get your hopes up."

He stepped closer, eyes narrowing. "You'll be lucky if you ever set foot outside these walls again. I'd suggest you get comfortable."

Socorra bit the side of her tongue, rage crawling up her throat like bile. "Just listen–" she clenched her jaw, trying to keep her voice level, to sound reasonable, controlled.

But before she could finish, one of the Doves cut her off.

"No, *you* listen, bitch–" He unsheathed his sword, brandishing it toward her.

"*Alexandre!*"

The name cracked through the air like a whip. The guard froze, sword still raised. His face locked into a mask of stoicism, but Socorra noticed the tremble in his knees. A bead of sweat snaked down his temple.

"Is that any way to speak to our *guests*?" The voice that followed was velvet and venom, a rich vibrato that filled the corridor with a deceptive warmth, like honey over poison.

Socorra craned her neck, squinting through the rows of bars.

A broad figure ducked through the doorway, imperious and dangerous. His great wings folded behind him, but still brushed the edges of the stone frame. He was clad in steel, his armor etched with a flaming sword whose hilt crossed the breadth of his chest and whose blade ran like a spine down his torso, etched into molded muscle.

He moved with the deliberation of a predator.

"Well?" He tried to keep his voice calm, but it crackled with tension. He stepped up to Alexandre, bringing his face so close their noses nearly touched.

Alexandre swallowed hard. "N-No, Sarge!"

"That's what I thought," Sarge whispered, the words slow and sharp as a blade unsheathing. He lingered a moment longer, breathing in the fear before pulling back with a curled lip of disgust.

Turning now to the other guards, Sarge's gaze flicked to the last scraps of Socorra's gear being pocketed. His shoulders lifted slightly, like a hawk tightening its wings.

"And what have we found–" he paused, voice low and thick with disdain "–*gentlemen*?"

"Traveling provisions." The guard coughed to cover the quiver in his voice. "A few days' worth of dried meat and medicinal herbs."

"Liquor?"

"No." He huffed, the disappointment slipping through before he caught himself. "But–" he added quickly, "–both were carrying weapons."

"A lot of good they did us!" Fatima snapped before Sarge could respond, her feathers puffed with indignation. "You've got a lot of nerve, ambushing us in the dark like cowards. Why don't you give me my knife back and fight me like real men?"

The guards chuckled, amused, but Sarge threw his head back and laughed, deep and genuine, like something about her fury delighted him.

"This one's got moxie. I like that." His smile twisted into something dark. "Alexandre!" Before the guard could react, Sarge seized him and slammed his face into the bars of Fatima's cell. The metal clanged; Alexandre groaned but didn't resist, Sarge's massive hand braced between his wings and shoulder blades.

"Stick out your arm," Sarge growled.

Alexandre obeyed instantly.

"Not at me, idiot." Sarge shifted, twisting Alexandre's arm and forcing his shoulder deeper into the bars. The guard wheezed as the pressure drove the breath from his lungs, his fingers now just a few feet from Fatima.

With one hand still gripping the back of the boy's tunic, Sarge reached for the scabbard at his hip. Alexandre's eyes widened, jaw slack, as the officer drew an enormous claymore.

Even Socorra gasped. The blade was monstrous, easily two heads taller than she stood, with a crossguard the width of her forearm.

Without fanfare, Sarge tossed the sword into Fatima's cell.

The pommel, an apple-sized gem of deep amethyst, struck the stone floor with a deafening clang. The vibration thundered through the Brick, jolting up Socorra's legs and into her spine.

Alexandre squirmed, trying to pull away, but Sarge held him fast, both hands braced against the guard's back. A cruel grin carved itself across the officer's face.

"Now, girl..." He turned his gaze to Fatima. "This braggart was terribly rude to your friend." He nodded toward Socorra. "I think you ought to teach him some manners. Don't you agree?"

Fatima's eyes widened, realization striking like a slap. "Are you insane?" she squealed. "I'm not cutting off the poor bastard's arm!"

"Even though he's the reason you're in here?" Sarge's words came out smooth and coy.

"He's defenseless!" she scoffed. "I'll fight him fair if that's what you want, cage-match style, but I'm not going to dismember him for your sick amusement."

Sarge tilted his head. "Even if it could earn you your freedom?"

Fatima opened her mouth to retort, but whatever she meant to say stuck in her throat.

"That's what I thought," Sarge murmured, satisfied. "If you manage to sever this pitiful excuse for an arm with my Zweihander, I'll let you and your friend go. No tricks. No strings."

She said nothing. Her eyes flicked from Sarge to the sword, then to Alexandre's outstretched limb, trembling against the bars.

"Well?" Sarge goaded. "Don't just stand there. Pick it up…if you can."

A bolt of panic lanced through Socorra as Fatima dropped to one knee, her expression sharpening into a look of grim resolve. Socorra lunged forward, gripping the heated bars between their cells.

Fatima, stop! she wanted to cry, but her voice failed her. The words jammed in her throat. Her stomach churned, bile rising fast. The pain in her palms was distant, almost unreal. Everything inside her screamed to intervene, but she couldn't move.

As grotesque as the moment was, one truth loomed larger than the rest: their freedom meant everything. For them. For Gideon. For Avis.

With a grunt, Fatima managed to wrench the sword from the floor. The massive blade wobbled in her grip, its weight forcing her arms to tremble. She staggered backward, struggling to lift it overhead. The tip flailed wildly, nearly toppling her as she fought to stay upright.

"No, *please!*" Alexandre cried. He tried to yank his arm back, but Sarge held him fast, one hand digging into the joint of his wings with terrifying glee.

As Fatima fumbled, a sudden glint of light caught the sword's edge. It seared across Socorra's vision like lightning, followed by a wave of heat pulsing through her gut. Her hands slapped the floor. The stone burned against her skin, but the fire inside was worse. Her stomach twisted.

She couldn't hold it.

The retching was violent and immediate, the vomit splattering in front of her with a sickening stench.

"Oh shit!" someone uttered.

Through the haze, Socorra looked up. Fatima had the sword *barely* hoisted above her head. Her face was rigid with focus, but her arms shook wildly beneath the weight. The moment broke. The momentum betrayed her. The blade crashed behind her with a deafening clang, dragging her down like a ragdoll beneath its bulk.

Laughter erupted behind the counter.

"Pity." Sarge's tone was flat and unimpressed, the word hanging sharp and cold in the air.

His face shifted, his jaw slackening, brows smoothing as if a lever had flipped inside him. Without a glance, he released Alexandre's tunic. The guard collapsed face-first onto the floor with a grunt.

Squealing like a wounded animal, Alexandre scurried away on all fours. His armor scraped against the stone, a miserable screech of metal on clay. He didn't stop until he collided with the boots of his fellow guards. They looked down at him with a mix of disgust and pity.

"Useless sack of shit," Sarge muttered, brushing past Alexandre like he was nothing but refuse on the side of the road. His attention shifted back to Fatima, that same smug curl twisting his mouth. "Well now, it's safe to say your *squawk* is worse than your bite." His voice oozed with condescension. "So be a good little girl and tell me what were you two doing all the way up in the Phoenix Mountains?"

Fatima didn't respond; instead, she picked herself up, slowly and deliberate, brushing the dirt from her robes. A strand of hair slipped from beneath her headdress; she tucked it back with the same composure she'd use to tie off a bandage. Then, without blinking, she spit in his direction.

Sarge's eyes narrowed, but he didn't wipe it off. "Tartarean sympathizers, then? Or just a cozy little supply run to Airam's?"

Fatima glowered. "What's it to you?"

He gave a crooked smile. "So it's the hard way." He turned on his heel with military precision. "Let's go, gentlemen."

The guards hesitated, exchanging uncertain glances.

"What about the other one, sir?" One of them nodded in the direction of Socorra's cell.

Sarge didn't even pause. "The concussed one who can't hold her breakfast?" He strolled to her cell, slow and deliberate. "I'm sure *she's* going to be helpful."

"You arrogant son of a–" Socorra tried to stand, but pain cleaved through the base of her skull. Her voice died in her throat. Hot, jagged bolts of agony radiated down her neck and spine, pulsing through her limbs. Another wave of nausea buckled her. She collapsed, cheek pressed to the stone, her skin burning on contact.

The world dimmed. The only sound was her breath hitching against the filth.

"What'd I tell you, boys?" Sarge gloated.

He loomed in front of her cell, blotting out the stained-glass light. From the floor, Socorra could barely make out his expression, but in the silhouette of his face, his eyes burned like twin cinders in the dark.

"Now, you two get comfortable." His voice was airy and sweet, like a lullaby gone rotten. "It's still early. You're not feeling the full strength of the Brick yet. But as the sun climbs..." He clicked his tongue. "These stones are going to cook you from the inside out."

A coarse chuckle rolled from his throat. "Pretty soon, you'll be begging to get out of this oven. *Then* the inquisition begins."

Chapter Fourteen

GIDEON

Cuckoo…Cuckoo

"Shit!" Gideon jolted, the sound cutting through the stillness. Flinching, his thumb scraped against the jagged brass of the keyhole. A biting sting bloomed beneath the nail, and he yanked his hand back, pressing the wound to his mouth.

"Shut up," he hissed through clenched teeth, shooting a venomous glare at the tiny figurine perched at the end of the plank. The paint had long since flaked away, but the carved wings and pointed beak were unmistakable. If he didn't know better, he might've thought the tiny creature was Nox.

On the third chime, the cuckoo retreated, the plank sliding back into its cache with a mechanical snap.

"Thank you," he muttered. Pulling his hand away from his mouth, he inspected the cut; it was shallow, barely bleeding. Still, it throbbed with indignity. With one final sneer at the clock, he turned back to the task at hand. He fitted the scalpel's edge into the keyhole with surgical care.

"Step one," he murmured, tilting his head to better see inside the lock, "get the door open." The blade scraped against the tumblers with a teeth-on-metal grind. He'd read so many stories where heroes popped locks in seconds, but he found the task much more complicated. Talking to himself helped, grounding him in the moment.

"Step two…" His voice faltered, lips tightening. "Find Cas."

Anything to take his mind off the monotony.

"Step three, get out and get back to the Noktern."

It was a simple plan. Not a great one, but it was all he had.

He'd spent two days now chewing through poss-ibilities, turning over contingencies like stones in his stomach. Every dead end made him queasy. Eventually, he'd convinced himself not to sweat the details. Just move forward one tumbler at a time.

"Simple is better," he whispered to himself, shaky but reassuring. "You can't plan for every eventuality."

Time passed slowly. Every *tick-tock* from the cuckoo clock drove a nail deeper into his spine, a relentless, mechanical reminder of how much time he lost.

"It's like Moda all over again," he groaned.

The clocktower of the Finch city loomed in Gideon's mind—the granite monolith that his father helped build standing guard over the citizens of Moda. The pervasive ticking had flooded the air there too, lacing through the cobblestone alleys, echoing between the smoke stacks. Those days felt impossibly long ago. He missed the scent of Wydah's bakery, the zing of citrus curd inside her orange tarts. He missed lounging beneath the great elm that shaded his bench, the burble of the fountain chasing away the weight of the world.

Cas.

The memories inundated him. Cas laughing, sprinting through Moda's winding streets while Gideon chased after him, panting and smiling. Cas lying beside him on the bench at night, whispering dreams while smog-shrouded stars winked through residual haze of the smelting factories.

A sob cracked in Gideon's throat before he could stop it. His fingers trembled, slipping against the scalpel.

"I have to get him out of here."

The next moments were a blur; a rush of adrenaline coursed through him before he realized what he was doing.

Tick. Tock.

Taking a step back, Gideon looked at the enigmatic cuckoo clock, the pervasive sound of the cogs twirling, catching at every second, every minute…time moving forward where he couldn't be productive…couldn't save Cas…

"Enough!"

The word erupted from him, his blood boiling. Before he knew what he was doing, he lunged at the clock, the ancient wood crunching beneath his fingers as he wrenched it off the rusty nail. He reeled it above his head, then hurled it across the room with a deafening crash. Splinters exploded in every direction as the clock slammed into the door.

Gideon stood dead in his tracks, his mouth parted in a soft, but horrified gasp. The damage was done. The sound must've echoed through half the castle.

"This was supposed to be the one part of the plan I could control."

His knees gave out. He fell to the floor, frantically scooping the broken pieces into a pile with shaking hands. His movements were erratic, as if by gathering the wreckage he could undo the noise and rewind the moment.

On Hawks & Harpies

"You're dead," he chided himself. "The Master's going to burst through that door any second and figure out what you were up to and kill you…or worse…"

His mouth went dry, the disturbing images of the change clawed into his thoughts, grotesque and unbearable.

"No. *No!*" He forced a breath into his lungs. "You'll figure it out. Just get this cleaned up, hide it, and–"

He reached for another fistful of shattered cogs, scrambling for a lie, any excuse that might buy him time.

A soft groan interrupted his thoughts.

The sound stopped him cold. His hand, brushing the door, had nudged it forward.

"You've got to be kidding." A heavy creak echoed through the room as the slab shifted ajar. "It's…it's been open this whole damn time?"

He knelt there, half-crouched, staring as a faint wash of torchlight spilled through the narrow crack, cutting across the floor. His mouth hung open. His pulse throbbed behind his eyes.

A searing heat rose in his throat, but it burned into something colder, emptier. "I'm so mad." A simple utterance—flat, quiet, and hollow.

With a heavy shake of his head, Gideon let the broken parts tumble from his hands. The shattered cogs scattered across the stone. Slowly, he stood and brushed the dust from his palms.

"Step one," he muttered, voice thick with sarcasm. "Check."

He turned to the open door, heart pounding.

Step two…" he hesitated, taking a deep breath as he stared down the open door, "…find Cas."

Gideon placed a trembling hand on the edge of the door.

"I should really clean this mess up," he stammered, stepping back toward the scattered clock parts. "What if something goes wrong? I can't have the Master–"

A sudden gust rushed down the corridor, strong enough to extinguish the torches behind him, plunging the room into darkness.

"*Gid.*"

The whisper was hoarse, distant. Barely louder than the rush of air.

Gideon flinched. "Cas?" His voice cracked in the silence. He couldn't be sure. The disembodied voice sounded off, distorted by the echo of the stone walls; but hardly anyone called him that.

"Besides Fatima," he reminded himself. "What am I doing?"

Before he could second-guess himself again, he leaned into the hall, bracing against the heavy doorframe. Smoke curled in the air from glowing embers of the torches. From somewhere in the corner of his eye, a figure flitted through the shadows.

"Cas?" Gideon hissed. "Is that you?" He tried to train his eyes on the dark figure, but the shape bounded down the stairs and was out of sight.

With a deep breath, Gideon stepped out into the hallway.

"Step two."

He plucked the scalpel from the lock, tucked it into his breeches, and slipped through the doorway, closing the door behind him with a soft *click*.

Moving quickly but cautiously, Gideon followed the path he'd memorized. "Brass chandelier…staircase with a broken banister…moth-eaten tapestry."

After a few twists and turns, Gideon made it to the main hall.

The entrance to the citadel stretched out before him, three stacked balconies running the length of the chamber like tiered jaws ready to swallow him whole. From his perch on the uppermost level, he heard the sharp shuffle of claws on the stone below.

He crept toward the iron balustrade and peeked over.

"At least six Harpies," he whispered, pulling back in alarm. "You need to be careful. If you get caught–"

He began backing away only to bump hard into a tall bureau, knocking an immense candelabra to the floor.

From below came a smattering of squawks as claws scraped and wings snapped open with a *thwap*. Gideon froze, paralyzed against the edge of the table. His throat seized.

"*Psst!*"

The hiss jolted Gideon out of his stupor. He whipped around, eyes searching for its source.

"*This way!*"

Bounding from the wall, Gideon sprinted to the open archway at the end of the balcony. The corridor beyond was narrow, barely wide enough for his wings. He shoved his way through, feathers scraping and tugging against the cold stone. The dim glow of the main hall vanished behind him as darkness closed in like a shroud.

Hands groping for balance, he felt the texture of the walls change; smooth marble gave way to craggy, time-worn rock. Under different circumstances, he might have paused to marvel at the ancient tunnel carved into the mountain's heart by long-dead Sapiens. But not now. Not with the bloodthirsty flutter of Harpies at his back.

Then, the passage turned abruptly. Gideon threw himself against the wall, breath held, spine flat to the stone. He listened for any sign that he was followed.

Clack. Clack.

A singular set of talons against the stone floor.

What do I do?

Panic gripped him, raw and cold, tearing into his gut like icy claws.

What can I do?

His mind raced in frantic loops, offering no answers. Over the footsteps, came a thin flutter that tickled at Gideon's ears.

"Wind." The word escaped Gideon's lips like a beacon cutting through the darkness. He stilled, straining his ears. Past the echo of claws, he heard it. Not the muffled sigh of wind brushing the castle walls, but the harsh whistle of a breeze cutting through a valley.

Peeling himself away from the wall, Gideon resumed his descent into the corridor, but the soft rhythm of his footsteps betrayed him. The clack of talons grew louder as the beast picked up its pace, but the Finch didn't have to go far before the scent of barren earth and rotting wood permeated the hallway. Pale flecks of moonlight kissed the stone ahead, just enough to make out a jagged opening in the rock.

"A window."

Hope surged in his chest. He rushed to the aperture and clambered onto the narrow sill. Spreading his wings, he embraced the cool air, ready to descend into the cover of night to flee the Harpy and abandon his prison sentence under the vengeful foot of the Master.

One leap, and he'd be gone, but his feet refused to budge.

"You can't," he choked.

A numbness spread through his limbs, his palms tingling where they pressed into the sill. He stared into the night as though it might give him an answer.

"Cas wouldn't leave you here to rot." Climbing off the ledge, he wiped the dirt from his palms. "He'd have found you days ago and gotten you out."

The Harpy was almost upon him now, the sadistic chirps and growls that emanated from its gullet sounding from around the corner.

"Cas wouldn't have let you get taken in the first place." Gideon's hand slid to the scalpel tucked behind his hip, his fingers trembling. "He would've done what was necessary to save Avis."

The breeze licked at his skin, and his cheeks flushed, heart hammering in his chest.

On Hawks & Harpies

The Harpy barreled around the corner, talons screeching against the stone floor, but Gideon's voice rose against the clamor.

"Cas would have been the champion everyone expected him to be."

Up-close, the beast was absolutely vile. Top-heavy and lurching, its oily gray hair draped a twisted grin of jagged teeth. Ungainly, but no less deadly, it bore down on him with sick glee.

"It's time to be the champion that Cas deserves..." Gideon's instincts screamed for flight, but he dug in, wings flaring wide.

"...The champion that Avis needs."

The Harpy let out a guttural screech and lunged, claws extended toward Gideon's throat.

What happened next felt like possession. It was as if Socorra or some warrior of old had taken over him. He dropped low, knees buckling, wings anchoring him to the floor. The Harpy's weight crashed onto him, and Gideon raised the scalpel on instinct.

They hit the ground hard. The world blurred. Gore slicked the floor beneath him, stealing his grip as the Harpy straddled his waist. The beast raised its talons, poised to tear him apart.

Gideon raised his arms, bracing for death, but the strike never came.

Lowering his arms, he saw the scalpel lodged in the Harpy's throat. The creature froze, confusion and pain mingling in its beady eyes. Its claws twitched, faltering.

With a jerking motion, it yanked the blade free and flung it aside as a stream of blood cascaded over Gideon's face.

Pain in its eyes, the Harpy tore its head back, its mouth twisted in a grisly screech; but no sound escaped. In its place, a geyser of gore erupted over the creature's jagged teeth. Abandoning its prey, the creature clambered to its feet, holding back the river spewing from its esophagus.

Gideon watched in a daze as the creature staggered, blood pouring from its throat like oil. Scrambling backward, he fumbled through the dark until his fingers brushed the scalpel. Gripping it tight, he turned his gaze back to the Harpy. The creature's gray skin had gone ashen, ghostlike in the waning moonlight. It staggered to the window, one claw scrabbling at the sill, but its slicked hand lost its grip.

"No!"

Scrambling to his feet, Gideon launched himself to the window, but he was too late. He watched in horror as the creature's limp body tumbled into the void beyond the castle walls. A distant crack of branches, then a dull, final thud echoed up from the valley floor.

Gideon stood at the window, staring out into the shadowed gorge of Raven Rock. A breath of relief passed through him, but it quickly curdled. Guilt knotted in his stomach, rising like bile in his throat. He looked down at the scalpel in his hand, reddish-black ooze trailing down the hilt and onto his hand.

"I'm sorry," he whispered in lament. "I didn't have a choice. I–." He swallowed hard. "I *had* to."

"*Yes, Gid, you had to.*"

Gideon's heart skipped a beat. He spun around, but the corridor behind him was empty.

"*Come on*," the voice instructed, soft, coaxing, distant. "*You're almost there.*"

He glanced once more at the window. The Harpy's silhouette had vanished.

"Step two," Gideon muttered, shaking his head. He forced his wings to relax and turned into the shadows ahead, deeper into the corridor.

Chapter Fifteen

Pelanor

Mantids darted through sparse flora, their buzzing a symphony over tranquil waves that lapped against the stony islet. Tucked between two olive trees, Pelanor scanned the rich blue of the Rainbow Sea in search of the Brick. His eyes followed the sprawling network of crystalline shallows that rose into white limestone croppings that pockmarked the area.

Despite the beauty that lay before him, Pelanor felt ill-at-ease given the rumors and sinister history of the region. The Owl had read of numerous battles from before the Great End where Sapiens were slain by the thousands, and those that survived were often driven from their homes. Even as civilization began to emerge in the early days of Avis, the tribes regularly waged war for control of the area. In recent times, many reported seeing ghost ships afloat the sea, or heard the phantom footsteps of armies patrolling the shores—a haunting reminder of the violence and brutality in the region. Several Finch merchants even claimed to have seen ghoulish figures lurking amid the waves beneath their ships—echoes of the past that neither the tides nor time could wash away.

"Aha!" Pelanor exclaimed in a hushed tone. Climbing higher on his perch of gnarled roots, the Owl squinted hard into the distance, gleaning all the detail he could. Despite its ominous reputation, the complex didn't look like much. The island was devoid of all vegetation save a few paltry ferns that dotted the perimeter of the prison complex. The outer buildings consisted of a two-story wooden outpost which desperately needed a new coat of varnish, and an alabaster watchtower; Pelanor could see three or four guards pacing the platform amid the haphazard colonnades, their silhouettes visible in the distance. At the center of the compound stood a squat black cube, a web of gray concrete scrawling between each brick.

"Bit of a letdown, isn't it?"

The words crept into Pelanor's ear like a spider. Flinching, his wings unfurled to their full length, knocking into the Avian who lurked behind him. Plunging his hand into the sleeve of his robe, Pelanor withdrew a hidden knife and whirled around onto his would-be assailant, but his foot slipped into the gnarled roots.

"Steady," Théo called out, catching Pelanor by his forearm.

Stunned, the Owl stared at the Dove, mouth agape. "What're you doing here?" He strained his abdomen as he tried to lift himself.

"What, no 'hello'?" Switching his bo staff to his off hand, the Dove placed his large palm on Pelanor's shoulder and helped prop the Owl up. "Not even a 'thank you'?"

Pelanor breathed deeply, trying to catch a whiff of Théo's breath, but he smelled nothing but the salt air. "Thank you!?" he squawked. "For what? Sneaking up on me? Giving me a heart attack?" He looked down at his ruffled robes and straightened them out. "I think not!"

"You really are something else." The Dove's tone hinged between admiration and frustration.

"So I've been told." Pelanor lifted his eyes to find Théo staring at him with a gentle smile. There was a strange calm that washed over the Owl, but it was quickly replaced by a tingle as a warmth rushed to his cheeks. "Now," he stammered, turning his back to the Dove, "tell me what you're doing here."

"I received word from our scouts that your friends had been captured by the Inquisition, but I suppose you already knew that."

"Naturally," Pelanor affirmed with a flair of pride in his voice. "What I didn't expect was for you to show up."

"Your visions have been wrong in the past." Théo gave a dismissive tilt of his shoulders, derision curling in his voice.

"We're not doing that right now," Pelanor chided, chasing away the turmoil that crept into his chest. "The failure of our relationship is off limits." Turning, he let his gaze lilt past Théo to avoid eye contact. "Besides, we have more important matters to attend to."

"Do we, now?"

"Absolutely," Pelanor beamed arrogantly. "You're going to get me into the Brick."

Théo was unfazed, his dark eyes still locked into Pelanor. "What makes you think I can do that?"

"Because," Pelanor stated matter-of-factly, "where my hubris often puts me in situations where I don't belong, I don't believe that you'd be here if you didn't have a plan to help Socorra and Fatima."

"Are you calling me a coward?" Théo smirked.

"No," Pelanor shook his head. "I'm calling you judicious."

Théo furrowed his brow. "That somehow feels worse coming from you."

"Is it any worse than calling you a drunk?" For the first time in their conversation, Théo's look hardened, but he remained silent. "I'm sorry." Pelanor exhaled, letting the tension out of his shoulders. "That was uncalled for." Taking a step forward, he reached a palliative hand to Théo's shoulder, but the Dove withdrew.

"It's fine," Théo gave a casual shrug. "As always, you're right. But that's enough repartee for one encounter. Besides, I'm sure you're eager to get to the matter-at-hand." Fiddling with his tunic, the Dove withdrew a small linen pouch from his trousers.

Clearing his throat, Pelanor gave his shoulder a shake, chasing away the tingle of regret he felt. "What's the plan then? We can't very well just fly over to the island and introduce ourselves to the guards."

"Won't have to." Théo tossed the satchel into the air for Pelanor to catch. His curiosity piqued, the Owl untied the knot and pulled out the only item within the pack.

"What's this?" Pelanor asked.

"Take a whiff."

Pelanor undid the clasp of the unassuming metal canister, the unmistakable smell of manure catching in his nostrils. "Preening oil?" He shook his head. "This must've cost you an arm and a wing."

"It's hard to come by in Tartarus. The Noktern won't supply it to us directly, but we have our ways," he answered coyly.

"Airam?"

Théo stared blankly, confirming Pelanor's suspicions.

"May I?" Théo took a few short paces toward Pelanor and held out his hand, a coquettish smirk on his face. Taking the canister, Théo directed Pelanor to turn around, and the Owl complied. Dipping his fingers in the thick gel, the Dove rubbed the salve into Pelanor's feathers with a gentle hand, and Pelanor could feel the heat flush his face.

"So this is your big plan?" Pelanor stammered, tamping down the fluttering in his stomach. Théo continued working on Pelanor's wings without answering. While only seconds passed, the silence felt interminable to Pelanor. "I suppose it's simple enough. We swim to the island to avoid having to fly. The Inquisitors would never see it coming."

More silence. Pelanor could almost feel Théo rolling his eyes from behind him.

"Stealthy, I guess," he continued. "But then what? They've got at least twenty guards stationed along the perimeter and who knows how many more inside. I know you're impressive with that staff, but the two of us can't just fight our way into the Brick–"

"Pelanor," Théo interrupted and the Owl turned to face him. "As much as I've always loved to hear you ramble, you're starting to drive me crazy." Extending his arm, Théo offered the canister to Pelanor. "Now do mine."

Wordlessly, Pelanor accepted the pot.

"Besides, we're not swimming to the island."

Fingers in the viscous oil, the Owl cocked his head. "We're not?" he asked dubiously.

"No, much better." Théo beamed. "We're swimming under it."

⚹   ⚹   ⚹

With enormous strength, Théo plowed through the depths, lunging his arms against the water. Pelanor held tightly to the Dove, his arms wrapped around Théo's neck as they dove deeper. Following the steep incline of the island down, the crushing strength of the ocean grew with each stroke of the Dove's powerful limbs. The saltwater burned Pelanor's eyes, but he kept them open as long as he could. In the growing dark where the sunlight could not penetrate, a cavern appeared where the island's base met the ocean floor. Corroded pipework surrounded the entrance, a hole into the abyss.

The space was pitch black and too narrow for Pelanor to continue holding onto Théo. He held back and let the Dove enter first, but the Owl stayed tightly on his trail. They pushed on for what felt like ages, the burning becoming unbearable in Pelanor's chest as his lungs failed him. Fumbling in the dark, Pelanor tried to feel for Theo's boot in front of him, but his hand found nothing. The pressure growing, panic started to set in as he flailed his hands. Kicking, he tried to propel himself forward, but he hit a wall. The fear rushed to his chest; he couldn't stop from inhaling, sea water rushing into his throat. He tried to scream, but nothing came out.

There was a firm grasp at the nape of his robe, and suddenly he was ripped upward. The sound of crashing water exploded in his ears as he broke the surface, stale air tearing into his chest.

"We're off to a great start, I see," Théo mocked. He gave Pelanor a hardy pat on the back and a cascade of saltwater sprayed out of the Owl.

"Thanks," he coughed, a chill creeping into his wet skin. It was too dark to see, but Pelanor felt the tightness of the space. "Where are we exactly?"

"Beneath the Brick." There was a spark and a quick whir as Théo lit a torch. Removing it from the worn and rusted sconce, the dim flame illuminated his face, his dreadlocks soaked and dripping with water. "This sewer system was built by Sapiens millennia ago and the Inquisition unwittingly built their prison on top of it. Airam and our runners have been using it for years to steal supplies."

"Poetic." The word came out more ambivalent than Pelanor had intended. "Stealing right out from the nose of the organization that would see your people extinguished. It's brilliant."

"Thank you." Théo flashed him a sincere smile. "But this won't be as simple as a supply run. We'll take this path up to the storage hold, but once we're inside, we'll only have a few minutes to find your friends and get out."

"Why only a few minutes?"

"It's baking hours," Théo answered solemnly. Handing Pelanor the torch, he wrung out his hair and the excess water from his tunic. "It may not look like much from the outside, but the Brick is beyond brutal. The air is so hot and dry that it isn't safe for anyone inside."

"Hence no guards."

"That's the upside." Théo flashed him a knowing stare and withdrew the two halves of his bo staff from his boots, screwing the bronze shaft together.

"Then why do you need that?"

"Always better to be prepared." Taking the torch back from Pelanor, Théo dipped his head to the left and proceeded down the tunnel without another word.

With a deep breath, Pelanor withdrew the hunting knife from his sodden sleeve and followed up the concrete pathway. He did his best to keep his footing on the uneven incline, the stone worn down by years of trickling water.

"Mind your head," Théo called back in a low rumble. Dipping down, the flames licked a network of roots that had broken through the walls.

After a quarter-hour, the pair made it to level floor.

"Here." Théo thrust the torch back into Pelanor's hands with no further explanation. Lifting his tunic, he revealed his strong figure, the flames dancing along the creases of his chest and abdominals. Pelanor tried to avert his gaze, but couldn't keep his eyes from lingering.

"Desire is the greatest of vices," the Owl muttered under his breath.

"What was that?" Théo cast him a sideways glance.

On Hawks & Harpies

"I asked what you're doing." Pelanor blushed, but hoped that Théo couldn't see in the dim.

"The stone is too hot to touch directly." He wrapped his tunic around his hands. "You'll understand in a second. Just brace yourself."

With a judicious shove, Théo pushed the stone slab, shards of light filtering in through the cracks; a grating echoed through the sewer. A trickle of heat poured down on them until the slab was fully removed. Then a wave of hot air burst through the corridor, searing Pelanor's face. Tying his damp tunic around his waist, Théo lifted himself up through the hole. He reached down and offered Pelanor his hand.

The alcove was tight, packed with crates, barrels, and baskets of all sorts of dried victuals. Once Pelanor was safely settled, Théo replaced the stone slab with a gentle thud and made his way to the edge where the recess met the hall.

"Mim, it's hot." Pelanor fanned his face with his hand, sweat beading on his forehead. He could feel the dampness of his robes starting to dry; the nape of his neck felt like it was on fire as the warming cotton rubbed.

"C'mon," Théo called in a harsh whisper. "The coast is clear."

"I thought we weren't worried about guards," Pelanor huffed. He wiped the dust stains on his robes, but it only spread along the tan linen.

"Better safe than sorry." The Dove rounded the corner and broke into a trot, Pelanor following right behind. Without stopping, the Owl took in the ghastly scene of the hall. They ran past oil braziers which cast an unearthly red glow along the black stone, shadows dancing along the walls.

"They may as well have called this place the Inferno," Pelanor mused.

"Dante Alighieri." Théo responded. "An apt reference. I'm sure that's what the Inquisition was going for."

"You've read it?" There was a pique of surprise in Pelanor's voice.

"The Doves of Pas read it to their children as a bedtime story," Théo answered solemnly. "It's easier to instill the fear of Hell in us when we're young."

Coming to a tee in the hall, the pair stopped.

"Which way?" Pelanor asked, but Théo hushed him. Digging at his collar to release the heat, Pelanor watched the Dove cup his ear and listen down each branch of the hall.

"Hard to say." Théo tossed his shoulders. "The prison cells line the outer walls, so they could be in any of the main chambers."

"Good thing time isn't of the essence."

"Hold on," Théo threw up his hand. "We have company."

A shiver ran through Pelanor as he listened. The sound was faint at first, but the unmistakable clack of boots rose from down the left hall.

"Get back to the nearest alcove," Théo directed.

"What are you–"

"Don't argue, just do it."

Pelanor flinched at the Dove's sternness, his neck reeling back. As much as he wanted to snap back, he could see the seriousness in Théo's eyes. Without further question, Pelanor did as he was told, returning down the hall from which they came with Théo close on his heels. Ducking into the nearest archway, they stood silently out of sight.

"Damn, Sarge!" The words resounded through the empty halls, the sound of footsteps growing louder. "Gives the fledgling wench a sword and forgets it so I have to play fetch during baking hours. Bullshit! The bitch would've cut off my arm if she weren't so damn small!"

Pelanor and Théo exchanged looks and peered out of the archway. Crossing into view at the intersection, the guard stomped along as he continued to mutter to himself. Without thinking, Pelanor laid a hand on the wall to steady himself, a searing pain digging into his palm. Unable to control his reflex, the Owl audibly whinged. Wheeling back, the guard drew his sword, his eyes landing directly on the pair. Before he could call out, Théo had already bolted from their hiding spot, bo staff drawn. With a quick flick of his wrist, Pelanor brushed off the pain in his palm and brandished his hunting knife, following in pursuit.

Shakily, the guard seemed to assess the situation. Trembling, he looked down the hallways on either side of him. Backing up, he darted into a sprint, turning back the way he came.

As Théo and Pelanor reached the intersection, the Owl went to follow the guard, but Théo placed a forceful palm on his shoulder. "Forget him."

Pelanor raised an eyebrow, his heart pounding. "He's calling for reinforcements! We have to–"

"The alarm's already been sounded," the Dove interrupted earnestly. "Best thing we can do is find your friends and get out."

"How do you propose we do that when we'll have the entire Inquisition breathing down our necks?"

"Now you're just wasting time." Théo broke out into a jog in the opposite direction. "You heard him," the Dove called back. "The fledgling wench is this way!"

The Brick was a small maze of harsh corners which led to more blank hallways. The further they drew on, the worse the heat became. Every once in a while, Pelanor looked over his shoulder to see if they were being pursued, but the halls remained empty.

"There!" Théo called out from half-a-hall ahead.

An open doorway led into yet another room. Skepticism weighed heavy on Pelanor's mind, but he pressed forward despite his body's urge to stop. Crossing the threshold, they found themselves standing amid a long row of prison cells.

"Fatima?" the Dove called.

"Socorra?" Pelanor echoed in a hoarse gasp, his breath wavering. The only response they got was a heavy grunt and the piercing grate of metal against metal. There was a moment of strained silence until an eerie groan resounded through the hall. A shadow amid the flame-licked walls, one of the cell doors swung downward until it crashed into the stone floor. From out of the cage strode a haggard looking Fatima, her face twisted in something between anguish and pride. Her dark robes were visibly heavy; soaked with sweat, her headpiece sagged at the shoulders.

"Can I help you?" she huffed, turning to face Pelanor and Théo.

"How did you–" Pelanor began.

"The hinges are pins," Fatima interrupted. "Very easy to undo when I figured out how to leverage the sword. But that doesn't matter, we have to get Socorra and go."

"Where is she?" Théo asked, but Fatima had already moved to the next cell. Lifting the sword above her head, Pelanor thought the fledgling might tip over. Despite the immensity of the weapon, Fatima managed to stabilize herself before bringing the sword down in an arc against the lock of the cell. Sparks flew in every direction and the lock shattered, falling to the ground.

With the final clack of the metal contraption, a ruckus arose from the handful of other prisoners, all pleading for their freedom.

"You'll have to carry her." Fatima raised her voice to be heard over the chorus of pleas. "She's passed out in there and not doing well."

Amid the already brewing noise, Pelanor heard calls ring out from the hall. They were still far, but it called for great concern. "Théo, grab her," he commanded, posting himself at the door.

Ignoring Pelanor's warning, Théo turned to Fatima. "Give me the sword."

"Over my dead–" She hesitated, her eyes cast to the floor in a moment of thought. Wordlessly, she handed the hilt over, pulling her sleeve up. Taking the weapon in his bare hand, Théo grunted from the heat, but did nothing about it.

"What are you doing?" Pelanor squawked.

"Making a distraction." Jotting down the hall, the Dove slammed the hilt of the sword into every lock, the prisoners bursting forth from their cells and filtering out the only door into the hall beyond.

Smart, Pelanor thought, though he wouldn't say it aloud.

Once he'd finished, Théo dropped the sword. He doubled back to Socorra's cell where Fatima was hunched over the Hawk, wiping the sick from her cheeks. Before entering, Théo turned to Pelanor. "Here!" With a gentle lob, the Dove tossed his staff into the air and Pelanor managed to catch it. Turning to Fatima, he whispered gently, "Don't worry, I've got her." Scooping his arms under the Hawk, Théo effortlessly lifted Socorra in his arms with all the strength of a bear. Swadling her in her own wings, the Dove cradled Socorra like a newborn fledgling and carried her to the door.

Following Théo out of the cell, Fatima froze, a slight panic stricken on her face. "Hold on," she blurted out before running back through the corridor.

"Fatima," Pelanor called after her. "Forget the sword, it's too heavy."

Ignoring him, she continued her pursuit, but didn't go to where the sword lay. Instead, she disappeared briefly behind a wooden counter. After some clinking and clanking of metal, she emerged a few seconds later carrying two light rucksacks and Socorra's spear.

"She'd kill us all if we forgot to grab it." Fatima's eyes widened, a small snicker escaping between her lips. "Fortunately, those idiot guards left it behind."

"Good thinking," Pelanor admitted. He felt a feather lighter knowing they wouldn't have to worry about that, but it did little to quell his nerves. "What's the plan?"

"There's no going back under the island, not with Socorra in this condition." Théo shifted the Hawk higher against his chest. "We'll have to fight our way out."

"Now that's my kinda plan!" Fatima brazenly strode through the door twirling the spear in one hand. Mid-swing, the butt of the spear knocked against the top of the stone frame and was thrown to the floor with a resounding clack.

Pelanor and Théo exchanged cursory glances.

"Don't say a word," Fatima snapped. "I'll figure it out." Collecting the spear, she stood off to one side continuing to practice, jabbing at the air in front of her and twirling the spear above her head.

"Pelanor," Théo blurted over the growing jeers and footsteps of the guards. "You'll have to take the lead in case we run into trouble."

"You mean 'when' we run into trouble," Fatima muttered.

"It shouldn't be too hard to find the exit," Théo continued, ignoring the fledgling's pessimism. "Just follow the hallways until we find the southern wall."

"Or just follow the trail of guards who're pouring into the main entrance as we speak," Fatima sassed.

"Or that," Théo scowled in her direction. "Is she always like this?" He turned back to Pelanor.

"Worse usually," the Owl shrugged. A smirk crossed his lips despite the knots in his stomach.

"And I thought I had problems." The Dove shook his head. "It may be dismal, but she's right. Let's get going before it's too late. And Pelanor…"

Passing through the door, the Owl turned back toward Théo.

"Try not to get us killed."

Chapter Sixteen
Kyte

Kyte tramped through the muddied paths that wound through the chaotic sprawl of tents that made up the Hawk's encampment. Many of the larger structures were held up by central posts on which the upper platforms sat, creating two, three, and even four-story tents that swayed precariously in the wind. The crimson canvas rippled and flapped, the taught guy lines straining to keep the makeshift shelters upright in the mid-summer breeze.

"Your quarters are just up here." The scout's voice barely carried over the din. Ahead, the officer's tent loomed above the rest, compartments jutting out at odd angles from the main structure, as if added hastily and without thought for symmetry. The whole thing looked as though it might collapse at any moment, yet Kyte knew better. What the Hawks lacked in aesthetics, they made up with sound engineering.

Kyte had felt eyes on him since the moment he'd arrived at the encampment, but in the inner rings, the soldiers seemed more brazen. As he passed, several paused to stare. Some leaned in toward their comrades to whisper while others openly smirked, nudging and pointing. Kyte kept his expression unreadable, though a pit swelled in his stomach with each pair of eyes he caught.

Arriving at the officer's tent, the scout drew back the canvas flap, the emblem of an ancient hawk embroidered into the make-shift door, and bade them enter.

"...Sagittarii legion's so desperate, guess they'll let anyone be an officer."

Kyte lingered at the back of the line, letting the others shuffle in first. He shifted his weight and tilted his head slightly to catch the conversation of two soldiers who stood just a few paces behind him. Their words, clipped and conspiratorial, blended with the hum of the camp around them.

"Shut up, Falco! He's right there."

"Like I give a shit! Let him hear me, I'll say it right to the cripple's face."

His blood boiling, Kyte clenched his jaw and dug his heels into the mud.

"I'd love to see him try to give me an order, I'd walk right up to him and…"

"Leftentant?" Kyte jumped as the scout called out to him. Using the momentum, he consciously turned into a strut without acknowledging the boy, pushing past into the tent. "General Melierax will be with you shortly to give you your orders."

Dropping the curtain, the scout left the officers standing in a neat row at attention. Joining them, Kyte mimicked their stance, spreading his legs shoulder width apart, folding his hands into the small of his back. He held his wing rigidly in a postured position, hyper-aware of the feathers grazing only one of his arms, the other feeling naked.

It was unbearably hot in the tent, only growing warmer as the minutes passed. The air was rich with the scent of anise, dried blossoms hanging around the tent, mixing with the smell of burning incense. While it was better than the putrid stench of sweat and piss outside, the smoke and odors clung heavily in the air. Wiping the sweat at the back of his neck, Kyte readjusted himself, shaking out the tightness in his legs.

"Wouldn't do that if I were you."

With a sideways glance, Kyte eyed the officer to his right—a short, muscular woman with rigid features. "And why's that?"

She didn't respond, barely letting her eyes dart in his direction.

"What, nothing to say?" Kyte shook his head.

She shook her head. "It's because Melierax–"

"Because Melierax–" a thunderous voice raised over the woman's, "is a bloviating tyrant who would sooner rip your wings off than tolerate any type of insubordination!" From behind a dividing curtain emerged an imposing figure; Melierax was a rotund Hawk, vibrations emanating through the earth beneath Kyte's feet with every step. Pausing in his egress, the general eyed each of the officers in turn, his gaze coming to rest on Kyte. "A poor choice of words I see. Nevertheless, I have a rigid sense of discipline and won't tolerate any shenaniganry from my officers. I hope each of you would expect the same from your troops."

"Yes, sir!" The other officers answered in unison, Kyte a beat behind.

Raising an eyebrow, Melierax scanned Kyte up and down, his eyes rolling over him for an uncomfortably long time.

"So, this is *the* Kyte Pandion?" He trudged over, his steps heavy beneath him. "Raised to leftenant for fighting off a hoard of mutant Crows." The stench of anchovies and pickled capers was palpable on his breath, flecks of spittle landing on Kyte's cheeks.

"Yes, sir."

"I've heard a lot about you, soldier." Boldly and without hesitation, Melierax grabbed at Kyte's arm and seemed to inspect his tunic, twisting and turning his body in every way possible. Seemingly content with his inspection, he waved a hand in the direction of the other officers. "The rest of you are dismissed."

Exchanging cursory glances, the other officers hesitantly shuffled their way to the entrance of the tent. "Sir," one of them called, a tremor in his voice. "If I may–"

"You may not."

"But sir–" another piped up.

"If one of you 'but sirs' me one more time…" He held up a pudgy finger, the skin of his hands as red as his face. "…I'll personally see to it that you're sent back to the Hawklands with broken legs!" His chest heaved, each breath like the grunting of a Zarpan boar. The officers said nothing, but looked at each other nervously until they cleared out of the tent.

Melierax held his position even as the tent flap fell behind the last of the officers. The color in his face receded to a soft pink, but he maintained his rigid stature, his lips moving rhythmically as if he were counting.

"…Ten! Alright, they should be gone by now." With a quick shake of his head, the general unwound his shoulders, letting his wings fall back to rest. "Sorry about that nonsense, good man. Have to keep up appearances, you know." Waddling his way to the far side of the tent, he flopped into a chair, the wood bowing beneath his weight, and grabbed a tray. "Can I offer you a biscuit?"

"I'm fine." Kyte wrinkled his nose, dazed by the sudden shift in Melierax. "Thank you."

"Suit yourself." He popped one of the coarse wafers into his mouth. "So fell me–" He stopped mid-word, jaw working furiously. "How doef a Hawk who can' fwy…" He coughed, swallowed hard, and grimaced. "Void's mercy, that's *dry.*" He smacked his lips, brushed crumbs from his armor, and tried again. "How does he manage to take down a small legion of those dreadful creatures?"

Kyte shrugged. "I just did what I had to do."

"How noble." Melierax went to grab another biscuit, but seemed to think better about it. "But that's not what I'm getting at. There were plenty of Hawks in Zarpa who sprang into action. Who did what they had to do. But how did *you* do what fully able-bodied Hawks couldn't do?"

Clenching his jaw, Kyte bit down his anger. "Like I said, I–"

"Leftenant Pandion," Mclicrax interrupted with an exasperated groan. "It's mostly a rhetorical question. I want you to think about why you've been invited here as an officer. You seem like a good man. Headstrong, but talented. And above all, a valiant leader from what I've heard. But understand that good men die on the battlefield all the time. Seeing as you're already at a disadvantage–"

"Sir!" Kyte growled, a tremor in his hands. "I think I've proven myself despite my wing." A warmth radiated through him; a feeling of wholeness settled in his stomach. "There's no need to bring it up anymore. I know what I've suffered. I don't need to be reminded."

Melierax seemed unaffected. Rising from his chair, the general looked, gave him another size-up, his lips curling gently into an almost imperceptible approval. "Hepha had me worried about you. She'd said your confidence had been shaken since your accident."

That wench. Kyte rolled his eyes.

"But I can see there's a fire in you yet. You'll need it out there."

"On the battlefield?"

"With your soldiers, leftanant. You'll be leading the Sagittarii legion..." With a heavy sigh, Melierax's eyes bulged. "They're a grounded unit for a reason—not exactly the sharpest swords among our ranks, if you catch my drift. What cruel things do you think they'll whisper behind your back? Some might be stupid enough to say it to your face."

Kyte thought back to that soldier outside the tent.

Falco, wasn't it?

"Be sure to set an example for them, Pandion." Melierax scrunched his eyelids in a stern look. "Courage is one thing, but not every soldier will be tamed through your heroics. Sometimes a forceful hand is necessary. I trust you understand?"

Letting Melierax's words roll through his mind, Kyte nodded.

"Good." Extricating himself from the chair, the General whisked open one of the desk drawers. After rummaging, he withdrew something. "Your orders." He handed Kyte a scroll sealed with the winged-sword insignia of the Hawk Elder Council. "It's time you were off to meet the Sagittari."

Without a word, Kyte took the scroll from him and saluted. Melierax rolled his eyes, meaning Kyte had done it wrong, but the general was silent. Turning on his heel, Kyte headed to the tent flap.

"Oh, and Pandion." Wheeling around, Kyte paused beneath the flap. "If you ever growl at me like that again, I'll tear off your other wing." There was a seriousness in Melirax's eyes. "Dismissed."

You'd have to catch me first.

A half-smile crawled across Kyte's lip. "Yes, sir."

✳   ✳   ✳

For half-an-hour, Kyte trudged through the trampled streets, mud pressed flat beneath the boots of soldiers. He could feel their stares—pitying, disgusted, reviled—all cutting into him. He kept his eyes forward, refusing to meet a single gaze, but the weight of their judgment clung to him all the same.

No matter how far he walked, he couldn't escape it. The names followed, echoing in his skull like drumbeats. *Useless.* The word struck first. *Damaged.* The things they'd called him since he'd lost his wing. *Broken.* His cheeks burned with rage. *Cripple.*

"Enough!" The growl was intense, but low enough that Kyte felt confident no one had heard.

They made you an officer for a reason, he reminded himself. *Own it.*

The training field sat at the edge of the encampment. Keeping an even pace, Kyte walked past groups of Hawks huddled with straw dummies practicing their swordsmanship. Others darted through the air sparring with spears. At the far edge of the field, a line of archers drew back their bows.

"Fire!" A surly looking Hawk called out and the whistle of arrows hit the air, streaming toward rough targets that dangled from the tops of the trees. "Maxim, Elia, and Falco..." the name pricked Kyte's ears. "Right on target. The rest of you, retrieve your arrows, then give me a running lap."

Huffing, the soldiers did as they were told, running into the thicket of brush and branch. Approaching the officer who remained behind, Kyte extended his arm to the Hawk. "Good afternoon. Sergeant Hiero, I presume?"

The Hawk pursed his lips into a thin line, the man's yellowing eyes darting back and forth between Kyte's hand and his face. "And who the hell might you be? Some new recruit who doesn't even know his place enough to salute a commanding officer?"

"Ah, of course." Kyte withdrew his hand and darted it into his pocket. "How silly of me. Feel free to salute me at your discretion."

"How dare you!" The words were more of a command than a question. "Insolence and insubordination won't get you far here, boy. Drop and give me–" The sergeant immediately shut up upon seeing the scroll Kyte had withdrawn from his breeches. "That's Melierax's seal, which means…" With a trembling hand, he took the parchment and unfurled the scroll. "Leftenant Pandion." The soldier put his hand to the brim of his leather helmet; Kyte returned the salute. "Sergeant Hiero, at your disposal. I apologize for my outburst, I didn't mean–"

"At ease, sergeant." Kyte clapped him on the shoulder, Hiero recoiling at the familiarity. From the corner of his eye, Kyte could see that a good amount of the soldiers had been watching them. "What do you say we get a line-up going so I can introduce myself to the ranks."

With a hasty salute, Hiero turned back to the copse and reared his head back. "Sagittarii legion, fall in!" The clump of boots on the earth pounded as the soldiers bound from the trees, some on foot while others leapt into a quick glide, hovering above the meadow before descending to their station. Only Falco, who Kyte watched intently, dawdled. Idly sauntering to where the other soldiers gathered, he tapped on the chests and shoulders of others who passed him, pointing and snickering in Kyte's direction. Despite his attempts to cajole his peers, Falco was met with uncomfortable stares and shaking heads.

With the last of the soldiers falling into their rows, the sergeant drew in a deep breath. "Atten–" There was a palpable pause. Looking over, Kyte could see the veins in Heiro's neck bulging as he held the word. "–tion!" A deafening roar rang out as the soldiers stomped their boots in unison, their bodies rigid with arms at their side. "It is my honor to introduce Leftenant Pandion." The group seemed unaffected. "Present arms!" With a deft swoop, the group raised their arms in a rhythmic salute, save Falco who rolled his eyes before giving a flimsy lift of his wrist.

"Falco–" Hiero blared.

"Stand down, sergeant." Kyte placed a forceful hand on the Hawk's shoulder. "I got this." Stepping forward, Kyte looked out to the group who maintained their rigid position. Kyte turned back to Hiero. "How do you get them to relax?"

"Sagittarii legion, ord–"

"No, no," Kyte interrupted in a hushed voice, raising his eyebrows. "I've got this. Just need to know the order to give."

With a cock of his head, Hiero seemed to search the field as he processed before sharing the order.

Releasing his grip on the sergeant's shoulder, Kyte turned back to face the legion.

"As Sergeant Hiero mentioned, I am Leftenant Pandion." His steps were methodical as he walked down the first row of soldiers. "I'll ask that you forgive my informality, but I prefer to go by Kyte." Breaking between two of the soldiers, he stepped to the second row, his eyes meandering the soldiers. "Ground infantry…" he let the words linger as his boots padded along the verdant green. "It's not very sexy, is it? Considering all of the *action–*" there was acrimony in the word, "–will take place in the air." A third of the way down the second row, he stepped between another pair of Hawks, walking towards Falco, his eyes trained directly on the delinquent Hawk. "But that doesn't change the importance of our role." There were only a few soldiers between him and Falco left; Kyte felt his shoulders tense, but did his best to appear unaffected. "We stand united as a front, protecting our sisters and brothers in the air."

Kyte's boots clumped in the grass as he came to a stop, turning to look the soldier in the eyes. "Falco, isn't it?"

The soldier had a harsh stare in his eyes, his lips thin as he clenched his jaw. With an air of defiance, the soldier nodded. "Yessir."

"Order arms!" Falco flinched as Kyte bellowed in his face, lowering his arm out of tune with the rest of the soldiers. "It's come to my attention," Kyte shouted brusquely, "that our Falco has a lot to say in the way of my leadership. " Falco didn't stir, but a snide smirk crossed his lips. "You have permission to speak freely."

A silence lingered between them, the only sound on the field was the buzzing of cicadas in the distance. Even the drills from other legions seemed to have ceased; Kyte wondered if they'd stopped to stare, but he didn't break eye contact with the soldier.

"Nothing to say for yourself?" Taking a step closer, Kyte brought the tip of his nose to the soldier's, his voice falling to a gravely whisper. "Now's your chance to say it to the *cripple's* face."

The soldier's cheeks reddened, a fire burning deeply in his eyes. "If you say so, sir." His lips twisted in a snarl. "Sagitarii is a joke!" He spat loud enough for the entire legion to hear. "When I signed up for this war, I expected to see some real action. But no, they've got us all on the ground. And now to add insult to injury, they've got us stuck with the likes of you." Taking a step forward, he put a meaty finger to Kyte's chest. "A battered leftenant who can't even get his arse off the ground." As Falco pressed forward, Kyte could feel the tip of the soldier's nose against his own. "You're no Hawk, not anymore. You even said it yourself; you're nothing more than a low-brow, good-for-nothing, crip–"

Before Falco could finish his sentence, Kyte had his arms wrapped around the soldier's neck. With a sweep of his foot, Kyte dug the boy's leg out from under him, felling him to the earth. Several of the soldiers flinched, but watched in earnest as Kyte rolled the boy onto his stomach before Falco had the wherewithal to react.

Face down in the mud, Falco flailed, his wings flapping viciously behind him as he tried to gain enough traction to fight Kyte off, but Kyte held him in place. One knee in the boy's back, Kyte grasped at one of Falco's wings, ripping tufts of feather until he found the sinewy limb of tendon and bone. With a tear, Kyte pressed it to the ground and maneuvered his free foot down atop the wing, the space between the avial ulna and radius clear even through the sole of Kyte's boot.

"I'll give you one last chance, Falco." Kyte kept an even tone despite the rush he felt in his chest. Something in him felt wickedly delighted, but he couldn't show it, not to the other soldiers who watched the scene unfold before them. "Still think I'm just a cripple?" He pressed his boot down harder.

"Get off me!" A slew of swears gurgled from the mud as Falco redoubled his efforts to free himself.

Kyte shook his head. "Then I guess I'll just have to show you." Maintaining the pressure of his boot on the soldier's wing, Kyte jerked the limb back with immense force until an audible *crack* resounded through the field, followed by Falco's palpable wail.

Avoiding Falco's retaliatory swipes, Kyte withdrew from the soldier and wiped his muddied hands on his breeches. He watched as the boy flailed around, his cries only interrupted by his need to breathe. Looking out into the crowd, Kyte saw a mix of pale faces and smirks roll out amid the rest of the battalion. All other activities had ceased through the field, and for the first time since losing his wing, Kyte relished knowing that all eyes were on him.

"Hiero." Kyte spoke the order, but the Hawk didn't move, his jaw ajar as he watched Falco writhe on the ground, beads of sweat dripping from his brow. "Hiero!" Kyte bellowed a second time and the Hawk snapped to immediate attention.

"Sir?" The sergeant's eyes were awestruck despite his rigid stance.

"Get Falco to the medical tent and out of my sight."

"Yes, sir." With a salute, Hiero rushed off to Falco's side and grabbed another two soldiers to help him. They lifted the still howling soldier and carried him off the field back toward the encampment, Falco's shrieks growing more plaintive.

"Oh quit your bellyaching," Kyte called after them. "It's a clean break—should be healed in no time!"

Another wave of swears and threats emanated from Falco as he was dragged off the field.

Once he was out of earshot, Kyte turned back to the battalion, stone-faced. "So," he squawked, the soldiers flinching back to a rigorous pose, "does anyone else plan on questioning my leadership?"

"Sir, no sir." The legion called out in unison, their eyes trained forward on Kyte, a sobriety in their stares.

"Good!" A quiet breeze ruffled Kyte's hair, the cool wind a welcome break along his sweaty, mud-caked skin. "Then back to your stations! We've got training to do."

*　　　　*　　　　*

The sun had already set well beyond the horizon by the time Kyte had made it back to the encampment. What would have been a five-minute flight turned into an hour walk, but for once, Kyte didn't mind. He allowed himself a slow gait; he reflected on today's actions, his stomach churning as he replayed the snap of Falco's bones beneath his boot. Walking past the tent that had been assigned to him—a few rows from the officers' tents, as there were no available units on the ground—he headed in the direction of the medical tent.

"Kyte!"

The scathing, yet familiar voice cut through the haze of his thoughts. Kyte twirled about looking into the dimly lit street. From the alley formed between two tents emerged Hepha, dragging three massive glaives behind her as if they weighed nothing. Her gruff presence seemed to fill the space, and Kyte couldn't help but feel a flicker of warmth despite his weariness.

"Hepha." Kyte greeted her with a curt nod; his mouth twitched in a flicker of a smile.

"Oh, don't give me that bullshit." Her grizzled face broke into a wide grin and Kyte returned it heartily. "Come here, you bull-headed badger." Setting the blades down with a *thud*, she pulled him into the traditional Hawk greeting, pushing her forehead to his, her touch grounding, a mix of stern affection and unspoken understanding. "I'm glad to see you."

"I'm glad to see you too, Ama."

"Are you?" She gave him a firm, but not unkind shove which forced him to stumble a few steps. "I wouldn't know it the way you locked yourself up on that boat. Did you even come out of that hold for food?"

Kyte's lip thinned as rocked on his heels, teetering like a fledgling caught red-handed.

"Well…" She shook her head. "Either way, I'm glad you seem to be doing better. At least you don't look like you're going to throw yourself off a cliff, anyway."

"Who, me? Never. I'm more of an impale-myself-on-a-spear kind of Hawk."

"Smartass," she huffed. "Anyway, I heard what you did out on the training field today."

"How did you–"

"I hear things." There was a hint of pride in her voice. "Are you thinking of making a wellness visit?"

Kyte raised an eyebrow. "I repeat, how did you–"

"I know things." She gave a cursory glance at her fingernails, picking iron filings out from under them. "And I know you." Looking back up at Kyte, she cocked her head, her eyes piercing through him. "Do you think that seeing him will somehow help?"

"I–" Kyte hesitated, his voice faltering. "I thought I could–"

"Make it right?" She gave him a wanton smile. "Kyte, you broke the kid's wing in front of the entire battalion. Hell, in front of half of the company! There is nothing that you can say or do for him that will make it okay."

"I thought I'd at least apologize."

Hepha's eyes darted from side to side. "Why?"

"What do you mean, 'why'? For everything you just said."

"Boy, you did what you had to do." She rubbed her temples. "Sure, you may have ruined that poor boy's life. But he'll fly again!" She gave a cursory glance that said, 'I'm sorry', but Kyte knew well enough she'd never say the words aloud. "What I'm saying is, you hurt one to help the many. Now your soldiers will respect you and they'll fight for you."

Kyte sighed heavily and nodded his head. "I know, Ama."

"Do yourself a favor. Don't go to the med tent. Don't make yourself look weak. Hell, besides Socorra, you're the strongest Hawk among us." Her wings and shoulders fell, her normal snap and veil of stoicism lifted. She put a hand on his shoulder. "I've seen what happens when Hawks rally behind you, Kyte. It's exactly what we need to win this war."

The two shared a tender silence; Kyte relished the calm that rushed through him until he could no longer bear the comfort. "You've never been this nice to me before. Are you dying?"

Hepha rolled her eyes so far that Kyte could only see the white. "Don't get used to it." With a quick nod, she started back down the path between the tents. "And stay away from the med tent! If you go anywhere near it, I'll consider you an enemy and take you out myself."

"I wouldn't expect any less!" Kyte called out after her, breaking into a fit of helpless laughter. It burst from him like a flood—raw, wheezing, uncontrollable. His stomach cramped, his ribs ached, but he couldn't stop. He couldn't remember the last time he'd laughed like this.

When the tears came, they caught him off guard. He ducked behind the nearest tent, pressing a hand to his face as the laughter dissolved into trembling breaths. For a fleeting moment, the world felt light again like before the war, before everything had gone wrong.

He wiped his cheeks with the back of his hand and leaned against the tent post, drawing in a shaky breath. The smile still lingered faintly on his lips when the low blare of a horn split the air.

Kyte froze.

The sound rolled through the camp like thunder, distant yet unmistakable. His stomach dropped, the fragile warmth of moments ago vanishing as the old, cold instinct took hold.

He barely had time to move before the ground began to tremble beneath his boots. The earth shifted, sending him sprawling into the mud. From somewhere to the east came another horn, closer and sharper. Then another from the south. And another.

Within moments, the camp erupted into chaos: the clash of armor, the bark of orders, the shrill call of steel being drawn. The night that had just held laughter now burned with the sound of war.

Kyte shook his head and picked himself up, steadying himself as the next shock hit the encampment. "Here we go."

Chapter Seventeen
Socorra

The scent of fresh earth mixed with smoke; it made Socorra's stomach wretch. There was the crackle of a fire somewhere nearby driving away the chill in the damp air. Her eyes still closed, she could feel a wool blanket draped around her, the material somehow comfortable despite the itchiness against her skin.

"Have you lost your mind?"

The words erupted from somewhere nearby, muffled as if coming from another room. Socorra didn't recognize the woman's voice. She tried to stir, but couldn't muster the energy.

"We don't exactly have a choice here." It was Pelanor. Even in Socorra's semi-conscious state, she could hear the frustration in his tone.

"She's not going, and that's final!"

"Pelanor…" A deep baritone interrupted, the voice familiar but just out of reach of her memory. "Between the Brick and now this, there's no way she can come with us."

Socorra had a flash of understanding; they were talking about her. Summoning as much of her strength as she could, she forced her eyes open. The unfamiliar room was dim, the only light coming from the faint glow of a wood stove in the corner. She tried to sit up, but her head exploded in a mix of colors.

"*Jangan bergerak.*" The voice was calm, a strange accent that Socorra couldn't place. A strong but gentle hand pressed against her shoulder, pushing her back down on the straw bed. "Don't move. You need to sleep and heal."

Her head pounding and body weak, Socorra didn't resist. She sank back into the cotton-stuffed pillow beneath her head, a luxury she had never known.

"Where am I?" she murmured, pressing a hand to her forehead. The pressure helped ease the pain slightly.

"*Kamu aman.*" There was a soft murmur as they breathed, like the steady rhythm of a grindstone. "You are safe."

The colors started to fade, but the pain was still excruciating. Her mouth felt dry, but she needed answers. "Who are you?"

"My name is Satu. I am *Harimau*. Or as your people call us, Bengalan."

A disquiet settled within Socorra. Memories of her father telling bed-time stories of the voracious and bloodthirsty creatures known as Bengalans roaming the lands of the far-east, preying on anything that moves. Her muscles tensed, though she couldn't bring herself into any type of defensive position.

"*Tenanglah,*" the cat whispered. "Be calm. I can hear your heart beating. I promise you are in no danger."

Sitting in the stillness, Socorra felt her fears gradually ebb as the cat continued to thrum, the sound melodic and soothing. In the placid quiet of the cat's purr, Socorra could hear the voices continuing their discussion.

"She needs time."

"...prophecy..." Pelanor was talking, but his voice was too faint to discern what he was saying. Socorra could only catch a few words here and there, but not enough to cobble together an understanding.

"What're they talking about?" The Hawk rolled over to address Satu, though she didn't open her eyes.

"It's not important." The Bengalan placed their soft paw on her shoulder. "Sleep now."

"Wait!" A sudden panic struck her. She instinctively tried to raise herself, but the cat kept her down with a firm grip. "Where's Fatima?" Her shoulders tensed, the back of her head on fire from where she'd been hit.

"The fledgling? She too is safe."

"Thank the Void." A wave of calm broke over Socorra, though the news did nothing to soothe her nausea.

"She is sleeping." Satu pulled their paw away and silently slid from the bed. "As you ought to be."

Her eyes still closed, Socorra could hear them fuss with something by the woodstove and the faint trickle of water. Returning to her bedside, the cat put one paw at the back of Socorra's neck and gently lifted her head. "Here, drink this. It will help."

Without arguing, Socorra drew the liquid from the bowl, the water hot, but not enough to burn. The flavor was completely foreign to her, though the sweetness of honey mellowed the earthy spiciness of the drink. "What is it?" Socorra coughed, sending a fresh pain radiating through her skull.

"*Teh jahe*." Satu withdrew the bowl and sloshed around its remaining contents. "It is tea, but I don't know what your people call *jahe*. I brought it with me from Bengala and have been able to grow it here." A toothy smile flashed across the cat's face, though there was a pain behind their eyes. "Airam and I have never come across it in our smuggling. It is believed to have healing properties. It's very good for your condition."

"Well, thank you." Rubbing her eyes, Socorra laid her head back on the pillow and drew the blanket up to her neck. "Now, what're they talking about?"

"Socorra–"

"Yes, I need to sleep," she interrupted. Her patience began to wane as the tea took effect. While her nausea receded, she could feel the grip of slumber already pulling at her, and she wanted answers before she was forced to sleep. "But I know they're talking about me. What're they planning? And what's wrong with me that I can't go?"

There was a long silence, the only sound Satu's purring. "They're going to rescue your Finch friend." Before she could move, the cat was upon her.

"I have to go," Socorra choked. "I promised to protect that boy. There's no way they're going without me. Pelanor will convince them! Help me up."

"*Nggak!*" Even without a translation, Socorra understood implicitly that the cat was not going to relent. "Socorra, you simply cannot go."

As much as she wanted to fight, she could feel her exhaustion weighing her down. The pain in her head was reduced to a minor throb, but the heaviness she felt pulled her under. She relaxed, her head falling deep into the softness of the pillow. "And why not?"

"You have already suffered much." Satu stroked her hand. "But more is still to come."

"Why won't they let me go?"

"You have a," the cat searched for the word, "*gegar* …a head injury."

"I've had worse," she lied. "What else aren't you telling me?"

There was a long pause; Socorra struggled to stay awake as she waited for Satu's answer.

"Socorra, you are with litter."

The Hawk scrunched her forehead. "What does that mean?"

"*Bangsat*," the cat swore. "You are…what is the word? *Hamil*…you are to have a kitten. Or I think your people call it a chick?"

Despite the exhaustion and the cloudiness of her mind, Socorra understood. A shiver ran through her temple, her chest brimming with warmth.

"I'm pregnant?"

Chapter Eighteen
GIDEON

Leaning against the wall, Gideon caught his breath as he looked down the next flight. The air was heavy and damp, the stench of decay flooding his senses.

"Why are there so many stairs?"

"*C'mon, Gid.*" Cas's disembodied voice called past the corner, just out of his vision. "*It's not much further.*"

With a resigned sigh, Gideon trudged down the steps. Wiping the sweat from his brow, he pressed forward through twists and turns, corridor after narrow corridor. The path felt endless until a familiar, acrid odor filled his nostrils. His skin prickled, the tips of his feathers ruffling involuntarily.

"The lab."

His feet hit the landing and Gideon found himself at a crossroads of identical stone walls, the ensconced torches casting an ominous glow. "Cas?" He called out in a hushed tone, the tingle in his toes crawling up his legs. There was no answer. He tried again, the sound of muffled screams perking his ears.

"Cas!" Tearing down the hall, Gideon's knuckles flared with pain as his grip tightened on the still bloodied scalpel. He had no idea where he was going, only that he had to follow the dampened wailing through the maze of rough-hewn limestone.

The sound growing louder, Gideon rounded a corner. "Shit," he whispered, dropping to a crouch. The sour odor caught like a blade in his throat.

At the end of the hall were two doors, windows peering into his mother's lab. From this distance, Gideon couldn't make out anything inside aside from the harsh lighting, but he feared being caught. Folding his wings tight against his back, Gideon lowered himself into a crouch and waddled toward the doors, the sleek steel standing stark amid the ancient rock of Fate's Folly.

"Enough!"

His mother's voice sliced through the plaintive cries of whatever poor soul she had tied to the slab. At the command, the world fell silent, a harsh disquiet crawling through Gideon's skin. The metal was cold against his palms as he shimmied up to peer through the grated glass, careful not to push too hard.

"That's a good girl."

Gideon's eyes darted about the room. Fortunately, the Master's back was turned away from the door, her wings glimmering regally in the fluorescent lighting as she sauntered back to her work station further down the lab. On the slab lay the victim, the Avian's head lilting from side-to-side as if tranced.

"Zokya." The whisper left a small puff of fog on the window. "At least it's not Cas." In his relief, the Finch forgot to check his weight. The door slowly gave way beneath him, a slight *pop* as the door pressed inward.

Pulling away from the door before it could open fully, Gideon threw himself against the wall, keeping his head away from the window. His heart pounding wildly, he listened for the clack of his mother's heels, but they seemed to be moving away from the doors.

"Get it together, Gideon." He breathed a sigh of relief. "You don't have time for this. Step two, find Cas. Remember?"

As soon as he peeled himself off the wall, Gideon's ears caught the sharp rise in his mother's voice.

"I do have to thank you, dear..." there was a clanking of glass, "...for collecting those Sapiens for me. And the guns were just a beautiful addition! I'll make sure to put those to good use."

Gideon's heart sunk in his chest.

Step two.

The words played in his head over and over, but he couldn't help feeling the intrigue pull him back to the window. "What is she planning?"

"It's a shame that you decided to betray me." She tapped her talons on the neck of a beaker full of purple liquid, the *clink* echoing through the chamber. "So what do I do, darling? Normally I couldn't let these things go un-punished." She shrugged her shoulders before pouring a vial into the container. "But I think I may have found a way for you to make it up to me. I need someone to test the newest version of Serum C." Her tone was clinical, detached. "The first successful change happened with that Dove boy...whatever his name was."

Rocque, Gideon mouthed, his jaw clenching.

"And after that was our dear Cas, and we all know how that went."

A pang of fury ripped through Gideon's skull, hot and unrelenting. His hands curled into fists, the blade of the scalpel biting into his palm. Blood trickled down his fingers, but the Finch barely noticed.

"He took to the change beautifully. Physically anyway…" Her voice was glib, as if she were amused. "His mind…well, that's another story altogether." Working as she spoke, glass vials clicked and clanked between her words. "Now the poor dear is so consumed in his hatred that he'd kill anything that dares to get too close."

Gideon's breathing hitched, fury welling in his chest ready to explode.

"I'm even struggling to control him at a distance. The beast almost killed my son at the Noktern." Her voice softened to feigned sympathy. "Gideon must've been devastated to see his friend like that. But," she added with a flippant toss of her golden hair, "what is one creature in the grand scheme of things? Scientific development must take precedence over some rudimentary friendship. Gideon must understand the bigger picture. Isn't that right, Zokya?"

There was no response. Looking over to where Zokya lay, the Finch watched as the Raven's head bobbed from side to side, her good eye vacant, the other still swollen shut.

"Well, I wouldn't worry too much, dear. He'll see things my way eventually."

"Never," Gideon seethed in a hiss.

"Now!" Cecilia clapped her hands, scanning the array of vials and containers before her. She took a small clear pipe and dipped it in a milky-white solution. With a few drips into the beaker, the purple concoction began to bubble, the mixture curdling into the black tar-like substance Gideon had come to recognize as the change. "So long as this new version takes, then the stage is set." From somewhere beneath her workstation, she withdrew a large syringe, wiping the needle with a damp cloth. "I'll create an army of superior Harpies—a force that no Avian could hope to oppose."

Siphoning the bubbling liquid into the syringe, Cecilia flicked the tip with her talon. "With my new army, we'll fly to Vines' Crossing where those imbeciles have gathered for war." With a fervent gait, the Master strode over to the slab. "My Harpies will ravage the land, devastate the war effort, and capture the strongest warriors that Avis has to offer. Once I've turned them, not even the Noktern will be able to stop me."

His hands trembling, Gideon's legs buckled beneath him. He could only watch as the Master grasped Zokya's arm in her talons, angling the syringe with the other. Letting his gaze wander, he tried to cast a pitiful look on Zokya only to stagger back in shock; the Raven was staring directly at him through the window, a pained and pleading look in her eye. Clutching his chest, his heart fluttering wildly, Gideon scuttled away from the door.

"Shit, shit, shit." The Finch ambled backwards, breaking into a trot back down the hall, trying to keep his boots from clacking against the stone. His breathing was uneven, his stomach fit to wretch. Stumbling through the corridor, he noticed the small trickle of blood he'd left behind.

Zokya.

Ducking into the first offshoot, Gideon pressed himself against the wall. His breathing labored, he wondered if he should go back.

She tried to capture me, maybe even kill me.

All the same, Gideon hated to see Zokya like that, strapped down in his mother's grasp like some poor creature caught in a trap.

"You can't worry about her now, Gideon." An image of Cas strapped to the slab flashed in his mind. "You have more important things to deal with."

Visions of fire, bubbling black goo, and cries of pain, any form of torture he thought his mother might devise if she caught him, raced through Gideon's mind. Adrenaline pulsed through the Finch's veins, his skin tingling with the rush. With a brief inhale, Gideon steeled himself and thrust his neck back around the corner, ready to find the Master barreling after him, a small detachment of Harpies ready to tear him to pieces.

Nothing but an empty hallway.

A pressure grew at the back of his neck, radiating up his skull and down his spine, a hollow sensation. "How did she not…?"

With a shake of his head, Gideon backed himself down the corridor, unable to shake the feeling of being watched. "Cas!" He called out in a harsh whisper, hoping that the disembodied voice might answer him, but he got no response. Meandering, his mind kept going back to the Master's words: *not even the Noktern will be able to stop me.* The thought made Gideon shudder. Trying to chase away the memory, he ran through his list.

"Step two, find Cas." He kept his eyes peeled for any downward path: sloping corridors, staircases. He'd seen the Harpies drag Zokya down this way when they'd captured her, so the dungeons couldn't be that far off.

"Step three, get out." He'd originally planned on going to the Noktern, but it seemed futile now given his mother's plans. "Then to Vines' Crossing. If we can defeat her on the battlefield, then this can all be over." A glimmer of hope lighted in the pit of his stomach, a light in the hollowness he'd felt.

Through more twists and turns, Gideon finally stumbled upon a hallway that dipped downward, a set of stairs plunging further down into the heart of the mountain.

"You can do this, Gideon." He took a deep breath. "One step at a time." Shaking out his wings, the Finch wiped his sweaty palms on his breeches, careful not to cut himself again with the scalpel. With a few paces forward, Gideon started down the stairs.

"Step two. I'm coming, Cas."

Chapter Nineteen

Zokya

Prick. Burn. Anguish.

Though familiar, the fire that coursed through Zokya's flesh was unbearable; one's body can never truly adjust itself to become used to the change. It tears at the insides, everything that makes its victim who they are; it breaks down every fiber of the being, rearranges it, and spits the subjugate out a new Avian. So many die from the agony, but not Zokya. She may have been a broken fledgling, but she was the true embodiment of a Raven. Stronger, better, more resilient.

The hot flashes stopped; the crawling beneath her skin died down to a low hum. Even torn to pieces, she felt more whole. Opening her good eye, the world felt more vibrant: the colors crisper, the stench of the lab more pungent than before.

Wrapping her fingers around the chains that bound her wrists, Zokya jerked upward, the metal links crumbling in her grip; she hadn't even exerted much force.

"It worked!"

The voice startled her; Zokya had almost forgotten that the Master was there. Clenching her jaw, she bared her teeth and broadened her shoulders. Flaring her wings behind her, she launched herself from the slab, the clasps around her ankles torn from their bolts.

"Tut-tut." The Master waved a finger as if scolding a fledgling, her eyes flashing a brilliant amethyst.

Before she could get any further, Zokya was immobilized, trapped in a half-lunge, her wings poised to propel her straight into Cecilia. "Let me go, you witch!" She struggled against the Master's hold, fighting tooth and nail against the pull of her own mind. Her fingers twitched, feathers bristled, but she wasn't able to break through.

"That's still more resistance than I would have liked." Cecilia shook her head and walked over to one of the metal shelves that sat along the wall. She picked up a pen, dipped it in the inkwell, and scribbled down a few notes in a journal. "But at least you can be controlled. That's progress."

"I'll kill you!"

"And you finally could." The Master turned and gave her a curt smile. With a few strides, she stopped an arm's length from Zokya's grasp. "You're welcome, darling." She stretched out her taloned hand and gave Zokya a quick prick on the nose, the tip of her claw gently breaking through the skin. "But I'm afraid it's simply not your destiny to kill me."

"Maybe not," she snarled. "But if I can't, then at least your little *brat* will."

The Master's face turned stony; she withdrew her arms to her side, her lips thinning, eyes pointed right into Zokya's stare.

"Hit a nerve, did I?" she smirked.

"Not at all, darling." Cecilia shrugged, the tips of her wings jilting lightly as she relaxed her frame. "How long have you been in my service, dear?" She began to walk in a tight circle around Zokya, slowly spiraling outward as she milled about the room. "A year? Two? Time seems so trivial when you're out to change the world. But in all that time, have you ever known anyone who could pull the wool over my eyes?"

Zokya waited for the Master to continue, the only sound the clacking of Cecilia's heels on the stone floor. "No," she finally admitted, giving the Master her clearly anticipated response.

"No." Cecilia retorted in a flat voice. "From the day I found you, I have been in complete control. At any moment, Craven could've tried to slit my throat, Rocque might have crushed me, even my own son tried to plunge a sword into my heart. And yet, I persist."

Zokya let out a snort, a reflex she couldn't contain.

"Don't be so naive, dear." The Master's voice didn't shift without even the slightest hesitation to Zokya's outburst. "Or did you forget I can see into your mind?"

Zokya squinted her eyes and tried to cock her head, but was met with resistance from Cecilia's control.

"I know you saw him…Gideon. You caught a glance of him in the window."

Fear crept into Zokya's chest. She didn't dare show it, but she knew that wouldn't matter. "So what if I did?"

"Well, you can dash any hopes that he'll escape and stop me. I know that's what you're thinking."

"But he heard you!" The words tumbled from Zokya's lips, threaded with breathless disbelief. "He knows your entire plan and he's on the loose in your castle. You really trust your Harpies to catch him, when he managed to slink down to your lab undetected? No, I think he'll escape and tell anyone in Avis who'll listen about your scheme to build an army of those brainless things."

A grin unfurled across the Master's face, so wide and sharp it seemed to stretch the skin around her jaw. Her eyes gleamed, wild with delight, and a single, guttural burst of laughter rolled from her chest. "And who, pray tell," she crooned, "do you think unlocked the door to his chamber?"

Zokya couldn't contain a gasp. "No."

"Yes, darling."

"But why?" She tried to shake her head, but all she could muster was a slight tremor. "If he manages to get to Vines' Crossing before you, won't that just allow them to prepare for your attack?"

"Precisely, dear." The Master strode back to the table where her instruments lay. Drawing a second syringe, she plunged the tip into the vial, drawing in another dose of the change. "In fact, I'm counting on it."

Chapter Twenty

Fatima

"Could you please stop sulking?" Pelanor leaned against the sloop's mast, rubbing his temples. "It's a grim enough situation as it is. I can't take your brooding on top of it."

Fatima braced herself as the boat crested a wave, jolting her into the side of the sloop. "I'm not brooding." She swallowed hard, fighting to keep down her meager dinner of hardtack and salted fish. "I'm just mad that you didn't even let Socorra decide for herself whether to come with us."

"More or less the definition of brooding." Pelanor teetered as the sloop lurched again, grabbing the boom, a wooden pole that held the bottom of the sail, to steady himself.

"*Nggak!*" Satu growled, their voice a low rumble. The rope ripped free from their grip as the boom swung to the bow. The boat pitched wildly; Pelanor fell to the floor, hard. Théo went sprawling. Fatima held her ground, barely. Her nails bit into the wood as a crate slammed past, crashing into the hull.

With a deft hand, Satu regained control though Pelanor was knocked to the ground as the boom came back into place. "Are you trying to kill us?"

Picking himself up, Pelanor brushed a layer of dirt and sawdust off his robes. "My apologies, Satu. I haven't quite found my sea legs."

Satu's dark eyes reflected the waning light shimmering off the sea, the harsh stare boring into Pelanor. A long silence pervaded the air, the whistling breeze and the rhythmic crash of waves the only sound until they resumed purring. "The three of you can go. It'll be easier on you if you fly. And for me as well."

"That'll be quite impossible until we have the full cover of darkness." Pelanor resumed his position on the mast, his face pale, legs trembling. "Fate's Folly will be crawling with Harpies. It's best that we stay here and wait until we reach the island."

"I think *'best'* is not truth." The cat's words hung heavy and pointed.

Fatima grunted as she heaved one of the massive crates back into place. "Pelanor always seems to know what's best for everyone. Wouldn't you agree, Théo?"

Coiling a length of rope, the Dove let out a dry laugh. "Don't get me mixed up in this, little one."

"For the absolute last time," Pelanor exhaled sharply, "you don't know what you're talking about. And that's my last word on the matter."

"So the fact that Socorra's pregnant has *nothing* to do with your decision to leave her behind?"

"Fatima!" Drawing in a hiss of a breath, the Owl clasped his hands together and placed his fingers to his mouth. "As I've already told you, Socorra has–"

Before he could continue, Théo rose from the floor and put a hand on Pelanor's shoulder. "I thought that was your last word on the matter?"

The Owl scowled, a low growl emanating from his throat. The two stared at one another, searching each other's eyes in a silent conversation.

"If you two kiss, I'm going to throw up." Fatima perched herself atop the crate, letting her wings droop over the sides.

Pelanor shook his head, but Théo chuckled with a toothy smile. He gave the Owl a light squeeze on the shoulder before turning his attention to Fatima.

"Socorra means a lot to you, doesn't she?" With a gentle stride, Théo walked over to the crate where Fatima sat. Folding his legs, the Dove plopped down onto the floor of the sloop, resting his arms on the bo staff that he laid over his lap.

Fatima's heart leapt a beat, a strange stillness settling within her. "Of course she does," she stammered. She had expected some kind of lecture; the question caught her off guard.

"Then you have to understand why she can't be here right now."

"Don't speak to me like I'm a fledgling."

Théo sighed deeply. "Fine." His voice dropped in register, the word direct, but not harsh. "But my point still stands. Socorra has a severe concussion. She's dehydrated and needs to rest and recover."

"I'm a child, not an idiot." She drew the hunting knife from her boot, gently gliding the blade across the wooden slats of the crate. "I understand fully that she's hurt. But I also know what's coming."

"Fatima–"

"No!" She snapped more harshly than she'd intended, but the adrenaline was already pumping through her. "There's nothing that you can say right now that'll change my mind. You're sidelining her for the next nine moons–"

"It's closer to ten moons for Avians," Pelanor interrupted offhandedly.

"Whatever!" Fatima scoffed. "Nine moons, ten, it's all the same. You're going to force Socorra into bed rest. We'll be without her and Avis is going to have to suffer for it all because you, Airam, and Pelanor think she can't handle herself while she's pregnant."

"You can leave me off that list," Pelanor hissed.

"I absolutely will not!" She stood and drove the blade into the crate, pointing an accusatory finger at the Owl. "You have some nerve–" Before she could continue, Théo interrupted.

"Fatima, don't." The Dove bolted to his feet, the force causing the boat to waver violently. A furious thrum erupted from Satu, but they didn't say anything, keeping their eyes on the horizon. "Believe me, I know it feels easy to blame Pelanor for everything…"

The Owl rolled his eyes. "I'm standing right here …"

"But Pelanor was on your side this time." Théo continued, paying Pelanor no mind. "He fought tooth and nail for Socorra to come with us."

Leaning over to see past the Dove, Fatima narrowed her eyes. "He did?" she asked, her voice laden with surprise, and Théo nodded. "Is that true, Pelanor?"

"I don't know that I'd go that far." The Owl gave a wry lift of his shoulders. "If you hadn't noticed, I lost that battle, which means I couldn't have fought very hard."

"And we all know how much you hate to lose." Théo's voice was deadpan, though the corner of his lips curled into a faint smirk.

"Wait," Fatima bellowed before Pelanor could respond. "So, what does this mean for Socorra moving forward?"

"Once she heals from the concussion, all of the decisions will be left up to her." Pelanor paused, then waved a hand vaguely. "Airam certainly seems to think that she should be on bed rest for the remainder of the pregnancy. Something about being stressed for the early stages. And Théo," the Owl lulled his head to the side, his eyes rolled to the farthest stretches as he stared acrimoniously, "seems to agree."

"I didn't say that. I–"

"It's of no consequence," Pelanor waved an effusive hand. "You're entitled to your opinion on the matter—even if it's the wrong one. But at the end of the day, Socorra will make up her own mind and do what she must."

Théo furrowed his brow. "You seem awfully assured that Socorra will do what you want."

"Am I not always self-assured?" A coy smile pricked his lips. "You yourself said only moments ago how much I hate to lose."

Théo crossed his arms and shook his head. "Pelanor..." Théo drew out the Owl's name. "What did you do?"

"I have no idea what you mean." With a flourish of footwork, Pelanor spun against the mast, ducking just beneath the sail to stand away from them, his back turned signaling that the conversation was over.

Fatima went to speak; she wanted to pry and figure out exactly what the Owl was talking about, but something stopped her. Maybe it was the way that Théo stared at the Owl through his scrunched brow, or how cooly Pelanor acted in the face of the accusations. Fatima couldn't be sure, but for some reason, she wanted to trust the Owl's intentions.

✳   ✳   ✳

The sky was painted black, clouds ensnaring any light from the moon and stars. There was no way to sense how much time had passed since they docked on the rocky beach beneath Fate's Folly. The minutes bled into hours as she and Théo waited for Pelanor and Satu to return, the silence between them palpable. She would have given anything for conversation, something to pass the time, but they didn't dare speak lest they give away their position to the Harpy sentries that flitted above the island.

The pair sat shoulder-to-shoulder under a jagged overhang. Fatima pressed herself against the cold rock, her body taut as a bowstring. Any time she moved, the decaying roots above them grasped at her headscarf like bony fingers. Every sound, every touch made her flinch.

"Stay calm," Théo murmured, his voice barely audible. He wrapped his hand around her forearm, squeezing gently, and she regained herself.

After what felt like an interminable wait, the crunch of loose stones sounded from up the beach. Fatima's grip tightened on the hunting knife she held to her chest. Focusing her breathing, she counted the footsteps and tried to envision who approached. The steps were light, trying to avoid making noise—three pairs of footsteps in total by her best estimate. It must be Pelanor and Satu returning from their work, but in the dark it was impossible to tell.

"Everything is set." Pelanor's harsh whisper reached her ears and Fatima relaxed, her muscles uncoiling as she slid out from under the hanging rock, Théo close behind her.

"Took you long enough." Fatima brushed the dirt from her robes, sheathing the knife back into her boot.

"Oh, I'm sorry to keep you waiting." The pair were close enough to see their outlines. Satu was carefully on all fours, Pelanor with a hand between their shoulder blades to keep together. "But unless you've unpacked and prepped enough black powder to explode a castle wall, then I don't want to hear any complaints."

"Hush," Satu growled.

At the cat's warning, they all crouched low; Fatima's heart hammered as the air seemed to thicken. From somewhere above them, the rhythmic drum of massive wings thundered like an oncoming storm. A piercing squawk rang out and Fatima's breath hitched, her veins turning to ice. The shriek rattled her insides, the wail a battle cry that promised violence should it find them.

No one moved; Fatima scarcely heard anyone breathe until the Harpy disappeared, the beating of its wings reeling to the east. Once they were certain that it was gone, Pelanor finally broke the silence in a strained hush.

"We have to move quickly. The explosives are scattered along the southeast of the castle. Once Satu sets them off, Théo and I will enter through the main courtyard and try to find Gideon. And Fatima–"

"Yeah, yeah," Fatima huffed. "I'm on scout duty because I'm the smallest and least detectable, blah, blah. We went over it twelve times in the boat, and I'd rather not debate the sexist implications again." Even in the darkness, Fatima could feel the Owl roll his eyes. "Now," her wings twitched behind her in anticipation, "let's save Gideon!"

Chapter Twenty-One

GIDEON

"Down, down, down."

Deeper and deeper, Gideon descended into the belly of the mountain fortress, reciting the lines from Alice's Adventures in Wonderland as he went. He found some comfort in the familiar words, even in the eerie red glow of the single torch at the bottom of the steps, its flame dancing along the damp stone bricks.

"I wonder how many miles I've fallen by this time?"

He could see his breath as he spoke. Wrapping himself tightly in his wings, his feathers shielded him from the bitter cold that tried to worm its way into his skin.

"I must be getting somewhere near the center of the earth."

After what felt like an eternity, he reached the bottom landing and came face-to-face with an imposing iron door, the crossbars held fast by bolts that could have fit neatly in his palm. The door resisted at first, the hinges stiff with rust, but after a few judicious tugs, Gideon managed to open it just wide enough to slip through. He winced as his feathers snagged on the jagged edges of the frame.

There was a heavy, unsettling air about the chamber; overhead lighting cast the room in an iridescent blue. It reminded him of something out of L'Inferno, like Dante traversing Cocytus, a frozen lake in the deepest, coldest circles of Sapien Hell. Moss and lichen snaked through the cracks in the stone walls. His boots echoed on the damp floor as he passed row after row of cells, all appearing to be empty.

"Cas?" His voice failed him, his friend's name forced in a choked cough. He swallowed hard and tried again. "Cas?" The name echoed through the chamber, the reverberation rattling his chest.

A faint, distant groan answered him.

His pulse quickened. "Cas, is that you?"

"Gid." The response was clear now. Cool if not biting. "You shouldn't be here."

Relief washed over Gideon.

"Cas, I'm here." He scanned the chamber until his eyes landed on the grates embedded in the floor, narrow openings meant to keep prisoners trapped below. "I'm here to save you."

"Why should you?" Cas's voice rose from another grate further down the hall, a despondent quality in his tone.

Gideon shook his head, stepping carefully from one grate to the next. "Why wouldn't I?"

"In case you forgot," there was almost a snicker in his tone, "the last time we saw each other, I tried to kill you."

"But you were under my mother–" The word curdled in his mouth, his stomach churning with disgust. "–the Master's influence."

"Oh, Gid." A sharp edge cut through Cas's voice, something between amusement and disdain.

Gideon pressed on, scanning each opening in the floor until–

"Cas!" He dropped to his knees beside a grate, fingers threading through the rusted bars. Cas didn't move. He sat slumped in the corner, his head lilting to the side. One leg was stretched out, the other bent so he could lean his elbow on it.

"Don't worry, Cas, I'm here."

"Worry?" Cas craned his neck to look up at Gideon. There was malice in his stare, his eyes burning like coals in a dying hearth, dark and simmering. "I'm not the one who should be worried, Gid."

Gideon's heart fell. "You're still like this? But my mo– the Master isn't even here to control you."

"She doesn't have to be."

Without any warning, Cas leapt off the cell floor and launched himself at Gideon. Fingers clamped around Gideon's collar, yanking him down. The bars kept Cas caged, but his grip was steel, his reach just enough.

With a frantic gasp, Gideon wrenched himself back, the fabric of his tunic tearing between Cas's fingers as he staggered away. His back slammed into the stone wall between two empty cells, breath coming in sharp bursts.

Cas laughed an unhinged, maniacal cackle.

"Oh, Gid, Gid, Gid…when're you going to learn?" "I don't want you dead because she makes me." His arms slithered back down the grate, a soft clack of his boots as they hit the ground. "I want you dead because it's what you deserve."

Gideon's heart pounded in his throat.

"Are you kidding me!?" His voice tore through the chamber, startling even himself. "Everything I've done... everything that's led me here...I did for you!"

The fear that had gripped him moments ago was gone, burned away by the anger seething through his veins. "I get that you're pissed because I left you at Goldfinch's." He pushed himself to his feet, wings flared rigidly behind him as he stormed back toward Cas's cell. "But you have no idea what I've been through."

Through the grate, Cas stood still, arms folded over his chest. He stared coldly, glowering upward, waiting for Gideon to reappear.

"I flew across the desert...I got shot at by Sapiens..."

Well, technically Kyte did, but that's not the point.

"I learned how to use a sword..."

If that doesn't speak for itself, I don't know what will.

"I fought Zokya one-on-one..."

Is it my fault that she's strapped to the lab table right now?

"I flew across Avis to the Noktern just to fight my own mother who, BY THE WAY, happens to be the worst evil that Avis has known since the Great End...so much so, that there's an entire prophecy dedicated to stopping her–"

His breath came in short bursts, his chest aching. Tears burned at the corners of his eyes, but he kept going, unable to stop himself.

"And despite all of that–" a tear slipped free, "–here I am."

The fire in his veins numbed him to the cold.

"If I had known even half of what I know now, then I would have come back for you the night of Goldfinch's dinner. I probably would have died trying, but I'd have grabbed a butter knife and shoved it through Zokya's eyeballs…and who knows? Maybe we could've gone back to Moda and lived our content little lives."

Did I really just refer to my life in Moda as content?

"But here we are, Cas." He swept his arms wide, motioning to the dungeon's damp, rotting stone. "In my mother's dungeon." The words were bitter on his tongue.

"At the very brink of it all, I picked the lock of my own prison cell…snuck down the deepest trenches of this fucking fortress…murdered a Harpy in cold blood." He pulled the scalpel from his belt, turning it in his fingers; the ruby rivulets like black ooze in the dim light.

He had to pause. Taking a deep breath, he chased away the ghastly vision of the poor, twisted creature plummeting into the crevasse below.

"And after all that…" He swallowed, his voice quieter now, but no less fierce. "I still showed up for you."

The silence was palpable, the dull roar of the torch outside rising in a crescendo as Gideon waited for something…anything.

Finally, a harsh clap cut through the tension. Then another. And another.

"Beautiful speech." Cas's voice was thick with feigned sincerity.

Gideon exhaled, steeling himself for the worst.

Cas pursed his lips, dragging a finger beneath one eye in a mock wipe of a tear. "I'm so proud that you've finally grown a spine." As quickly as he'd put on the front, Cas's demeanor grew harsh, his lips twisting into a scowl. "Just in time for me to snap it in two."

"Fu–"

Gideon barely got the swear out before Cas launched himself at the grate again. For a split second, he thought he was safe and out of Cas's reach, but the grate was wrenched free from the floor, the iron snapping like twigs. Stone shards exploded outward as Cas burst through.

Gideon didn't even have time to brace himself. Cas slammed into him hard, driving them both into the wall.

Pain lanced through Gideon's spine, radiating down his legs. He tried to scream, but Cas's hands were already at his throat. Gideon fought back. Bucking beneath him, he gasped for air, but Cas didn't budge.

Cas's gaze bore into him, his dark eyes furious and unrelenting. "Should've stayed away, Gid," he growled. "I'm gonna enjoy this."

Fingers still latched around Gideon's neck, Cas wrestled him flat on the floor. He threw one leg over Gideon's side and straddled his torso, pinning his arms down with his knees.

Gideon tried to maneuver the scalpel in any way possible, but his hand was pressed tightly into the floor.

"C-a-ssss," he choked, his voice strangled.

But Cas didn't budge; he only tightened his grip. The last scraps of air bled from his lungs, leaving nothing but a raw, burning tightness in his chest. His limbs numbed.

The lights flickered. A moment of darkness. Then a groan.

Gideon's feathers bristled.

Still, Cas wouldn't relent. He just stared, his eyes cold and wicked.

The dungeon shuddered. Soft at first, crescendoing into a deep, rolling tremor, the iron bars rattling like the cage of some monstrous beast. Dust billowed from the cracks in the stone, curling through the air.

A chunk of the ceiling cracked loose, slamming Cas in the shoulder.

He snarled and jerked his head to the side. The shift in weight was small, but enough.

Gideon yanked his arm free.

His fingers tightened around the scalpel as he lifted it above his head, his muscles straining to drive it down into Cas's leg.

But Cas was faster, his hand snapping around Gideon's wrist.

With a flick, the scalpel was gone. It clattered against the floor, spinning out of reach until it fell into one of the grates with a clink-clink.

His grip tightened. "Did you really think stabbing me would work again?"

From somewhere above, Gideon thought he heard a muffled boom. Another tremor rolled through the dungeon, the walls quivering like they might cave in.

Cas smirked. "You already got away with that once at the Noktern…with your little sword routine."

Cas leaned in, his breath was warm against Gideon's ear.

"This time, you're mi–"

A deep, grating crack split the air and another chunk of ceiling collapsed, slamming into the back of Cas's head; he reeled, a sharp grunt tearing from his throat.

Pebbles rained down and pelted Gideon's face, but Cas took the brunt of it. Freeing his arm, Gideon reeled back and drove his fist square into Cas's groin.

Cas let out a scream that ripped through the air, his face twisted into something raw and furious, but the sound was drowned out in the now roaring tremors. Another rock crashed down, clubbing his wing, and his grip on Gidoen's throat was shattered.

Air flooded back into Gideon's lungs. The release was abrupt, overwhelming. His vision threatened to go dark, but he couldn't stop now. Through the lingering haze, he wrenched himself free. Twisting onto his stomach, he scrambled out from under Cas.

"Get back here, Gid!"

Behind him, Cas clambered off the floor, unsteady but relentless. His hands latched onto the nearest prison cell, fingers curling around one of the rusted bars. Gnashing his teeth, the iron shrieked as he wrenched the bar free. Reeling it over his head, Cas launched it like a javelin.

With a rush of air, the bar whizzed past Gideon's head, missing his wing by mere inches before burying itself deep into the far wall.

A flow of ice ran through his veins, a pit settling in his chest.

Gideon hadn't even regained his breath, but his legs moved beneath him before his mind could catch up to what was happening around him. The tremors shook the floor, each footfall threatening to send him sprawling to the ground; still, he weaved through the falling debris, pressing forward until he reached the door.

He squeezed back through the narrow gap, Cas's footsteps pounding behind him. The chamber was too cramped for Cas to fly, his bulky frame struggling against the violent shockwaves.

"Nothing's gonna save you now, Gid!"

Gideon barreled up the steps, lungs burning, vision swimming. Each breath felt like fire clawing through his ribs. He thought he might collapse.

Behind him, there was an explosion of metal against stone—Cas had ripped the door from its hinges.

Don't stop.

Pushing through the pain, Gideon lunged up the rest of the steps. His mind was blank. No time to think, no time to second-guess.

Left, then right. Straight—no, left again.

Gideon had no idea where he was…the corridors all looked the same.

Suddenly, the ground shuddered beneath him, a fresh tremor rolling through the castle. From somewhere up ahead, a chorus of chirps and squawks erupted. The sound of Harpies.

The main hall.

It would be risky with all the Harpies, but at least there was a way out. He could slip out in the confusion…

What about Cas?

"Gideon!"

His name tore through the halls, raw and guttural like a rabid animal. There was an explosion of stone from somewhere behind him. He ran without looking back; he didn't need to.

Cas had torn through a wall searching for him.

You can't help him.

The corridor widened, the floor angling into a steep incline. Able to spread his wings, Gideon lifted himself into the air, just above the floor, pressing himself upward.

Finally, the light of the main hall bled through the archway ahead. The sound of battle filled his ears: the rhythmic clash of metal on metal, the squeals of the Harpies.

Gideon's heart seized. He'd expected chaos, but not full-out fighting.

Who could…

He didn't have time to finish the thought. His feet hit the floor in a running stop. Beating his wings, he fought to slow his momentum, bracing against the wooden arch. The air burned as he gulped it down, but it was refreshing, nourishing.

Over the din of the battle raging in the hall, Gideon listened, straining for any sign of Cas behind him. He caught the faint rumble of shifting stone, though they seemed sporadic and more irregular than the tremors had been.

On Hawks & Harpies

Poor Cas.

Gideon imagined him down in the bowels of Fate's Folly, punching at random walls, not even attempting to navigate the corridors while in pursuit. It was fortunate in a way; it had given Gideon time to escape. Still, he shook his head.

I have to find some way to help him. Maybe the Noktern will have an answer.

Shoving off the wall, Gideon stepped onto the balcony that overlooked the atrium. His boots were muffled by the runner that ran the length. Cautiously, he peered through the balustrades.

He couldn't believe his eyes. Two Avians fighting against a sea of Harpies, at least a dozen. But the pair held their own.

The first was a tall Dove, wielding a staff with breathtaking precision. Gideon didn't recognize him, but the ferocity of his movements was mesmerizing. He spun the staff overhead, each strike fluid and practiced, knocking back any Harpy that dared get too close. The other–

"Pelanor!" Gideon cried, his voice cracking with desperate relief.

Below, the Owl's head snapped up, his cacao eyes widening. He moved to call back, but a Harpy lunged with its claws drawn. He barely had time to parry, catching the creature's talons on his short sword. Longsword in his other hand, he swiped in a viscous arc, slicing clean across the Harpy's stomach. It let out an agonized screech, crumpling to its knees before collapsing to the floor.

Pelanor twisted back to Gideon. "What're you waiting for, an invitation? Get down here!"

Gideon hesitated a moment, but he climbed atop the railing and jumped. His wings flared, pressing to slow his descent.

About halfway between the balcony and the floor, one of the Harpies spotted him. Launching itself in the air, it screeched ferociously, barreling straight for him. It drew back its lips, revealing its razor-like teeth.

Gideon fumbled for the scalpel, but remembered that it lay at the bottom of the dungeon. He braced himself, but the Dove darted forward with two swift beats, ramming the butt of his staff into the creature's throat. It choked out a strangled cry, slammed backwards into one of the pillars, and fell to the floor.

Gideon shook his head to process as his boots skimmed the ground.

"Thanks," he swallowed.

"No problem." The man nodded, a hand briefly clapping Gideon's shoulder. "I'm Théo."

"Nice to–"

"No time for pleasantries!" Pelanor's voice cut through the chaos. Three Harpies closed in on him as he ran to join them.

Théo dropped into a defensive stance, his bo staff held lengthwise across his chest.

Pelanor barely slowed as he shoved his longsword into Gideon's hands. "Take this for now."

Gideon's fingers curled around the hilt of the sword. He swung it once, testing the weight. It wasn't as heavy as his sword had been, but it still helped him to feel at ease with a real weapon back in his hands.

Théo moved like lightning. A deadly dance, he pivoted on his heel and thrust the staff sharply, the butt cracking the Harpy's temple. The creature's eyes rolled back as it collapsed unconscious.

The remaining two flanked them, circling like ravenous foxes, teeth bared, claws flexing.

Back-to-back-to-back, the trio tightened their stance into a defensive triangle, weapons raised waiting for the inevitable attack.

Feeling a nudge at his waist, Gideon caught a flick of Pelanor's head, his feet edging toward the main gate. Gideon followed, Théo not far behind.

They hadn't made it more than a handful of steps when the earth rumbled again.

Pelanor stiffened. "That can't be right." His voice wavered. "Satu couldn't have lit the next explosive yet… they would've had to have flown."

"That wasn't an explosion." Théo's grip tightened on his staff. "We'd have heard the blast."

The rumble deepened, the low growl swelling into a roar. The stones beneath them shuddered. Even the Harpies froze, wide-eyed and rigid.

A chill crawled up Gideon's spine with a sudden realization.

"We have to go."

Pelanor shot him a look. "That's the general plan, Gideon." His tone was somewhere between mocking and dread.

"You don't understand." Gideon didn't think twice. Without any concern for the Harpies, Gideon broke from the circle and bolted for the door. "That's Cas."

"What!?" Pelanor squawked.

Gideon didn't answer. He just ran.

Footsteps thundered behind him, Pelanor and Théo keeping pace. Then came the shrill, piercing cries of the Harpies as they gave chase.

Pounding rang in Gideon's ears. Without stopping, he turned around in time to see the wall explode. A cloud of dust and stone ripped through the chamber, the shockwave knocking the Harpies off their feet.

The debris settled and Cas emerged from the wreckage, his face twisted in a gruesome nightmare. The veins in his neck bulged, his wings flared viciously behind him in a ruthless display.

"You're not getting away from me again, Gid!"

With a single, powerful stroke, Cas vaulted into the air.

The Harpies shrieked wildly, the sound jarring like nails on slate. Gideon flinched but kept moving, throwing the occasional glance over his shoulder.

Picking themselves up off the floor, the Harpies threw themselves into the air and converged on Cas in a coordinated strike; they latched onto him, talons digging into his arms, teeth gnashing at his flesh.

Cas snarled, struggling, his movements jerking with the pain. He twisted, trying to shake them loose, but they clung on tight.

Veering wildly, he slammed one against the nearest pillar. There was a sickening crunch, the Harpy's spine snapping like a stick. His arm freed, Cas snatched the other by the throat and ripped it off his shoulder. With a violent twist, he broke the creature's neck. He looked at it, his eyes cold as he let its lifeless form drop to the ground.

The Harpies dispatched, Cas turned his gaze forward and resumed the hunt.

They were almost there, Gideon could taste freedom in the air through the main gate. The smell of stale, dead wood and scarred earth flooded into the hall, but it was sweeter than anything he'd known in weeks as a prisoner of Fate's Folly.

The final stretch.

So many thoughts, so many emotions clawed at him. But there was no time to process a single one. His lungs burned, begging for air. Between being choked half-to-death and the endless sprinting, his body was on the verge of collapse.

His mind was drained. Too many plans, too many desperate choices. He was running on empty.

His heart was shattered.

He'd finally done it. He'd found Cas. He'd fought for him…almost died to get to him. And it meant nothing. His friend was gone. The Master–

No. My bitch of a mother…

–had taken him away.

Rage reignited him, his legs pressing harder to the gate.

Escape.

Cas's wings pulsed behind them, the heavy, erratic beats gaining on them.

The threshold of the courtyard was dead ahead, just a few more steps and they'd be able to disappear into the night. Gideon flared his wings, ready to take off.

Boom!

An explosion tore through the night, somewhere on the mountain just outside the main hall. The sound hit first, a deafening crack that plowed through Gideon's chest like a physical blow. Then came the impact—a violent quake that rattled through the chamber, shaking the very bones of the castle.

The floor lurched beneath his feet and Gideon's legs buckled beneath him. He fell hard, slamming into the floorboards. He barely had time to register the pain before a shadow loomed through the swirling debris.

Cas barreled through the air, coming straight for Gideon, Pelanor, and Théo, all sprawled across the floor. They were prey, ripe for the picking.

Gideon tried to pick himself up, fingers laced around the hilt of his sword.

As the stone seemed to settle in the aftermath of the shockwave, there was another crack. And another. And another until a symphony erupted like crevasses etching themselves into glass.

The columns began to give way. They groaned, stone grinding against stone. The nearest fractured at the base, the entire structure tilting forward like a felled tree.

Gideon's breath caught in his throat.

It fell straight onto Cas. The beam swatted him from the air like an insect. He had no time to react, the full weight driving down on him, crushing him under its momentum. The impact shattered against the far balcony, wooden beams splintering like dried twigs.

"Cas, no!" Gideon's voice cracked. He scrambled to his feet, the sword clattering to the floor as he lunged forward.

Théo's powerful arm snapped around his waist.

"Forget it, Gideon!" Pelanor's voice cut through the chaos, urgent and raw. "The ceiling's about to go!" He turned and bolted for the door, his voice trembling. "Get him out of here, Théo!"

Gideon fought viciously. He twisted, flailed, pressed his wings in desperate bursts, but Théo held him firm.

"Cas!" Dust caught in Gideon's throat, the call hoarse and broken. He pushed harder, tears streaking through the dirt on his face. "I have to help him!"

Théo said nothing, only tightened his grip, dragging the Finch toward the gate.

Gideon watched in horror as the first stones cracked loose from the ceiling, tumbling in a cascade that expanded across the hall.

"No!"

Théo hauled Gideon through the threshold, both of them tumbling into the courtyard as the rubble came crashing down behind them.

There was a final, thunderous crash as the castle swallowed Cas whole.

Chapter Twenty-Two

Socorra

Fucking Pelanor.

Socorra pushed herself upright on the bed. The sudden motion sent a wave of nausea rolling through her gut, but she swallowed it down. Moving with more care, she propped herself against the pillow, elbows braced on her knees, and reread the letter she'd found tucked in her boot.

Socorra,

Since you're reading this letter, I assume Airam has been giving you the powdered Tylenol. I told her it was Frankincense. Mim forbid ~~the forest witch~~ she give you anything that isn't homeopathic. But don't worry, it won't hurt the fledgling.

You're welcome.

What a smug ass...Still, I do feel better.

Socorra's gaze dropped from the letter. Her fingers trembled slightly as she rested a hand on her stomach.

It won't hurt the fledgling.

The thought felt foreign, almost unreal. Aside from dehydration and a dull headache, nothing felt different. There was no great change, no tangible proof, just the knowledge that a life was growing inside her. It was overwhelming, terrifying, and exhilarating all at once. She had always imagined having fledglings with Kyte one day, but never like this. Never under these circumstances.

With a sharp flick of her head, she shook the thought away and refocused on the letter.

On to business. I'm going to provide you with information and you need to trust me on it. Yes Soccora, even if I haven't given you a reason to.

Yeah, no kidding.

Socorra hadn't forgotten Pelanor's transgressions. From the start, he'd withheld the truth about Kyte being alive, despite knowing exactly who she was. When Kyte was injured, the Owl had all but abandoned her at the Noktern. And to top it off, he was downright insufferable.

But…he did rescue us from the Brick.

She rolled her eyes.

~~*But Kyte is in danger.*~~

Even on her second read-through, Socorra's heart skipped a beat. The etching over the words was just faint enough to be legible, no doubt deliberate. Pelanor wanted to shake her, to light a fire under her. A calculated push to call her into action.

But Kyte is currently on the front lines at Vines' Crossing. While he can handle himself in battle, something is coming for him. I had a vision...I suppose I'll have to explain myself at some point, but just go with me on this. Gideon is going to divert us there should we save him. I don't know any of the details, but I can't imagine it's for anything good.

Obviously, your pregnancy throws a wrench into all of my plans. ~~Frankly, it feels irresponsible of you~~

Socorra's knuckles tightened around the paper.

Airam and Théo made their position clear that you weren't to accompany us on the rescue mission. However, she cannot stop you from continuing your duties to Kyte, and to Avis. With that said, ~~I am not completely heartless~~ I understand that I cannot make any decisions on your behalf. What you do from here is completely up to you, and I will support whatever you choose. Should you join us at Vines' Crossing, I and all of Avis would be eternally grateful. If you choose to ~~abandon~~ focus your energies on the pregnancy, I cannot fault you. ~~I know you'll make the right decision~~ I will respect your decision.

Warmest regards,

P.S. I left two pills and a glass of water on the end table. Take them before you leave. They'll help with any residual pain.

Twice more, Socorra read the letter, each pass stoking a storm of emotions: frustration, anger, joy, confusion until they knotted into something dense and impenetrable in her chest.

Her mind went numb, the steady throb in her temples drowning out thought. Without ceremony, she set the letter aside and swung her legs over the bed. The wooden floor was coarse but warm beneath her feet as she crossed to the end table. She scooped up the pills Pelanor had left, each stark white, about the size of a large peanut, deceptively harmless.

She popped them into her mouth and chewed, grimacing as bitterness coated her tongue, the chalky remnants clinging like dust.

Pelanor!

Grateful for the glass of water within reach, she seized it and drank deeply, swishing the last mouthful in a futile attempt to wash away the bitterness. Still, the taste clung to her tongue, stubborn and sour.

She set the glass aside and braced herself against the table, pressing her weight into the solid wood as if it could steady her. Her head bowed, eyes unfocused on the blurred lines of the floorboards.

An exasperated huff escaped her. Her wings drooped low, feathers brushing the ground. The guilt that followed wasn't sharp like she expected; it came as a slow, heavy ache, spreading through her chest until she could hardly breathe.

This should be harder.

But the knot in her chest slowly unraveled as her resolve stiffened. She wrenched herself up and threw on her boots, tearing about the room as she rifled through whatever of her personal effects she could find. Her knapsack still had some provisions left, including a clean change of shirt and breeches. Fumbling beneath the bed, she found her spear, its weight in her hands bringing her immediate comfort.

"And what do you think you're doing?"

Socorra whipped her head around to the door. Instinctually, she pulled herself into a defensive position, foisting the spearhead in front of her. As she looked, she was awed by the woman's wings: one black, one white.

Airam.

She'd caught enough snippets of conversation while she was half-asleep, but she was taken aback by the woman's presence. Domineering, yet aloof, the woman's stare scorched deeply into Socorra.

"Packing my things," Socorra answered brusquely, shoving a rolled-up pair of breeches into her knapsack.

"I can see that." Airam folded her arms over her chest and leaned in the doorway. "The question is more *why* than what."

The Hawk let out an exasperated sigh. "Airam, I appreciate everything that you've done for me, but my friends need me…my family needs me."

Airam shoved off the doorframe gracefully, her feet lacing in front of one another as she strode forward. "And what of your fledgling? Don't they need you?"

The words hit like a punch to the gut. Socorra stiffened, her fingers tightening around her spear. "That's none of your business."

Airam stopped, the finality of her step punctuated by the clack of her heel. "Of course, dear." Despite the sharpness in her voice, something softer flickered in her jade eyes. "But from one woman to another, I need to know…why?"

Socorra furrowed her brow, her mouth dry. "Why what?"

"Why are you so willing to throw this away?"

Socorra's lips curled. "I'm not throwing away anything."

Airam tilted her head, "Dear, you misunder–"

"I misunderstand nothing," the words snapped like a whip. "Look, Airam, I value your concern. But, from one woman to another, I won't let you guilt me. It's my decision."

Breaking from Airam's gaze, Socorra turned back to the bed and scooped up her remaining sundries, shoving them into her pack. "I'm going to Vincs' Crossing, and I will fight." Throwing the knapsack over her shoulder, she pushed past Airam, their wings grazing in the narrow space.

"And if you lose the fledgling?" Airam's tone was even, though there was an accusatory edge to it. "What then?"

Socorra froze in the doorway, a heaviness settling in her chest as the real plausibility sunk in. "That's a risk I have to take."

A silence stretched between them. Finally, Airam spoke, her voice barely above a whisper.

"You have no idea what that pain is like…"

Socorra turned, ready to fire back, but the words died on her lips. Airam hadn't moved, hadn't turned around. She stood with her gaze locked on the dying embers of the woodstove, her wings trembling.

"The pain of losing a fledgling is…" her voice cracked, "…more than anyone should have to endure." She cleared her throat and wiped at her face. When she finally turned to face Socorra, her charcoal liner was smudged. "I just want to make sure that you don't regret your decision."

A lighthearted smile etched the corner of Socorra's mouth. "Thank you, and I mean that. But there is no choice for me. My people are in danger, and I have to fight. It's who I am. A huntress and a warrior."

Pride swelled in her chest, her feathers bristling.

"And if this fledgling–" her hand found her stomach, the strap of the knapsack slipping to her elbow. The words caught in her throat, adrenaline twisting into something raw and overwhelming. "If they make it through this war, then they'll be all the stronger for it."

Airam studied her, lips curling in silent resignation. "I still think this is a mistake." Undoing the sash at her waist, she stepped forward. Socorra went rigid but didn't move from the doorway. "But at least take this."

Without waiting for approval, Airam wrapped the lace sash around Socorra's hips and knotted it deftly. "Red is the color of a healthy birth."

Socorra furrowed her brow as Airam whispered something in a language she didn't recognize. There was something strange about it, something ancient, but oddly comforting. For a brief moment, she was back in the cell beneath Cherub Farm, Tama bustling about, caring for her.

The memory ebbed as Airam pulled away, her fingers lingering on Socorra's stomach longer than she'd have liked.

"Come." With a graceful sweep, Airam threw an arm over her shoulder and led her down the hall. "I'll show you the way out."

Chapter Twenty-Three

GIDEON

The Harpy lunged, its beak-like jaws snapping at Gideon in the dim hall. There was no fear, only a hollow stillness as he swung the scalpel into the creature's throat. Blood drained onto the floor in a torrent of crimson mire at his feet.

Haven't I done this before?

The beast shuddered. Its ashen skin peeled back, revealing the Avian beneath. A flush of warmth spread across its cheeks, scraggly hair smoothing into chestnut locks. Gray feathers deepened into a vibrant red.

Cas.

Gideon went cold, a numbness spreading from his chest to his limbs.

Cas's hands clutched at his throat, trying to staunch the bleeding, but the blood oozed through his fingers like water through a broken dam.

"It's okay, Cas," Gideon's voice shook. "You're gonna be okay."

He reached out, desperate to help, but before his fingers found Cas, the hallway vanished. A darkness swallowed them whole, and his friend was wrenched some thirty yards away.

Across the void, Cas collapsed. His body buckled as his knees caved, shoulders sinking, chest imploding as if the air had been ripped from his lungs. For a fleeting heartbeat, his arms flailed before snapping rigid at his sides. A wet, awful sound filled the space between them, bones grinding, joints popping.

"Cas!" Gideon cried. He tried to launch himself forward, but an unseen force held him back, rooting him in place. He thrashed, flailing against the invisible grip, but nothing he did broke its hold.

Cas's mouth opened in a strangled scream, his body compacted inch by inch, crushed under a pressure that Gideon couldn't see. His pale, bloodshot eyes flicked to Gideon one last time; the fury in them melted away, widening into confusion and fear.

Then, with a sickening crunch, he was gone.

Gideon jolted awake, a scream tearing from his throat, only to be swallowed by the wind roaring past him. Panic surged as he lunged forward, grasping for something, anything to feel secure.

"Hey!" A sharp, authoritative voice cut through the chaos just as his body pitched forward.

Disoriented, his breath coming in ragged gasps, Gideon struggled to gather his bearings. Everything blurred, a dizzying rush of wind and motion. He was strapped to Théo's back, leather bindings cinched tight across his chest, his wings tethered to the Dove's.

"Pelanor!" Théo's voice strained against the gushing wind. "A little help here!"

In the first light of dawn, Gideon watched as the sprawl of the open sea stretched below.

Hands gripped his tunic from above, steadying him.

Using the leverage, Théo flapped his wings; Gideon's followed in suit, bound to the rhythm.

"Gideon." Pelanor's voice was level, unwavering, but it barely reached Gideon's ears through the roar. "I need you to stay calm."

No!

How could he? He had to fight, tear himself free, and reach Cas to wrench his friend from the rubble, from the crushing weight that was breaking his body apart.

A cavernous ache carved through him, a pain deeper than anything he'd ever known.

Even his father's disappointment, his mother's betrayal felt like nothing compared to the stilling emptiness that wrapped through his very being.

"Gideon?"

The Finch couldn't explain it, but there was a kindness in Pelanor's voice, and it broke him. Numbness spread, the fight draining from his body. With a ragged sob, he buried his face against Théo's back.

He cried hard and unrelenting tears. His body trembled with the force of it. He couldn't be sure how long it lasted; if anyone spoke to him, the words were lost. Wracked by the loss, exhaustion finally claimed him, and he fell back asleep.

✶   ✶   ✶

Over and over, the nightmare played out without reprieve, relentless.

Jolts of turbulence had startled him awake more than once during the journey, but the exhaustion always dragged him back under. By the time they finally landed on a windswept peninsula, far south beyond the sight of Lake Shore, he was too numb to care.

"Gid?" Fatima's voice was soft but firm as she plopped down beside him beneath a linden tree.

He lifted his head from his hands, staring at her blankly.

"I know…"

She kept talking, her words washing over him in an indistinct blur. He caught fragments, sparse words and half-formed thoughts, but none of it made any sense to him as she droned on.

The images in his head were already too much, each one gnawing at him like teeth sinking into raw, exposed nerves. Her voice only intensified the pain. His skin prickled, a sting flaring in his chest, creeping up into his throat. Where his wings met his back, his muscles burned, tension coiling them tight like drawn bowstrings.

"Fatima!"

The name tore from his throat, his voice cracking under the weight of it. Tears threatened, but he swallowed them down. Guilt ripped at him, for everything that had happened at the castle, for snapping at her, but he couldn't contain himself. He felt helpless.

But Fatima didn't flinch; she didn't bristle or recoil. She simply watched him, her eyes steady, waiting with quiet patience. No judgment. No pity. Just understanding.

Gideon struggled for words, but nothing came. Finally, hoarse and broken, he managed, "I'm sorry."

Fatima's lips curled wryly. She shrugged. "Don't be." Her voice was tender, gentle. "You've been through a lot."

She placed a hand on his knee. A flicker of something stirred in him, some distant awareness of how young she was, a contrast to how composed she seemed. The realization stung, not in bitterness, but in quiet frustration at himself.

"I'm here if you want to talk."

He expected her to get up and walk away, to leave him to his solitude. Instead, she shifted herself, tucking her wings to the side and settling more comfortably against the tree. Without reservation, she rested her head on his shoulder.

Gideon stiffened, his wings going rigid at the sudden contact. But Fatima didn't move, didn't press him, simply existed beside him. And slowly, the tension bled from his body. He let his wings splay behind him, his back molding against the rough bark of the tree, the sweet scent of honey filling his senses. His heartbeat fell into an easy rhythm, matching the rise and fall of the waves crashing somewhere beyond the cliffside.

He had no idea how long they sat there. Minutes? Hours? Pelanor wouldn't have allowed them to linger for long, but for the moment, time felt irrelevant.

For the first time since Cas died, the world was quiet.

"You loved him…didn't you?"

The question hit him like a fist, shattering his brief respite.

"I'm sorry." Fatima pulled away, her eyes brimming with a mild shame. "That wasn't…I didn't mean–"

"It's okay," he rasped, though his throat felt like it was closing in on itself. He swallowed hard, blinking against the sting in his eyes. Then, inexplicably, his lip twitched into a smile, small, broken, and aching. Another wave of tears welled up.

"Yeah." The word came out fractured, barely held together. "I did–"

The past tense nearly destroyed him. He couldn't say it. Wouldn't.

His pulse thundered in his ears as he forced the correction past trembling lips. "I do."

Saying it aloud felt like stepping off a precipice, a weight finally removed from his shoulders. Terrifying, exhilarating, freeing. There was nothing to stop him now. No more pretending. The truth had always been there, buried beneath fear and hesitation, tucked away in precious moments, longing stares, tender embraces.

I love you, Cas.

What he wouldn't give to go back and say that to him now.

From the corner of his eye, Gideon caught sight of Théo and Pelanor returning. They had gone on a walk to give Gideon a few minutes alone to grieve; they had tried to get Fatima to come along with them, but the fledgling refused to budge.

Théo grasped Gideon by the forearm, the pressure causing Gideon to wince. "How're you holding up?"

"I'm…" Gideon stammered, looking for anything to say that would even remotely come close to how he felt. "I'm okay."

Why am I lying?

Gideon shook his head to chase away the thought.

Théo forced a smile. "Glad to hear it."

"Yes, very happy," Pelanor's interjection was quick and biting. "Now, as you know–"

Gideon braced himself. His wings tensed, shoulders hunched inward, chest tightening like a fist clenching around his ribs, prepared for whatever admonishment Pelanor was ready to dole out.

Fatima let out an exasperated sigh. "Pelanor, don't."

"What?" The Owl's voice was cool, edged. "We don't have a lot of time, so forgive me for not tiptoeing around feelings."

Fatima opened her mouth to argue, but Gideon gently laid a hand on her arm, silencing her with a knowing stare.

"It's fine." He gave her a curt nod, his lips curling gently, but with resignation. "Pelanor, I'm sure you're going to give me some lecture about duty and responsibility."

The Owl's gray eyes bore into him, passive, unreadable. He didn't say anything, holding himself stoically, hands folded into the sleeves of his robes, listening intently.

Gideon exhaled slowly. "But that's not going to help." He rubbed at the back of his neck, swallowing hard. "I just lost my best friend, the person who I–"

Love.

The word tangled in his throat. Saying it to Fatima had felt freeing, but saying it to Pelanor felt wrong somehow, like ripping open a wound that had only just begun to heal. His face burned, and he cast his eyes downward.

There was a soft squeeze on his hand. Fatima. When he looked up, her eyes were full of compassion.

He cleared his throat. "I'm going to miss…" He shook his head, inhaling sharply. "I'm deeply saddened…" His thoughts tangled, the words muddled and lost.

A heavy silence settled between them. Then, to Gideon's astonishment, Pelanor stepped forward, closing the space in a few deliberate strides. The Owl hesitated only a heartbeat before pulling him into a firm, almost clumsy embrace. His arms stiff at first, then tightening with a quiet certainty.

What's happening?

For a moment, Gideon couldn't breathe. Pelanor's feathers were cool against his cheek, his scent faintly of oil and wind and ash. It was the kind of closeness Gideon had never imagined he'd be offered in his state of grieving, least of all from *him*.

"I'm very sorry for your loss, Gideon."

The words were low, almost rough, but sincere in a way that made something in Gideon snap. His body buckled. A strangled sob tore from his chest as he buried his face into the crook of Pelanor's neck. The Owl said nothing, only steadied him with one hand pressed firmly between his shoulder blades, the other pressed on the top of his head, fingers gently brushing through his hair, anchoring him while the grief tore through him and left him trembling.

"Thank you."

Gideon pulled back a fraction, ashamed of how small his voice sounded. Gradually, the torrent began to ebb; his breathing slowed, the ragged sobs giving way to steady exhales.

When Pelanor finally pulled away, his hands remained firmly pressed on Gideon's shoulders. "If you need time, take it. Stay here. Fly to Lake Shore and hide out for a few days. Do what you need."

Gideon sniffled, caught off guard by the unexpected kindness. He glanced at Fatima, her brows knitted in bewilderment. Even Théo looked stunned, his head cocked slightly as if he were seeing Pelanor for the first time.

Withdrawing his hands, Pelanor straightened up, resuming his usually staunch composure. He tucked his wings neatly against his back, folding his arms into his sleeves. "But the rest of us have to go on and fight. Time is a luxury we simply don't have."

Exhaling shakily, Gideon squared his shoulders. "Cas is gone." Saying it aloud felt like being struck. He forced himself to continue, even as his throat tightened. "I will grieve him every day until I die. But the best thing I can do now is to make sure no one else suffers like this." Tears blurred his vision. "The Master has taken too much already. I won't let her take anything else…Anyone else."

Pelanor sighed a quiet relief. "Then we're off to Vines' Crossing." With a practiced flourish, he pivoted southward, wings unfurling in one fluid motion.

Gideon instinctively moved to follow, but something gnawed at him.

"Wait!" The wind caught his feathers as he hesitated. "How did you know that's where the Master would attack?"

Pelanor rolled his eyes, exasperation flickering across his face. "We have *so* much to catch you up on," he huffed, lifting off the ground. "We'll fill you in on the way."

Chapter Twenty-Four
Kyte

Red in the face, General Melierax squawked at the handful of officers who'd managed to fall back into the command tent. "Someone give me a status report!" He rubbed the dark bags under his eyes and shoved another kola nut into his mouth, his third since Kyte had arrived.

Colaroja, one of the officers Kyte had spoken with on the day of his arrival, stepped forward. "Sir, much of the southern camp has been completely wiped out by flying boulders, including the armory. The northern one is still intact, but our resources are depleting." She brushed a mat of sweaty hair off her forehead. "We've also lost the med tent. There were no survivors from the attack but…"

So I sentenced Falco to death…great.

A pang of guilt lanced through Kyte, but he tamped it down, focusing on the war ahead. Others were still counting on him, and he wasn't going to let them down because of his feelings. He shoved the thought aside and refocused on Melierax.

"What of our attempts to disrupt the Crows' defenses?"

"Nil, sir," another officer replied, a captain, judging by the three-star patch stitched to his armor. "Any attempt to approach from the air has been disastrous."

"Have we at least managed to get eyes on whatever the hell is costing us so much damage?"

"A few reports from Virgo legion." The captain flitted his wings, stirring the humid air in the tent. "They've acquired some kind of heavy-duty machinery. Looks almost like a massive slingshot on wheels. They load the boulders in and launch them at our flight parties."

Melierax wiped his brow. "So what options does that leave us?"

Silence. The officers glanced at each other, wary, defeated.

Melierax snapped his fingers. "Not a rhetorical question, people. Any idea is better than no idea."

"Full aerial assault."

The words came with a crisp confidence, called out by Sergeant Harlan, grandson of Brutus Harlan from the Hawk Elder Council.

Melierax didn't look up. His eyes fixed on the floor, expression flat. "I know I said *any* idea is better than none," he muttered, "but damn it, Harlan, thank you for proving me wrong. You're dismissed."

"Sir, I–"

"Did I stutter, sergeant!?" Melierax stomped toward the boy, wings flared, his voice rising. "A full aerial assault would mean certain death for half of our company, if not more!" He jabbed a thick finger into Harlan's chest, berating him with spit-laced fury.

Whatever came next was lost on Kyte. His mind was already racing, an idea swirling in his head. "What if it's the perfect idea?" His voice cut through Melierax's tirade like a hot knife.

The general froze, still looming over Harlan. Slowly, he craned his neck, fixing Kyte with a narrowed glare. "Not you too, Pandion." His voice was low, gravelly, hissed through clenched teeth.

Kyte met his stare. "Sir, if you'll give me a chance to explain…"

The purple in Melierax's face slowly faded, his expression shifting from anger to cautious curiosity. "This had better be good."

"At the risk of losing soldiers, we haven't been dispatching the full forces of our arsenal. Why not send in a full assault? It's risky, sure, but it would force the Crows into a true defensive stance, maybe even get some of their soldiers off the ground."

"Pandion," Melierax snarled, "in case you've forgotten, that's exactly what we tried at the start. They decimated our troops. Why would I send them back up there? For target practice?"

"No, sir." Kyte scratched at the back of his neck, the sweat stinging his already irritated skin. "What we lacked last time was a coordinated ground offense."

The general's lips thinned. "I'm listening, Pandion, but make your point quickly."

Approaching the planning table, Kyte looked over the map that Melierax had unfurled with the position of the Crow camp. "I'll lead half of Sagittarii through the forests to the east." He pulled several of the statuettes off to the side to mark his plan. "Sergeant Hiero will take the other half to the west. While the Crows are tied up in aerial combat, we hit them from the ground on both sides. First a volley from our archers to weaken their defenses, then a charge with hand-to-hand combat."

"A brilliant idea."

All heads in the tent turned, protocol forgotten as they looked toward the entrance at the Avian who had spoken out of turn.

Kyte shook his head wearing a crooked half-smile. "Pelanor."

The Owl gave Kyte a curt nod. "They certainly won't see that coming. Unfortunately, we have much bigger problems to attend to."

"We certainly do!" Melierax bellowed, his brow furrowing. "How did you get past my guards?"

"Have you seen the state of your camp?" Pelanor raised an eyebrow. "Every guard I passed was busy putting out fires. Mostly metaphorical, but I'm pretty sure one of the living quarters was actually aflame."

"That's none of your concern, Owl." Melierax flared his wings. "Now, get out before I pluck your feathers and drag you out of here myself!"

Pelanor tsked. "I suppose, then, you'll have no problem fighting off the Crows and the approaching army of Harpies?"

Kyte's heart skipped a beat.

Melierax's stoicism cracked for only a moment, but Kyte saw it, his pallor draining. The general planted his hands on the table to steady himself, his legs trembling.

"Pandion." He lowered his voice. "You've fought these creatures before, haven't you?"

"Yes, sir," Kyte replied, uneasy. "But that was only a dozen or so." He turned to Pelanor, dread creeping in his chest. "How many are we talking about?"

"All of them." Pelanor was stone-faced, but Kyte could read the slight flicker of his gaze, his eyes dancing around the tent. The Owl was nervous. "Gideon believes–"

"You got Gideon back?" Kyte cut in, a wave of relief breaking through the fear.

"We did." The Owl's tone was clipped, nonchalant. "But he said that there's at least a hundred, if not more. We killed a few during the rescue, and some are bound to have died when we blew up the castle."

"You blew up Fate's Folly?" Kyte bellowed, his voice a mix of shock and admiration.

Pelanor shot him a sidelong glance. "Kyte, you know how much I *love* being interrupted, but can I just explain, please?"

Kyte let out a sharp exhale, but raised his palm in surrender, gesturing for him to continue.

"Thank you," the Owl chided. "As I was saying, the Harpies *should* attack at twilight, and they'll be led by the Master. For those of you new to this, I don't have time to explain what that means. But it's bad."

The tent fell into silence. The officers, Melierax included, shifted uneasily. Kyte felt their gazes prickling against his skin.

"Very bad," he murmured. A disquiet settled in his bones. Slowly, his hand drifted over his shoulder, fingers brushing the raised skin, the last remnants of where his wing should have been.

"Not to mention the stock of rifles she's acquired."

"You're kidding." Kyte's voice came out flat, but the alarm in it was unmistakable. Around the tent, officers exchanged bewildered, if not dubious glances, some scoffing under their breath. For many of them, guns were nothing more than a fairytale, bedtime stories used to scare fledglings into behaving. His own father used to warn that a wild Sapien might shoot holes in his wings, and he'd never fly again.

Guess the joke's on me, dad.

"They're real." Kyte's voice cut through the muttering, silencing the tent before Melierax could sneer a word of doubt. Gripping his collar, he yanked it down past the shoulder, exposing the twisted scar beneath. Raw, raised flesh puckered around a still-scabbed crater.

Gasps rippled through the officers, but Melierax lips twisted in a grimace. "Now I've heard it all." He shook his head, brushing off the front of his leather tunic with feigned calm, though Kyte noted the tremor in his fingers. "I won't hear any more talk of this rubbish." His tone was final, deflective. "Do whatever you will, Owl, but I'll be damned if I let the Noktern dictate this war any more than it already has."

Pelanor raised a finger, consternation scrawled on his face, but Melierax barreled forward, speaking over him. "Pandion, regardless of this Harpy attack, our first order of business must be to disarm these weapons "

"Trebuchets," Pelanor interjected, staccato, but loud enough to cut over Melierax.

Melierax's head snapped toward him. "So the Owls are aware of this technology?" The general fumed, venom in his glare. "Are we to assume that the Noktern has sided with the enemy, then?"

"Hardly," Pelanor scoffed. "We've only read about them. Sapien technology, ancient by even their standards. No one's ever used them in Avis until now."

The general's scowl deepened as he turned his gaze back to Kyte, the muscles in his jaw ticking. "Whatever you call them…these 'treb-you-shays' have brought enough ruin to my command."

"General, if I may–" Pelanor began, but Melierax raised his voice to drown him out.

"Pandion, I'll trust you to execute your maneuver." He slammed a palm on the stratagem table, scattering figurines of troops. "Take a squadron from Virgo for your aerial attack, and lead the Sagittarii as you've outlined. Everyone else, fortify the northern flank. If these Harpies come, that's where we'll break them."

The tent fell into charged silence as he swept statuette after statuette off the table, each one clattering to the floor like a death knell.

"Dismissed!" he roared.

The officers obeyed, boots scuffing against canvas as they filed out. Only Pelanor remained, jaw tight, his frame unmoving despite the current of bodies jostling past him. His eyes never left Kyte.

When the last soldier cleared the tent, he stepped forward and placed a hand on Kyte's shoulder, his grip firm, his slender fingers sliding beneath the edge of the pauldron.

Kyte retied the front of his tunic and met the Owl's stare, his eyes like daggers.

"We have to do something." Worry was etched in the Owl's brow, his voice acerbic.

Kyte exhaled slowly through his nostrils. "And what would you have me do, Pelanor?" He flicked his eyes toward Melierax, who still watched from across the tent, his upper lip twitching, feral.

Laying a hand on the small of Pelanor's back, Kyte guided him toward the exit, his touch firm, insistent, but not unkind. "You know I can't go against my orders." Pushing past the tent into the open, Kyte used his free hand to shield his eyes from the sun. "And frankly, you've no one to blame but yourself. I'm only here playing soldier because you told me to."

"Then you have a good habit of doing what I say, so why stop now?" Pelanor pried himself loose from Kyte's grip with a quick flick of his wings. He spun to face the Hawk, a slight flush in his cheeks. "I'm telling you, Kyte, this is serious."

"As if a war isn't serious? Which *your people* threw us into, if you need to be reminded."

Before Pelanor could muster a retort, the ground shook beneath them. In the distance, screams tore through the sky, sharp and distant.

Pelanor sniffed. "Fine. Point taken, but there'll be serious repercussions if the Hawks and Crows–"

"I'm gonna stop you there." There was a quiet force in Kyte's voice; not harsh, just firm, undeniable.

Pelanor froze, arms mid-gesture, his mouth hanging open in exaggerated disbelief. "There you go again," he exasperated. "Interrupting me mid-sentence. What is it with you Hawks? So disagreeable."

"Okay, Pelanor." Kyte pinched the bridge of his nose. "Look, it's not that I'm ignoring you. I hear you, loud and clear. But I have my orders. I'm leading the legion. If *you* can convince the Crows to stand down–"

"Already in motion," Pelanor interrupted smugly. "Gideon and Fatima are on it."

Kyte gave him a dry look. "Wonderful, but don't interrupt me again." He let out a quick exhale, his lip curling in a smirk

Pelanor blinked. "Unbelievable."

"If you get a ceasefire, I'll get Melierax to shift his focus to the Harpies. Deal?"

Pelanor folded his arms, unreadable. The air between them stretched thin as the chaos of the camp spun around them, soldiers lifting off into the sky, others barreling through the muck, shouts echoing the drumbeats of war.

"Pelanor…"

"Oh, I'm sorry," the Owl flared his wings in mock apology. "I didn't want to interrupt."

"You're such an ass," Kyte muttered, dragging a hand through his tangled hair. It was filthy, knotted, and crusted from days of sweat and blood. He barely felt Avian anymore. "I have to go."

"Kyte…"

"Don't." Kyte's tone dropped, low and gravelly. "I *get* it. Don't pretend I don't know what we're dealing with."

Pelanor opened his mouth, finger lifting in protest. Then stopped dead.

Kyte stilled. He knew that look.

The light behind the Owl's eyes dimmed, his focus sliding elsewhere. He stood upright, but his breath hitched, and a tremor licked down his spine. Even now, it unsettled Kyte. Watching Pelanor seize with a vision was like watching a corpse remember how to breathe.

He does love to make a spectacle.

As soon as it had come on, the episode ended. Pelanor drew in a slow breath, as if the weight of something massive had just slipped from his shoulders. A glimmer sparked behind his eyes.

"What is it now?" Kyte masked the thrum of panic in his chest.

Pelanor didn't answer right away. He just smiled, brushing his black hair from his face, straightening his robe with an infuriating grace. "Nothing," he answered smoothly. "Do what you must, *Leftenant Pandion*." He clicked his heels together, chin lifted in a crisp nod. "I have other matters to attend to."

Kyte watched him go, a pit yawning in his gut.

That's not ominous.

✱   ✱   ✱

It was far from the silent operation Kyte had envisioned. None of the Hawks were well-trained in a wooded environment, their home being sparse of trees.

Branches snagged feathers, thorns tore at skin, and every step seemed louder than the last. Still, his soldiers pressed on, silent and determined.

As they neared the edge of the Crow camp, Kyte signaled for a halt. He dropped low into the brush and motioned for the others to follow suit, bows drawn and eyes sharp.

Peering through the foliage, he surveyed the enemy lines. Crow soldiers milled about the outskirts of their camp with casual indifference, as if unbothered by the war they were fighting.

Unlike the Hawk encampment, which sprawled like a miniature city, the Crows had formed a barricade of stark gray tents in a tight, linear formation that stretched across the isthmus like a blockade.

On the northern edge, a row of trebuchets loomed— hulking wooden beasts spaced a hundred yards apart, each attended by a small crew. Kyte's stomach churned as he watched one group roll a boulder into position. A strap dangled from the arm like a noose. With practiced ease, the crew rotated the machine on a groaning piston mount, aligning it with grim precision. Once in place, the machine groaned to life with a single pull of a lever. The boulder launched skyward, cutting through the air. Heading straight for Virgo legion.

The soldiers of Virgo broke formation as the boulder hurtled toward them, half of the unit climbing higher in the air, others steered themselves to the left and right. But with only one projectile, they were able to come together in the v-pattern, spears and javelins at the ready.

A horn blared from within the Crow lines, but their soldiers barely reacted. Calm, unhurried, they worked in unison, methodically loading each trebuchet like cogs in a war machine. One fired. Then another. Then another, each launch punctuated by the groan of timber and the deep rush of air.

The closer Virgo moved, the more treacherous the barrage became.

"Sagittarii!" A dozen heads snapped to Kyte, bows already in hand. "Forward fifteen paces. Notch." The soldiers moved as one, stepping from the trees into the open brush, drawing arrows to cheek. Kyte followed, notching his own. "We'll use the trebuchets as strong-points." His voice was low, but brusque and commanding. "Pick off the crews. Take control of the machines. Then move to the next. Break their rhythm, and we break their line. Understood?"

"Sir, yes sir!"

"Fire!"

The sharp pluck of bowstrings rang out, arrows hissing through the air like angry wasps. The three Crows manning the first trebuchet dropped where they stood, caught completely off guard. Kyte advanced with his unit from the rear, leading the charge as the Hawks surged forward to seize the position.

"Hold here!" he ordered, his voice piercing as his soldiers scrambled to recover usable arrows and take up defensive posts around the captured machine. He moved past one of the fallen Crows but caught the empty, glassy stare in her eyes. A chill traced down his spine.

On Hawks & Harpies

Pelanor's words echoed in his mind: *You're the best shot we have to cut the bloodshed and save lives.*

For a heartbeat, Kyte hesitated, the weight of it all pressing in.

There has to be a better way.

But the war didn't wait. A heavy *thunk* cracked through the air, and Kyte tracked the next stone as it smashed into a Hawk mid-flight, sending her spiraling from the sky.

"Notch!" He shot out his command just as a Crow soldier at the next trebuchet turned, head lifting, eyes narrowing. She froze for half a second—long enough—still shoving a boulder with a comrade. The next volley of arrows cut both down where they stood.

From behind the trebuchet, a third soldier lurched up, spinning on his heel, wings flaring wide. Kyte loosed a quick shot. The arrow caught the Crow square in the back as he tried to take flight.

They pushed forward. The Hawks took the second trebuchet, then a third, then a fourth, each time striking fast and hard, driving the Crow soldiers back and claiming the siege weapons.

At the fifth, Kyte paused to assess. The rhythm was broken now, the Crows' steady barrage disrupted. Virgo legion was pushing deeper into the battlefield, dangerously close to the enemy line. Maybe Hiero was coordinating something similar from the other flank

Kyte shifted to the edge of the formation, scanning the next target. He opened his mouth to give the next command.

Thunk.

The sound sent a chill through him. The sixth trebuchet had turned, its base rotated on some kind of concealed mechanism, pivoting with ease and precision.

Now the sling was leveled, aimed directly at them.

Crack.

Wood shattered. A barrage of splinters and stakes exploded outward as the stone slammed into the Hawk's newly claimed trebuchet. Kyte and a handful of others managed to dive aside, narrowly escaping the impact. Around him, six Hawks lay broken, crushed or skewered by flying debris.

But the chaos wasn't over yet. One of the Crow soldiers surged forward, wings flared as they descended on the Hawks. Still on the ground, Kyte yanked the sword from the scabbard on his hip and scrambled to rise, but the Crow was already upon him, the curved blade of the fauchard arcing toward Kyte's throat.

Before the strike could land, a spear hissed through the air, piercing the Crow clean between the wings. He tumbled; with a guttural squawk, he crumpled in a heap of feathers and dirt.

Kyte's breath caught. His knuckles were bone white around the sword's hilt as he staggered upright, turning in a wild circle, heart hammering in his chest.

Socorra!?

His pulse jolted as she spiraled down from the sky, wings gleaming in the fractured light. For a heartbeat, the war fell away: the clamor of steel, the cries of battle, and the roar of the trebuchets all dimmed beneath the shadow of her wingspan.

"What in the Void are you doing here?" His voice was strained, meant to sound even, but the rawness of his worry slipped through, or was it relief?

"Saving your ass, apparently." Socorra landed with a sweep of her wings, knees bending to catch the fall with effortless grace. "You're welcome, by the way."

Kyte's lips twitched, a rare flicker of a smile breaking through his mask. "Thank you." He pulled her in without thinking, arms locking tight, hands grazing the curve of her wings.

How're you here right now?

He wanted to ask. He should've asked. But those were precious seconds they didn't have to waste.

"I've been worried about you," he murmured, the words rough-edged, scraping out from somewhere deeper than he meant.

"Yeah, well…" She cocked head, her eyes flicking past him, sharp and restless, scanning the field beyond, ensuring their safety in this brief aside. "I'm a big girl." She gave a light punch to his good shoulder before curling into him and kissing his cheek. "I can take care of myself."

"Of course you can. It's part of why I love you." He buried his face in the crook of her neck, fingers stroking softly between her wings. He inhaled her deeply; she smelled of licorice, sweet, unmistakably *her*. Even here, far from the anise fields of Zarpa. It unspooled something tight inside him.

But the clash of steel snapped him back.

"When we're not about to die," he caught her stare, "you'll have to tell me all about how you became a fugitive of the Noktern." Without waiting for a response, he tore himself from her, eyes sweeping the chaos. The battlefield surged, chaos alive again: Virgo had broken through the trebuchets, Hawks clashing in vicious knots of combat, some still skimming the air to avoid the killing arcs of stone. Across the field, the war horns shrieked. The Hawks were mobilizing, coming to press the breach.

"Kyte…"

Socorra's fingers caught the back of his tunic, but her voice barely reached him. His mind raced: the scattered survivors of his legion, Virgo pushing forward, the Hawks pouring into the fray. Even as his thoughts reeled, his hand found hers without thinking, fingers threading tight.

"Sagittarii!" Kyte's voice rang out, leaden with command. He drew a breath, ready to rally his troops, to pull them back into formation where they could do more for the battle.

"Kyte!" Socorra snapped as she yanked him back, the rasp of his name cutting through the roar of battle.

Kyte stumbled, heart still pounding thinking of the fight, but the look in her eyes stopped him cold. She didn't need to speak. He followed her gaze.

A dark form rose on the horizon. At first, he thought it might have been smoke, another encampment set up by the Crows, drifting on the wind. But the shape was wrong, the movement of the form too erratic, too quick. His stomach dropped as the truth came into chilling focus.

Harpies.

They were still far in the distance, but closing in fast. At a glance, Kyte guessed there had to be at least two hundred. Far more than Pelanor had estimated.

Heat rushed to his face, his breath catching in his throat. He turned back to Socorra, panic flickering in his eyes. She was breathing hard, chest rising and falling, eyes wide, but steady.

They locked eyes and, for a moment, the world shrank away.

Kyte exhaled, the breath slicing through his teeth as a shiver crawled down his spine. His lips pulled into a lopsided grin, stubborn, refusing to let his fear show.

"Are you ready to go?" His voice came out rougher than he intended, but the words steadied him.

Socorra drew a breath, rolling her shoulders, wings flaring behind her like a banner.

"Shit," she whispered. "Hold on."

For a heartbeat, Kyte's grin faltered. Her eyes darted, sharp and wild, scanning the ground. Then she was gone from his side, striding toward the slumped Crow she'd felled. He watched in a strange stillness as she planted her foot on the soldier's back and wrenched her spear free, the blade slick with blood.

For the first time, Kyte really looked at the fallen Crow—a young man, no older than twenty. Long black hair coated in dust and dirt, unmarred alabaster skin, his cheeks void of any color. He thought of Falco, probably buried somewhere, either in the ground if the Hawks had been able to, otherwise under a pile of rubble. The weight of their deaths crashed onto Kyte's shoulders. Enemies in different ways, but casualties in a war that none of them had chosen, that had been thrust upon them by the Noktern. Lives broken beneath something darker, shadows that had been creeping through Avis all along.

Her spear free, Socorra lingered, just a breath, as if honoring that truth. Then she turned back to him, weapon poised in hand, her eyes alight. "I'm ready."

Chapter Twenty-Five

GIDEON

"Welp," Fatima huffed, giving the chains binding her to the support beam an unhelpful tug, "that could've gone better."

"Could've been worse," Théo shrugged, his own chains rattling as he shifted. "General Corvinus could've just ordered our execution."

"I'd've liked to see him try." She rolled her eyes. "We fought worse at the Brick!"

"'Ey!" one of the Crow soldiers squawked. "Qvit it vit de talking! And stop fiddling vit dose chains. Dere's no getting out til de general decides vat to do vit you lot."

Gideon's ears pricked at the distinct accent.

Dinar.

His mind flashed to Goldfinch's kitchen. The rich smells, Gatya—Altuna's chef—bustling about the stove-tops.

What I wouldn't do for a slice of one of her tarts.

There was a low growl in his stomach.

Not the time, Gideon...don't lose focus.

"I'm Gideon." He forced a steady smile despite the raw burn of iron at his wrists. Gatya's voice flickered in his memory: *De Crows of Dinar, ve are a varm people.* "And you are?"

The guards exchanged wary glances.

"Rook," the first muttered, trilling his 'r'.

Gideon calmly turned to the second, holding his gaze. "And you?"

There was a pause before the second gave a soft clack of his tongue. "Jackdav." His posture eased slightly, the tip of his fauchard dipping an inch. "But ve shouldn't be talking to you."

"I understand…"

Gideon's gut twisted; he hated small talk, playing polite. It wrenched everything inside him. But there was a bigger picture here. He drew a slow, steadying breath and shifted his wings carefully, rising just enough to look taller, more deliberate. The guards tensed, spears lifting, but they didn't advance.

"But please, just hear me out."

He felt a strange swell inside—an urgent pride crashing against the fear tightening his chest. Maybe, just maybe, he could reach them. The general hadn't listened. But these two? Maybe.

His mind ticked through his books, the ones that had shaped his heart. *The Tale of Despereaux. Charlotte's Web. Pollyanna. The Secret Garden.*

How many stories had been changed by a simple act of kindness?

"Look, we're not–"

A deafening whir split the air. The blare of a war horn.

Gideon flinched as the walls trembled. Everyone in the tent froze, the sudden stillness pressing in.

The guards exchanged a sharp glance.

"Vat do ve do?" Jackdav asked under his breath.

Rook grimaced and stepped toward the entrance, lifting the tent flap. Blinding afternoon light poured in, and with it the unmistakable roar of battle: shouts, the pounding of boots, wings slicing the air, the rush of Crows surging forward.

Fatima cocked her head, giving an impish grin. "By the sound of things, you boys should get going." She rattled her chains lightly. "Don't worry, we'll be right here."

The guards hesitated, eyes flicking between the prisoners. Then, without another word, they turned and slipped into the chaos outside.

As the flap fell closed, Gideon let out a long huff, his shoulders sagging.

"Don't worry about it, Gid," Fatima murmured. She slipped her fingers into her headscarf, careful not to shift it too far back. With practiced ease, she drew out a bobby pin and knelt by her cuffs. "I'm sure it was going to be a beautiful speech."

She worked the pin carefully, the tiny *click click* of metal on metal almost drowned beneath the rising din outside. "Almost there," she murmured, eyes sharp, fingers steady. "And…"

Clink.

"Yes!" she hissed triumphantly, immediately turning to Gideon. "Give me your hands."

"Grab me my staff first." Théo's voice was gruff. "I'll see what I can do while you get Gideon free."

Without question, Fatima darted to the side of the tent, scooping up the hunting knives the Crows had confiscated, tucking them haphazardly at her waist and boot. Seemingly satisfied, she snatched up Théo's bo staff and hustled back.

"Just put it through the chain. I'll take care of the rest."

As commanded, she laced the staff between the chain and his wrists. With the staff firmly in place, Théo started twisting it, straining the links. Fatima turned back to Gideon, working at his cuffs.

The Finch strained against his chains, eyes fixed on the tent walls as shadows pulsed and raced past. Outside, he could *feel* the battlefield: the hammering of the trebuchets, Crows shrieking, the snap of bowstrings, the clash of arms.

"Would you stop fidgeting?" she chided, her fingers nimble at his lock.

"Easier said than done," Gideon muttered. "People are dying out there."

"Almost…there…"

As the cuffs sprang loose, Gideon let out a breath, rubbing at his raw wrists. "Fatima… you're wonderful."

She shot him a curt nod. "I know." She held up the bobby pin triumphantly before turning to Théo. "How about you? You wanna tell me how amazing I am or–"

The Dove answered by wrenching the chains apart, the staff unbending despite the force he exerted. His arms trembled for a moment, his muscles swelling before the links snapped free.

Fatima and Gideon stared.

"What?" Théo shook off the loose metal.

"Nothing," they mumbled in unison, Gideon feeling his cheeks flush as Fatima dropped her gaze.

Rolling his eyes, Théo strode to the tent entrance, lifting the velour flap with Fatima and Gideon close behind.

"Wait!" Gideon blurted, pausing at the threshold. "I don't have a weapon. What am I supposed to do?"

"Just stay close to me. You'll be fine." Before Gideon could argue, Théo grabbed his forearm and hauled him out, weaving fast between the lines of tents. They darted through a narrow gap, emerging onto the edge of the battlefield.

Gideon's heart plummeted. "They're actually fighting each other…"

"Looks like Pelanor had as much luck with the Hawks as we did with the Crows," Théo mumbled grimly.

"You'd be correct," came a voice behind them.

Fatima whipped around on instinct. "*Ya Allah!*" she shouted, her fist flying. Her punch landed square in Pelanor's stomach.

The Owl doubled over with a choked grunt, dropping the sword he clutched. Crumpling to his knees, he wrapped his arms protectively around his middle.

Gideon let out a gasp.

Beside him, Théo doubled over, wheezing uncontrollably. He clutched his stomach as a deep, guttural burst escaped him, shoulders shaking with the force of it. Tears streamed down his face.

Pelanor sucked in as much air as he could, his face pinched.

"What's the matter with you!?" Fatima shook her head, extending a hand out to the Owl.

"Mim forbid I try to help," he grunted. "But maybe I deserved that."

"Yeah, well, maybe next time don't sneak up on an ally in an active warzone."

Pelanor let out a faint, pained chuckle, more a dry cough than real humor, as he hauled himself upright, one arm still wrapped around his ribs.

Gideon managed a shaky smile, a flicker of relief warming his chest. But it didn't last. His gaze lifted past Pelanor, beyond the tents, beyond the forest. His heart stopped.

"Guys…" His voice came out thin, trembling. His knees nearly buckled beneath him. The others froze. Slowly, they turned, following his outstretched finger to the sky.

Dark shapes gathered on the horizon. A roiling mass of wings upon wings, like a thundercloud swallowing the light.

Fatima sucked in a sharp breath. Théo's expression tightened, and Gideon's throat went dry. All three let their eyes fall to Pelanor.

"Don't look at me," the Owl muttered softly, shaking his head. "This is Gideon's gambit."

Gideon blinked. "*What?*"

"I'm going to have to agree with Gideon here," Théo added dryly, not taking his eyes off the approaching cloud. "*What!?*"

Pelanor stepped closer, calm despite the rising wind. "Gideon. Don't you remember the prophecy?"

Gideon stared at him blankly. "I mean, yeah…But it never said anything about *stopping a war*!"

"Didn't it?" Pelanor's eyes gleamed. *"If the champion does not succeed at first light, the earth will run red, and the pillars of Avis will fall."* He gestured at the battlefield. "Tell me, how much blood has been spilled today?"

"Pelanor," Théo snapped, his patience cracking, "that's a hell of a stretch, even for you. You can't seriously —"

"No." The word escaped from Gideon. His voice, small at first, then steadier. "No," repeated louder, cutting Théo off. "He's right."

Fatima and Théo both turned to stare at him.

"I failed to stop my mother when I had the chance. *Succeed at first light.* And now the earth's running red." His fists trembled at his sides. "The pillars falling must mean the tribes…and now they're at war and it's my fault." His voice cracked. "We're running out of time."

Pelanor inhaled deeply, his visage alight with what Gideon thought might be pride. Extending his arm, he offered Gideon the sword he'd been carrying. "Then, what would you like to do about it, champion?"

No pressure at all.

Gideon tugged the leather cord loose from his tunic and quickly lashed the sword to his belt. "We need to rally the Hawks and Crows, and *fast*. Something big. Sweeping." Gideon's mind spun, searching. Fatima tapped her foot, impatient. Then, an idea clicked. "We need to find the herald, or a standard-bearer or something."

"A what?" Théo's eyes thinned, his brow furrowed.

"A flag person." Gideon explained, flaring his wings. "They're the ones who keep the war horns to signal units. If we can get one, we can–"

"How would you even know that?" Théo interrupted.

Gideon shrugged. "I like to read."

Théo and Fatima exchanged a confused look, but seemed to accept the answer.

"Good thing I'm way ahead of you." Pelanor reached into his sleeve and pulled free a polished black war horn, its body laced with silver inlay.

Gideon blinked. "How did you–"

"Gideon," Pelanor sighed, his shoulders sagging. "I thought we'd be past that question by now."

Fatima narrowed her eyes. "So you've known his plan the whole time…" She shook her head, her words somewhere between a question and exasperated statement. "Do you realize how much time you wasted? How many people are probably dead because you didn't just blow the damn horn yourself?"

Pelanor sniffed, wrinkling his nose. "I can guide the future—not shape it. That part's up to him." He took the horn and pressed it into the Finch's grip. "Besides, Gideon had to make this decision on his own."

The horn was heavier than it looked. Gideon turned it in his hands, the carved goat horn humming with responsibility.

"Okay. I'll fly out, get the armies' attention. Fatima, find Kyte. Get him on the same page and have him redirect his troops. Théo, hit the far end of the line. Break up the ground fighting where you can. Pelanor, take to the skies—warn the aerial units. Get them braced for what's coming."

He looked around at the others, each poised at the edge of motion.

"Everyone got it?" He was startled by the resolve in his own voice.

Where did that come from?

It felt like a switch had gone off in him. He was still the same person—anxious and timid, but there was a new sense of purpose within. It hadn't even been a day since he'd lost Cas, but something had changed. He had no more room for doubt. His grief had already calcified into something solid. It was heavy, but reliable; his heart was torn, but his will had solidified. He had to move forward.

That's what Cas would've wanted.

Théo gave a curt nod, already leaping into the air.

Fatima grinned, half-exasperated, half-reverent. "Sir, yes sir!" She saluted playfully, but with a nod of deference, and then took off.

Pelanor lingered a moment longer. "Good luck, Gideon." There was pride in his voice.

Then, he too, vanished into the chaos.

Alone in the center of the Crow camp, Gideon's heart pounded. The wind tugged at his tunic as he spread his wings and kicked off from the ground, lifting into the air with one hard beat, then another. He rose fast, slicing through the air until the battlefield stretched below him, a mosaic undulating as soldiers sought their footing.

He flew farther back, beyond the first ridgelines, where the noise dulled and the sky opened wide. Hovering over Vines' Crossing, he steadied his breath, pressed the horn to his lips, and let out a long, clear blast. The note rolled across the valley like thunder. It vibrated in his ribs, echoed across the isthmus and seemed, for a heartbeat, to hold the world still.

Nothing changed. Steel still clashed, war cries rang out, and trebuchets were loosed with whiplike snaps.

The Finch's stomach dropped.

He let out another blast from the horn, the note fuller and sharper, expelling all the desperation that filled his chest. The call cut through the plain and something shifted. Small pockets of stillness began to form as wings faltered, heads turning as they searched for the shrill blare. On the outskirts of the chaos, scattered bands of Hawks and Crows hesitated, drawing together in uncertain truce.

But the center still churned, a maelstrom of steel and fury.

A glance over his shoulder sent an icy chill through him. The sky behind them was darkening fast. A swarm of Harpies tore through the clouds, a ragged mass of wings and clawed limbs, talons glinting like hooks in the fading light. Rifles caught the sun on their barrels.

They'll be on us in minutes.

He surged forward, diving into the chaos with the horn pressed to his lips. The call rang out again and again, a piercing signal that climbed higher each time, shrill and desperate, impossible to ignore.

"Stop fighting!" he roared, voice shredded by the wind. "Over there! The Harp–" A spear whistled past his cheek. He twisted hard, barrel-rolling sideways before catching himself and diving lower.

Another blare.

This time, the reaction came faster; soldiers jolted upright, some raising weapons, others lowering them. Confusion rippled through the crowd like a wave hitting stone. Below, Gideon watched as General Corvinus of the Crows ripped into the air, calling for his Crows to halt. From the corner of his eye, he caught a glimpse of Pelanor banking hard to the left, leading a mixed knot of Hawks and Crows who had already fallen into a V-formation. Their eyes followed Gideon, expressions tense but alert.

Steadily, the tide began to turn.

Crows and Hawks alike lowered their weapons, fighters peeling away from one another as they fell into their lines. Trebuchets turned and reloaded, hands moving with frantic precision, all attention fixed on the dark swarm bearing down from above.

Gideon swept through one final pass, lungs burning, the horn falling silent in his grip. His wings ached with every beat, muscles trembling from overuse. He was running on fumes now. Scanning the teeming field below, he searched for any familiar faces.

Near the eastern ridge, he found his people.

"Fatima… Kyte…" His eyes caught a flash of auburn hair. "Socorra!" A laugh bubbled out of him before he could stop it. He dipped into a shallow dive and shot toward them, wind whipping through his feathers.

The huntress looked up just in time to see him land hard beside her. "Gideon!" She threw her arms around him, crushing him in a tight hug.

He let the sword hang limp at his side, arms wrapping around her in return. "I'm so glad to see you," he murmured, voice cracked and dry.

"Me too." She pulled back just enough to look at him, hand still on his shoulder. "That was brilliant. I can't believe you pulled it off."

He could only muster a crooked, breathless smile. Her words steadied him.

Only a few feet away, Kyte's voice cut through the clamor like a blade.

"Pull the archers back another ten paces—tighten the middle line, don't give them a gap! Get these trebuchets loaded, now!"

And they listened. All of them. Crows and Hawks alike moved with purpose, with unity.

Fatima arrived at a run, the tension in her face undercut by the gleam in her eyes. "Lines are locked. Where do you need me, leftenant?"

Kyte didn't miss a beat. "You and Socorra stay with me. We'll protect the rows of archers and keep the Harpies off their backs."

Socorra wrinkled her nose, casting him a dry look. There was a silent exchange between them, a knowing glance that said she wasn't happy about his decision, but she didn't argue.

Gideon, still catching his breath, stepped forward. "What about me?"

"I can't tell you what to do, Gideon." Kyte's stare softened, his lips curling. "I don't give orders to the Avis' champion."

A flicker of something warm stirred in Gideon's chest. He gave a short nod and turned back to the oncoming threat, sword drawn, wings folded tightly at his back.

Deafening shrieks filled the sky and a round of gunshots echoed through the field. A windstorm of dirt and debris flooded the battleground as a burst of gunshots tore across the field just in front of the frontmost line of archers, kicking up plumes of earth and feathers.

"Fire!" Kyte's voice cut through the chaos.

Gideon raised the horn once more. His chest ached, but he let loose one final thunderous blast, the trebuchets answering in kind. The massive stones launched skyward, slamming into the tight nest of Harpies with devastating force. Squeals of pain tore through the sky as clusters were crushed beneath the weight, their bodies scattering like autumn leaves stirred by a gale. Wave after wave, the volleys came, and bodies fell to the ground.

But the Harpies surged on, unyielding and merciless.

Their next volley of rifle fire tore into the front ranks. Gideon watched in horror as a handful of Hawks and Crows crumpled to the ground; two were rent from the sky, their wings flailing wildly as they dropped to the field with a sickening *thud*.

From above, a violent scream rang out—Théo giving the signal for the air forces to surge forward. Ground forces followed, Avians leaping into the sky by the dozens, blades drawn, cries echoing as they joined the fray in full.

Gideon wavered for a beat, looking to Kyte and Socorra for a better sense of what to do. Socorra clutched her spear tightly, wings flared ready to join in the aerial assault, Fatima beside her, coiled like a spring. Kyte had one hand on Socorra's arm, seemingly urging her to stay grounded; but Socorra simply leaned in, kissed him quickly on the cheek, and leapt into the air. Her wings snapped open, catching the wind. Fatima followed right after, silent as a shadow.

Gideon's heart surged. He clenched his jaw, gave Kyte one final look, and kicked off the earth. His wings snapped open as he launched into the air, sword drawn, his pulse thundering in his ears. Wind tore past his face, thick with the stench of sulfur from the gunfire.

A raw cry burst from his throat as he dove into the chaos, his blade a flash of silver through the smoke. The first Harpy never stood a chance; Gideon's sword punched through its collarbone, the crunch of bone and snap of sinew vibrating up the hilt. The creature let out a strangled shriek before tumbling into the dark, a storm of feathers and blood spiraling in its wake.

He slashed back instinctively, wild and wide, driving one back, but another clipped his shoulder. Pain seared down his back as its talons scored his skin. He staggered in the air trying to right himself, eyes spinning. The creature struck out again, claws aimed at his neck.

Before Gideon could react, a blur shot up from the air beneath him.

Fatima!

Slamming into the Harpy with brutal force, she clamped down on the creature's back, her knives flashing, stabbing deep into the skin between its wings. The Harpy shrieked and spiraled down with her still clinging on. She rode the fall halfway to the ground, then kicked off the beast and climbed back into the air. Her wings beating furiously, she rose through the chaos with blood-slicked blades, a fire roaring in her eyes.

"Better keep up, Gid!"

Breathing through the pain in his shoulder, Gideon veered hard left and vaulted after Fatima, his wings slicing through the turbulent air. She moved like lightning, her twin knives flashing silver as they found their way into the gray flesh of the Harpies. He mimicked her path, dodging arrows and boulders alike. One of the creatures lunged at him with a spear—one it must've stolen from a fallen soldier. Tilting his wings, he dipped backward, the air above his head whistling as he dragged his sword across the creature's torso. Flailing his wings, Gideon regained the air as the creature spiraled to the ground below.

Somewhere to his left, a rifle crackled with a sharp and mechanical *clip*. Turning in time, he watched as six soldiers fell from the sky, the Harpy's thin lips curling into a manic grin as it cackled. With a flourish of its ragged wings, the creature spun valiantly in the air, brandishing its weapon wildly.

They're killing Avians?

On Hawks & Harpies

Gideon froze for a breath too long; he lost altitude. Feeling the air rushing past him as he faltered, he shook off the realization with a flap of his wings and caught himself.

They're supposed to be capturing them...for the change...not slaughtering people.

Without warning, a flicker caught at the edge of his vision. Gideon twisted sharply, feathers cutting the air as a Harpy lunged, a blur of claws and steel slicing through the storm. He spun midflight, heart seizing as the creature's talons missed him by inches and tore into a Hawk behind him. A crimson mist burst across the sky as the soldier pitched sideways, wings collapsing before he plunged toward the ground.

A sick heat rolled through Gideon's gut as another volley of gunfire cracked overhead.

Deal with that later.

Shoving the thought aside, Gideon tucked his wings tightly and let himself fall, plummeting through the mess of tangled skirmishes and spiraling bodies, vanishing beneath the storm of wings and metal. Then, with a sharp snap, he flared his wings and caught the air, leveling into a low glide before angling upward again. He surged back into the fray from below, rising fast through the crush of movement. The armed Harpy loomed just above, still spraying bullets into the crowd.

It never saw him coming.

Driving the blade up, Gideon buried the sword to the hilt into the Harpies side. The creature let out a guttural rasp, the gunfire sputtering to a halt as blood frothed at its mouth.

On Hawks & Harpies

The weight of the creature threatened to drag him down, but Gideon clenched his teeth and held steady, flapping his wings as wildly as he could muster. One hand gripped the sword lodged in the Harpy's ribs, the other wrapped around the rifle's stock.

He tipped forward with a grunt, bracing his wings against the shifting air, and yanked the blade free. The Harpy lurched, clutching the gun with one last, desperate plea; its fingers gave out, limp and useless. It slipped from his grasp and dropped like a stone through the air, vanishing into the carnage below.

Gideon tested the rifle's heft in his hands. It was lighter than he'd expected, almost deceptively so. He'd need both hands to use it, but he didn't want to drop his sword.

Focus. Regroup. Find the Master.

He dove to the ground, angling his wings to cut speed. Dirt and feathers kicked up around him as he skidded into a rough landing, boots thudding into the packed earth slick with gore. Weaving through fallen warriors, he sprinted to a rare open patch of earth. Without hesitation, he slammed his sword into the ground, the hilt vibrating under his palm as it struck stone beneath the surface. Then he turned his gaze skyward, rifle locked against his shoulder.

He had no idea what he was doing.

How hard could it be?

In the swarm above, Harpies dove and twisted, clashing with Hawks and Crows midair, dragging Avians down in their claws. One broke from the havoc, its black eyes locked onto Gideon. It dove, talons splayed like curved blades.

Gideon didn't breathe. He aimed. Fired.

BOOM.

The gun exploded backward against his shoulder. He stumbled and dropped hard, landing in a patch of red-slicked mud, a coppery odor filling his nostrils. His hands were covered in blood; he stared at them, heart hammering, body trembling. The raw power in that one pull of a trigger; it was thrilling. Horrifying.

No one should have that much power.

He'd killed before—to defend himself, but that had required effort, some skill and luck. This was…different. Distant and too easy.

The Master.

She had to be here somewhere, flying above it all like a puppet master pulling on the strings of her marionette.

He raised his eyes to the sky, wincing as a flare of white light nearly blinded him. He squinted, shielding his face.

The sun?

Gideon flicked through his memories of the battle of the Noktern—the massive clouds that cast a darkness like night over the tundra. His breath hitched with the sudden realization.

She's not here.

Hollowness cracked through him, followed by a rising fury. A trap. It had to be. She told him this was the target—this field, this moment. Had he misunderstood? Been manipulated? Was this just a distraction?

He clenched his jaw.

I should've known better.

Chapter Twenty-Six

Agnes

But at that moment a breaking sea dashed on her bows, and right after it the white whale himself smote the ship's starboard bow, till men and timbers reeled. Some fell flat upon their faces. The entire ship's frame reeled and shivered like a blown sapling in a storm. Retribution, swift vengeance, eternal malice were in his whole aspect...he now completely dashed the shivered boat to splinters; and with a frightful, soundless maw, he ground the oars and gunwales to bits.

"For a book set on the ocean," Marta began, her knitting needles clicking lazily, "it's incredibly dry."

Agnes, balanced in her chair and propped against a bookshelf, lifted her gaze in a slow, unimpressed stare. "Good thing ye're nae the one readin' it, then."

Marta paused, mouth open to retort, but a thunderous pounding silenced her before she could get the words out.

Bang, bang, bang.

The sound echoed through the great chamber of the Noktern, low and brutal. Scholars lifted their heads from the scrolls and tomes they poured over. Even the waterfalls near the entrance seemed to hush in the wake of the boom.

Bang, bang, bang.

The sound came again and whispers ruminated through the hall.

"What do you think that is?" Marta hissed. Her usual sharp edge faltered, smothered by a tremor in her voice.

Agnes wanted to snap back with something barbed and clever, but her fears dampened her habitual sarcasm. "I don't know," she breathed, her voice a ghost of itself.

Bang. Bang. BANG.

The rhythm turned staccato, hammering faster, harder. Each strike rattled the shelves, sending books thudding to the stone floor. The river winding through the chamber surged, sloshing over the banks of polished granite. Chairs scraped violently as scholars lurched to their feet in alarm.

A chorus of gasps erupted as the lights blinked out.

Seconds of darkness stretched on like an eternity until the red floodlights flared to life. The pounding returned, now deafening. Agnes clutched her chest, sure her heart was beating in time with the assault.

Bang, bang, bang.

Marta sat frozen beside her, pale as parchment. The red light deepened the shadows under her eyes, but it couldn't hide the terror as the blood drained from her face.

BANG! BANG! BANG!

With the redoubled force, the Noktern erupted into pandemonium. Chairs were overturned and scrolls scattered. Scholars stumbled and shouted over one another, their cries echoing off stone walls now pulsing with red light. The pounding continued like a monstrous heart hammering just outside the walls, each blow closer than the last.

And then, at once, everything stopped; silence fell like a guillotine. The red lights persisted, but the chamber itself froze in a breathless, unnatural stillness.

Agnes stood rigid, chest heaving. Sweat pooled cold along her brow despite the icy air, and her fingers twitched with instinctive urgency. She stepped back, one foot sliding behind the other as she turned toward the river's narrow bridge.

"Marta!" Her voice was a hoarse whisper. "Marta, c'mon. We need to go."

But Marta didn't move. She sat petrified in her chair, eyes wide, staring up at the doorway that led up to the fortress's exit. Her lips parted slightly, her hands clenched in her lap.

Agnes took another step. "Marta–"
BOOM!

A deafening explosion cracked through the air from somewhere above. The mountain shuddered; the vaulted ceiling of the Noktern splintered, cracks webbing through the tilework as chunks of stone rained down. A burst of dust and gravel struck Agnes's shoulder as she ducked, shielding her face with her sleeve.

Then came the mist. A strange, dense fog plowed down from the upper doorways, rolling like smoke, but heavier, darker. It slithered down, pouring over the balcony and down the steps, swallowing the chamber in seconds.

Panicked cries echoed in the thickening haze. Scholars stumbled blindly, some reaching to protect their precious tomes, while more shouted for help or screamed obscenities into the haze.

Agnes didn't hesitate. She turned back to where they had been sitting moments before and grabbed Marta by the wrist, lifting the smaller Dove in a swoop. Marta barely had time to find her footing before they took off running. Together, they plunged into the mist. Agnes pushed forward, pulling Marta along as they weaved between tables, toppled chairs, and frantically fleeing Owls. Their boots skidded across the slick tile, the floor coated in a fine film of water and grit from the collapsing ceiling. They had to reach Ordranor's bunker—somewhere safe, somewhere hidden. Somewhere tucked away from whatever horror descended upon them.

Agnes couldn't see anything; every step felt like plunging deeper into a nightmare. The mist clung to her feathers and seeped into her wimple, penetrating deep into the fabric. The dampness prickled her skin, but she didn't stop running. So long as she could make it to the far wall, she'd be alright, she told herself.

Somewhere behind the Doves came a screech, a sound horrifyingly unavian. Wings beat through the air with a dreadful, wet *snap*.

There was a sudden shift in the floor and Marta stumbled, yanking Agnes off balance. Both of them crashed hard to the stone, a sharp cry tearing from Agnes's throat as her elbow slammed into the ground.

"No!" She twisted around, groping wildly in the mist. "Marta?"

No answer.

"Marta!"

She reached back, searching, her fingers sweeping across the ground where Marta had been only seconds before. But there was nothing.

Another scream tore through the haze. Then came a wet, sickening *crunch*.

Agnes went cold. Tears blurred her eyes, but she scrambled back, forcing herself to stand. She had to move. She had to live. Her limbs screamed in protest, but she pushed forward, staggering blindly until her hand met the wall. Her fingertips grazed the frigid stone, then followed it desperately, one hand bracing the surface as she fumbled her way along the chamber's perimeter until she found a break in the wall.

Blessings. The feckin' hallway!

Agnes lunged into it, desperate to be free from the roiling storm cloud, the cries and shrieks behind her muffled slightly as she pressed into the corridor. She stopped, shoulders heaving, and turned back to the fog, willing Marta to emerge from the haze.

But there was nothing. No one.

She took a step back, one trembling hand braced against the wall, the other pressed to her chest. Her heart plummeted like a stone. For all the arguments, the eye-rolls, the never-ending jabs, Marta had been her only friend at the Noktern all these years. The one constant in this cold, dim existence.

"I'm so sorry, Marta."

She said a silent prayer for her sister in God, and ran.

Chapter Twenty-Seven

GIDEON

A bonfire raged at the center of Vines' Crossing, climbing high into the dawn sky, serving as a fiery monument to the fragile armistice between the Hawks and the Crows. Leaning against the thick leg of a battered trebuchet, Gideon watched as flames devoured the mangled bodies of the Harpies, the acrid stench of burning feathers and singed flesh curling on the southerly breeze.

A heavy silence hung over the battlefield. The wounded had long since limped back to their camps. The bodies of fallen Hawks and Crows had been recovered—those from Zarpa prepared for the journey home, while the Crows had already begun digging solemn trenches along the edge of the forest.

Suddenly, a burst of *pops* cracked through the air. Startled murmurs rippled through the gathered soldiers, shoulders tensing, hands reaching reflexively for their spears.

"Don't worry," Pelanor murmured, stepping closer. He placed a steady hand on Gideon's forearm. "It's the bullets still loaded in the rifles. They're 'cooking off,' I believe is the term."

Gideon inhaled sharply, scanning the fire. "No one's going to get hurt, are they?"

"The guns were buried deep in the pile," Pelanor replied, tone even and flat. "There shouldn't be any danger."

Gideon gave a small nod, the tension in his shoulders easing. "Good."

There had been plenty of debate over what to do with the rifles. Both armies had angled for control of them, but in the end, they had deferred to Pelanor's judgment. Mercifully, neither General Melierax nor General Corvinus seemed to know of his disbarment from the Noktern.

Pelanor, in turn, had made a point to involve Gideon in the decision-making. For the Finch, the choice was easy. The rifles had to be destroyed.

After a while, the Crows drifted back to their tents, and a hush settled over the field.

"We have about half-an-hour before the generals arrive for negotiations." Pelanor stepped away from the trebuchet. "Would you like to join me in the officers' tent for some tea?"

Gideon drew a steadying breath of the cool morning air. "I appreciate it, but I think I'll stay here."

Pelanor lingered, gently biting at his bottom lip before asking. "Is there anything I can do?"

A surge of emotion rolled through Gideon's chest, but he forced it down. "No, but thank you." The Finch put on a gentle smile. "I'll be alright"

"Okay." Pelanor's tone was clipped, as if he had more to say but held back. "Then we can just sit here."

"Pelanor…" Gideon settled onto the base of the trebuchet. He crossed one leg beneath his backside, letting his other dangle just above the ground. "You don't have to–" He paused, then shook his head, massaging the knot at his neck. "Really, I'm fine. Go get your tea."

"No, that's quite alright." Pelanor gave a small shrug, but his eyes lingered on Gideon a moment longer than necessary. Then, quietly, he moved to sit on the opposite side of the trebuchet, wings folded neatly at his sides. He rested his hands in his lap, thumbs gently circling one another as they sat in silence.

Gideon exhaled softly. Part of him craved solitude; another part found comfort in Pelanor's quiet company. This Owl was not the distant scholar he remembered; he was softer, more down-to-earth.

Still an ass.

Gideon stuck his tongue in his cheek and rolled his eyes.

But better.

They lapsed into a peaceful silence, the summer breeze rustling Gideon's feathers. His thoughts drifted to darker moments—Cas, the Noktern—so he focused instead on the trebuchet's mechanics, tracing its elegant clockwork.

"These pistons are immaculate," he murmured to himself. "And the escapement levers, perfectly balanced."

"It's a work of art," Pelanor replied evenly. "Finch craftsmanship at its deadliest."

The phrase snagged in Gideon's mind.

Finch craftsmanship...

With a pang of disquiet, he rose and circled the machine, inspecting more closely.

The counterweight attachment's essentially the pendulum in a grandfather clock, and the pins in these axles are clock arbors.

"Everything alright?" Pelanor's voice broke his reverie.

Gideon's fingers brushed a small bronze plaque bolted to the frame:

L211 | 1600 spans | Max: 110 kg

E. Thrush

Made in Moda

Gideon stiffened. "No," he whispered. "It can't be."

Pelanor stood, concern darkening his brow. "What is it?"

"My father. Erasmus Thrush." Gideon's voice was low, tight with bitter irony and disdain. "Moda's most celebrated clockmaker."

Pelanor stood there, tall and regal as usual; he was still, silent, waiting for Gideon to continue.

"I shouldn't be surprised." Gideon exhaled through his nose. "That man would sell his own heart if someone offered enough gold."

Behind the Owl, the outline of four Avians emerged in the plain. As they neared, their silhouettes flickered in the shadows cast by the sunlight filtering through the trees. Fatima was the first to come into clear view, darting a few paces ahead of the others. Her laugh rang like a bell, sharp and bright. She twisted and turned to everyone, leading whatever conversation they were having. She had been the first to believe in him, even before he'd believed in himself. Through every doubt, she'd never once looked at him with disappointment. She was the sister he'd never had.

Behind her, Kyte and Socorra walked shoulder to shoulder. The breeze swept Socorra's auburn tresses over her face, poised, relaxed. She said something softly, and Kyte chuckled under his breath before slipping his wing around her, tugging her closer. The gesture was natural, easy. It made something tight in Gideon's chest unwind.

Socorra was a fierce and resilient woman—present and protective. Kyte was stoic but steady, a man needing few words.

Gideon had followed them separately in his time of need, and now he knew he'd follow them anywhere. Neither of them were old enough to be his parents, but he saw in Kyte the father he'd should've had—someone to hold him accountable, but with kindness and care too. And in Socorra, the mother he'd thought he had—powerful, but present and protective.

Trailing just behind, Théo moved with quiet authority. His bo staff thudded against the dirt in rhythm with his steps, doubling as a walking stick. He may have been the last to join their odd group, but in two days–

Maybe less?

Time twisted oddly since the battle, and yet, in that brief time, Théo had offered him more warmth than many had in his entire life. It was like he'd always been meant to be.

Gideon's eyes drifted back to Pelanor; the Owl stared at him, poised and unreadable as ever. But Gideon had seen past that veneer, past the rigid etiquette and barbed remarks. In those rare moments, the brief flashes of honesty, there was a gentleness. Pelanor was an anchor, someone that had kept him rooted when he'd flown too far. He wasn't sure what family member the Owl was…maybe a distant cousin or strange uncle…

All that mattered was that Gideon felt home.

"Good morning!" he called as the others arrived. It was all he could do to chase away the tears pooling at the corners of his eyes.

They exchanged their pleasantries, though there was little energy to be had among them. No one had the occasion to sleep as negotiations were called for immediately, but after the battle, the morale was low.

The group shifted and started toward the officers' tent.

Fatima kicked a loose rock as they walked, arms behind her head. "So…" she exhaled heavily. "What're the odds that we'll be able to end the war and focus on stopping Gideon's mom?"

"Fatima…" Théo's voice issued a slight warning.

"It's fine," Gideon said with a casual flick of his wrist, feeling no particular way about it.

"Unlikely." Kyte shook his head solemnly, returning to Fatima's question. "The Hawk Council won't stand down unless the order comes directly from the Noktern. Too much pride. Too many dead."

"The Crows might agree to a ceasefire," Pelanor sighed, "but not if it's one-sided. And they still have the trebuchets at their disposal, so the Hawks won't have an easy time of it."

"As a Hawk, I hate to say it," Socorra chimed in, "but they do have a right to defend themselves. Especially given the circumstances."

"True and fair," Pelanor acknowledged. "But you know as well as I do that the Hawks could easily conquer the Crowlands with minimal bloodshed—especially with the two of you at the helm. The trebuchets mean equal fighting…equal deaths."

Something sparked in Gideon's mind. He slowed, falling a step behind the others, turning to look once more at the machines they'd used to destroy the Harpies. His father's machines.

"Why don't you guys go on ahead," he offered, his voice calm. "I'll catch up in a bit."

Fatima blinked, turning back. "What? Why?"

"Just something I have to do." He gave a faint shrug. "I won't be long, promise!"

There was a slight pause, a shared hesitation among them.

Pelanor waved a permissive hand. "Do what you need to do, just be sure to join us when you're done with …" he paused, his tone laden with speculation, "whatever it is you're up to."

Gideon nodded and peeled off toward the trebuchets as the others continued toward the tent. He circled the first of them, slipping into the scaffolding. He searched for a bit, his hand moving with precision.

He pulled the first axle pin, thick and slick with grease. He worked it free with a grunt.

That'll keep them from being able to aim.

Then the trigger mechanism pin. Smaller, deceptively simple, but without it, the firing arm would lock in place, rendering the machine useless.

He tucked them into the leather pouch on his belt and moved to the next machine. One by one, he dismantled them. Quiet sabotage. Subtle enough that the Crows wouldn't notice until it was too late. Twenty minutes passed in a blur.

Stepping back from the last trebuchet, he wiped the light sweat from his brow, feeling the lubricant smudge on his forehead.

"Take that, Erasmus."

Looks like being the clockmaker's son wasn't a total waste after all.

As he started back toward the tents, a shrill *caw* split the quiet of the morning, echoing from above. He turned, his hand instinctively shielding his eyes from the sun.

A black speck circled, growing rapidly larger as it descended.

"Nox," he breathed. There was a quiet sense of relief as the raven swooped down in a graceful arc, landing neatly on his outstretched arm. But as her talons dug into the sleeve of his tunic, the quick bite of her claws in his skin called back his fear. What news could he possibly be receiving from the Noktern?

"Well, hello," he murmured softly, extending his hand. Seemingly content, she allowed him to nuzzle the soft down on her chest and neck.

"Please tell me you have some good news."

She tilted her head, her beady eyes bright and knowing. Using her beak, she extricated a tightly rolled scroll from the leather tube tied to her leg, coaxing Gideon to take it.

Gideon's fingers still trembled, tired from the delicate work of adjusting trebuchet gears as he accepted the scroll. It felt unnaturally heavy and rigid, as if something solid lay coiled at its core. He began to unroll it, but Nox, still perched on his wrist, tugged insistently at his tunic.

"Oh, uh," he stammered, patting his waist. "I'm sorry, I don't have any food for you this time. I left my pack at Fate's Folly."

As if she understood, Nox shook her head in swift arcs, ruffled her feathers, and delivered a quick nip to his fingertips before darting off toward the forest's edge.

"She'll be back," he told himself, forcing a light chuckle that did nothing to banish the knot in his stomach.

He unfurled the parchment to reveal a small metallic box tucked inside. Rotating it between his fingers, he noted tiny divots and prongs like the teeth of a mechanical key. Etched on one side was the label: *USB*.

Whatever that means.

Returning his attention to the letter, Gideon noticed that it was penned in a hurried scrawl, smudged in places—but the handwriting was unmistakable: the same hand that had delivered his first message while he'd been a prisoner.

Gideon,

The Noktern has fallen. The Master has seized control of the Parliament. Our life-support systems are failing.

The Finch's stomach lurched, then clenched.

He read the words again, slower this time, stupidly hoping that he'd misunderstood. But there they were. Unmistakable.

His hands shook, knuckles pale around the parchment. A bitter taste welled in the back of his throat, acidic but familiar. He sucked in a sharp breath, but it caught halfway, refusing to settle. The trees around him blurred for a moment, colors bleeding at the edges of his vision. Not from tears—he'd wasted too many of those on her—but from rage.

"She *used* me," he growled, the words tearing raw. "She set the trap and I fell right into it."

He wanted to scream, to tear the letter in half, or crush the USB in his palm until it splintered open. But he didn't. He stood frozen, jaw clenched so tight it ached, his breath coming in short bursts as he returned his attention to the letter.

She's looking to get her hands on the kill code.

Kill code? That sounds ominous.

She'll stop at nothing to get her hands on it. That's why I've put it in this letter. Be sure to keep it <u>safe</u>. We may need it one day. Good luck.

—Ordranor
(No point in keeping it a secret anymore)

Gideon flipped over the scroll.

Blank?

"But where's the co–" His words cut off as realization flickered behind his eyes. He twisted the USB between his fingers.

What could my mother want with this?

Gideon scratched at the back of his neck.

Whatever it is, it can't be good.

He drew in a long, steadying breath and started toward the Crow officers' tent. After only a few steps, he heard a soft whisper of wings. Nox landed neatly on his shoulder, her beak streaked with blood and carrion.

Gideon wrinkled his nose but kept walking. "Will you stay with us now that the Master's taken the Noktern?"

Caw.

Nox shook her head, she tapped the leather strap on her leg.

"You're waiting for a message?" Gideon sighed with heavy relief. "So Ordranor's alive?"

She made no response, only stared, something rueful in her beady eyes.

"You don't know, do you?"

She shook her head again, and a bead of blood splattered Gideon's tunic.

Opening the flap to the officer's tent, every face turned as he entered. Eyes went wide and jaws dropped. Socorra and Fatima shared a quiet, knowing smile; Pelanor's gaze softened, reverent but unreadable.

General Corvinus rose from behind the parchment-strewn table. "By the gods…is that what I think it is?"

"She's a raven." Gideon cleared his throat. "Her name is Nox." He widened his stare hoping to convey a sense of urgency. "Pelanor, can I see you outside for a minute?"

Whispers ran out among the dozen officers on both sides.

Pelanor seemed to consider for a minute before standing. "Of course, Gideon." Pelanor rose slowly from his seat. "I'm sorry, generals, but I need a private word with the Noktern's champion."

Melierax lurched to his feet, protest curling on his lips, but Pelanor's tone brooked no argument. "Feel free to deliberate amongst yourselves. Perhaps you'll find peace before we return."

He escorted Gideon back toward the tent entrance, careful not to jostle Nox as she teetered on Gideon's shoulder. The others—Kyte, Socorra, Fatima, and Théo—slipped silently to their feet and followed.

"Pandion," Melierax bellowed, his face turning a vibrant red. "Have you forgotten where your allegiances lie? Sit down."

Kyte's jaw tightened. He fell silent, eyes flicking to Socorra. Leaning close, he murmured something in her ear before he folded his arms and returned to his chair.

The tent flap fell closed behind them as the morning light spilled across the clearing. Without a word, Pelanor sprang into the air, his wings unfurling with a snap. Nox followed, her talons briefly catching on Gideon's sleeve, and Gideon leapt after, his own wings flaring wide. The others rose close behind until they hovered in a loose ring above the waking camp. Below, soldiers stirred in their bedrolls. The first cookfires hissed into life.

"Is there a reason you had us fly up here?" Théo folded his arms.

"Privacy," Pelanor answered brusquely, as if the answer were sufficient. Holding out his hand, he turned to Gideon. "If I may?"

Hesitating, the Finch exchanged anxious looks around the circle, then placed the note and USB into Pelanor's extended palm.

The Owl's eyes scanned the jagged handwriting. As he read, the color drained from his face. "This isn't good."

"Care to elaborate?" Théo huffed.

Silently, Pelanor passed the letter to Théo, who read it with Fatima leaning in over his shoulder.

"So what do we do?" Fatima asked as Théo passed the scroll to Socorra.

Pelanor didn't answer. For a moment, Gideon thought he might be having a vision, but none of the signs were there. No shudder, no dimness behind the eyes.

"Pelanor?" Gideon pressed, waving a hand.

Still nothing.

Socorra finally broke the tension. "We could rally the Hawk army and–"

"Unlikely," Pelanor cut in, voice sharper than usual. "Once news of the Noktern's fall reaches the major cities, we'll be dealing with chaos, not support. The Hawk Elder Council only agreed to war based on the Noktern's recommendation. If Parliament has been..." He paused, searching for the right word, "...dissolved...then Mirabel and the rest of the Elders are likely too hot-headed and stubborn to reasonably call off the war—no offense."

Socorra tossed her shoulders lightly. "None taken."

"The Hawks will need someone to blame," Pelanor continued, "and for as much as we've tried, I don't think we'll convince them that the Crows don't also have something to do with this bit of news as well."

"But they fought the Harpies together!" Fatima exclaimed. "Shouldn't Mclicrax know better that–"

"Why is a raven like a writing desk?" Pelanor interrupted flatly.

Fatima blinked, confused.

"Sometimes," he continued evenly, "there's no rhyme or reason for what people choose to believe. We'll do our best to shape the narrative, but for now, we must assume that we're on our own. The Hawks and Crows will be too distracted by their pointless war, and the Finches too busy profiting from it. The Owls of Krepusk and Veta don't have the resources to be of assistance. And the Doves..." Pelanor inhaled deeply, casting a concerned glance toward Théo.

"With the Noktern gone," the Dove began quietly, his shoulders tightening, "the Inquisition will have the freedom to act without consequence."

"Precisely," Pelanor nodded.

"Then we need to–" Théo began, but the Owl held up a hand to silence him.

"No." The word was pointed, but flat—a command rather than a suggestion. "For now, we wait and gather intel. No bold moves."

"Are you kidding?" Gideon snarled. His wings flared with sudden force, sending him tilting in the air before he righted himself with a few sharp flaps. "If my—if *the Master* is at the Noktern, then we need to stop her immediately."

Silence fell, heavy and expectant. All eyes turned to Pelanor.

"You're really leaning into your role as champion." There was softness on the Owl's face, but irritation laced his words. "But even breached, the Noktern is still a fortress. She'll probably have a small contingent of Harpies with her, and if she remains there, she'll likely have barricaded the place, or laid traps. There's likely nothing we can do, not yet."

"But we have to–"

"Gideon." Pelanor's voice didn't rise, but there was a firmness. "Even if we stormed into the Noktern ourselves, we don't know what we'd find. Once *the Master* realizes what she's after isn't there, she might retreat. She might lash out. She might disappear entirely. We need to anticipate every possibility, and right now, we can't. Not without knowing what we're up against both inside the Noktern, as well as what's shifting *outside* it."

He held up the USB between two fingers. "And this may be the key to all of it. If Ordranor chose to protect it and she wants it, then we may be able to use it to help."

Gideon furrowed his brow. "You think so?" There was a dubiousness in his voice as he extended his hands, nudging his wings forward to take the kill code back.

The Owl seemed hesitant to relinquish the USB, though he acquiesced as Gideon's fingers caught the metal. "It must be important, otherwise Ordranor likely would have just destroyed it."

"That's true, I guess…" The words lingered on Gideon's tongue, A fragment from Tvanor's journal flickered in his memory.

Was this the backup plan she mentioned?

His thumb brushed over the smooth surface.

It would help to nourish the world…make the world flourish…?

"Then what could the Master possibly do with that?" Gideon mumbled.

"Care to share your ideas with the rest of the group?" Pelanor asked lightly.

Gideon blinked, snapping his attention back to the circle of faces. "So—" he stammered, "what do you suggest we do?"

Pelanor raised an eyebrow but didn't comment on Gideon's mutterings. "We go back into the negotiations," he answered. "Play along. Act surprised when the peace talk falls apart. Then we regroup at Airam's. We'll plan our next move from there."

Gideon's jaw clenched. The thought of standing still and going through the motions made his skin crawl.

"Fine." He stuffed the USB into the leather pouch alongside the trebuchet pins. "We'll do it your way. Like we always do."

Without waiting for a response, Gideon fluttered to the ground. His boots hit the dirt with a soft thud, the others trailing behind him as they tromped back toward the officer's tent.

A heavy silence settled within the group, thick with tension.

Gideon's cheeks burned.

Maybe Pelanor's right.

He chided himself bitterly, embarrassed by his outburst. Rationally, he knew waiting was the smarter move. With everything he'd been through, he'd learned to trust Pelanor, at least mostly. But waiting didn't sit right with him.

Not while the Master still has Avis in her talons.

He sucked in a breath through his teeth, trying to calm the churn in his gut.

"Soon enough," he whispered to himself, drawing the tent flap back. He held it open and let the others pass, catching the unease in their eyes, their resolve tangled with worry.

"It'll be okay, Gideon." Pelanor paused, placing a hand on his shoulder before brushing past him into the tent.

Gideon lingered at the threshold, staring out across the scarred field, the smoke of the bonfire still rising high into the sky.

You don't get to win, Cecilia. Not this time. Not again.

Epilogue

The Eve of the Dzuly Half-Moon

Grand Inquisitor Sarge,

We have received word via emissary that the Noktern has fallen. Already, the vacuum of its influence ripples across the continent.

If ever there was a moment to strike at the Godless settlement that is Tartarus, it is here and now. Devoid of the Noktern's interference and protection, these heathens will soon understand that indulgence and depravity will no longer be tolerated within the sacred borders of the Dovelands.

There remains, however, the lingering threat of the witch of the woods, Airam. See to her eradication with the full force of your command. You have the unreserved backing of the High Priesthood of Pas.

One condition only I place upon your crusade : spare my son, Théodore. Bring him home to me alive.

With cordiality,
Hierophant Gabriel

Acknowledgments

This past year has brought me so many things: joy and turbulence, love and loss; there's been a real beauty that can only come from living the good and the bad. Despite everything that life had to throw at me, I've tried so hard to look at it all through a lens of wonder…something I hadn't done in years.

The reception of *On Ravens & Riddles* has been more than I could've ever hoped for. Thank you to my friends, family, students, colleagues, and everyone in between who's supported me along the way. This project has been a labor of love, but it took a true community to bring it to life.

I'd like to offer a special thank-you to my friend and colleague, Kristin. After reading my first book, she made it her personal mission to uncover the artwork that inspired my writing. She reached out to her friends who helped her to cross-reference release dates with my age and the avian theme, and then scoured the internet chasing fragments of what I thought was a lost or made-up memory. Somehow, they found it. The images that ignited my imagination all those years ago belonged to a product ad for *Fire Emblem: Radiant Dawn.* Opening that file and seeing those images truly breathed new life into me in a way that I don't know that I could ever explain; it felt like rediscovering a piece of myself that'd been missing for longer than I can even remember. I can never repay her or her friends for giving me that amazing gift. Thank you, Kristin, from the bottom of my heart.

Another special thank-you to my friend, Steve. After *On Ravens & Riddles* was released, he worked tirelessly to help me navigate media outreach. I didn't expect anything when he offered; after all, who was I to deserve any kind of attention? But, amazingly, Steve worked his magic and was able to connect me with several outlets across the tri-state area. I was, and still am, blown away that he was able to do that for me. Steve, your work and expertise have been so vital to me and I'm so grateful for everything you've done for me throughout the years.

After agreeing to edit *one* book, my childhood friend Emily has continued to act as my personal editor, poring through every chapter to help make them the best that they could be. She always answered every call, never knowing what she was going to get: a quick hello, an hours-long discussion about some random plot point, or a total crash-out. Despite more than *we both* bargained for with this trilogy, I'm grateful to have had you with me through the journey. Thank you for always being there for me and helping me make my dream a reality no matter how much of a lunatic I can be sometimes.

Much like Mr. Bemis in the 1959 Twilight Zone episode *"Time Enough at Last,"* I always thought of myself first and foremost as a *reader*—something I've always been proud of. Growing up, I always adored stories. Just like Gideon got this love from his mother, so too did my mom pass on this love to me and my siblings. Frankly, I never aspired to be anything more in the literary world. I was content to sit by quietly and hope that someone else might write the story brewing in my mind—at least something similar. But when I first sat down to write, my mother was my biggest fan and encouraged me to keep going. I know I wasn't an easy kid to raise, but I'm so grateful for the relationship that we've built. From reading buddies to travel partners, thank you for giving me an appreciation for the things in life that are the most meaningful. I am, in many ways, the man I am today because of you.

My friends, Mike and Daniella once again sat with a rough draft, reading through spelling errors, missing quotation marks, misaligned formatting, and rushed wording (though it probably wasn't *as bad* as it was in my head). I'm so sorry to have subjected them to that, but I'm so appreciative of what they do. Their feedback solidifies the story in the end and helps to make it the best that it can be. Thank you both so much, and I'm so excited for your thoughts on the final installment, *On Finches & Folly*!

My friend and work-wife, Christina has seen me through so many ups and downs over the past few years. She has always been there to listen over a glass of wine, offering me advice. More often than not, I didn't listen (I am a flawed human being); but I always came crawling back to tell her she was right. After a quick celebratory dance and giving me a well-deserved "I told you so," she always did her best to lift me back up out of the dumps. Thank you for collecting me those many years ago and for continuing to encourage me no matter how dumb I can be. I wouldn't be half the person I am today without you.

In the months when so many things felt uncertain, Stephanie became a compass, guiding me back toward who I was always meant to be. On many occasions, she assured me that I did the hard work for myself, but her steadiness and care made it possible to find my way. When she read my book and spoke of my characters as though they were old friends, it felt like she'd glimpsed a part of my soul. Through our conversations, I've been able to unearth and reclaim a version of myself I was afraid I'd never see again —someone who doesn't struggle in the dark—someone who can find joy, wonder, and love in even the hardest of times. Thank you so much for everything you've given me and for getting me where I needed to be.

Once again, Alexandre has transformed imagination into something tangible and breathtaking. What I pictured in my mind was nothing compared to the stunning work that now binds these pages. Thank you for breathing such beauty and vitality into my world; your talent continues to amaze me, and I'm endlessly grateful for it. I look forward to working with you again in the future!

Since coming to Cranford, I've been continually struck by the sense of community that defines this place. From my first year here, it felt familiar—like stepping back into the small, close-knit town where I grew up. Back then, school was the center of everything; I spent most days there from 7 a.m. to 9 p.m., surrounded by teachers who wound up becoming a second family to me. I've had that same feeling of belonging and shared purpose since coming to this wonderful town.

The enthusiasm of my students, collaboration with my colleagues, and the support of our administrators have created something truly special—a place where creativity and care flourish side by side. I'm deeply grateful to be part of such a community, one that celebrates its own and lifts one another up. To the Cranford community, thank you for your faith in me, for cheering me on as both teacher and author, and for reminding me every day what it means to feel at home.

And finally—though maybe most absurdly—I'm so grateful for all of the hardships that I've had to endure the past two years of writing have really shaped not only who I am. They've had such a huge role in what I feel makes this story so special. From the deaths of loved ones, to feelings of self-doubt—the loss of meaningful relationships, and wondering if I'm good enough…all of these have played such a crucial role in defining these characters. There's a reason I chose the dedication that I did.

Without all of that hurt, some of the most meaningful parts of this story wouldn't exist as they do. I've had to learn that even in the darkest moments, there is something beautiful to be found. Something worth transforming. To turn sorrow into art, to create meaning from the mess— that's its own kind of magic.

Thank you all again. My life is so much fuller and richer for having you all in it. I hope you've enjoyed the story thus far, and I can't wait for you to see what's next.

With courage and honor,

Monsieur Sean W. Bagan

P.S. I'm sorry that was somehow sappier than the acknowledgments in book one…I have a lot of feelings. Please don't judge me.